MOLLY

ALSO BY MAX EHRLICH

THE
CULT

MAX EHRLICH

SIMON AND SCHUSTER   NEW YORK

DESIGNED BY ELIZABETH WOLL
MANUFACTURED IN THE UNITED STATES OF AMERICA

1   2   3   4   5   6   7   8   9   10

LIBRARY OF CONGRESS CATALOGING IN PUBLICATION DATA

EHRLICH, MAX SIMON, DATE.
    THE CULT.

    I. TITLE.
PZ3.E334CU   [PS3509.H663]   813'.5'4   77-18188
ISBN 0-671-24053-6

ACKNOWLEDGMENTS

Margaret Druckman, my research assistant and editorial consultant, worked unceasingly with me on this manuscript, and her critique was invaluable. Don Flint, student counselor at San Marcos High School, and Gil Horne, psychologist, both of the Santa Barbara City School System, contributed insights into the behavior patterns of young people. Attorney Gerald Levie of Los Angeles was generous, both in his patience and in his expertise in criminal law. Linda Price, Marc Jaffe and Peter Schwed, my editors, in their own special ways brought this book to life, and Scott Meredith, in his own special way, also made it come true.

To all of the above, my thanks.

FOR MARGARET

They love it every time I remind them how Jesus and I got to walk together hand in hand, and I love it when they anoint my head with dollars.

— BUFORD JOE HODGES
Born-again as
The Master

PROLOGUE

Sometime during the night, it had stopped snowing.

The footprints leading to the tree had, by this time, almost been buried. In a little while the cold wind would drift more snow over them, obliterating them entirely.

The tree, standing alone in the soft-white waste, was a gray-barked rock maple.

It stood tall and stately, a lone sentinel etched sharply against the pale winter dawn. Its rich and brilliant autumn plumage had long been gone, and now its branches were stark and bare; they groaned and cracked and moved fitfully in the bitter wind.

The body itself hung from a lower branch.

It was that of a young girl. She wore a shapeless monk's robe of gray cloth. The robe was unbelted, and it flopped open to reveal her thin, pathetic, naked body. The monkish hood had slipped partially over her pinched face, twisted in its last death agony.

Her flesh had begun to turn blue now. Her body had the stiff, frozen look of some forgotten scarecrow. There was a sandal on her left foot, but the right foot was bare. At the moment of impact, the sudden jerk had caused the sandal to fall off, and it lay below, buried in the snow, only its tip showing.

The girl hung like some broken toy, her legs spread grotesquely. Tiny, obscene icicles had begun to form on the hairs in her crotch.

Tied to the branch, and twisted around her neck, was a braided rope. Its color was green. Clearly, it was the belt that had held her robe, and it was this she had used to hang herself.

Now and then, when the wind gusted, the body swayed gently, and the rope creaked just a little, in sympathy with the naked branches above.

PART
ONE

1

The Devil was lying on the bed, flat on his back, smoking a cigarette.

Idly, he blew smoke rings, watching them float upward and finally flatten against the ceiling of the hotel room. Occasionally he glanced at his watch, and frowned.

The Devil was waiting for a phone call.

Actually, he wore no horns, nor did he sport a tail. And of course, he had registered at the hotel under another name. But there were those who regarded him literally as Satan himself. Or to be more exact, the human incarnation of Satan. They cursed him daily in their prayers; they warned the innocent and gullible to be constantly on their guard, never to listen to the seductive whisperings of the Antichrist in their ears, nor to yield to the temptations he offered. They would have gladly consigned him to Hell. But they knew, of course, this was useless since it was, after all, his home.

To those who really knew him, the Devil had no earthly home. Today, he was in New York. Tomorrow it could be Chicago. Or St. Louis. Or Miami, Houston, Seattle. He was nowhere, and he was everywhere. The Devil's work was never done. He was dedicated, and he was diligent. And he always struck without warning.

The man they variously called the Devil, the Evil One, Satan, or Lucifer, or simply the Antichrist, or very often just *him*, was in his late forties. Even at this age, he had the lean, lithe body of an athlete. Women would have admired him, men would have liked and trusted him. He could be cold steel, or he could be completely charming. He had a rough-hewn, craggy kind of face, bright ice-blue eyes which could either snap or sparkle, and light brown hair. It was a face you could easily overlook in a crowd, and this was to his advantage. He had all the natural cunning you might expect of the Devil himself; a quick brain, a gift with words, and he was very very expert in the art of persuasion. He knew when to whisper sweet reason. But he also knew when and where to strike for the jugular.

Finally, the phone rang.

Languidly, he reached an arm out and picked up the phone on the end table. The voice at the other end of the line shook a little. It sounded frightened.

"This is Williams. Stanley Williams."

"You're a little late."

"I know. I was turning your deal over in my mind."

"And?"

"I've decided to accept it."

"No more haggling? On my terms?"

"You're asking a hell of a high price."

"Not for the services I intend to render. You can still back out, Mr. Williams . . ."

"No. I'll pay it."

"Fine. Now, you understand this can be dangerous?"

"Yes."

"If you fail, you could be in big trouble."

"I know that. But I'm willing to take the risk." The quaver in Williams' voice was more pronounced now. "I'd gamble everything I've got on this."

The Devil was sympathetic. "I don't blame you. If I were

in your position, I'd do the same. Now—you agreed, when we last met, to follow my instructions. To the letter. It's vital you do so. Do you understand?"

"Yes."

"You've made all the preliminary arrangements?"

"Yes. We're ready for you."

"All right, Williams. I'll take the next plane out."

"If you'll phone me the airline, and the flight number, I'll meet you at the airport . . . "

"No. The airport's a public place. Too many eyes. It'd be wiser if we're not seen together. Sit tight and wait. *I'll* contact *you.*"

The Devil hung up. He buttoned his shirt collar, tied his tie, and put on his jacket. He slipped on a pair of dark glasses. He always wore them when he traveled, day and night. A small bag, already fully packed, stood on the baggage stand. The Devil always traveled light. There was only one thing missing from the suitcase.

He went to the bureau, and picked up a Bible. The covers of this particular Holy Book were frayed and well worn. Its pages had been thumbed many times. And he never went anywhere without it.

He took the elevator down and checked out at the desk. He paid his bill in cash.

He walked out, hailed a cab, and said to the driver: "Kennedy Airport."

He sat back and stared out of the window. It had already been drizzling, but now it began to rain hard. Suddenly the lunch hour crowds on the streets became animated. They turned up their coat collars, raised umbrellas, ran for shelter, and waved for cabs. The cab driver cursed at the clogged crosstown traffic.

The Devil was barely aware of his surroundings. He was deeply absorbed in his own thoughts. He was beginning to feel the old, familiar excitement. A kind of ecstasy, even exaltation. He was already on his way. Everything was all set. The pact had been made. And he thought, *here we go again.*

I'm going to steal another one from Jesus.

And after this one, another one, and another, *and* another.

He paid the cab driver, walked into the terminal, went to the counter, and bought a first-class ticket for a flight leaving in a half hour. He paid for it in cash. The Devil always rode first class. It wasn't just a matter of status. He was tired, and he needed all the rest he could get, for there would be much to do.

At the gate entrance, a clerk checked his ticket before he boarded. The ticket read *Denver*.

But actually, the Devil was bound for a place called Gath, which was in the country of the Philistines, the place where David, fearing still that he would perish by the hand of Saul, dwelt for one full year and four months.

2

The name of the man driving the Mercedes was Frank Reed. He was a big man, with a rugged, windblown face, and he was forty-five years old. By profession, he was a civil engineer, and his home was in Montecito, California, a prosperous suburb of Santa Barbara. His wife, Kate, who sat next to him, was two or three years younger.

The time was eight o'clock on a hot Sunday morning in July. The highway was Route 101, and at this moment, they were heading south toward Los Angeles, hugging the Pacific on their right. It was still a little early for the real beach traffic to develop, and they moved at a steady sixty through Carpinteria, Punta, Sea Cliff, and Ventura.

Kate Reed glanced at her husband anxiously. Her face was haggard.

"You're sure we'll get there in time?"

"No problem."

"But by the time we get into the Malibu area, we'll run into heavy traffic . . ."

"I've made allowances for that."

"I just hope we can find the place . . ."

"We'll find it," he said. "We'll find it. The directions they gave us are clear enough." Then suddenly, irritated: "For Christ's sake, Kate, try to relax."

"How can I?" she said. "How could anybody?" Then: "Frank, I'm afraid . . ."

"Take it easy. There's nothing to be afraid of."

"I keep thinking of that man on the phone. His voice. The way he sounded. So—so weird. You were listening on the extension. You heard . . ."

"I know. All these creeps sound the same way."

"What did he say his name was?"

"Abijah."

"Abijah. What kind of crazy name is that?"

He shrugged, and they were silent for a while. Kate Reed felt exhausted, emotionally drained. Both she and her husband had been up most of the night, unable to sleep, thinking of the morning, and the rendezvous. She opened her purse and reached for her cigarettes. Next to the pack, she felt the sealed envelope. Her hand closed tightly over it for a moment, as though it could conceivably provide an instant answer to their dilemma. Fervently, she hoped it would.

She lit a cigarette and leaned back, closing her eyes, listening to the hum of the motor and the singing of the tires on the road. Then suddenly, the agony burst from her, she could contain it no longer:

"My God, Frank, I don't believe this. I *still* don't believe it. Why did this have to happen to *us?*"

"Don't ask me," he said, grimly. "Ask *him.*"

Just beyond Ventura, he swung the Mercedes away from 101 and onto Route 1, the Pacific Coast Highway. From Point Mugu to Leo Carrillo Beach, the traffic thickened. Parking space was already at a premium along the sides of the road opposite the beaches, and in the public parking lots, cars were jockeying for space.

They drove by Malibu Colony. The ocean was calm today, lead-blue in color, its surface heaving gently like some great bosom, rolling small waves shoreward like long undulations of molten glass, and finally spilling a token and apologetic surf upon the hot sand. A group of disconsolate surfers, wearing their rubber suits, loitered, waiting hopefully for the sea to change. A lone jogger ran doggedly along the beach, head up, arms flailing. Two young men threw and caught a Frisbee at incredible distances. The sun was bright, it razzle-dazzled the ocean, and there was no sign of smog.

All in all, reflected Frank Reed, a beautiful morning. Not the kind of morning for a mission such as theirs. This was the wrong backdrop. There should be black skies, rain, fog, thunder perhaps. The way it usually was in movies, on occasions like this. The day, being contrary, seemed malicious, it seemed to mock them.

Now they passed a miscellaneous assortment of motels, restaurants, fish places, and fast food chains. On the left rose the Malibu hills, topped by houses standing at crazy angles, some on stilts. The hills were very dry, of a brown and pinkish cast, cut through by the various canyons.

"We should be at the turnoff by now."

"It should be coming up any second."

"Maybe," she said, anxiously. "We missed it. Maybe it was one of those other canyons back there . . ."

"No," he said. "I've been watching. Better get the map out now. We're going to need it."

She took the map from her handbag. Just as she did, he saw the landmark the Voice had designated on the phone, the orange sign on the high pylon.

"There it is," he said. "The Gulf station. That's where we turn left. Topanga Canyon."

He made the turn, and they began to move upward.

"How many miles from the turnoff, Kate?"

She checked the map. "Four and three quarters."

"And then?"

"Then you turn left on a dirt road. It's just before some place called Thatcher Village."

The canyon was a series of curves. Frank Reed slowed the Mercedes, taking them carefully. It was remarkable how quickly the country changed, from the car-choked Pacific

Highway and its gas fumes below, to this mountain wilderness. The air was clear and slightly aromatic with the odor of eucalyptus.

They got caught behind a truck on the two-lane road. Kate was upset by their lack of progress.

"We'll never get there in time."

"Just keep your eye on the mileage."

"They warned us not to be late. Not even one minute late. Or else . . . "

"What time is it now?"

Nervously, she looked at her watch.

"Eight forty-five." She studied the map. "And we've still got a ways to go."

He blew his horn at the truck. The truck driver ignored him. He blew it again and again, in frustration. Still the driver of the truck made no effort to pull his rig over to the side of the road.

"That son-of-a-bitch."

He set his jaw, and suddenly swung the Mercedes to the outside. He was on a blind curve. Kate gasped and shut her eyes. If another car came around the curve, going downhill, straight at them, there would be no room to move. The canyon dropped steeply on her left. She prayed a little, and opened her eyes. They were around the curve, and safe, just missing a Mercury coming down fast. The truck driver behind them blew his horn again and again, outraged at their insanity.

She felt faint. The yellow dividing lines on the road blurred and wavered before her eyes. She knew it was not wholly from the close call they had just had. The nausea in her throat was rising now, because of the ordeal which lay ahead for them.

Not really for them. For her alone.

They had been very specific about that. It was *she* they would deal with, and nobody else.

"There it is," Kate said, suddenly. "The dirt road."

He had almost overrun it. He slammed on the brakes, turned sharply left. A rude wooden sign, in the shape of an arrow, pointed up the road. The sign was weatherbeaten, the letters almost indistinguishable.

Ashtaroth.

That was all. Just the single word. Ashtaroth. The dirt road seemed to climb steeply along the side of the mountain. It was one S-curve after another. He threw the car into low gear, and they struggled upward. The switchbacks seemed interminable. The canyon to the left dropped perpendicularly to the distant valley floor. Far off, they could see the ocean.

Finally, they came to another dirt road, this one rough and rutted, branching off to the right. And again, the sign: *Ashtaroth.* Only this time, it was lettered in white paint on a huge rock. Beside the rock, a wooden sign threatened: *Warning: This Is A Private Road! Trespassers Keep Out!*

"How far up this road, Kate? What does the map say?"

"Three tenths of a mile."

Frank Reed took the road carefully. It consisted of one switchback after another, hairpin turns veering off into nothing but deep canyon. These bastards really liked their privacy, he thought. And maybe they had good reason.

Suddenly, they came to Ashtaroth.

It burst upon them as they turned the final S-curve. It was located on a flat area that seemed to be cut out of the mountain itself. At first glance, it appeared to be the campus of some small college. There was a large building, set back, which seemed to be a kind of administration building, from which radiated walks leading to a number of other buildings. The grounds were well kept, the lawns mowed. The buildings themselves looked fairly new, perhaps four or five years old.

But on closer examination, it was obvious that this was not a campus, but some kind of compound.

There were a couple of odd things about Ashtaroth.

The first oddity was a huge golden cross, perhaps fifty feet in height. At the moment, as the Reeds stared at it, its reflection in the sun was blinding. It did not stand on top of any church or chapel, but on the roof of the main building itself. On its vertical bar, they could make out the letters SFJ. And each of the other, dormitory-like, buildings was topped by a similar but smaller cross.

The second oddity was the high metal fence that completely surrounded the compound. There was only one gate and that was tightly shut. The gate had no handle on the outside; it could be opened only from within.

The sign on the gate was emphatic.

Private! Keep Out! Area Forbidden to Strangers! Gate and Fence Are Electrified!

Frank Reed brought the car to a stop in front of the gate.

Suddenly, as though sensing their presence, or catching their odor on some wind, a pack of dogs began to howl from somewhere within. Kate Reed turned to her husband, startled. She shivered, felt the goose pimples spring up on her arms and back.

"Frank, I'm afraid. I can't do it."

"You've got to."

"I just can't go in there alone."

"God knows, I wish I could come in with you. Do you think it's going to be any fun, sitting out here in the car, waiting for you, wondering what the hell is happening in there, what they're going to say to you? But you know what this Abijah creep said on the phone. Only you go through that gate. And he was pretty damned emphatic about it."

She stared at the gate. Fear constricted her throat. The dogs continued to howl, desecrating the silence of this mountain retreat. They sounded as though they were held back and, if allowed loose, would automatically rend and tear. She felt his arm around her, holding her close, reassuring her.

"We've got to do it their way, Kate. Either that, or turn back." He waited a moment. "Do you want to do that? Do you want to go back, without seeing him?"

"No," she whispered. "Oh, no."

"The thing is, you've got to really talk to him," said Frank, almost fiercely. "You've got to make him see what he's done, make him understand."

"I'll try, Frank. Oh God, I'll try . . . "

"You're his mother, Kate. He won't listen to me. But he'll listen to you. He's *got* to!" He leaned over and opened the car door for her. "Don't be afraid. Nobody's going to hurt you. I'll be waiting right here."

She got out of the car and walked slowly to the gate. There was a communications setup at the gate for visitors, a panel on which you pressed a button, spoke into a speaker. She hesitated a moment, drew a long breath, and then pressed the button.

"Who is it?"

A voice answered. It had a harsh, metallic sound. It came over a public address system somewhere, and it could be heard over the entire compound. It sounded not only loud, but obscene.

"Who is it?"

"This is Mrs. Reed. Mrs. Frank Reed."

"Mrs. Reed," the voice repeated.

"Yes. I'm expected."

There was a long silence. The howling of the dogs stopped abruptly, as though someone had suddenly corked their mouths.

"You are to enter alone, without your husband, as agreed. You understand?"

"Yes."

The electric gate slid open. She stepped inside, and it closed noiselessly behind her. Again, the tinny voice:

"You are to walk toward the building, straight ahead of you."

She started down the long driveway, toward the building topped by the huge gold cross. The place seemed entirely deserted; the silence was eerie, almost obscene in itself, broken only by the crunch of her shoes on the gravel drive. Kate Reed could feel the perspiration break out all over her body, she could feel it seeping through her clothing.

It was all some kind of nightmare. What was she doing in this place, on this bright Sunday morning in July, this beautiful sunny morning? She noted the mountains, earth-colored against the blue sky, and far off she could see the ocean sparkling in the sun, and she knew the beaches now were covered with bathers, playing and resting and plunging into the surf. To everybody else in this world it was a hot July Sunday like any other, and normally, she and Frank would be home in Montecito, and it would be just after breakfast, and they would be planning to go to the Club for a round of golf, or perhaps swim in the pool, or perhaps do nothing, except lie around the house, reading the paper and doing the little household chores people did on Sunday mornings...

Suddenly, she saw four men come out of the building and walk forward to meet her.

They were all lean, all had an emaciated look. They were dressed in rough gray monks' habits, wearing cowling or hoods, their robes held by rope belts. Their leader wore a long white beard, and his belt was white. The others were clean shaven, and younger; their belts were red. To Kate Reed, they looked like sinister apparitions from the Dark Ages, like the monks of the Inquisition.

They walked toward her slowly, in measured cadence. Then they stopped. Their faces were stony, as they stood there silently, watching her.

Finally, the older man, the bearded man with the white belt, held his hands up, and placed his left forefinger across his right forefinger, to form a cross.

"Jesus loves you," he said.

The other three followed suit, forming the same kind of cross with their forefingers, and intoned in unison:

"Jesus loves you."

Kate Reed was bewildered. She did not quite know how to reply. She took it as some sort of blessing, or greeting, some ritual of recognition. She started to stammer something, then stopped, confused. Finally, she said:

"I—I came here by appointment. I spoke to—to someone named Abijah. He said I was to be here at ten o'clock..."

"You are standing on sacred ground," said the leader. "This is a church, and we call it Ashtaroth, after the name in the Bible. We are all Souls for Jesus—born again in Christ, and disciples of his Messenger, whom we call The Master. I am First Elder of the Souls for Jesus here. My name is Nehemiah." He nodded toward his three companions. "And these are my Deacons—Zedekiah, Hattush, and Azariah." Then: "You have brought the money?"

28

"Yes."

"Exactly as Abijah has directed?"

"Yes."

The First Elder held out his hand: "Then I will take it."

Kate made no move to open her purse. She stared into the blue eyes of the First Elder.

"First, I want to see my son."

"Your son? And who is your son?"

"Jeff. Jeff Reed."

"There is no Jeff Reed here," said the First Elder.

"He is here. I *know* he is. He told me, over the phone . . ."

"Your son is dead," said the First Elder.

"Jeff? Dead?"

Her mouth fell open. Her heart seemed to stop. She stared into the cold blue eyes of Nehemiah. His face was impassive.

"Dead?" She choked. "He's . . ."

"I repeat, Jeffrey Reed is dead. This was his earth-name. There is no longer anyone here by that name. You came here to see Simeon."

"Simeon?"

"When he became a Soul for Jesus, a Neophyte in the Church, he was born again as Simeon. It is Simeon you wish to see. But he is no longer your son."

"What do you mean?"

"He no longer belongs to you. You are only his earth-mother. He belongs to Christ, now." The First Elder held out his hand again. "If you will give me the money now, as Simeon requested."

Suddenly, she was no longer afraid, but angry. She set her lips.

"I want to see my son."

"That is impossible."

"I don't care what you say, I'm his mother. And I insist on seeing him."

A faint smile flitted across Nehemiah's stony face. "That may be true. But he does not wish to see you."

"I don't believe it," she flared. "You're lying."

"To speak thus to a First Elder of the Souls for Jesus is

blasphemy." The blue eyes blazed. " 'Speak not evil one of another.' " Suddenly, his face softened, became beatific, benevolent: " 'So saith the Lord. Let all bitterness, and wrath, and anger and clamour, and evil speaking, be put away from you, and with it all malice.' "

The three Deacons intoned, "Amen. Praise Jesus and give ye to Him your Soul."

Kate Reed stared at the four men. Their faces were rigid, set. Their eyes seemed glazed. They seemed to be looking through her, instead of at her.

"I'll say it again," she said. "I won't leave here until I see my son." Then: "And unless I do, I'm taking the money with me."

"I repeat. Simeon does not wish to see you."

"You mean, you won't let him see me."

The First Elder smiled. He turned to one of the Deacons.

"Hattush, summon Simeon to come to us."

"But is this wise, Nehemiah? He is still a Neophyte still going through Holy Purification. Perhaps he is not ready . . ."

"Have faith in the Lord, Hattush. We are here to see his miracles. Do you question it? Then you are a fool. Read Proverbs again, and take heed: 'A fool's mouth is his destruction, and his lips are the snare of his soul.' "

The Deacon named Hattush reddened at the reproach. He turned toward the main building, and signaled with a wave of his hand. A moment later, Kate·Reed saw her son come out of the door, and walk slowly toward them.

She stood rigid in shock, staring at him.

Oh God, she thought, Ohgodohgodohgod, what have they done to him?

Suddenly, she wanted to cry.

She hardly recognized him. He had been here about a month, and now he looked thin, half-starved. His face was pale, it had the pasty look of prison pallor, and his hair was long and wild. But it was his eyes. They were glassy, dead, they seemed spaced out. He stared at his mother like some robot, some zombie, almost without recognition. He wore the rough, gray monk's robe and cowl, like the others—but the rope belt he wore was green in color—green for the Neophyte, the new Soul for Jesus.

He held up his forefingers, crossed them in the sign, and spoke the ritual greeting to the First Elder in a kind of dead, reflex monotone.

"Jesus loves you, Nehemiah."

"Jesus loves you, Simeon." Then, gently: "Your earth-mother has come to Ashtaroth. She has brought the money. But she would not give it to the Church until she could see you. We had hoped to spare you this ordeal. But we must also find out if you are ready for it."

Kate Reed was still in shock.

"Jeff," she blurted out, "oh, my God, Jeff!"

He stared at her. His mouth quivered. He trembled a little. He seemed under stress, some inner conflict.

"Don't call me Jeff. My name is Simeon now."

"Jeff, please . . ."

"Simeon." His voice suddenly became shrill, angry. "You and *him*. My earth-father. You never understood, you never listened to me. My name is Simeon now. *Simeon*."

"All right, darling. Simeon." She was on the verge of tears now. "Simeon, I . . ." She was suddenly conscious of the First Elder and the Deacons, standing in a small circle around them. They seemed far less interested in her than they were in Jeff. She turned to the First Elder.

"I'd like to speak to my son alone."

"He is no longer your son. True, you bore him first as a child. Now, he has been born again. He has a new spiritual mother and father, a new family."

She wasn't prepared to argue with him. The man was insane, what he was saying was crazy. But they were in authority here. For the moment, she thought, *do it their way.*

"I'm sorry. I'd like to see *Simeon* alone."

"This is forbidden."

"But I have a right to speak to him alone."

"You have no rights here in Ashtaroth. You belong to the world outside—the world of Satan. Here, there are no secrets among us. We are always together, in what we do and what

31

we say. It is so written in the Bible, in Ephesians and Galatians. 'We are members one of another. Bear ye one another's burdens, and so fulfill the law of Christ.' "

" 'If we walk in the light,' " said Jeff, suddenly, " 'as He is in the light, we have fellowship one with another.' "

Jeff's eyes were vacant, he intoned the words by rote. The First Elder smiled, pleased.

"Very good, Simeon. And the reference?"

"It is from the First Epistle General of John."

"Excellent, excellent."

The First Elder looked at the Deacons. They all beamed the same approval. Then he turned to Kate Reed:

"Mrs. Reed, it is best that you simply give the money to Simeon and then go . . ."

She ignored him and looked directly at Jeff. She met his eyes square on. She spoke gently, softly:

"Darling, your father's waiting outside. We've come to take you home. We don't know why you and Cindy Hyland came here to live. We know now, your father and I, that we made mistakes. Maybe we paid too much attention to your older brother, to Ken. Maybe we didn't show you the love you needed. Maybe we just didn't understand you, maybe we didn't even try. But your father and I love you, Jeff."

It seemed to her that his eyes had softened. That she was getting to him. His mouth was trembling again. It was almost as though he were choking up, making a hard effort to keep from saying something he wanted to say. The First Elder and the Deacons were watching him closely. She went on:

"Jeff, come home with us. Home to your family, to those who love you. Take Cindy out of here with you. Come home to your family, to those who loved you. Dad, and myself, and your brother Ken. All your friends keep asking for you, Joe Peterson, Tom Lacey, everybody." Her voice brightened. "And your father. He'll be home for a few months. He was talking about taking you to Colorado, on that camping trip you've always been talking about, and it would be wonderful if just the two of you . . ."

She began to falter. Something she had said had suddenly turned him off. She knew what it was. Mentioning his father. Telling Jeff his father loved him. Her son's eyes were suddenly glazed again, there was in them no longer any glimmer of warmth or memory; his face became stony; his mouth stopped trembling and became a thin, hard line. He stood rigid.

She kept talking, and her frustration became sharper and sharper, as the expression on his face remained unchanged. She was aware that the Souls for Jesus were listening to her monologue now in an amused kind of way. They were, in fact, relishing it, relishing her desperate attempts to get through Jeff's shell, to reach him again, somehow. Her face felt hot in her humiliation. But she continued to try:

"Darling, look. You've been accepted at Stanford this fall. You've got your whole career ahead of you. If it's Christ you want, if it's Him you're looking for, you can find Him in your own church. Oh I know, your father and I, we haven't been very good Catholics, but if you feel this way, we'll all go to Mass every Sunday, as a family. Darling, don't you understand, we love you . . ."

"You do not even know me. And I do not know you. My home is here. I am here to do the work of the Lord. To go home, as you call it, would only be to serve Satan. You have come here to tempt me." Jeff was shouting at her now. "You are not my mother. You are evil, a daughter of the Devil, spawned by Satan. And you are wed to a son of Satan, who was once my earth-father."

"My God," she said. "What have they done to you?"

"Done to me? They have shown me the way. They have taught me how to love God and each other. This is what they've done. But you wouldn't understand. You are a harlot, come here to tempt me. And the man who once was my earth-father is no better. He is scum, the vomit of a pig, an adulterer, a hypocrite."

"Please, Jeff. Please. Stop . . ."

He did not even hear her. "He cares only for the lusts of the flesh, in filling his fat belly with food and drink, lying and stealing and kissing the ass of the Establishment, the whole lousy system for his filthy dollars. You say he loves me? Him? *Him?*" Jeff laughed harshly. "He is filth, unclean, and so are you. He is shit. Shit, shit, *shit*. I am no longer of your rotten, stinking, flesh family. Don't you understand? I have been reborn in the spirit of Jesus, I have given him my soul. I do not know you, and I never want to know you. You and yours defile this earth. Do you know what Jesus himself said? 'And a man's foes shall be they of his own household.' It's right there in the Bible."

He turned to look at the First Elder, and suddenly he seemed to come out of his trance. He held his hand out to her: "Give me the money."

She kept staring at him, in shock, still unable to believe what she had seen and heard. Then she heard herself saying, "Jeff, they'll only take it from you and . . ."

"It's my money." His eyes blazed. "Not *his*. Mine. I made it myself. Give it to me."

She opened her bag and took out the fat envelope. All this seemed like some kind of dream to her now, some surrealist nightmare. What was she doing here, in this strange place, standing here in the hot, bright California sun, dealing with these grotesque zombies in robes and hoods, reviled and rejected by her own flesh and blood?

Reluctantly now, she handed the envelope over to her son. Suddenly, the anger in her welled up like bile in her throat. She saw the smiling faces of the robed men through a red haze. She wanted to slap the smiling, hypocritical face of the First Elder. She saw Jeff standing there, looking so thin, so pathetic.

She hardly knew him now. He was a stranger, talking this strange language, mouthing the Bible and speaking this filth and garbage, all in the same breath. She wanted to leap at his seducers and tear their eyes out with her nails. It was just as well that Frank hadn't come into the compound with her. She knew he would have gone wild at the sight of Jeff. She knew he would have waded into these four hypocrites in their obscene monk's costumes, he would have fought like a fiend, trying to smash in their smiling faces. Perhaps they had guessed at this possibility, and that was why they had insisted on seeing her alone.

She watched Jeff hand the fat envelope over to the First Elder, who put it in a pocket of his robe.

"Praise God, Simeon," he said, smiling. "Ye have done as the Lord has commanded, as written in the First Epistle of Paul the Apostle to Timothy. 'The end of the commandment is charity out of a pure heart, and of a good conscience, and of faith unfeigned.'"

With that, Kate Reed exploded.

"You damned, pious, Bible-quoting hypocrite," she flared. "If I could strangle you with my own hands, I would. Look what you've done to my son. You've made a zombie out of him. You've stolen his mind, and starved his body, and destroyed his spirit. And he's coming home with me. Now."

"Is he?" The First Elder laughed.

She turned to Jeff. "Jeff, for God's sake, take off those ridiculous clothes. We'll walk out of here together. They won't dare stop us. Your father's waiting outside. Let them keep the money. But we've come to take you home."

Jeff turned abruptly and began to walk toward the cross-topped building. Kate Reed ran after him. She was crying now.

"Jeff, please, don't go with them, come with me, please..."

He shook her off, as though she were something dirty. She was hysterical now, crying out his name. The First Elder came up to her and said: "Calm yourself. And go."

She slapped his face, hard. The three Deacons closed in on her. They seized her roughly and started to push her toward the gate. She fought like a tigress, tearing at their faces. But they were strong. Finally they reached the gate and opened it. Still, she fought them. They wrestled her through the gate.

Frank Reed saw them as soon as they opened the solid iron gates. He had been waiting impatiently. Now, he jumped out of the car and came at them. But he was a moment too late. They pushed her out and slammed the gate in his face.

Kate Reed put her face on her husband's shoulder and wept uncontrollably.

3

A few minutes later, the entire colony of Ashtaroth was summoned by loudspeaker to gather in the main hall, otherwise known as "The Church."

They came quickly from their dormitories and kitchens and study rooms, the young boys and girls in the robes and green belts of the recently converted—the Neophytes—and the red-belted Deacons. There was an altar at one end of the room, on one side of which was a golden statue of Jesus, lying limp on the Cross; at the other side was a huge, blown-up photograph of the Master himself, the Messenger of Jesus, His Divinity, leader and founder of the cult. He looked down at them with a loving smile, and a hand raised in benediction. The Church was empty of pews and chairs, and the hushed assembly sat on the hard floor, facing the altar.

Seated on the altar itself were the five Elders of Ashtaroth. Their faces were solemn, they fingered their white belts. In the center was Nehemiah, the First Elder. On his left sat Jeroboam, the Elder in charge of Witnessing, or recruiting new converts, and Henoch, the Elder in charge of Purification, Prayer, and Penitence. On Nehemiah's right sat Hezekiah, the treasurer in charge of tithes and revenues, and finally Rehoboam, the Chief Sexton of Ashtaroth, whose concern was administration, maintenance, and supply.

The curtains were drawn. Huge tapers set in candlesticks were lit at the base of the altar, throwing an eerie flickering light over the faces of the Elders, and sending dancing shadows through the hall itself.

Everybody was hushed. They knew this had to be some kind of event. They were rarely called together like this on a Sunday morning.

The First Elder arose and made the sign of the cross.

"Jesus loves you," he intoned.

Everyone in the crowded church made the same sign with crossed fingers.

"Jesus loves you, Nehemiah."

"The Master loves you," he said.

"Praised be the Master," intoned the crowd, "Messenger of God and our Beloved Leader."

"Ordinarily, I would not interrupt your Bible studies and meditation on this sacred day. But something has happened at Ashtaroth this morning which deserves your attention." He looked at the young people wearing the green belts. "And especially the attention of those of you newly born-again in Christ, those of you now undergoing Purification in His name and memory. As written in Timothy, all scripture is given by inspiration of God, and is profitable by doctrine, for reproof, for correction, for instruction in righteousness. We have tried to teach you this here at Ashtaroth. One of our members has learned this well, and today he was inspired by God, and remembered.

"As you know, Satan takes many forms, comes in many guises, man or woman, and offers many temptations. Today, he came to see our new brother Simeon, in the form of his earth-mother. She tried to pollute his Purification, to shake his faith. But he knew who she was, smelled her evil. And he rejected her, and his earth-father as well, for his real family. For you. His spiritual family. Let all of you profit by his example. Your mothers and fathers are no longer yours. They are of flesh, and yours are spiritual. Simeon here has taken a long step in his Purification. He has overcome and hurdled a great test. There will be others. And some day he will change his green belt for red. Praise be to Simeon."

"Praise be to Simeon," shouted the crowd.

"I have said," continued the First Elder, "that Satan takes many forms, comes in many guises. But there is one he favors, most of all. We have told you who he is. We have shown you photographs of him. You would all know him if you saw him?"

"We know him," they responded.

"Then be on the watch for him," warned the First Elder. "He is anywhere, and everywhere. His business is to steal Souls for Jesus, wherever he can, and convert them into Souls for Satan. Beware of him, be always alert, for he is the Antichrist incarnate in the guise of an ordinary man. His technique is to strike at our God Squads as they gather tithes on the street. If you see him, report him at once to your Deacon leader." The First Elder paused for breath. "But enough of this unpleasant subject. This is a joyous occasion. We have seen our young brother Simeon pass our hardest test."

The First Elder raised his arms and smiled.

"As it is written in Psalms, make a joyful noise unto the Lord. Sing, O ye Heavens. Shout, ye lower parts of the earth. Turn on for Jesus!"

Suddenly, a group of Deacons rose and opened large cabinet doors at the side of the Church. They took out electric guitars, rolled out a small piano and a set of drums, and quickly set them up. At first, the drummer played alone. A moment or two later, to the steady beat of the drummer, the entire congregation began a low chant:

My Soul belongs to Jesus! Hallelujah!
My Soul belongs to Jesus! Hallelujah!
My Soul belongs to Jesus! Hallelujah!

The chant began to increase in intensity. Neophytes, Deacons and Elders alike seemed transfixed, hypnotized. They shouted the chant, glassy-eyed. A kind of mass hypnotism seized them. They began to sway back and forth, rocking from side to side.

"My Soul belongs to Jesus! Hallelujah!"

Finally, at a signal from the First Elder, the chanting stopped. There was a moment of silence. Everyone surrounded Simeon now, in a great circle. Then the monk-robed band started to play, and a singer at the microphone started to chant a hymn to the Glory of God, the lyrics composed by the Master himself. The lyrics were set to rock music, and the Souls for Jesus began what they called the Sacramental Dance. They joined hands and swung around Simeon, singing praises to the Lord as they danced. They twisted and gyrated, and went into individual patterns now, as the rhythm built up, the beat of the piano increased, the sound of the drums grew louder, and the two electric guitar players swayed back and forth as they twanged the strings.

The sound crashed through the Church, the dancing became wilder and more frenzied. Some of the dancers began to scream hysterically, as though possessed; they rolled their eyes upward, and waved their arms; they went into odd little dances of their own, swaying their hips and shaking their heads to the sound of the music.

The only one who did not dance was Simeon.

He stood in the center of the swirling, whirling crowd, careening wildly around him like dervishes, as though intoxicated by the music and possessed by demons. He watched them raptly, his face flushed. This particular Sacramental Dance was in his honor. By ritual, he was not supposed to dance, merely stand and watch.

Suddenly, he began to feel it come. He felt hot all over, he began to sweat. There was so much pressure on his chest that he could hardly breathe. He knew exactly what was happening to him, he had seen it in others. He was being possessed by the Holy Spirit.

He raised his hands and began to moan softly.

The First Elder, who had been watching Simeon, signaled

the band to stop abruptly. The dancing stopped. They all stared at Simeon, waited expectantly.

He felt ecstatic, exalted. He felt relaxed, incredibly light, as though he were floating among clouds. He knew he was not controlling his own behavior, he was being manipulated in some supernatural way. He was in a complete trance now. Something, or somebody, was using his vocal cords. His tongue began to move of its own accord. He could feel it moving, he could hear his own words, as he began:

> *Ki lada dada ko camana.*
> *Kiamo dado amus boronba.*
> *Snan verta, shan piro sun kalana.*
> *Camana, camana. Dio, io . . .*

Everyone listened raptly. One of the Deacons took a tape recorder from a cupboard and turned it on, to take Simeon's words down for posterity. The First Elder raised his hands high to the heavens, and announced solemnly:

"Praise be to Simeon. Now he is speaking in tongues. He is speaking the language of the angels. God's language. The Holy Spirit has possessed him, and now speaks through his mouth."

And all present chanted: "Praise be to Simeon, and to our Lord who has blessed him."

And Simeon continued, his eyes closed, still babbling, the words pouring from his mouth:

> *Hano, hanta, brago, domi,*
> *Shum, domi, O, domi,*
> *Daga, cristas, jono, opono,*
> *Laga, laha, vilia, vidi,*
> *O, madaga, madaga . . .*

He seemed to be dancing in a shaft of light. His body shook, he felt alternately hot and cold. Waves of passion poured through him, he felt the surge of indescribable power. His head reeled, his brain seemed ready to explode, he felt insanely wonderful, as though on the verge of an incredible orgasm. His lips continued to move, his tongue continued to chatter gibberish. He did not understand it, but he knew he was not really speaking, he was being spoken *through*.

He fell to the floor, and started to roll over and over. And still the heavenly words came pouring from him:

Dolo, dovala shun lana,
Mobo, brada, son moga, moga,
Decium, doora, doora, doora,
O, madaga, O madaga ...

Finally, the words began to fade and became indistinct, until they were mere mutterings. Simeon's tongue and lips stopped moving, and his mouth closed. Slowly, he came out of his trance. There were tears in his eyes. He was soaked with perspiration, sweat poured down his face. He looked about him, bewildered. The faces of the others came out of the mist.

He began to weep. And he cried, over and over again: "Hallelujah, I believe! I believe, I believe, I *believe ...*"

There was one Neophyte who did not press forward to congratulate Simeon.

Her born-again name, the biblical name assigned to her, was Athaliah. But her earth-name had been Cindy Hyland. She and Jeff had gone together on the "outside," and they had been "witnessed," or proselytized—recruited into the cult—together.

It was Jeff who had been eager to come to Ashtaroth, just to see what it was like, and she had reluctantly gone along. Now she realized how they not only seduced you into joining, but how they kept you in the cult, once you passed through that electric gate and it closed behind you.

Some deep instinct told her this whole Souls for Jesus thing was evil. She knew they were trying to steal her mind through the Purification procedure and the other techniques they used to make new believers out of the Neophytes. She did not quickly succumb, as did the others.

41

She knew that in time she would, that finally they would get to her, as they had gotten to Jeff and the others. No one could withstand their onslaught forever. She had to steel herself not to panic, not to show them how frightened or disturbed she was. Sometimes, when they kept at her with the recordings, and the Bible quotations, repeating them over and over, and drumming in her ears day and night that Jesus loved her, and so did they, she felt hypnotized, felt herself falling over the edge. But somehow, she always pulled back, remembering who she had been, desperately holding on to her identity.

At night, unable to sleep, she would toss and turn and tell herself, I am not Athaliah, I am Cindy Hyland, Cindy Hyland, *I am still Cindy Hyland.* She would repeat this over and over again, until she fell asleep, trying to plant it so deeply in her mind that they could never take it away from her.

Now, watching Jeff as he continued to accept congratulations, she was terribly worried.

She could see he was getting in pretty deep, and soon he would be too far gone. She had to talk to him. Get through to him. Make him understand what they were doing to him. She had to find some way to get out, and persuade Jeff to go with her. And it had to be soon.

But how? They were trapped here, prisoners. They never let you alone with anyone else. Never. Not for a moment. There was always a Deacon or an Elder nearby. Watching. Always watching. To be alone, in their view, was dangerous. If you were alone, you had a chance to think.

Suddenly, she felt an arm encircle her waist. A body pressed against hers from behind.

"Ah, Athaliah. It's a great day for Simeon."

She turned to see that it was the Deacon Tobiah. Tobiah was her mentor and Bible teacher. He was middle-aged, overweight, and had a bloated body that looked huge under his robe. He seemed to perspire all the time, he suffered from acne. His small eyes were always fixed on her greedily when he discussed the Bible with her, and when he leaned over to show her a particular passage, he loved to lean his face against hers. He had bad breath, and its stink repelled her.

"I suppose you cannot wait until you get through Purification, Athaliah."

"No, Tobiah."

"Then study your Bible well." He kept his arm around her waist and smiled benevolently at her. "Work, hard, Athaliah, and the time will come. I shall help you all I can." He smiled again. "You see, I cannot wait, either."

He left her then, and she watched him go. She shuddered. She knew exactly what he meant. After Purification, she would no longer be untouchable, when it came to her flesh. She would be available. And she knew Tobiah had already chosen her.

She pictured the night she would be summoned to his room. She imagined him stripping her of her robe, his eyes eating her naked body. She thought of how it would be, that overripe wet red mouth crushing hers, those fat fingers and sweaty hands fondling her breasts, and finally, caught in his embrace, smelling the stink and sweat of him, crushed under that fat belly, penetrated by him—in effect, raped, yet submitting because it was inconceivable that a young Neophyte would dare reject a Deacon, an important officer of the Church, next only to an Elder. And rejecting him was also inconceivable because they were both children of Jesus, everybody loved everybody, and everybody was obligated to comfort everybody, not just by prayer, but in every other way. . . .

She gagged at the very thought of lying naked with Tobiah, caught in his wet and hairy embrace. She was sure she'd kill herself before she let that happen. She knew he would do everything he could to rush along her Purification, because he wanted her quickly. There must be some way to get out of here. She had to think, *think*. And talk to Jeff. Make him listen. Try to make him understand what they were doing to him.

If it wasn't too late.

4

The next day, Frank Reed was in the office of his friend and golfing companion, Joe Haines, an assistant district attorney of Santa Barbara County.

He had called Haines the first thing in the morning, asking to see him immediately. Haines had known Reed for a long time. They had been classmates at Stanford, and he had always known Frank to be a very cool man, quietly tough when he had to be, and absolutely unflappable. But this was another Frank Reed he was listening to over the phone. He canceled another appointment to fit in his friend.

Reed told Haines that about two weeks ago, he'd received a call from Jeff. Jeff had been down in the Malibu–Santa Monica area. He had, in fact, been away for two weeks before that. His excuse was that he had been surfing. The fact was that he had met some girl down there. Some girl named Cindy Hyland. He had brought her home once, and she seemed nice enough. She lived somewhere in Santa Monica, and obviously Jeff and she were shacking up together somewhere down there.

Joe Haines smiled.

"And that's what's bothering you?"

"Hell no," said Reed. "That's something I would expect—kids being the way they are these days. Both Kate and I understand that—it's a whole different world. Of course, when he suggested that this girl and he spend the night together in his room at our house, just as if they were married, Kate got a little upset, and I put my foot down. I thought it showed a lot of gall. I told Jeff that while they were staying under our roof, there were certain customs we expected to maintain. Well, Jeff didn't like that much. He got into a huff about it, and we had an argument, and he told me, in so many words, to go screw myself, he wouldn't spend the night home at all, and they both drove off." He hesitated, looked at Haines. "It's funny, I get along with his older brother, Ken, we really get along together, we see eye to eye on everything, but Jeff—?" He paused, looked at Haines, and then, apologetically:

"Sorry, Joe. I know you've got a tight schedule. I didn't mean to get off the track."

"You were saying about this phone call . . ."

"Oh. Yes. I got this phone call. It was from Jeff, and he sounded strange. I don't know, sort of weird. As though he were spaced out—on drugs, or something. He told me he'd decided not to go on to college in the fall. He was quitting school, and so was Cindy, and together they were going into the service of the Lord."

"The *what?*"

"The service of the Lord. They had become born-again Christians, and they were getting on what he called the God-wagon, and they were going to become Souls for Jesus. They were going to work to save the world from its sins, and live with their new family at the Church, this big commune-type place in Topanga Canyon they called Ashtaroth."

Haines stared. "Jeff? He's joined a cult?"

"Would you believe it? A Hope Ranch kid doing a crazy thing like that? *My* son?"

"Look, Frank. I can't really see Jeff staying with this, I mean, not seriously . . ."

"That's what I thought," said Reed, grimly. "And then I got another call. From Jeff. A week later."

"Yes?"

"He sounded weirder than ever. What's the word these kids use? Stoned. I'm convinced these bastards have him into drugs, Joe. Anyway, he told us he wanted to give everything he had to Souls for Jesus, and he'd already given them his car. A Porsche I bought him last year. It was a couple of years old, but I paid ten thousand for it, and he'd *given* it to them, for God's sake. Not sold it, *given* it to them. Not only that, he had three thousand dollars in a savings account of his own. He said he couldn't go get the money himself, but he'd written a letter to the bank, instructing them to turn the money over to his mother, and close out the account."

"Why all this rigamarole? Why didn't he just go down to the bank and take out the money himself?"

"I asked him that. He said he couldn't do it, because he was going through something they call Purification, and he couldn't leave the Church for a period of time. There was still another reason. He couldn't take out the money unless he presented the passbook, and he'd left it home. Anyway, what he wanted us to do was take out the money and mail it to him, so that he could give it to Christ. Meaning the cult, of course."

Haines smiled thinly. "I can imagine what you said to *that*."

Reed nodded. "I really blew my top. I told him I'd be damned if I was going to do that. Or let Kate do it. We weren't going to mail him one dime. I told him these creeps were milking him of everything he had, and begged him to get out of there and come home. But I don't know, Joe, it was like talking to someone else, someone really spaced out, a stranger. I had the feeling that I wasn't even talking to my own son, but to someone else entirely. Then he came on with the blackmail."

"Blackmail?"

"He said the money was his, and sooner or later he'd collect it. But he wanted it now. If he didn't get it, he'd never see us again. He laid it on to Kate, she's always been so permissive to him. She was listening on the extension, and he really broke her down. He told her he never wanted to see or hear from her again. She started to cry at that. Then he said he'd make a deal with her. She could come up to this Ashtaroth, where he was staying, and bring the money in cash. Only then would he see her."

"And naturally, Kate went for it."

"Naturally. He wasn't interested in seeing *me* at all. And the thought of never seeing Jeff again was too much for her to bear."

Then he told Haines what had happened on their visit to Ashtaroth. Kate had been hysterical all night. She was under sedation now, and he was afraid she could go over the edge and into a nervous breakdown.

"Joe," said Reed. "I need your advice. These people aren't just robbing him blind of everything he's got. They've turned him into some kind of zombie. How can I get him out of there—away from these creeps—and back home, where he belongs?"

"How old is Jeff now?"

"Eighteen."

Haines shook his head. "Then, legally speaking, there isn't a thing you or we can do."

"Why not?"

"If he were a minor, you'd be responsible for his welfare and protection. But according to California law, anyone who passes the age of eighteen is legally an adult. The fact is, Jeff can do anything he wants without your permission."

"But when he does something crazy like this . . ."

"*You* think it is. He doesn't. As an adult person, he has the right to worship as he pleases, join any church he wants to. It's part of the First Amendment. Freedom of religion."

"But goddamn it, Joe, this isn't a legitimate church. It's a cult. A religious ripoff run by weirdos."

"You know that and I know that. But a lot of people look at it differently."

"But they *took* Jeff's car and his money. Isn't that some kind of fraud?"

"Hard to prove," said Haines, patiently. "His answer would be that he gave them the car and money voluntarily. As a gift or contribution."

"But for God's sake, they had him hypnotized . . ."

"Take it easy," said Haines, soothingly. "Take it easy . . ."

"Look, there must be *some* kind of legal action you can take . . ."

"It's out of my jurisdiction, Frank. Ashtaroth is in Los Angeles County. I can talk with the people down there, but I'd just be wasting my breath. I doubt if you'd get any action. There are a lot of other parents who have the same complaint you do. Some of them, particularly in the East, have formed organizations to combat the cults. They've been putting on some legal pressure, but the cults have plenty of legal muscle of their own. The cults, and especially this Souls for Jesus, are loaded with tax-free money, and they've got all kinds of political clout. They've had protest meetings with Senators and Representatives in Washington, hollering about their right to exist. They've got a lobby in Washington you wouldn't believe."

"And these congressmen are falling for it?"

"Look, Frank. Anybody will tell you. Nobody in government, on any level, national, state or local, likes to screw around with any religious issues, or investigate any particular religious group, no matter how weird it is. It's a very delicate area, it can blow right up in your face. The first thing you know, you have the ACLU and a lot of other organizations getting on your back, screaming bloody murder, yelling violation of religious freedom and the First Amendment. Even the established churches haven't officially attacked the cults to any great extent. They want to protect their position, as free institutions . . ."

"Joe," said Reed, quietly, "I understand the problems. But somehow, I'm going to get my boy out of that Ashtaroth place. We've made some mistakes bringing up Jeff, some bad mistakes, and a lot of it is my fault . . ."

"Frank, Frank, why do you think *you're* so different? We *all* make mistakes. These kids we're bringing up today are all little monsters, including mine . . ."

Reed didn't seem to hear him. "Kate and I both love Jeff. I'm not going to just stand by and let these pious bastards waste him, ruin him. I'm not just going to stand by and watch Kate slowly go out of her mind." He was white with anger, his voice shook in its intensity. "I've got to *do* something, Joe. I can't fly a plane over Ashtaroth and bomb it out of business. Isn't there some way I can go? Isn't there a bottom line, somewhere?"

Joe Haines was silent for a while. He lit his pipe and studied his friend in a speculative way. Calculating. Carefully. Wondering. Finally, he said:

"There's a man I know who may be able to help you."

"Yes?"

"A man named Glennon. George Glennon."

"Glennon?"

"The writer. Ever hear of him?"

"No."

"Then you're not up on your best-sellers. He used to work out of San Francisco, but he lives in Santa Cruz now. He's an expert on this cult. Probably knows as much about it as anybody, if not more. In fact, he's writing a book on it—a kind of exposé."

"What can this Glennon possibly do for me?"

"Why don't you just go and see him?"

"Yes. But why?"

Haines seemed irritated. "Frank, you ask too damned many questions."

Reed became irritated in turn.

"I keep asking. But I don't get any answers."

Suddenly, Haines was angry. "Look," he snapped, "I'm not opening my big mouth any further. The fact is, I'm sticking my neck out for you right now. Way, way out. If word of this conversation ever got out, I could get my ass in a real jam, not only with my own office here, but with the County Bar Association. So—forget what I just told you. We never had this discussion." Haines' gray eyes were veiled, almost hostile. He opened a reference pad, wrote a phone number on a slip of paper, and handed it to Reed. "Now, Frank, would you mind getting the hell out of here? I've got a busy day."

5

It was five o'clock in the morning at Ashtaroth, and time for the daily Mass.

All four hundred Souls for Jesus, Elders, Deacons and Neophytes alike, a great congregation already robed and hooded and sandaled and ready for the day, sat cross-legged on the bare floor and listened raptly to the recorded voice of the Master as he conducted the Mass.

This same recording, on this same morning, would be played in over a hundred SFJ church-communes throughout the country, holy places with names like Hazor, Mizpah, Shimron, Jericho, Chaldea, Edom and Moab, after the names of the Bible.

"Jesus loves you," said the Master's Voice.

"Jesus loves you," intoned the congregation, responding to the recording. "Praise be to the Master, Precursor of the Messiah, Messenger of Christ."

"To those of you who labor in our God Squads, who venture on the streets to spread the words of the Master, to collect tithes, to sustain and nourish the Church, blessings. Work hard and labor long in the vineyards of the Lord, with good heart and clear conscience."

"Praise to the Master," chanted the congregation.

"To those who witness, and therefore seek new Souls for Jesus, I give blessing."

"Praise to the Master."

"Now," said the Master's Voice. "Let us all meditate in His name."

The only light came from a single candle on the altar. The rest of the church was dark. Each Soul for Jesus bowed his or her head, engaged in a kind of transcendental meditation. They did not use a personal mantra, or exotic word, as suggested by Maharishi Mahesh Yogi, and used by hundreds of thousands of TM devotees throughout the country. Instead, each congregant used the same word as a key to the meditation, and the word was *Love*. The Reverend Buford Hodges, when he had started the cult, had never hesitated to borrow from other religions or techniques in forming his own.

While everyone else was repeating the magic word silently, over and over, listening to its sound, letting his or her thoughts drift, trying to reach the state of "pure awareness," Cindy felt a hand slip under her robe.

It was cold and clammy. She opened her eyes to see that Tobiah was sitting next to her. He had moved over in the darkness to be next to her. His eyes were closed. His sweaty hand moved farther up the inside of her thigh, caressing her soft warm flesh, savoring it.

His face was wet with the perspiration of his excitement. He reeked with body odor. Cindy sat rigid. His hand moved farther up. It was too dark for anyone to see. No one would possibly notice. She wanted to vomit. She wanted to scream. She wanted to die.

For Tobiah to touch her like this, before she had completed Purification, was forbidden. A true Soul for Jesus, a Deacon no less, would never dream of violating such a rule. To show such lust was to show possession by Satan. But Tobiah, under cover of the dark, had dared to do so.

She could yell out, tear his hand away, accuse him of fondling her. But who would believe her? She was only a Neophyte. They would simply call her a hysterical young girl, they would think she had gone mad. Tobiah was a Deacon. But more than that, he was a favorite and a protégé of Henoch's. It was incredible that he would be capable of such sinful behavior, that he would foul his love for Jesus by yielding to a woman's flesh before she was purified, and eligible.

His hand moved up to her underpants. His damp fingers hesitated for a moment, then began to probe. She heard him breathing heavily. She began to tremble violently. Revulsion choked her. She could feel the gooseflesh pop all over her body. She sat very still, paralyzed. She did not dare push his hand away. He would resent the rebuff. In his mind, he was sure that she wanted him as much as he wanted her. If she rejected him, he could make life unbearable for her at Ashtaroth. She could do nothing but simply sit there, submit, endure this humiliation.

She prayed for the end of the meditation. She prayed for the lights to come on, and rescue her. But they did not. She felt his greedy fingers slip under her underpants. They fondled her pubic hair for a moment.

She turned to look at him. He wore a beatific smile. His lips moved silently, mouthing the sacred word of meditation. *Love, Love, Love.*

Ohgodohgodohgod, she thought. I want to die.

She remembered that Jeff and she would be working in the kitchen all day. He was scheduled to be on the dishwashing detail, and she was waiting on tables. But it wasn't until dinner that Cindy was really able to talk to Jeff for a few moments.

The Sexton, Rehoboam, the Elder in charge of Administration and Supply at Ashtaroth, was always in the kitchen during the serving of the meals, and he kept a sharp eye not only on the food, but on the Neophytes working in the kitchen. By edict of the Master, all Souls for Jesus were vegetarians, and Rehoboam made sure that each plate was not oversupplied. More than this, the Neophytes were to remain silent and do their work. Because the kitchen was hot, and because they were more efficient in work without them, they were permitted to remove their heavy monk's robes while they worked.

Suddenly, the First Elder entered the kitchen and motioned to the Sexton to leave. Apparently he had something to discuss with Rehoboam, and the kitchen was no place to do it.

Cindy immediately set down her tray and went over to Jeff. The tank shirt he wore was soaked through with perspiration, and rivulets of sweat ran down his thin face as he soaked the dirty dishes in a huge tub of hot, soapy water.

He looked up to see Cindy coming and said, "Jesus loves you, Athaliah."

"Jeff, will you cut it out? This biblical crud they're feeding us? I'm Cindy, remember?"

"My name is Simeon."

"Okay," she said. "I haven't got time to argue with you now. We've got to find some way to get out of here."

He stared. "Get out? What for? I like it here."

She had noted that his mind seemed to fluctuate. Sometimes he appeared normal, at other times he lapsed into a spaced-out state. At the moment, he seemed rational enough. "This is my home, my place."

"This is nowhere," she said fiercely. "This is Crazyville. Jeff, can't you see what they're doing to you? They're turning off your mind, spacing you out. They're really getting to you now. Pretty soon it'll be too late. All that talking in tongues—hearing God speak to you. Don't you see how crazy that is?"

"I heard Him," said Jeff. His eyes began to glaze. "I heard the Lord. He spoke to me, I felt Him inside of me."

She saw that he was slipping away from her. She tried again, desperately: "Jeff your folks are waiting outside for you. They love you. They want you to come home."

His eyes blazed frantically. "That's shit. They never loved me. They loved my brother, Ken, but not me. And my earth-father. You think he cared about me? All I ever heard from him was 'What's the matter with you, boy?' or 'Why are you

54

goofing off?' Or 'Why can't you be like your brother?' You think I want to go back to *that?*"

"Jeff," she began, brokenly.

"Don't call me that, ever again, Athaliah. My name is Simeon. Jesus loves you, Athaliah. And now, you betray Him. Do you know what the Lord has spoken about backsliding? It is there in the Bible in Jeremiah, Athaliah. 'Turn, O backsliding children, saith the Lord. I had planted thee a noble vine, wholly a right seed: how then art thou turned into the degenerate plant of a strange vine unto me?' "

One of the most important ways they programmed the Neophytes at Ashtaroth was to force them to study the Bible incessantly, memorize key passages from it, learn them by rote, be able to quote them to suit any occasion. You could not complete Purification, you did not qualify as a pure Soul for Jesus, you could not win the red belt and become a Deacon, until you passed rigid Bible exams, conducted by Henoch himself.

She knew now that she had really lost him. It was too late. He had gone over the edge. Now, like the others, he *wanted* to stay.

Jeff turned, and plunged his hands deep into the tub of soapy water. Cindy, out of the corner of her eye, saw the Sexton coming toward them. She snatched up a tray, already loaded with food, and walked into the dining room. She was serving a table of Deacons. The Deacons and the Elders had separate tables, but the Neophytes ate at long, rough wooden tables, and were required to eat in absolute silence.

She tried hard to keep from crying. She knew if they saw tears, they would begin to interrogate her. They would torment her with questions, over and over. Why was she crying? Wasn't she happy here at Ashtaroth? How could she, now in the service of the Lord, be anything *but* happy? This was a happy place, to be a Soul for Jesus was to be in ecstasy.

Tell us, child, why do you weep? Is it Satan? Has he been near you? Has he tempted you? Have you sinned, Athaliah? Confess to us, have you sinned? If so, how? How have you sinned, Athaliah?

Over and over, until they drove you crazy. Until you went mad. Until you were ready to say anything, do anything, just to make them go away.

Acknowledge thy transgressions, Athaliah. Declare thy iniquity, and the Lord will be merciful. He will heal thy Soul.

She clenched her teeth as she put the New England boiled vegetable dinners in front of the Deacons. One of them looked up to notice her tear-streaked face. He watched her curiously for a moment, and she froze in an agony of fear. She had the presence of mind to take out a handkerchief and wipe her whole face, as though swabbing away the perspiration. Then she smiled at the Deacon: "It's so hot in here, Absalom."

This was one of the Deacons she knew. She had taken Bible lessons from him. He frowned a little, nodded curtly, and turned away, satisfied. He had accepted her explanation, but had been on the verge of a reproach. Neophytes did not ordinarily address Deacons, at least in the dining hall.

During the rest of the meal, a vague plan began to form in Cindy Hyland's mind. A plan to get out of Ashtaroth, to physically break out and be free. It would take some doing, she knew. She'd have to keep cool, and not panic. The important thing was to make them believe her.

Or rather, *him*. One man.

She looked over at the Elders' table. The Elder in whom she was particularly interested was Hezekiah. He was a tall, thin man, bald, with a pinched face and shrewd gray eyes. Hezekiah. His name suited his job and his personality. He reminded Cindy of a tight-fisted Scrooge in monk's robes. He was the Elder responsible for Tithes—which meant everything financial connected with Ashtaroth: the collections made by the God Squads, the money acquired from the Neophytes, the sales of their cars and other worldly goods, the sale of SFJ literature—and the general treasurer of Ashtaroth.

Hezekiah.

He, Cindy decided, was the key to her freedom. The problem was to turn the key, and open the door.

6

Reed phoned George Glennon that afternoon. The writer agreed to see the Reeds the next day. He sounded affable and relaxed on the phone, and not at all surprised by the nature of the call. He gave the impression that he had received others of the same kind many times before.

They drove up to Santa Cruz. Glennon lived in an old Victorian house, overlooking Steamer Lane and the sea. It was a relic of another day, with turrets, bay windows, baroque scrollwork and huge porches. The author was about thirty-five, bearded and partly bald, clad in jeans and a bright red shirt. He greeted them warmly and conducted them into his study. He introduced them to his wife, Ellie, who was also his research assistant. She served them coffee, and then vanished into the kitchen.

Basically, Glennon told them, he was a reporter. He had done a lot of freelance work for the *San Francisco Examiner*, and had been a roving reporter for *Rolling Stone*. Now, in view of the national interest and concern about the cults, and the magnetic pull they had for thousands of young Americans, he had been given a contract to write a book on the subject.

Glennon asked Frank and Kate's permission to record their conversation, for research purposes of his own, and they agreed. He started the tape recorder going, and Frank told him everything that had happened. Glennon listened quietly, nodding now and then. As though all this were familiar, a story he had heard, with some variation, many times before. Finally, Reed said:

"Haines said you might be able to help us get our son out of there."

Glennon nodded, but corrected Frank. "Put it this way. I wouldn't be involved personally. But I have a contact who's an expert in this kind of thing. He *may* be able to help you. It depends . . . "

"On what?"

Glennon was vague. He seemed to study the Reeds, trying to make some kind of value judgment.

"On a number of things. Whether he's available. Whether he wants to get involved, at this point. A lot depends on how he assesses your particular situation."

He was aware that the Reeds were a little puzzled by all this, and he added, quietly: "He's a friend of mine, a very good friend, and there's a big risk involved here, so in a sense I'm screening you for him." Glennon was looking directly at Frank Reed now. "Before he commits to anything, he'll insist on meeting you personally. He'll want to know *who* you are, and how you'd react in a stress situation."

"I don't quite understand."

"I'll make it plain. To get your son out of that cult is going to be a very complicated operation. It's going to take careful planning, and a lot of guts on your part. I might as well tell you going in, Mr. Reed, that you'll be heavily involved personally, and it could be dangerous." He eyed Reed closely. "If that turns you off . . . "

"It doesn't. I'll do anything to get my boy out."

"All right. Before we get down to the nitty gritty, and in view of what you propose to do, it's important that you have a few facts on the SFJ. These cults have become a kind of weird and disturbing national phenomenon. They've been able to attract thousands of our young people, mostly teenagers. All of them are led by father figures of one kind or another.

"There are hundreds of cults in America, but the Souls for Jesus is by far the biggest, richest, and most powerful of them all. It's a conglomerate, and the millions it takes in are all tax-free. It's dwarfed the Moonies and the Hare Krishna put together, when it comes to sheer numbers. The membership lives in closed groups, in communes, or 'churches,' as they like to call them, going outside only to recruit members or solicit funds."

"How many of these communes are there?"

"Ashtaroth is only one of them. The SFJ owns and operates over a hundred compounds like this, each called by a biblical name. But the cult has a secret membership living outside these communes. They rank as Deacons in the SFJ hierarchy, and serve the cult in their own ways. Recruiting new members, or 'witnessing,' as it is called, for example."

"You said this outside membership was secret."

"Yes."

"Why?" Reed wanted to know.

"Because the people involved may be performing undercover services for the cult that aren't exactly legitimate. Moreover, they don't want to be labeled as crazies or weirdos by the rest of the community. The fact is, they're just as dedicated as the members inside the walls, just as fanatic, and there are a surprising number of them everywhere. And all, of course, ready and anxious to serve the Master."

"The Reverend Buford Joe Hodges."

"Right. Sometimes called His Divinity. Spiritual leader and founding father of this huge, tax-exempt gold mine. He's supposed to be the Messenger sent to precede the Messiah, announce his coming, and prophesy the Armageddon. Actually, the SFJ religion isn't too clear to anybody outside the cult. In general, it's a kind of garbage soup of other religions and sects. It's got a pinch of medieval Catholicism, the monastery and monk bit; it's heavy on fundamental Baptist and highly Pentecostal in character; there's a lot of hellfire-and-brimstone evangelism, and speaking in tongues. His Divinity has also borrowed a few exotic gimmicks from some of the Oriental cults, just to make it more interesting."

"But who is he, really?" said Kate.

"Actually, before he got the message to save all those souls, he was born Buford Joe Hodges, in a backwater county in southern Georgia, son of a barefoot revivalist preacher and an alcoholic mother. For years, he was an itinerant farmer and sometime preacher."

"But how did he make it so big?" Reed wanted to know.

Briefly, Glennon outlined the Master's meteoric rise to his present eminence. Then he said, "The thing about the Reverend Hodges was that he had an eye for a fast buck. And he knew how to pyramid what he had. The cult owns extensive real estate, on which its buildings are located; a national chain of thrift shops; a publishing house; a recording company; and a film and television production company. And whenever it buys something, it's never by check. It's in cold cash. And then there are the SFJ God Squads."

"God Squads?"

"They're made up from the Neophytes in the commune, and each is supervised by a pair of Deacons. These squads go out on the streets daily, soliciting money from passersby, selling a small booklet called *Sayings of the Master*." Glennon smiled faintly. "I suppose the Reverend Hodges got the idea from *The Sayings of Mao*. Anyway, it probably costs a quarter to make, and the kids sell it for two dollars a copy. And I mean, they sell it hard. The God Squads bring in hundreds of thousands of dollars all over the country. Some of these kids bring in from a hundred to two hundred dollars a day. All, of course, in cash and unreported."

They were silent for a while. There was no sound but the very faint whir of the tape recorder. Then Kate burst out: "Mr. Glennon, I've got to talk about Jeff. I mean, what they've done to him. To his mind. There must be some kind of law against—well, whatever they did—"

"I'm sorry, Mrs. Reed," Glennon said, gently. "But there's no law on the books against brainwashing anybody. Charles

Manson was convicted of murder, but nobody convicted him of warping the minds and stealing the brains of the kids who joined his cult—kids like Squeaky Fromme and the rest. In a sense, the crime he committed against their minds was just as bad as the murder. You could say the same about the Symbionese Liberation Army. Their brainwashing Patty Hearst. They actually kidnapped her psychologically, which in a way was even worse than kidnapping her physically."

Frank Reed shook his head.

"I don't understand it," he said. "I just don't understand it. Kate here and I have kept asking each other why. Why? Why? Why do these kids join these cults at all? What in God's name do they see in it? Why do they stay?"

"Well, I don't know your son or his girlfriend," said Glennon, "so I can only answer you in a general way. In the sixties, teenagers like Jeff and Cindy were activists, rebels. There was Vietnam to get excited about, the Civil Rights movement, and all the rest. Now, in the late seventies, these same kids are still rebels, but passive. They've got nowhere to go with their passions, no place to diffuse them. So they pick the Establishment as a target, and part of the Establishment is organized religion, the profit system, their own families, you name it."

Frank Reed shook his head. "I *still* don't get it."

"Put it this way. The kids I just spoke about feel alienated. They feel lost. The cult represents a new family to them. A loyal group of their peers, brothers and sisters, and a new and spiritually pure Father figure, all working toward the same end—salvation."

"Something I'm curious about," said Reed. "You're going out of your way to help us. And we appreciate it. But why?"

"Because the SFJ is such a goddamn fraud," said Glennon. "More than that, it's a threat to the kids of this country, and it's growing like a cancer." He smiled. "That's the idealistic part of my reason. The other is more practical. I'm writing a book, remember? And it's almost finished. I want an exclusive from you on everything that happens from here in—at Ashtaroth. *If* anything happens. You give *me* the detailed story, no one else. Fair enough?"

"Fair enough. Now—about this friend of yours. How do we get in touch with him?"

"He moves around a lot," said Glennon. "As far as I know, he has no permanent address. I don't know where he is at the moment, but sooner or later, he'll get in touch with me. He always does. Then I'll try to bring you together." Then, to Frank: "Incidentally, you won't get in touch with him. He'll contact you."

"You still haven't told us," said Kate, "who he is."

Glennon grinned, knocked the ashes from his pipe, and turned off the tape recorder.

"That's something you'll find out for yourselves. Later."

7

After dinner at Ashtaroth, the evening began with hymn singing from the Master's hymnal. This lasted for perhaps an hour.

After that, long stretches were spent in silence, with each person praying as the spirit moved him. During this silent prayer, two or three members of the group mumbled in tongues. Some bowed their heads and closed their eyes. Others prayed silently on their knees, looking upward, their palms pressed together in supplication. Still others used chairs as "altars," kneeling on the floor and supporting their upper bodies on the seats of the chairs, burying their faces in their hands.

The First Elder signaled the end of silent prayer by uttering what was called a "gate keeping" prayer:

"Dear Jesus, and to thy Messenger, His Divinity the Master. We just want to thank thee for bringing us here, and for being here with us, to help us in our prayer and to purify it. Guide us, O Lord, give us the gift of prophecy so that we may divine Thy will."

After this, there was a chorus of "Thank you, Jesus" and "Praise the Lord."

Finally, the meeting would end when one or two of the members confessed to temptation, or depression, or a faint doubt of total commitment to Jesus. They would ask to be prayed for with "laying-on-of-hands." A number of the members, usually Deacons in this ritual, would gather around the tormented person, lay hands on his head or shoulders or hold both his hands, and pray aloud. In this way, the "baptism of the Holy Spirit" was sometimes granted to newcomers and, hopefully, healing would ensue.

Jeff Reed, on this particular evening, was seated near Cindy. This was rather rare, since the cult frowned on any intimacy between new members who came in together. It was better to keep them apart, since one might have doubts and affect the other. He saw that Cindy's robe was loose, and he could see much of her naked breast beneath it, the sweet curve of it, and suddenly he was infected by lust. His groin tightened. He prayed hard for Jesus to forgive him for this sin of the flesh. He tried hard to think of her as Athaliah, her born-again, pure spiritual name. But despite himself, for this moment he could think of her only by her earth-name.

He wanted to get up, reach into her robe and cup her rich, round breast in his hand. He wanted to kiss her full on the mouth. His flesh cried out in his anguish.

Now, dimly, as though it were long, long ago and on some other planet, he remembered meeting her on the beach, a tanned, slender seventeen-year-old, with hazel eyes and a soft red mouth, and long chestnut hair that flowed down to her hips. There had been some kind of instant electricity between them. He recalled Cindy and himself together, driving up and down the Pacific Coast Highway, looking for the waves. He remembered the times he had finally stripped off his wet suit, and together he and Cindy had lain close together on the beach. She wore a very brief bikini, and the smell and the feel of her flesh, perfumed by the sea and warmed by the sun, really blew his mind. Later, they slept together at a friend's pad in Santa Monica.

The time came when they could never get enough of each other, there was never enough, and thinking of her body now, her naked body, he slipped his hand under his voluminous monk's robe, almost going mad in his desire to put out the fire, and right in the middle of prayer . . .

Then the Holy Spirit prevailed and possessed him again; he started to murmur in tongues, and his erection went down. He had been on the verge of asking for a laying-on-of-hands, of confessing his lust and temptation, but at the last minute he refrained, knowing they would consider this kind of backsliding very serious, and fearing it might set him back. His lips began to move, and he was out of it, and he thought, Praise Jesus, I am saved again.

Startled, he heard a voice. Torn out of his reverie, he turned to see a Deacon standing next to him.

"Hezekiah wishes to see you in his vestry, Simeon."

"He wants to see *me*, Micah?"

"At once."

The face of the Deacon was expressionless. Apprehension gripped Jeff. Fear bit into his vitals. Had they known what he had been thinking? Had they looked into his mind, and seen how weak he had been, how he had given in to lewdness? Hezekiah was one of the Elders, and to Jeff, they seemed omnipotent. They seemed to know everything, they sensed what was going on in the spirit. He, Simeon, had lusted after Athaliah, and he had not confessed. It was a hard rule at prayer meeting, and part of Purification. If one felt lust, or other unworthy thoughts, he was to speak out, to confess, to beg forgiveness, and to submit to healing. Panic gripped him.

They knew. He was sure of it.

He walked the length of the chapel and went up the stairs to the second floor. He passed the rooms reserved for Bible study and confessionals, and walked up the vestry corridor, where the Elders of Ashtaroth conducted their business, each in a separate study. When Jeff came to Hezekiah's door, it was closed. He knocked on the door timidly, and was told to enter.

Hezekiah was sitting at his desk. He was drinking wine in

a silver goblet and going over some accounts. On one wall, there was a bronze figure of Jesus carrying the Cross up Calvary, and on the other a huge portrait of the Master, smiling down benevolently. Hezekiah had untied the collar of his robe, and now it flapped open, exposing his hairy chest. They exchanged the ritual greeting, and for a moment there was silence. Jeff stood there, trembling. There was no expression on Hezekiah's thin face. He studied Jeff for a while, seemed to look directly through him.

Then, suddenly, there was a smile on the pinched face and he said, "Simeon, I have spoken to the other Elders. We are very pleased with your Purification. You have done well."

"Thank you, Hezekiah."

He was still shaking, astounded at this warm greeting.

"So well, in fact, that we believe you are ready to serve on a God Squad. To go out on the street and collect tithes for the Lord. Normally, you would not enjoy this privilege for at least three months. You have been here less than a month. But you have come along very quickly. You have learned your Bible, and you have spoken in tongues." He paused, then smiled. "I trust you are pleased, Simeon."

"Praise Jesus," said Jeff, fervently. He could not conceal his delight, nor did he try. "I promise you I will work hard in service to the Lord."

"Yes, yes, of course," said Hezekiah, drily. "That goes without saying for all of us. You understand, of course, that each God Squad must reach a certain quota in selling the wisdom of the Master. The Church needs new converts, it needs new facilities, it needs money to spread the word of the Lord everywhere, and to defend itself against the attacks of Satan, in his many different guises."

"I understand."

"And, of course, Simeon, it needs money to help the poor. As it is written in Matthew: 'If thou wilt be perfect, go and sell that thou hast, and give to the poor, and thou shalt have treasure in heaven; and come and follow me.' This is a cardinal tenet of the Master, Simeon. Remember it well."

66

"Yes, Hezekiah."

"I have assigned you to God Squad Three. It is an excellent group, and led by two of our best Deacons, Ephraim and Shechem. Listen to them well, and learn. As you know, when we go forth on the streets, we wear earth-clothes, not these robes. You will go to the Wardrobe Room in Building Four to be properly fitted for your task. I have already told them to expect you." He studied Jeff critically, and then: "Also, your hair is a little long. Be sure and have it cut before you go out."

"When do I begin?"

"The day after tomorrow."

That night, Jeff lay wide awake on his bed. Or rather, on the canvas army cot that served as a bed. Lights were out at nine, and the hour of rising was five each morning.

The male Neophytes slept on one floor of the huge dormitory building called Hachilah, which was the place where Saul pitched his tent when he pursued David into the wilderness. There were no bedrooms or even sleeping cubicles. The beds were lined up in rows on each side, in the manner of army barracks. The female Neophytes slept on the upper floor of Hachilah, and, of course, the Deacons had their own dormitory, Tiberias, named after the sea on the shore of which Jesus stood when he showed himself to his disciples.

It was impossible for Jeff to fall off to sleep. He was too exuberant, too excited. He knew he had already come a long way in his Purification. If his performance was good on the God Squad, if he worked hard and collected enough money, he would be well on the road to becoming a Deacon.

And that meant privileges. It meant that he no longer would have to remain celibate. He could go to bed once a week with any Deaconess of his choice, or a Neophyte, for that matter. He would have better food, and he would be allowed to leave the compound occasionally—in the company of others, of course, but more or less on his own.

He felt happy here, at Ashtaroth. Very happy. He didn't

have to make any hard decisions of his own. All he had to do was have faith in the Master, and do what he was instructed to do. He felt spiritually at peace. He was no longer drifting and confused "out there." He was safe from his earth-father, Frank Reed, who was always putting the pressure on him. Always pointing to his older brother, Ken, who was a football star at Stanford, setting him up as a shining example.

But he didn't have to take that anymore. He was Simeon of Ashtaroth now, dedicated to serving the Lord. He was guaranteed survival when the holocaust came, the Apocalypse. The Master himself, God's messenger on earth, had said so.

But more than that, he felt that he *belonged* to something. Something special and exclusive. He belonged to a group, they were all brothers and sisters here. There were people who cared for him, and cared about him. *Really* cared. There was nothing but love at Ashtaroth. Love for Jesus, love for the Master, love for each other, from the First Elder to the newest Neophyte. And a fierce loyalty.

Of course, the rules were strict, the Purification hard to take. It was all necessary, he had been told, to learn humility.

But even during Purification, it wasn't all work. Twice a week they sang and danced to their gospel songs, played in rock style, with bass, electric guitar, piano and drums. An hour a day, just after lunch, they had free recreation. They could walk around the grounds, play touch football, or simply lie beneath the trees and talk. Jeff was usually hungry; he had lost quite a little weight. But abstinence was part of Purification, mortification of the body elevated the soul.

After Purification, and an interim period they called Purgatory, he would be a Deacon, perhaps in a year, and the food would be better, and more plentiful. Now and then, he thought of the hamburgers he used to love, the barbecued chicken and steaks, but he thrust them from his mind. The Master preached that God made all living things, and that the killing and eating of animals was as much a sin as the killing of human beings.

He was worried about Athaliah. She didn't seem to be really happy at Ashtaroth. He felt a little responsible, because it had been he who had persuaded her to join. He must talk to Athaliah, show her the error of her thinking. It was good, sitting so close to her this evening . . .

Then suddenly, it came on him. The picture of her soft, rounded breast peeking from under her robe. The breast he used to fondle, and snuggle his face against, the red sweet nipple he used to kiss. He tried to thrust the memory from his mind. He couldn't. His erection came on quickly, straight and hard. The Neophytes slept naked beneath their rough cotton sheets and he could feel the tip of his prick rubbing against the cloth, exciting him still further. In desperation, he reached down and grabbed it, as though it were some kind of villain, as though he could kill it, make it droop again.

He tried thinking of the Bible, some of the quotations he had learned about lust.

His mind went blank. He could remember nothing. He tried to think pure thoughts. It was no use. His thing was still standing up straight and hard, hot and throbbing. He thought of it now, buried between Athaliah's spread-out legs, he imagined it deliciously imprisoned in that hot, wet place, he imagined himself sliding it in and out, he heard Athaliah moan in her ecstasy, felt the surge of her own body up to his as she met him, as both approached climax . . .

He threw the sheet from him and went into the community shower room.

He turned on the cold water and stood under it for a long time, shivering. This procedure was recommended by the Elders when Satan had burst through with one of his most effective temptations, sexual desire.

He came out of the shower. His erection had shrunk now. As he was about to leave the shower room, another Neophyte came in. Jeff knew him as Zephaniah. Zephaniah was obviously there for the same purpose. His erection was painfully stiff and straight. The two looked at each other, totally unembarrassed, completely understanding. *We are all together here. What happens to one of us, happens to all.* Zephaniah smiled weakly at Jeff, and Jeff returned the smile.

"This is the worst part," said Zephaniah. "This is the part

of Purification that really drives me crazy. I used to love screwing. I used to ball a chick a day, sometimes two. Just couldn't get enough, you know?" He shrugged. "But now . . ."

"It won't last forever," said Jeff. "And it's worth it."

"Yeah," said Zephaniah. "I suppose it is."

He took a long breath, stepped in the shower, and stood there, gasping. Jeff wiped himself on a rough towel and went back to the cot. He lay on his back, for the moment, calm.

But it came back again. Thinking of Athaliah. But now he could think of her only as Cindy. Cindy with the round breasts, and the curved hips, and the provocative way she walked, the swing and the smell of her, the sultry eyes, and the soft warm mouth pressing down on his mouth, her hand straying down toward his prick, and then caressing it, first with her fingers, running her fingertips up and down, and then gently cupping it, and then stroking it and squeezing it.

He knew what he had to do now, in order not to blow his mind. He had to relieve himself. His hand strayed down under the sheet. He closed his eyes. He began writhing in ecstasy, and finally he arched his back, as he approached climax. Then he exploded, and he came, the hot white semen sticky in his hand, drooling over his palm.

He felt enormous relief. He opened his eyes, intending to go back into the shower room and clean himself up.

He was startled to see a Deacon named Zimran standing over him. Zimran had bedcheck duty for this particular night, and Jeff stared at him, horrified. Expecting some kind of wrath, some harsh reproach, some crying of shame.

But Zimran only nodded and smiled benevolently. His face was full of love. He understood.

"Jesus loves you, Simeon. Goodnight, and sleep well."

"Goodnight."

When Zimran walked away, Jeff suddenly remembered something. Something that had happened a long time ago. When he was maybe twelve or thirteen, he didn't quite remember. But he was in the bathroom, and masturbating over the toilet. He had forgotten to lock the bathroom door, and his mother had walked in. She had said nothing but it was all in her eyes, in the shocked look on her face. This was a dirty thing to do, a horrible thing, the kind of thing young boys should not do. He had wanted to hide somewhere; he had felt dirty, degraded, ashamed.

But here, it was different. Nothing was dirty or degraded when spiritually you were clean. Everybody understood. Everybody loved everybody. Here, love was everywhere.

And again, and above all, you were never alone.

God Squad Three met in the small chapel at eight in the morning.

There were ten Neophytes, five boys and five girls, under the direction of their sales managers, Deacons Ephraim and Shechem. Other squads were meeting elsewhere in the compound, and in a half hour they would all join for the bus trip to town, to be dropped at their assigned locations.

The boys were dressed in gray slacks and smart red blazers with the SFJ insignia sewn on one of the pockets. They wore white shirts and striped blue ties. Their hair was combed and their shoes shined. The Deacons were dressed in the same way. The girls wore blouses and long skirts, their hair neatly combed and braided. They were all young, fresh-faced, and eager to get started. On a table in the chapel stood stacks of the little blue booklets, embossed with the title: *Sayings of the Master*.

All this was new to Jeff, and he watched the proceedings eagerly. It felt strange to be wearing shirt, slacks and jacket, after a month of wearing the rough, gray monk's robes. In a way, he found it a little frightening to be leaving these walls and moving out into that other world, the world he had once known, the world which the cult regarded as the territory of Satan. Then he decided not to be nervous. After all, his friends would be there, close to him, working with him.

Ephraim seemed to be the Deacon in charge. He stood in front of them and asked for a silent prayer. They bowed their heads and prayed silently for a minute. Then Ephraim broke the silence: "What are we going to do today?"

71

"Sell!" cried the members of God Squad Three. "Sell, sell, *sell!*"

Ephraim waved his arms like a cheerleader, exhorting them.

"And *what* are we going to sell?"

"The *Sayings of the Master*," they roared. "The true Messenger of Jesus Christ."

"And how are we going to sell?"

"Hard, hard, *hard!*"

"And for whom are we getting this money?"

"For our Heavenly Father."

"And who are we going to take it away from?"

"Satan, Satan, *Satan!*" roared the group. "We're going to send Satan back into hell with this money, Brother. We're going to cut off his horns and his tail!"

"And what shall we do with this money?"

"Save souls," they chanted. "Save souls for Jesus! We are going into the streets, and save souls for Jesus."

"Jesus loves you," shouted Ephraim. "He loves you all."

"And Jesus loves you, Ephraim," they roared back.

At this point, the programmed question-and-answer pep talk ended abruptly. Now Shechem, the Deacon who was second in command, stepped forward, and said in a conversational tone, "Brothers and sisters, we have a new salesman for the Lord with us today. Simeon." They all crowded around Simeon, telling him they loved him. "Teach him what you know, so that he may sell well. You know what our quota is each day. What each of us is expected to collect. Simeon may fall short for a few days, since he is new, but he will learn fast." Then, with a touch of pride: "I talked with Hezekiah yesterday. Of all the God Squads at Ashtaroth, we now rank number two in tithes."

There was cheering and handclapping; then Shechem continued: "I must remind you, as I have before, that when you are selling the *Sayings of the Master*, be polite, yet persistent. Be aggressive, but do not engage in physical contact with people. By that I mean, do not seize their arms, or in any other way try to detain them physically, while you are trying to sell them the booklets. A few people have complained to the police about this and, of course, we do not wish this kind of trouble."

He paused to let this point sink in. "Now, let me make a point or two here for Simeon's benefit. These are things you experienced salesmen already know. Generally speaking, male prospects are more receptive to our girls approaching them, and females to our boys. Be cheerful, be smiling, and always be sincere. Remember, you are selling the most beautiful and purest product in the world—the word of God, as brought to you by the Master. Do not be afraid to raise your voices a little higher than usual when you are selling. Sometimes you can force a possible prospect into buying in this way, because he knows others can hear, and he is too embarrassed to refuse. Also, use your wits. Size up your possible sale instantly. If it's an elderly person, tell him the money for the booklet goes to our Old People's Home. If the prospect is a woman who looks like a motherly type, tell them it's for the SFJ orphanage. And so on. Almost everyone is vulnerable to one appeal or another." He paused. "Any questions?"

There were none, and now Ephraim stepped forward. He picked up his briefcase and took out a large photograph in color. It was a blowup of the same picture that was posted on the bulletin boards of each building in the church compound, like the "Wanted" pictures you saw in post offices. Only this was just a front view of a man's face. There was no profile view to go with it.

The face was that of a man in his late forties.

"You all know who this is," said Ephraim. "I remind you again that for all you know, he may be nearby while you work. Watching, waiting to catch you off guard. He moves like a shadow, he will strike when you least expect him. If he catches you, he will steal your soul, and consign it to instant Hell. And you, sisters, beware of him. He is capable of rape and murder. The man you see here is Satan incarnate. You have seen pictures of his human disguise here many, many times. But I remind you once again, beware of him. If you see him, report him at once to Shechem or myself."

Ephraim put the photo away. "Now, go thee forth, all of thee, and labor for the good of the Lord, and enrich his vineyard, and for this, He will nourish and protect you, and bless you with His Holy Spirit."

The members of God Squad Three picked up their allotted booklets, and marched briskly out to await the bus.

8

The man they knew as the Devil was in the middle of a dream.

Or, to be more specific, a nightmare.

He had suffered this nightmare, off and on, for the past three years. Now, tossing and turning in his bed, drenched in sweat and moaning softly to himself, he lived it all over again.

Sidon.

He was dreaming about Sidon again.

Sidon was the place where a Greek woman, a Syrophenician, had come to Christ, and had fallen at his feet, and told Him that her daughter had an unclean spirit, and besought Him to cast forth the Devil out of her daughter. And this He had done, and told the woman to go her way in peace, and the daughter lay on the bed, and the Devil was gone out of her. And after this miracle, Jesus had gone on, to the Sea of Galilee . . .

But this nightmare was in another Sidon, at another time and place, and even by day, he thought of the hated word, Sidon, Sidon, *Sidon,* but in the dream, he was seeing it all again, just as it had happened . . .

The phone rang, waking him. He lay there for a moment, limp in his own sweat, exhausted. The phone rang again, and he picked it up.

"Mr. West?"

"West?" he said, blankly.

There was a pause at the other end. "You *are* Mr. Charles West, aren't you? I mean, this *is* Room 22."

"Oh. Yes. I'm sorry."

"You left a wakeup call for eight o'clock, sir. It's two minutes past eight now."

"Thank you."

He hung up, lit a cigarette, and sat up, head propped against the pillow, still half-drugged in sleep.

Let's see. Where was he this morning? What was this place? His mind was really fuzzy. Oh, yes. He remembered now. He remembered, too, that this was Sunday. He had to make a phone call in a little while. After that, he expected a visitor.

And after that . . .

Funny. He had almost forgotten the name he had used when he had checked in the night before. The name he had told George Glennon he would use here, when he had phoned Glennon from Denver. But then he had used so many names in the past three years, a different one in every place he went, every city and hotel and motel, and he wondered whether he had begun to repeat himself. Vaguely, he seemed to remember using the name "West" when he had hit Hiddekel, near Seattle. Or was it the job at the Makkedah commune, in northern Florida? He grinned mirthlessly at the memory of Makkedah. That one had turned out badly. The Devil had blown one, or rather his accomplice had.

He reflected wryly that he had almost forgotten his real name. But it paid to keep a low profile at all times, keep them in the dark as to where you were at any given time. There were members of the SFJ everywhere, not just inside the communes. If they ever located you, they could really be rough. More than that, lethal.

He wouldn't put it past the Master to do anything. He

knew the Reverend Hodges would not hesitate to kill him, if he could. After all, he had a twenty-million-dollar empire to protect.

He reached for the phone, dialed nine, and then a local number. A man answered, his voice shaking a little, expecting the call:

"Mr. Prentiss?"

"Yes."

"John Morse."

"Oh. Yes." Then: "When did you get into Memphis?"

"Flew in from Denver. Last night."

"Where are you staying?"

"The Starlight Motel. You know where it is?"

"Yes. It's that big motel. On Route 40." Prentiss seemed surprised. As though he wanted to say, why a motel, and why out of town? But instead: "We're all ready to go here. When can we meet?"

"Later this afternoon. Pick me up at four—"

"We could make it earlier. I could come down now—"

"No. I have some things to do. Now, how far are we from Cana?"

"From your motel, you mean?"

"Yes."

"About ten miles. It's out in the country."

"Okay. I'll want to take a good look at it. Get a clear idea of the geography. Plan our strategy."

"Mr. Morse, why don't you come over to the house for lunch? Of course, we've already met once, but you're a stranger here in Memphis, and if we're going to work together . . ."

"Thanks. But as I said, I've got things to do. See you at four."

He hung up, reflecting that it was just as well; he'd be seeing a hell of a lot of Gerald Prentiss before they were finished in Memphis. He ran the electric razor over his face, showered, and dressed. Then he picked up the newspaper he had bought the night before as he had left the airport.

It was a late edition, and it had what the Devil was looking for. The TV listings for Sunday morning, the religious programs. He ran his finger down the page. At nine o'clock, "The Reverend Ed," "Gates of Heaven," "The Orrin Deakes Tabernacle," and the "Road to Rapture" were on. At nine-thirty, there were four other programs dedicated to spreading the Word, ministering to the faithful, and cautioning the backsliders. The Devil found the program he was looking for on channel seven.

The "Souls for Jesus Hour."

The SFJ hour was not on the network. It was filmed and then syndicated each Sunday over some 70 stations throughout the country.

Morse was a great fan of the show. He grinned, wondering whether they knew how much the Devil loved it. Wherever he was on Sunday, he never failed to tune it in. The Reverend Buford Hodges brazenly copied some of the program material presented by certain sincere, honest and dedicated evangelists who were on the air every Sunday. But he always had some new twist or new gimmick each week and, through his pipeline to heaven, always came up with a new message from the Lord.

Morse settled back, wondering what the greedy old bastard would come up with this time.

The program opened in the usual way. A choir of young voices singing the signature hymn:

> *Jesus loves you, give him your soul,*
> *Jesus loves you, make heaven your goal,*
> *Jesus loves you, and you can be sure*
> *The Lord is eternal*
> *In Him you're secure . . .*

Gradually the lights came on to reveal the choir singing beneath a huge, glittering, bejeweled cross, sparkling and shimmering in the light. The boys and girls in the choir all wore simple blue robes, and all wore beatific smiles on their faces as they sang. All of them were well-scrubbed, well-combed, fresh-faced youngsters, all as American as apple pie.

He had to give old Buford credit. It was all good showmanship to have these fresh young faces on the screen. Evangelism was show-biz, like anything else. And to use a bad pun, the Master was a past master when it came to putting on a show.

The camera cut to a large audience, most of them young people, sitting in the amphitheater of the studio. They applauded vigorously. Most of them looked as fresh-scrubbed and clean-cut as those in the choir. There were plenty of Souls in this audience. The Master had brought them in from nearby communes to pack the house.

An Elder of the cult, dressed in his earth-clothes—a sober, square business suit—stepped forward. He announced that the subject of the Reverend Hodges' program today would be "Has God a Plan?" No monk's robes here, on television, thought Morse. None of that medieval mumbo-jumbo to turn off the viewers. That was something exotic the kids could go for behind the walls of the commune.

As the choir continued to sing, four or five young couples came out of the shadows, hand in hand, and sang along with the chorus. The men were handsome in a plastic way, the women young and fresh and lovely in the same plastic way, and they all had beautiful white teeth, and the spotlight picked them up in all their wholesome glory as they sang along.

Finally the young couples faded back into the shadows. The set darkened, and a big spotlight came on. Into it walked the Reverend Buford Hodges.

He was a tall man, wearing a sober business suit and a conservative striped tie. He had snow-white hair and a short, white beard, and reminded Morse of Colonel Sanders. But, he thought, the Reverend and the Colonel were in the business of selling two entirely different products. The Master was wearing a benevolent smile, and his voice was soft, seductive, persuasive and very sincere. The southern drawl was faint but still there.

"Many Christians have asked me, 'Has God a plan?' Has he a plan for all of us? My answer to that, through his word and Holy Spirit, is *yes*. He *does* have a plan, my friends. But in order to be part of that plan, you must give Him your soul."

He waved toward a dark area of the stage. The lights came up to reveal a rock band: guitar, piano, bass. And standing in front of them a long-haired young man, dressed in blue jeans and checked shirt. Morse recognized the boy instantly. So did most of the rock-loving kids in the nation.

His name was Bob Biddle, and he was a nationally known rock star and composer. As part of the Blue Electrics, his records had sold in the millions.

Morse whistled. He was really impressed. The Reverend Hodges had caught a big one here.

The audience stood on its feet and applauded wildly. Biddle walked forward to the Master's side. He carried a microphone in his hand.

"You all know this young man," said Hodges, beaming. "You've seen his face on billboards, on millions of records, on the talk shows like Johnny Carson and Merv Griffin. This is Bob Biddle." The Master put his arm around Biddle's shoulder. "Now tell us what happened, Bob."

"I lived the life of the fleshpots," said Biddle. "I lived a life of sin and decadence. I smoked grass and took LSD. Between engagements and road trips, I lay around in crash pads and went naked, and engaged in carnal relations with women. I checked out on God, and listened to this certain guru, who was always at my side, whispering in my ear . . ."

"And who was this guru, Bob?" asked the Master.

"He was Satan," said Biddle. "The Devil incarnate. Whispering lust in my ear, talking temptation, trying to take my soul into his hot hands . . ."

"Then what happened?"

"I met a girl who was a Deaconess. She showed me the error of my ways. She showed me the way to salvation. She showed me the meaning of true love. 'Only give your soul to the Lord,' she said, 'and ye shall be saved.'"

Biddle put his hand out toward the right side of the stage. A pretty girl emerged from the shadow and walked into the spotlight, joining them. She wore a long gown of snow-white chiffon. "Thank you, Ellie, for bringing me to the light." He kissed her on the cheek, then turned to the audience. "This is the girl who I am going to make my wife. So that together we can pray and praise the Lord."

The audience applauded again. Then the Master announced that Bob Biddle had written a new song, with lyrics to match. It was a gospel number. He had dedicated it to all the Souls for Jesus out there. It was called, "If the End Is Near, Never Fear."

He sang the lyrics, and the band played quiet rock behind him. The lyrics made it plain that Armageddon could be just around the corner. The world was tottering on the brink of destruction. But if the end is near, never fear, give your soul to Jesus and hold him dear, and ye shall be saved.

Morse listened intently. The song was part of a kind of pop music ministry that was sweeping the country. Some of the other entertainers were recording albums of this new style gospel music, set to quiet rock. And the kids seemed to be buying it, on thousands of records and tapes.

Bob Biddle finished to tremendous applause, then stepped back out of the picture and left the Master alone in the spotlight.

The Reverend Hodges launched into his sermon.

It was hard-core Pentecostal in type, all hellfire and brimstone, and almost conventional in evangelical terms.

He spoke of the Rapture and the end of the seven-year Tribulation, and Armageddon, and the Second Coming, a time when Christ would appear from parted heavens and snatch millions of Christians from their jobs and homes and summon them to the clouds. There was the Millennium, and the Antichrist, and all of this proven by the Bible, chapter and verse.

Say what you would about the Godfather of the SFJ, the self-proclaimed Messenger of God, the one and only human pipeline to Up There—he did put on a great show. He was a terrific standup preacher, he had that old-time charisma, and it was no wonder he had been able to gain so many converts, and the assets thereof.

The sermon ended, the choir sang another hymn, and this time the Master stepped forward for the sales pitch, which was actually the most important part of the show.

First, he held up his booklet, *Sayings of the Master,* which actually, he explained, was composed of quotes from the Bible to enrich your daily life, and was only two dollars a copy, and the money would go to save a soul somewhere. It would help some young person to drop his terrible drug habit, perhaps, and instead, turn on to Jesus. Two dollars each, and create a Christian.

Aside from these, he had tapes of some of his sermons, eight-track and cassette, which could be played not only in your home, but also in your car, and each of these sold for ten dollars; send a check, care of your station, to the Reverend Buford Hodges and you would be blessed.

"Our church needs money," pleaded the Master, his hands thrown out in supplication. "It needs money to spread the Word. So those of you out there, good Christians, if you cannot afford two dollars or ten dollars, then send us one dollar, we appreciate them just as much in spirit, those wrinkled one-dollar bills, sent to us by wrinkled, toil-worn hands ..."

Morse stared at the big closeup of the Reverend Hodges, and the hate rose to burn in him; he wanted to get up and smash that pious hypocritical face. For a moment he was tempted to put his fist right through the tube and smash that bearded image to smithereens. But he told himself to take it easy, take it easy. His anger passed as quickly as it had come, and he told himself to stay cool, stay cool, there were other ways to get the son-of-a-bitch, and so far, he, whom they called the Devil, was being very successful at it, and was becoming more so, each week that passed.

Finally, the Master finished the sales pitch. He was standing square in the spotlight, the rest of the set was dark. The choir began to hum a hymn. Softly, very softly, the Master closed his eyes. He stood there for a moment, as though listening. Then he raised his arms toward heaven, and his mouth began to move:

82

Sphona shan kadia dada shan veria ko,
Conda amus borobono aako,
Kaga sombo poyentre zandre,
Shindri katari pili zhindra . . .

Morse stared. He could believe neither his eyes nor his ears.

This, he told himself, was sheer gall. Here was the Reverend Buford Hodges, speaking in tongues. On *television.*

As far as Morse knew, this was a first.

The Master's mouth moved. So did his tongue. But they seemed removed from him. His eyes remained closed. The look on his face was ecstasy. He was talking with God now. Speaking his language. Filled with the Holy Spirit.

Shanta kali deamo no ma diamos,
Shintar kae.
Sazhandra mesantro ama conda mala,
Nesantro limetaki lapatsomo.

The derivation of the phrase "Speaking in tongues," Morse knew, was from the Bible. From a passage said to be spoken by Paul in 1 Corinthians 13:1: "Though I speak with the tongues of men and of angels . . ." Others quoted Isaiah 28:11: "So it will be with barbarous speech and strange tongue, that this people will hear God speaking . . ."

But the scientists and linguists identified "speaking in tongues" with another word.

Glossolalia.

Glossolalia had long been familiar in religion, especially because of its use by Pentecostals, but it went back to the very beginning of Christianity. There were thousands of tongue-speakers today, and not all of them were in the traditional Pentecostal churches. By many it was sincerely interpreted as a spiritual gift given directly by the Holy Spirit, and just as valid today as it was in the time of the Apostles. Morse had no quarrel with that. But he believed, as did many others, that in certain cases it was infantile babbling, done in some kind of trance, a kind of psychological abnormality, usually ascribed to hysteria, ecstasy, or catalepsy. Others believed it to be some kind of demoniac possession, the kind that took place in African voodoo.

But whatever it was, thought Morse, the Reverend Hodges was really laying it on now. He was in no trance. He knew exactly what he was doing. Those who believed, out there, would believe his performance. They would really believe that he was conducting a dialogue with the Holy Spirit.

And the dollars would keep rolling in.

9

Frank Reed paid the cab driver and walked into the coffee shop of the Starlight Motel. He had called Morse from the airport, and this is where they had arranged to meet. It was almost noon, and the place was beginning to fill up.

He moved to a rear booth where Morse was waiting, and they shook hands.

"You know," said Reed, "after what George Glennon told me, I expected you to wear horns."

Morse grinned. "Sorry. No horns. I sent them out to be sharpened and polished."

Morse signaled a waitress, ordered bacon and eggs and coffee. Reed said he had had breakfast on the plane, and just ordered coffee.

"Have a good trip?"

"Stopped off in Chicago last night. Had some business there. Then came on here."

Reed was conscious of the hard blue eyes appraising him. Analyzing him. Dissecting him. But Frank Reed was a man who was not easily intimidated. He said:

"Something I'm curious about."

"Yes?"

"I'd like to know why I had to fly all the way from California. Just so you could get a look at me. You wouldn't even discuss a deal over the phone." Frank Reed was annoyed, and he made no pretense of hiding it. "You put your clients to a lot of inconvenience, Morse."

"True. I've had other complaints on this score." Morse grinned. "But you're here, aren't you?"

"Okay. I'm here."

"Which means you need my services a hell of a lot more than I need your fee. Otherwise, I'd have flown to California to see *you*. Right?"

Frank bristled a little. He was about to make some kind of angry reply, when Morse smiled. The smile was warm, friendly, disarming. The blue eyes stopped studying him.

"I'm sorry, Reed. No offense meant. It's just that I'm in a very peculiar business, and I have to be very careful. I really have to know who my client is before I sign on."

"But why?"

"To satisfy myself that he has the maturity and the guts to do what he has to do."

They were silent for a moment. Then Frank said, "Well? Do I pass?"

"I think you'll do. George Glennon screened you first, of course. His impression was favorable. Otherwise you wouldn't have made this trip at all. Part of this procedure is very physical, and you look big and strong. The other part involves a certain amount of determination and will power. My impression is that you have both, and I'll gamble on it. And you'll do anything to get your son out."

"That's right," said Reed, quietly.

"All right. I buy you. Do you buy me?"

"I guess I don't have much choice."

"No, you don't."

· "Then we're in business?"

"We're in business."

The waitress came with the food, and they were silent until

she left. Then Morse asked, "How much has George Glennon told you? About what we have to do, how it works?"

"He just gave me a general idea."

"All right. Let me be more specific. The only way to get your son out of Ashtaroth is to take him out bodily. In effect—and let's use the plain old dirty Anglo-Saxon word—to kidnap him. You understand that?"

"Yes."

"That's your job. Yours, and some friends you'll need to help you. I won't be physically involved in the actual kidnapping myself." Morse's smile was frosty. "For reasons of self-protection. For one thing, I don't want to blow my cover, as they say in the CIA movies. But I'll be in the background, helping you to plan it, showing you how it's done. There are certain procedures you'll have to know, and follow to the letter. I want you to understand, going in, that this can be personally dangerous for you, and perhaps illegal."

"I understand that."

"If you fail, if this thing doesn't come off, you and your wife will probably never see your son again. The first thing they'll do is shift him out of California, to a commune somewhere across the country. You understand that, too?"

Frank Reed felt a little sick at the thought, but he said yes, he understood that, too. Morse went on:

"Sometimes, things go wrong. We had an incident in New Orleans. At a Souls for Jesus commune called Bethany. I was working with a father who was trying to get his daughter out of there. At the last moment, he froze. The whole operation fell apart. He was almost beaten to death by a couple of Bethany's Deacons. Some of them can be pretty damned rough—real hardballs. Especially, when you try to steal one of their Souls."

"I don't intend to freeze," said Reed quietly.

"No. I don't think you would." Morse paused a moment. "Just on a hunch. Ever been in the army?"

Frank nodded. "In Korea."

"What division?"

"The 24th Infantry."

"Right," said Morse. "I know it well."

"In what way?"

"That's a whole other story. But let's get on with the briefing."

"All right," said Frank. "I kidnap Jeff. Now what do *you* do?"

"You already know. Glennon told you."

"I'd like to hear it from *you.*"

Morse grinned faintly. "I'm beginning to like you more and more, Reed."

"Thanks."

"My job is to reorient your son, back to reality. To debrief him, purge him of the poison he's been infected with by the cult. In other words, to defuse him, to deprogram him. To put it on the table, Reed, I'm a professional deprogrammer, and I work for pay. There are only a few of us in the country, and we have more work than we can handle, trying to rescue kids who have been caught and brainwashed by these pseudo-religious cults. Okay?"

"Clear enough. Only a question."

"Yes?"

"If I could get Jeff back home, where he'd be with myself and his mother, maybe we could make him see some reason, make him understand that, well—we love him, and want him . . ."

"It wouldn't work," said Morse, flatly.

"You're sure about that?"

"I guarantee it. In two weeks he'd be back with the cult, and transferred to another commune somewhere else in the country, and you'd never see him again. You don't quite seem to understand, Frank. The *real* kidnappers here are the people in Ashtaroth. They've already kidnapped him—psychologically —manipulated and stolen his mind. They've taken away his ability even to *think.* He no longer even has a will of his own. The bastards program him until he becomes a robot, a kind of zombie. They half-starve him, and make him work ten hours a day. They never let him rest, not for a moment. They won't allow him a normal night's sleep, until they're sure of him. They keep banging away at him with their crazy ideas and grotesque rituals. They teach him to hate the country, hate the system, hate his parents. The Devil is everywhere, everything outside those walls is Satan country. They separate him from his career, his friends, family, everything he owns and knows. He no longer has any idea what the hell reality even is. Just having him home isn't worth a damn. He's too far in, and he needs professional help to get out."

Frank Reed took a little time to think this over. He drained the last of his coffee. Then: "There's something we haven't discussed. Your fee. What's this going to cost me?"

"Twenty thousand. Plus expenses."

Morse's face was bland as he saw Reed react, startled. He smiled a little at the Californian's almost belligerent stare. He'd been through this with other clients. Reed was a businessman, and his reaction was an automatic reflex he couldn't help. Morse understood that, and it always amused him. He also knew what Reed was going to say next.

"Isn't that pretty steep?"

"Depends how you look at it."

"Glennon tells me the whole thing takes you about a week. At the maximum, no more than ten days."

"So?"

"I'd call twenty thousand a hell of a lot of money for a week's work."

"True. But I render a unique service." Morse grinned, mirthlessly. "How many other people do you know in my line of work? Besides, the week or ten days Glennon told you about is only the actual deprogramming time. If I come out to California, I'll have to spend some time in surveillance looking things over, and advising you on how to move. What we're talking about here is your son's future, his health and maybe his sanity. Are you trying to tell me this isn't worth twenty thousand dollars?"

"No. Of course not."

"Something I want you to know, Reed. In this business, I charge what the traffic will bear. I soak the rich, as they say, but in some cases I've done this job for nothing. Just because the parents of the boy or girl concerned couldn't afford it. You can. George Glennon checked out your resources for me. You live in the wealthy Hope Ranch residential district of Santa Barbara. Your house is worth about half a million dollars. You're a partner in the engineering firm of Wallabee and Reed, you're way up in the high brackets, and your Dun and Bradstreet rating is very good indeed. I might point out, while we're on the subject, that my particular operation is expensive. It isn't just myself. I have an organization of a kind; I have others to pay, in special situations." Morse paused a moment, then shrugged. "The price is twenty thousand. Plus expenses. And it's non-negotiable. Take it or leave it."

"I'll take it," said Reed.

"Good. We have a deal, then. If you can steal your son's body from the cult, I'll steal back his soul."

"You sound pretty confident."

"Put it this way. I'm a professional, but I'd be a fool to guarantee my work. Still, I've got a pretty good batting average. I've deprogrammed over a hundred kids. And I've only lost two or three who have backslid into the cult. If you get Jeff out, and I lose him, I'll return your fee. Okay?"

"Fair enough. When can you come out?"

"I can't pinpoint the time. Hopefully, sometime within the month. I've got a job to do here first."

Reed studied Morse. Now that the deal had been made, he wanted to know more about this man. He was conscious of some deep anger or intensity in Morse, somewhere just under his skin, ready to bubble and burst through to the surface.

"Something I'm curious about."

"Yes?"

"George Glennon told me you're not interested in deprogramming kids from Hare Krishna, Moon's church, or any of the other cults. The only ones you'll touch are those in Souls for Jesus."

"So?"

"He seemed to know the reason, but he wouldn't tell me. I thought maybe you . . ."

"It's a long story," said Morse curtly. "And I don't want to get into it now. Let's just say it's a personal matter."

"How did you ever get into this line of work, anyway?"

"That's something else I'd rather not discuss."

Morse spoke harshly. Frank Reed was startled at the quick transformation that had come over the man. The eyes were aflame now, the face contorted into a burning, almost fanatical hatred. He had opened a door that Morse had slammed shut in his face, so to speak, and Reed was embarrassed.

"I'm sorry. I didn't mean to pry . . ."

"Forget it," said Morse, rising. His voice was still harsh. "Let's get over to my room. I've got to brief you on procedure before I leave. You're going to have a lot to do back in California, before I even get there."

Shortly after Reed left, the phone rang. It was George Glennon, calling from Santa Cruz.

"Well, John? What did you think of Reed?"

"I like him. I think he can cut it."

"Then you made the deal."

"Yes."

"When can we expect you out here?"

"I'm not sure. Hopefully, within the month. How's the book coming?"

"Rolling along. Coming down the home stretch. You keep sending me material, and I'll keep sending you clients."

"That's our bargain."

"Right." Morse heard Glennon chuckle. "Wait till you read what I already have. This isn't just the usual exposé I've done. I put my heart into all the other books, but I've put my venom into this one. In effect, what I hope to do here is shove a stick of dynamite up the ass of the Reverend Buford Hodges, and light the fuse."

Morse grinned. "Sounds great."

"Hopefully, when I'm finished, he's going to have trouble staying low and away, even on that big yacht of his. Between us, John, this has the smell of a best seller. The whole country is cult crazy. If we're lucky, the Reverend Buford Hodges is going to be better known than Aimee Semple Mac, Sweet

Daddy Grace, Billy Sunday, and Billy James Hargis, all put together. Only he isn't going to like his publicity very much. By the time you finish in Los Angeles and get up here, I should have it about done."

"I can't wait."

"Got some news for you."

"Yes?"

"*Time* Magazine is planning to do a cover story on the Reverend Hodges. And of course, the SFJ."

"You're sure?"

"*If* they can get enough stuff on him. They've already sent a couple of what they call reporter-researchers around to see me."

"And?"

"Naturally, they've heard of you. They know the cult calls you the Devil and would love to turn you into a hopeless cripple, if they could find you. They know your real name, and they've talked to a number of the kids you've brainwashed back to normal. They'd like to talk to you, *if* they knew where you were. Naturally, I was not about to tell them. They suggested an off-the-record type of meeting with you, all names confidential. It seemed to fire their imagination. You know, a hoodoo-voodoo mumbo-jumbo secret meeting with the Devil himself. You could see them drooling over copy like this. I told them I'd discuss it with you—*if* I could ever find you."

"You know my answer to that," said Morse, firmly. "No way."

"I agree. By the way, I suppose you've already heard. The kid you deprogrammed in St. Louis is going on television, telling how the Souls of Jesus screwed him up. And the last kid you cleaned in Denver's giving this big story to the *Denver Post*. I talked to a friend of mine on the paper. And *he* talked the editor into doing the piece. Nice?"

"Very," said Morse. "You're beautiful, George."

"Thank you, John. As you know, my tentacles are everywhere. And I can tell you, the Master is very, very upset at you. And, of course, there's a damned good reason why you're the far-and-away favorite in the SFJ rogues' gallery. Every

kid you pull out who then goes on to blast the cult is another
hotfoot for His Divinity. To use the cliché, another nail in
his coffin. Keep them coming, John. You're really getting to
him now. You're hurting him."

"It's not enough," said Morse, quietly. "Not nearly enough.
I want to kill him."

10

The next morning, Frank Reed phoned Ken at Stanford, told him he needed his help, and explained why. His oldest son asked no questions.

He asked Ken to drive down to Santa Barbara that afternoon, so that he could orient Ken as to the preparations they would have to make.

He also talked to Joe Peterson, a fellow surfer of Jeff's and perhaps Jeff's only close friend. Frank Reed told Joe why he needed him. He carefully explained the risk involved, made it plain that somebody could get hurt, and that what they were going to do might, under certain circumstances, even get them into legal trouble.

In spite of this, Joe did not hesitate to volunteer. He considered Jeff a little far out, but he didn't care. Not only was Jeff great to go surfing with, but he really liked Jeff as a person, and anything he could do, he would do. Joe Peterson was a husky boy, as was Ken, and Frank Reed knew he would need all the muscle he could get.

The next day, Frank Reed and his two young companions drove to Los Angeles. From there they took the San Bernardino Freeway, and turned off into the mountain area where Big Bear Lake was located. He needed an isolated area just a couple of hours from Los Angeles. When he was a child his family had had a cottage at Big Bear, and he knew the area well.

In the town itself, he saw a real estate agent. What he wanted was a house he could rent for a month or two, something out in the woods, away from the shore of the lake, which would be somewhat populated. He wanted to get away from it all.

Business was a little slow at this time of year—Big Bear was really a winter place for skiers—and the agent was anxious to please. He showed Frank a roomy two-story rustic cottage, furnished, and set back on a dirt road leading through the woods. Included in the rental charge was heat, if they needed it. It could get pretty cool at night, up here in the mountains, even during the summer.

Reed paid the agent the rent he asked for, two months in advance. The man, whose name was Ernst, felt a certain amount of curiosity, wondering who his clients were, and for what purpose they would really use the cottage. But he was happy to make the deal, and he asked no questions. He gave Frank the key and left.

After that, they took the dimensions of all the windows and doors with a tape measure.

They drove to Lake Arrowhead, had dinner, and stayed overnight at a motel.

The next day, they drove down the mountain and bought a couple of mattresses and a large supply of foodstuffs, mostly canned, which they stored in the cottage. They looked for a lumber yard, found one near Crestline, and bought a number of strong wooden boards. These were cut into short lengths, according to specifications. They loaded them into the trunk of the car. Then they stopped at a hardware store, bought a couple of hammers and a quantity of nails. They delivered all this to the cottage as well.

It was late at night when they finally returned to Santa Barbara.

And Frank Reed thought, It's over and done.

All we can do now is wait for the Devil.

PART
TWO

11

The sleek yacht stood alongside the dock in San Francisco bay. It measured ninety feet from bow to stern, was painted white, and its name on the hull clearly identified it as the *Messenger of God.* Its mahogany superstructure shone, its fittings gleamed. It had enough cabins, aside from the crew's quarters, to sleep at least ten people. It was driven by twin motor GM diesels, and it had a range of almost three thousand miles, without refueling.

This was the floating home of His Divinity, the Master, and therefore, by definition, the Mother Church of the Souls for Jesus. All members of the crew, of course, were members of the SFJ, and when the ship was in dock, they wore their monk's robes, as though to emphasize to the general public, and especially to the IRS, that this was indeed a church, therefore tax-exempt, and rightly so.

Occasionally, the *Messenger of God* appeared at one of the big ports in the United States. It was in San Francisco now, because the Master had to come ashore to tape his television show and to confer with his associates. In addition, the engines needed a routine overhaul.

Usually, the *Messenger of God* was at sea. Here, released from landlocked details, the Reverend Buford Hodges could meditate in peace, commune with Christ, compose his pronouncements to his Elders and their fiefs throughout the land, and at the same time maintain a kind of personal mystique, not only to the members of his own cult, but to the public at large. It also eliminated the necessity of his having to face interviewers who, for the most part, were hostile, and insisted on asking embarrassing questions.

On this day, however, the Reverend Hodges had decided to grant one of his rare interviews. When he wanted to, he could be completely charming, but he was also shrewd. And he had good business reasons for being amenable to this particular interview. Now, in the beautifully appointed and luxuriously furnished main cabin, he waited, attended by three of his Disciples, to receive a delegation of prominent Jewish officials.

The Reverend Hodges knew the New Testament very well, and he was not above using parts of it in his own behalf, whenever he found it useful. He had surrounded himself with twelve Disciples, all answering to the classic biblical names, although only three were present at the moment. They were the trusted confidants and advisers of the Reverend Hodges, defenders and protectors of the cult, and helped make its policy.

The Master himself wore the simple rough, gray robe of the monk, the standard cult costume. It was tightly fastened around the neck, with the cowl dropped back over his shoulders. This seemed rather odd, since the air-conditioning system about the yacht was temporarily out of order and it was warm in the cabin. His robe was held together by a golden belt, symbol of his exalted office, and he wore golden sandals. The Disciples wore robes as well, in the same manner, tied together with black belts, indicative of their office.

The delegation came aboard. The spokesman introduced himself and his colleagues: "Reverend Hodges, my name is Louis Goodman. I represent the American Jewish Committee.

100

This is David Shapiro, who is with the B'nai B'rith Anti-Defamation League. And this is Rabbi Joseph Epstein, president of the Rabbinical Council of America. We appreciate your taking the time to give us this interview."

"Not at all, gentlemen." He smiled and raised his hand in a benevolent blessing. "Jesus loves you."

The delegation looked startled at this. Goodman said, blankly, "He does?"

"Surely, you must know that, my friends. You are His Chosen People. So the Bible says. He Himself was a Jew, before He showed Himself as the Son of God." He turned to Rabbi Epstein. "You know the Bible, Rabbi. Is that not true?"

"A Jew, yes," said the rabbi. "As to the other—it is a matter of opinion. Or faith. Or whatever you believe."

"Ah, well," said the Master, smoothly. "I know you have not come here to argue theology or the Scriptures today." He waved to his associates. "These are three of my Disciples. Matthew, Luke, and Peter."

"Jesus loves you," they chorused.

The Master waved to some chairs. "Please be seated, gentlemen. Can I offer you some refreshment? I regret we cannot offer you anything alcoholic. It is forbidden to us, by the Bible itself."

They all declined. They couldn't help staring at the strange, robed figures. The faces of the Disciples were stony. They stood with folded arms, waiting for the command of the Master, listening respectfully. These medieval figures seemed utterly incongruous. Part of some weird stage play. Certainly, they seemed sinister. They looked like some Mafia of monks, headed by a smiling Godfather. To the delegation, they were an unpleasant reminder of Torquemada, and the Inquisition, and other untold black instances of the role robed and cowled priests had played in the history of the Jewish people.

The Master noted their uneasy and curious reactions, and smiled broadly. "I know we must appear strange to you. But these are the symbolic garments of humility, abstinence, and dedication to God," he said. "The Souls for Jesus considers

101

itself far more enlightened and closer to the Holy Spirit than the Vatican and its Catholic Establishment. But here and there, we've borrowed a little from the Mother Church. According to our ritual, these robes are worn only in our churches. And this ship, of course, *is* a church." He paused, his eyes shrewd, as he studied his visitors. "Now, gentlemen. What can I do for you?"

"Among other things," said Shapiro, "we're here to register a formal protest."

"Yes? About what?"

"The branch of your church near Philadelphia, Shimron by name, is headed by a First Elder named Ozem. He's just made a highly anti-Semitic statement that, unfortunately, has already received widespread publicity."

The Master stared at the delegation.

"What kind of statement did he make?"

"He said, and I quote him exactly, that 'The six million Jews who perished in the Holocaust were paying indemnity for the crucifixion of Christ.'"

The Reverend Buford Hodges looked shocked.

"You have some proof of this, gentlemen?"

Shapiro handed him a clipping from a Philadelphia newspaper. "The remark was made in an interview over a local television station. Afterward, he tried to retract, but by then it was too late."

The Master's face darkened as he scanned the clipping. He returned it to Shapiro. Then he said, with quiet anger, "Gentlemen, I regret this incident. The First Elder, Ozem, was stupid and misinformed. I promise you that he will be removed from Shimron by nightfall, his position revoked, and I will see to it personally that he receives proper punishment. Believe me, gentlemen, it in no way represents our policy and attitudes toward the Jewish people."

"Just what is your official policy toward the Jewish community?" asked Goodman.

"I'm surprised that you ask that."

"We think we have good reason," said Rabbi Epstein. "There have been certain rumors about the SFJ."

"I know. Spread by my enemy. Satan. Delivering whispers of poison into the ears of the naive, the gullible. Gentlemen, you've asked me for my position, and I'll give it to you plainly."

"Fine, Reverend," said Shapiro. "We'd appreciate that."

"We of the Souls for Jesus love the Jews. We see them as God's timepiece and the people of prophecy. God promised they would survive, and planned it that way. Long ago, God made a promise to Abraham. That his seed would bless all nations. And that this seed would bloom into its sacred fruit as the Messiah. My Church believes in the coming of the Messiah. And the Jewish people have already fulfilled their prophecy by returning to their promised land—Israel—and bringing us closer to the most important vision of our lives. The coming of the Messiah. Let me make this absolutely clear, gentlemen. We totally support the people of Israel and their land, in their God-promised, God-ordained right to exist. And anyone opposing this isn't just fighting Israel. He is fighting God and time itself. He is a creature of Satan."

The men in the delegation looked satisfied. They expressed their appreciation, when the Reverend Hodges promised to make a public statement of his position, and then left. The Master and his Disciples watched them walk along the dock as they headed for the car.

Then they turned to smile at each other.

"By God, Buford," said the Disciple called Luke. He was really delighted. "You really handled those Jew boys. You know what? I damned near believed you myself."

"Thank you, Billy."

"Old silver-tongue Buford," said the Disciple called Matthew. "You've really got it, Brother Hodges. Had them nuzzling out of your hand, like a horse nosing for sugar. If you ask me, there isn't any place you can't go."

The Master grinned. "Yes. It was very worthwhile, Dick. Good public relations. Your specialty, and you should know. It's important to get the support of the Hebrews. And they're very sensitive on the issue of freedom of religion."

"And so are we," said Matthew. "Naturally."

"Naturally."

"And some of them are heavy supporters of the American Civil Liberties Union."

"Love the ACLU," said Luke. "Because it loves us."

The Disciple called Peter loosened his tight collar, whipped off his belt, and took off his robe. The others followed suit. They were all dressed in street clothes. "Goddamn it," said Peter. "These things get pretty hot, Buford. You wear them ten minutes, and you start to sweat like a mule. Not only that, they itch."

"Always like to give them a little show, Ray," said the Master. He slid open a door to a cabinet and took out a bottle of Jack Daniels for himself, Scotch for the others. He drank only sour mash or bourbon. Finally, after they had refreshed themselves, the Master said:

"All right, boys. Let's get down to business. Your report first, Billy." The man he called Billy, otherwise known as Luke, was actually William Digby, of the prestigious firm of Mason, Anders and Digby, investment counselors. "How'd we do on the last television special?"

Digby, with his expertise, acted as business manager and financial adviser to the cult. Actually, all the Disciples of the Master were only nominally members of the SFJ. They lived outside the communes, and they were all professionals in their highly specialized fields. They were top lawyers, public relations executives, accountants and media experts. The Master paid each of them a retainer, and gave them a piece of the action to keep them happy.

Now, Digby drew a computer readout from his briefcase.

"Got the figures right here," said Digby. "The money's rolling in. Almost a half million in contributions, and still coming." He grinned. "All those wrinkled dollar bills, from those wrinkled, toil-worn hands. By God, Buford, I have to hand it to you. You really know how to turn a phrase."

"Jesus loves you," said the Master, smiling.

They went over the figures for the SFJ publishing company, which printed the *Sayings of the Master* and the other SFJ literary output; the recording company, which recorded his sermons on both records and tape cassettes; the syndicated TV film company, which distributed the Master's evangelical programs; and the thrift shops, used as outlets for some of the worldly goods given up by the Neophytes. All these came under the financial umbrella of the Reverend Hodges Evangelistic Association, Inc., which was now a multi-million-dollar colossus with an annual budget of twenty million dollars, and still growing. The Master, under Digby's careful guidance, and for tax purposes, had been very careful that his "Association" did not involve itself in any business outside religious work.

All these enterprises showed a healthy profit for the past month, and now the Master said, "Let's get to the churches."

Digby submitted a list of the various church communes, over a hundred in all, and their collection figures from the God Squads. Most of them did well. The computers had come up with an average of a hundred and twenty-five dollars a day for each Neophyte-salesman. A few of the church communes, like Bashan, near Tacoma, and Samaria, near Houston, hadn't done so well, and gone under their quotas.

"What seems to be the trouble at these two locations, Billy?"

Digby shrugged. "Maybe it's the weather. You get lots of rain, and collections go down. People stay off the street."

"My guess," said the Master, "is that the God Squads at Bashan and Samaria are sitting on their asses. Not working hard enough."

"What do you suggest, Buford?"

"Cut their rations."

Digby stared. "But they're on a pretty low subsistence diet now."

"I can't help that. You take any alley cat. The hungrier he is, the harder he hunts. Of course, it could be the leadership up at Bashan and Samaria. Some of these Elders get lazy after a while. They don't provide any incentive. Send them each a note, in my name, Billy. Tell them I'm displeased. Tell them if they don't get off their asses and produce, we'll get us a couple of new boys. Think that will shake them up a little?"

105

Digby grinned. "It should. Speaking of Elders, what are you going to do about this Ozem? The First Elder at Shimron."

Hodges' face darkened. "I'm going to break the stupid son-of-a-bitch back to Deacon. And then transfer him out of there in a hurry."

The Elders were tough. They were really religious fanatics, most of them rebels and cast-offs from certain Pentecostal churches, too extreme even for the most extreme. They lived and died by the word of the Bible, and any rebuke from the Messenger of God, His Divinity himself, would galvanize them into action. They would get better performances from their Neophytes and Deacons, even if they had to beat them with whips.

The next item of business on the agenda was public relations.

Here, the Disciple Matthew, whose earth-name was Richard Caswell, of the well-known public relations firm of Caswell and Steen, took over. His report was brief, but important.

"*Time* Magazine is doing a cover story on you, Buford."

"I heard a rumor about it."

"I checked. It's definite."

"What have they got so far?"

"Not a hell of a lot. They haven't been able to really get to anybody yet. They've talked to George Glennon, of course. I don't really know how much they'll get out of him. If he's writing a book, he's liable to keep the stuff he's got close to his own chest, instead of giving it away."

The Master turned to the Disciple Peter, otherwise known as Raymond Garvey, senior partner in the law firm of Garvey, Donan, Bell, and Wall.

"This damned book of his. What about it, Ray? Anything we can do about stopping this thing before it gets off the ground?"

"We're giving the publisher a hard time now. Some of them have weak stomachs if you press hard enough. And any attack on a church is like walking on broken glass. You have to be very careful. Maybe we'll threaten to sue beforehand. Without even seeing Glennon's work. It probably won't work, but the publisher *may* feel his feet getting cold, and tell Glennon to go easy."

"Why not?" said the Master. "We might as well. We're suing everybody else."

The cult was not meek when it came to its detractors. Unlike the biblical admonition, it did not turn the other cheek. It always counterattacked, and viciously. It sued for slander, libel and in the case of the Reverend Hodges personally, defamation of character. It recoiled ferociously at every assault.

"To get back to this *Time* Magazine thing," said Caswell. "Naturally, Buford, they'll want to talk to you."

"And?"

"My advice is to say 'no.' "

"I agree with Dick," said Garvey. "Do what you've been doing up to now. Be unavailable. Keep a low profile."

"Gentlemen," said Hodges, "I disagree with all of you. If *Time* wants an interview, I'll give it to them."

"Buford, you're out of your mind."

"I don't think so. We're being hurt badly by these damned kids John Morse has sprung loose and deprogrammed. They're sticking it to us, every time they go on television or get into the newspapers. We can't just sit back and keep taking it. We've got to hit back. And this may be the time and the place and the way to do it."

"You do and you'll be sticking your neck way out," said Caswell. "As it stands, you're great magazine copy, Buford. But if they can't get to you, if they can't profile you personally, it's possible they may drop the whole project, because the main centerpiece, which is you, would be missing."

"I'll still talk if asked, Dick. And don't worry. I can handle it. If our image is being tarnished, I'm going to try and shine it up a little. And I think I can do it."

"Okay." Caswell shrugged and sighed. "You're the boss."

"Exactly," said Hodges. "I'm the boss. Now, let's go on to the next item on the agenda. The Devil himself. John Morse." He looked at Garvey. "Any luck?"

Garvey shook his head. "We've had our investigators trying to get a location on him. He keeps covered too well, and moves around too fast."

"Ray, we've got to find the son-of-a-bitch. I want him off my back. He's really sticking in my craw."

"We'll keep trying."

"You do that. Now, if you boys will excuse me, I've got another engagement."

He grinned at them, and they all smiled back, picked up their briefcases, and left.

12

The Master walked aft and entered a large cabin which served as his bedroom. In the big double bed a lady was waiting for him. She was blonde, and young, in her early twenties. She was sitting upright, back propped against the pillow, knees drawn up, reading a magazine and smoking a cigarette. Her nightgown was thrown across her chair. She had thrown the bedclothes back, and her naked body, with its ripe, beautifully rounded breasts and long, smooth white thighs, was reflected from the full-length wall mirror in sensuous images.

"Buford, *where* have you been?"

"At a business meeting."

"You know how long I've been waitin' here?" she asked petulantly. "You know how long I've been waitin'? An hour and a half, that's how much."

"I'm sorry, Rebekah."

"Buford, will you cut out that silly Bible crap, and stop calling me that Jew name?" She was originally from the South, but she had been away from home so long that she now talked "northern." "My name is Evelyn May Langley, and you *know* it."

He grinned, teasing her, and started to undress.

"This is a church. We're supposed to use biblical names."

"Oh, shit," she said.

"Fine language for a Deaconess."

She put down the magazine and watched him for a moment. Her petulant mood changed abruptly. Her eyes became hungry, sultry. Invitation to the Dance. She brought her hands around to support the back of her neck, so that her breasts thrust further forward. The pink nipples were hard.

"I've been so hot and ready so long, I've been going crazy. Make it quick and get in bed with me, Buford."

Ostensibly, Evelyn May Langley was a Deaconess of the Souls for Jesus, and officially, the Master's secretary. At least, this was the way she was listed on the ship's roster. They had just returned from a leisurely cruise through the Bahamas and among the islands in the Caribbean. And on those sun-drenched days and moon-washed nights, she had served him well. In fact, when it came to "work" she was insatiable.

He felt good now, *good*. The Jack Daniels he had drunk warmed him, the news that *Time* was going to do a cover on him stimulated him, the sight of Evelyn May lying there, stark naked and pulsing to be penetrated, fired him. He was stirred by the musky smell of her, the mix of hot flesh and perfume, the *female* smell of her, and now his groin hardened into a large lump, like a clenched fist. Although he was now in his fifties, the Reverend Buford Joe Hodges was a vital and virile man. He liked to think he was the best-hung Holy Man in the business. He liked young girls, and he was in the habit of taking a different "secretary" on every cruise, because he liked variety. He had never had a complaint from any of them, simply squeals of delight, and awed compliments.

No doubt about it. He had been lucky, and anointed in oil, as the Bible said.

He had been baptized by hard-shell Pentecostal preachers

in a dirty stream in southern Georgia, and saved by a miracle on a railroad trestle in Tennessee. He had squeezed the juice out of that miracle, and made it go as far as it could go. There had been witnesses to its authenticity, it was on the public record, it had been in all the newspapers, and people still talked about it. Shrewdly, he had realized that you could never get big, *really* big, in the evangelical business, unless you had a visitation, unless you could produce a miracle; and you could not get very far as a prophet unless you personally spoke to God, or he spoke to you. Look at Moses, look at Mohammed. So he had parlayed his miracle into a "vision." And then had, forever, pledged himself to the Lord.

This was the same Lord who giveth and also taketh away, and in his case, the Lord had seen fit to give. He had divinely blessed the Reverend Buford Hodges between his legs. And the stiff ramrod he could produce there, any time and on demand with almost any reasonably attractive female, had been a very important part of his career, his rise to glory and eminence and wealth. The truth was that long ago, by a curious twist, it had probably been the key to his career.

He took off all his clothes, and stood stark naked, standing over Evelyn May, smiling down at her. His erection thrust out, straight and hard, swollen and glorious, and Evelyn May stared at it, completely mesmerized.

"Buford, it's so *big!*"

He stood for a moment, watching his various reflections in the wall mirrors, pleased by what he saw. Then she said, huskily:

"For God's sake, Buford, just don't *stand* there. Get into bed with me!"

After they had finished, she lay on her back, eyes closed, and sighed contentedly. "Buford, that was the best. The best ever."

"Why, thank you, Evelyn May."

"No wonder they call you the Master. And I don't mean because of your preaching."

She thought for a moment. "Tell me something, honey."

"Yes?"

"What does the Bible say about sex? You know—about—well, fucking."

"It's for it, if you've taken unto yourself a wife, and wish to procreate and spread your seed. Otherwise, it's against all fornication and lust. As it says in James 1:15, 'When lust hath conceived, it bringeth forth sin.'"

She giggled. "Then you're a sinner."

"We're all sinners, Evelyn May. In the eyes of God, and before Jesus. His whole being was spiritual, holy. He had no truck with lust or weakness of the flesh. You know, Evelyn May, you may be possessed of Satan. You could go straight to hell, for a remark like that."

She didn't seem to be frightened. Instead, her hand slid along his thigh, and then to his groin.

"Maybe," she said. "But right now, I'll take my heaven—right here on earth." Then, as she caressed him: "Buford," she said, suddenly, "let's get out of here."

"What?"

"Let's go back to where we were. You know, the Bahamas, and the Virgin Islands and all those places. All those nice warm places, with the lovely beaches and things. We were having such fun. Why did we have to come back here?"

"Because I have things to do."

"But you have all those Disciples and Elders working for you. You've been so busy here, I've hardly seen you. How long will we have to be here?"

"Three weeks. A month, perhaps."

"You'll take me with you again?" she asked anxiously. "I mean, it won't be someone else..."

"Of course not, Evelyn May," he said. "Now, why would I do a thing like that?"

He turned his head and kissed her, and she seemed reassured, and started to chatter aimlessly about many things. He did not listen. His mind was drifting elsewhere now. The fact was that he had had enough of Evelyn May. She had been aboard with him for two months now, and that was longer than most of them stayed. She was very good in bed, but not really very bright. Already, he had his eye on a certain Deaconess he had seen at Elam, which was one of his churches located near Tahoe. What was her name? He'd made a mental note of it, but it was one of those hard ones to remember. Oh, yes. Jehosheba. That was it. The daughter of Joram, and the sister of Ahaziah. The reference was 2 Kings 11:2. If there was one thing he prided himself upon, it was his knowledge of the Bible. He had it down cold.

Anyway, he was sure that Jehosheba, who was about twenty, with dark eyes, raven-black hair, and a soft, delectable mouth, would be delighted to cruise south with the Master. She would consider herself blessed, and filled with the Holy Spirit. And of course, he would do just that. She would give her soul to Jesus, and her body to His Messenger. Fair enough. Everybody got a piece of the action. He smiled to himself at the prospect. He had not seen her body, since she was wearing her gray, coarse ritual robes. But he had a good imagination, and was sure she would do.

In a way, he would miss Evelyn May. She came from an impoverished but aristocratic North Carolina family, real "Gone With the Wind" southern gentry, who long ago had owned a huge plantation, and boasted of a general in the Confederate Army, Thaddeus Randolph, who had been killed at Antietam. It intrigued him, and was a tremendous sop to his ego, to have Evelyn May Langley lying next to him, warm and naked and willing, and stroking him the way she was, cooing to it, admiring it, adoring it, and loving it.

Long ago, when he had been a poor damned illiterate rednecked cracker, he had had about as much chance to get into bed with the likes of a Langley as a buck nigger did. Poor white trash was poor white trash, and there was nothing you could do with it. Or so people said.

But here he was, in bed with a real, honest-to-God Langley, under soft linen, on his own yacht, and with a couple of million stashed away in a numbered account in Switzerland, and the money rolling in every day.

113

Yessir, he thought exultantly, you've come a long, long way, Buford Joe.

Considering from where you started.

He had been born in Clinch County, near the town of Headlight, in southern Georgia.

Every once in a while for some strange reason, he recalled his childhood most vividly in terms of certain odors. In his memory, he recalled once again the smell of the red dust of the back country, and the smell of the fruitjar whiskey on his mother's breath—the whiskey that had finally killed her— and the astringent smell of lye soap in the old black washpot behind the shack in which they lived, and the stink of the big intestine when his father killed a hog and then rendered it down for lard, and he remembered the stench of the outhouse they had near the pigpen, and how he had almost gagged whenever the old man made him clean it.

But more than anything else, he remembered the stale, rancid smell of his father's sweat-stained body after a preaching, after he had hooted and hollered and waved his arms and jumped up and down, exhorting his listeners to praise Jesus or go to hell.

Of course, there were the more pleasant odors, hominy, and fried possum and sweet potatoes, and all these were eaten off a big oilcloth spread on the table. As a boy, he had had his first meeting with Jesus on that tablecloth. Its entire surface was decorated by a picture of the Last Supper, painted in many brilliant colors, with Christ sitting there, his halo shining, flanked by his Disciples, each identified by name in golden letters.

At the age of sixteen, when his mother had died, he had drifted away from home, working the land wherever he could for wages. But after a time he had decided that preaching was easier on the back than working, and he had gone forth to preach the word, as his father had. But because he was a nobody, with no credentials, few came to hear him, and he almost starved.

One day he read an ad in a North Carolina paper, and

answered it. The Universal Life Church, it read, would ordain you as a minister, practically free of charge, and thus enable you to perform weddings, funerals, and baptisms legally. More than that. The Universal Life Church believed that anybody had the right to interpret God according to his own theory or concept. And anyone interested in starting a church of his own could send for a charter and pledge a two-dollar monthly donation to be kept in the records.

After that, he could officially call himself the Reverend Buford Joe Hodges, with a certificate to prove it. And he had kept the idea of starting a new church in the back of his mind.

He had a persuasive tongue, the hellfire delivery beloved of southern Baptists, and a kind of magnetism and charisma even then, that seemed to attract people. He made a little money by preaching on street corners, or fields, in small towns throughout the South—wherever he could find some kind of audience—and then passing the hat for dimes and quarters. He could not afford a car, so he hitchhiked, and sometimes walked, from town to town.

But it was the Miracle, and the Vision arising out of the Miracle, that had put the name of the Reverend Buford Joe Hodges into the newspapers and wire services, and made him an instant celebrity.

It had all happened in the mountains of Tennessee, south of a town called Rogersville, on the Holston River in Hawkins County.

He had spent the night in a shabby whorehouse, roaring drunk, and was still a little high when early morning came. He had wanted to move south across the river and into Greene County, but the pedestrian bridge was a couple of miles upstream, and at this point only a railroad trestle spanned the river. He decided to take a shortcut by walking across the trestle.

The Madam warned him it could be dangerous, but he did not listen or care.

The river ran through a wide, deep gorge. It was a cold morning, and foggy, and he was halfway across the trestle when he heard the rumble of the train coming on behind him.

It seemed to be moving fast. The engineer apparently had no idea that any pedestrian would be stupid enough to be on the trestle; besides, it was strictly forbidden, and there were warning signs everywhere.

Even now, lying here safely in bed with Evelyn May Langley, Buford Hodges broke out in a cold sweat at the memory. He remembered the smell of death, the *distinct* nauseating smell of death, when he realized that the train was coming on too fast, the engineer could not see him in the fog, and there was no way it could stop in time before it knocked him down and mashed him beneath its wheels, or knocked him off the high trestle. To jump was suicide, because the river was shallow, and its bottom strewn at this point with jagged rocks.

He had whimpered and cried and begged God for help. He started to run ahead of the train but, of course, that was both useless and pathetic, just the reflex of a doomed and trapped animal.

The train was coming up on him now; the engineer finally caught sight of him in the fog, and put on his brakes, and the wheels screamed sparks on the rails, but, of course, they both knew it was too late.

That was when the Miracle happened, and he had made the most of it, and it had taken him a long, long way.

He became famous then, and the whole country came to know about him. Suddenly he found himself preaching to large crowds. In one of these crowds was a fifty-year-old woman, who was the Widow Banning at the time; she had this big house outside of Atlanta, and a few million dollars. She was also a devout Christian, Pentecostal in her leanings. When she heard him speak of his Vision, she believed and was converted to him, and his mission.

After that, she had taken him under her wing and into her house; she had hired tutors for him, and sent him to a Baptist school and, seeing his future now, he studied hard and dedicated himself. In passing, he also married the Widow Banning. He had been twenty-five at the time, and she was fifty-five, and now, lying here next to Evelyn May, who smelled so young and sweet, he remembered the odor of Eleanor Ban-

116

ning, whose flesh smelled rancid and sour and *old*. She was insatiable in bed and, many times, he had decided to leave her, but he had hung on, and finally he had been rewarded.

At the age of sixty, she died, and left him over a million dollars to carry on God's work.

He bought some time on a small TV station in the South, and then he caught on, the network of stations increased, and his converts came in by the score. He was shrewd enough to recognize that his future depended on the young, and moreover, they wanted something new, something different from the established religions. And so he had begun a whole new religion. He had started his church as the Kids for Christ, but then he decided that everybody should be eligible to receive the Word. And of course, it was more profitable.

After that, he had established his churches, or communes, and as time went on, the seeds he had planted multiplied, as the Bible put it, and now the Souls for Jesus was the biggest thing of its kind in the country.

He came out of the past, aware that Evelyn May was still caressing his member, and he felt it stir, and then thicken.

Then she rolled on top of him, and sat up and straddled him, spread her legs wide, and slid him into her.

This was the exact opposite of the so-called "missionary position," which was the only one considered permissible by the old-time missionaries. Any other way, they thought of as sinful. But although he, Buford Hodges, was a religious man, he reflected that he wasn't *that* religious.

Yessir, Buford Joe, you've come a long, long way.

He was in a deep sleep when the phone on the bedside table rang, and awakened him. Sleepily he picked it up.

The voice at the other end was trembling, agitated.

"Is this His Divinity?"

"Yes."

"Jesus loves you, Master."

"Jesus loves you." He looked at his watch. It was 5 A.M. He wondered who would be calling him at this ungodly hour. "Who is this?"

"I am Amon."

"Who?"

"Amon. First Elder at Cana." The name didn't register at all. He had a lot of Elders, and, much of the time, he couldn't remember their damned names, anyway. Still drugged by sleep, he couldn't even remember where Cana was.

"Cana?" he said, blankly.

"Your church near Memphis."

"Oh. Of course. What seems to be the trouble, er—"

"Amon."

"Yes. It's very early in the morning, here in California. Why are you calling?"

"Under ordinary circumstances," said the Elder, "I would not dream of disturbing the Master's sleep. I gave it considerable thought before I decided to do so. But then I decided I must do so, since it is a matter that would demand your immediate attention . . ."

The Master thought savagely, Get on with it, for Christ's sake, get to the point, and let me get back to sleep.

"What *is* it, First Elder?"

"The Devil has appeared among us this morning."

The Master sat bolt upright.

"The Devil? Where? How?"

"On the street. We did not see him, of course. But we saw others do his work. He has stolen another Soul from us. A female Neophyte, Esther, by name. She is in the foul hands of Beelzebub now. Even now, he must be busy, corrupting her soul with his satanic filth . . ."

"Yes, yes, First Elder," said the Master, impatiently. He had to shut off this fool and think. "You were correct in calling me immediately. Thank you. And Jesus loves you."

He hung up on the Elder. His sleepiness had vanished, his mind was now alert. Evelyn May had awakened, and now she was sitting up in bed, staring at him.

"What is it, honey? What's happened?"

"The son-of-a-bitch has done it again."

He knew what would happen next. Morse would deprogram

118

the girl. Then, through certain contacts he had, through George Glennon and others, she would be given space in newspapers, or time on television. She would damn the Souls for Jesus, and tell the public how she was seduced into it, then brainwashed. Then there would be talk of another investigation, and perhaps action taken on it. It had happened that way many times before, and the kitchen was beginning to get too damned hot.

He knew that John Morse was not just out to destroy the Souls for Jesus. The Devil was out to get him, Buford Hodges, too. This was a personal matter, a vendetta. Morse wanted the body of the Reverend Buford Joe Hodges raised high on the red-hot tines of his pitchfork. He wanted to cast his well-tailored body into the eternal fires of hell, singe and toast it first, and then watch it burn to a sizzling crisp. The Devil was really beginning to press him too hard. He was more than just a damned nuisance any more, he was a real threat, out for blood.

But sometimes, there was a substitute for blood.

For a few weeks, he had nurtured an idea. Now, it was an idea whose time had come. The thing was, he had to get to Morse somehow.

He got out of bed, went to a desk, and took out a telephone memorandum pad. He riffled the pages until he found Dick Caswell's home telephone number.

Caswell's voice slurred with sleep over the phone.

"Dick, Buford."

"For Christ's sake, Buford, it's five in the morning. Whatever it is, couldn't it wait?"

"You work for me, Brother Caswell. I can call you any damned time I please."

"Okay," said Caswell. "Okay, okay, what is it?"

"I've got a job for you to do, today," he said. "And it's the kind, Dick, that'll take delicate handling. You're going to be my emissary. On a very important matter."

"Okay. Just what do you want me to do?" Caswell was impatient to get back to sleep. "What's this all about?"

"It's a course of action taken directly from the Bible."

"The Bible? Buford, what the hell *are* you talking about, anyway?"

The Master chuckled. "You'll find it in Matthew 5:24-25. 'First be reconciled to thy brother, and then come and offer thy gift. Agree with thine adversary quickly, whiles thou art in the way with him.'"

Then, he quickly gave Caswell his instructions.

13

George Glennon sat at the desk in his study. It was nine o'clock in the morning; both Ellie and he were drinking coffee when the phone rang.

"You answer it," she said. "I'm going in and make some more coffee."

It was his editor, Rollie Stern, calling from New York.

"How's the book coming, George?"

"Just about finished."

"Good," said Stern. "Good. Glad to hear it. That's marvelous."

Stern tried to sound as though he meant it. But Glennon was instantly alert. He detected a false note in his editor's voice. Something he was worried about. Stern sounded a little *too* cheerful.

"What is it, Rollie?"

"What is what?"

"If you just called me about the weather, it's cloudy with a chance of scattered showers. But I know you didn't. Something's bugging you."

"Yes."

"What is it?"

"George, they're putting the pressure on us. Hard. I mean the SFJ, of course. They're not even waiting for you to finish the book. They're demanding that we withdraw it now."

"And?"

"If we don't, if we ever publish the book, they say they'll sue us from here to hell and back. For libel. And for millions."

"So?"

"You're not concerned?"

"No. Why should I be? What did you expect them to do—give us a medal? Buy out ten or twelve editions and distribute them to their members? Make a best seller out of it?"

"George," said Rollie, plaintively, "these people really mean business. They've got batteries of high-priced lawyers you wouldn't believe. We've received calls from prominent people, and I mean really important people, advising us that it would be both bad taste and bad judgment to publish. And they're getting very jumpy upstairs. Ralph Farrow's upset at all this hullabaloo." Farrow was the president of the publishing firm. "Especially when it's building up so early."

"What do you want *me* to do?"

"George, you don't quite understand. We're attacking a *church*, for God's sake."

"A cult."

"Call it any damned thing you want. But officially speaking, it's classified as a church."

"Give it to me straight, Rollie. Are you really trying to tell me that Farrow's getting cold feet? Wants me to back off? Doesn't want to publish the book at all?"

"No, no," said Stern, hastily. "I didn't say that at all. I'm just saying be careful. Be damned careful you document everything you say about the SFJ—in triplicate. If they sue, and you can be damned sure they will, even if it's only an automatic reflex, we don't want any holes in the line they can pour their running backs through."

"Deefense! Deefense!"

"Exactly. Facts, George. Quotes from other sources. No editorial opinions. You know."

"Yeah," said Glennon. "I know. I also know your lawyers will go over my manuscript with a microscope. Try to emasculate it. But I'm not going to let them, Rollie. I'm writing an exposé here. And a good exposé has to have balls. Especially if you want to sell a million copies. I'll have to do it my way. If Farrow doesn't like it, then I'll have to take it elsewhere."

"All right, all right, George. Look, I'm not trying to edit you at this point. All I'm trying to tell you is that Reverend Buford Hodges is turning on the flack right now, and they're getting restless upstairs." He tried to be cheerful, turn optimistic at this point. "But of course, we all remember the last book you did. Always get the same jitters about this time. Par for the course. But the book sold—how many?"

"Two hundred thousand hard cover. Four million paperback."

"Right. Give my love to Ellie. And keep punching."

When Stern hung up, Glennon leaned back in his chair. He stared out of the window at lawns, which now looked like green velvet, at mazes of hedges revealing great cement vases, made to look like alabaster, overflowing with geraniums and cyclamen, the wisteria in arbors, and the roses climbing trellises. He was always refreshed by the view in back of his old Victorian house, but now he was hardly aware of it. Stern's call had troubled him, and he felt vaguely uneasy.

The natives back in New York had been restless during the time he had been writing his last book, an exposé of the charity racket in America, but they had gone through with publication and it had been, as Stern had pointed out, a smash. But something told Glennon they were much more concerned about this one. Rollie Stern was right. He had better be careful. Damned careful.

The more Glennon had gotten into the subject, the uneasier he had become about the SFJ. In the beginning, he had thought the cult was simply some fad, something for the kids to go for, another version of Jesus freaks. But he had seen it grow and grow, and now it was insidious, it was a *force*. It used its power sometimes overtly, sometimes covertly. It deluged members of Congress with mail. It had the money to bribe the right people, and it did. It cajoled and threatened and lobbied. And it had clout in certain important areas of the media itself. The SFJ, in fact, ran a shadowy power structure of its own.

But what really disturbed Glennon was the fact that the SFJ was seducing more and more kids into the communes. They sold an attractive package. Get out of the rat race. Screw the Establishment, it's lousy and corrupt. Come in with us. Purify yourself. We'll give you a new family, one that loves you and makes no demands. We'll take care of you and, together, we'll change the system. And, he reflected, any number of kids could be vulnerable to all this. Suppose, thought Glennon, these thousands of brainwashed robots ran into the millions. Headed by a charismatic and power-drunk leader, they could wield tremendous clout, social and political. He shuddered to think what would happen to the country then.

Impossible? Maybe. But it had happened elsewhere in recent history, and it could, conceivably, happen here.

His phone rang, and he picked it up.

"Glennon, this is Richard Caswell. In case you don't know who I am . . ."

"You must be kidding, Caswell. Why, *everybody* knows who you are." Glennon grinned, lit a cigarette. He had a feeling he was going to enjoy this conversation. "This is an unlisted number. How did you get it?"

"Oh," said Caswell. "It's not important. Let's just say I have friends. How's the book going?"

"Just dandy," said Glennon. "You'll love it. And so will your client."

"I'm sure we will. *If* it ever sees print." Caswell paused a moment. "You know, George—er, do you mind if I call you George?"

"Why, of course not, Dick."

"You know, I was thinking you might get tired writing this book. Decide you didn't want to submit it at all. You know—

abandon it entirely. Naturally, of course, you'd have to return your advance. What was it—a hundred and fifty thousand?"

"Something like that."

"In that case, my client, recognizing this loss, would be glad to make up the advance, plus a reasonable bonus, for all your trouble."

"How much is a 'reasonable bonus'?"

"That's something we could negotiate later. And I guarantee, you'd be happy with it. Very, *very* happy. What do you say?"

Glennon smiled. "Look, Dick, this is something you just sprung on me."

"I understand that."

"It's something I'll need a little time to think about. Right?"

"Of course. But may I report that you really will consider it seriously?"

"Oh, I will. I will. Very seriously."

"Good. Now there's another matter. Actually, it's the main reason I called."

"Yes?"

"The Reverend Hodges wants to talk to John Morse. Personally."

Glennon sat up. He took a little time to absorb what Caswell had said. Then: "Is he serious?"

"He's very serious, George."

"Why?"

"He wants to make a deal with Morse."

Glennon chuckled. He had to restrain himself from laughing out loud.

"Dick, are you trying to tell me the Messenger of God, Chief Soul of all the Souls for Jesus, wants to make a pact with the Devil? My God, man, that's blasphemy."

Caswell's voice turned cold. "I'm sorry you find this amusing. But I can assure you that the Reverend Hodges wants peace with John Morse. And he is prepared to come forward and make an offer."

"As they say in the movies, an offer he can't refuse."

"All right. Put it that way."

"Okay. I will. But why call me?"

"We don't know where to reach Morse. But you do. That means you can relay this message to Morse. And if he's interested, please ask him to call my client, since my client can't call him. Okay? Will you pass on the message?"

"Why not? It sounds fascinating. I wish I knew more about this deal—you know, the details."

"I don't know them myself. The question is, will Morse be interested?"

"Oh, he'll be interested, Dick," said Glennon. "I can practically guarantee that right now."

"Talk to you again, George."

"Peace, Brother."

Glennon hung up. He grinned. Ellie came in with the coffee, and he told her the story. "Oh, my God," she said, "I've heard everything now."

"No, you haven't," he said. "You haven't heard *anything* yet."

He checked his watch, picked up the phone, and put in a person-to-person call to Mr. Charles West at the Starlight Motel in Memphis.

14

It was just before dawn, on a Sunday in Ashtaroth.

Cindy Hyland stood on a grassy knoll with a group of other Neophytes, waiting for the sun to peek over the mountain.

When it appeared, they began a slow dance, a choreographic prayer dance in tandem with God. They held each other's hands throughout, to symbolize their unity and love for each other.

This was a dance sequence derived from the *Agnus Dei,* or Lamb of God liturgy taken from the Catholic Mass. One of the tenets of the Souls for Jesus was that you did not merely pledge your soul. You gave Him your body, too, and this was expressed in the symbolism of the prayer dance, as in other, more intimate, ways at Ashtaroth. The prayer dance had an ancient history, tracing back to Old Testament times and the early Christian church.

Sunday was a day not only of worship, but of rest and recreation, and after the Morning Mass and breakfast everybody went out into the fields, and played run-and-tag games like "Last Man Out Is Satan," and "Hide and Seek the Messiah."

Cindy Hyland did not participate in the games. Instead, she lay on her back in the shade of a tree, thinking hard. Twice, she had gone to the Elder Hezekiah and asked to serve the Lord as a member of one of the God Squads. Twice she had been refused.

They had sensed that she still had some resistance, that she was not totally brainwashed as yet, and not yet a full Soul for Jesus. Not that this worried them. They knew that if they continued to work on her a little longer, they would finally have her for good.

And she realized with despair that they were right. She felt herself constantly drawn in, caught up, almost *ready* to be one of them. The effect was hypnotic. She had lived with her mother in an apartment in Santa Monica, and now even the face of her earth-mother was blurred in memory.

But lying here now, under the tree, an idea came to her. She remembered what had happened in Jeff's case. When he had broken into tongues, after he had rejected his parents, they had put him on a God Squad. Now that she thought about it, she recalled that a number of the Neophytes who had suddenly spoken in tongues had also suddenly been selected to go out on the streets and solicit tithes.

To the Elders of Ashtaroth, this seemed to represent some kind of breakthrough.

Cindy knew that in order to get out, in order to get away from Ashtaroth, and this crazy life, and particularly Tobiah, who haunted her, she had to get out on the streets, somehow. Once there, she would keep alert, look for her chance, make a break and then run for it. It was no use talking to Jeff about it. They really owned him now. He loved it here.

The way to impress them, Cindy decided, was to suddenly break out and speak in tongues.

But that came out of hysteria. And it was almost impossible to fake, unless you made it sound real. And she just couldn't improvise some gibberish they would believe, dream up such drivel . . .

She watched the Neophytes idly, as they played "Last Man Out Is Satan." They were yelling and screaming as they ran all over the field. In this game, one person played the Master, and he would chase all the others, trying to tag them. Once he tagged someone, that quarry became his Disciple. Together, they would chase other Neophytes, tagging them into Disciples. After they caught you, you all held hands and professed your love for each other. The last man out was supposed to be Satan. When you caught him, he too changed, and became loving, giving his soul to Jesus.

Last man out. Last man out is Satan . . .

Cindy Hyland sat up straight. The name of the game gave her an idea. Long ago, as a little girl, she had played a kind of counting game with her friends. It was a game where they all sat in a circle and recited this childish doggerel, pointing a finger at each girl as each word was spoken. Now she remembered how it went:

Impty, mimpty, dibity fig,
Deeah, dyah, dominig,
Eichey, beichey, domineichy
Om pom tusk
Oliga, boliga, boo . . .
And out goes
Y-O-U!

The girl tagged with the last letter of the last word was out. Then they would go around the circle until the next girl was counted out. And so on. Cindy worked hard to recall the second verse:

Cora, bora, coola, lam,
Doro, oko, boola, bam,
Oodoo, boodoo, alakahoodoo
Om pom tusk
Hoko doko, dado, doo,
And out goes
Y-O-U!

She shook a little in her excitement. It was worth a try. Maybe she could get away with it. It was all such gibberish, anyway, nobody really knew what it meant. All she had to do was to drop the end of each stanza, the out-goes-Y-O-U part of it.

The problem was that you not only had to babble the words, you had to make it *look* good, act as though you were really in some kind of trance. And she had no idea whether she had the talent to fake it.

Still, she intended to try.

And the place to try it was at Prayer Meeting, that evening.

The hymn singing was finished. The Elder Henoch, who was in charge on this particular evening, spoke on "The Wisdom of Jesus." Then everybody went into Silent Prayer.

During this part of the meeting, Cindy Hyland prayed as fervently as any of them. She prayed to God that her courage would hold out long enough to make it work, to make them believe her.

She waited until the "laying-on-of-hands," toward the end of the meeting.

When Henoch, from his seat on the platform beneath the altar, asked if anyone felt the need of hands tonight, Cindy got in quickly, before anyone else could, and cried out:

"I do, I do."

"Who is it that speaks?"

"I. Athaliah. I ask for hands to be laid upon me, and prayer to be said for me."

Henoch opened his arms wide, as though embracing them all. "All ye who are near to her, comfort her, and lay hands upon her, so that she will know and feel the love and solace of the Lord."

Several members of the group rose and gathered around her. They laid their hands on her head and her shoulders, held both her hands, began to pray aloud for her. Cindy knew that in this way, in traditional churches, the "baptism of the Holy Spirit" was sometimes granted to newcomers. Such prayer and laying-on-of-hands was often asked for, when the supplicant needed help in overcoming temptations or depression.

But she also knew that on such an occasion many of the Neophytes had begun to speak in tongues for the first time. And this was the ritual in which it would seem the most natural, the most believable.

She took a long breath, raised her head, and uttered a loud cry. She shut her eyes tight, and raised her hands. The others fell away from her, and formed a circle about her, sensing what was coming.

Cindy stood there, immobile, trembling. She was perspiring, she could feel her heart banging away in her breast. She prayed that she could remember the words. She prayed now that she would not go blank, like some actress, terrified that she might miss a cue or forget a line.

And then she began:

Impty, mimpty, dibity fig,
Deeah, dyah, dominig . . .

There was silence through the chapel, except for an occasional murmur of "Dear Jesus," or "Praise the Lord."

Eichey, beichy, domineichy,
Om pom tusk . . .

Cindy kept her eyes closed. She stood rigid, fists clenched. Someone called out, "Praise Jesus, He is speaking through her now," and someone else shouted, "It is the Holy Spirit, speaking prophecy . . ."

As Cindy continued, she forgot everything around her. The words of the childish doggerel poured from her mouth. Her tongue seemed to be working now, her lips moving, all by themselves, without any help from her. Out of her memory came a third stanza of the game she had played as a girl so long ago. And then a fourth stanza, both long forgotten, neither of which she had remembered when she had walked into the Prayer Meeting.

Suddenly, she felt transported. Light. Free. As though floating on a cloud. She was babbling now, as though in some kind of trance, some dream. Her mouth was speaking words. New words. Words she had never heard of before.

Daka mena moota arko da.
Maka mio ventra dro,
Preco, laga, cristo, ooma,
Raffa, amos, sonda . . .

But it wasn't really her mouth speaking. It was *someone* speaking inside of her, using her tongue, her mouth. The words continued to pour out. She could hear them clearly, she marveled at them, but she could not control them. The *someone* was telling her something, the meaning of which she did not know.

Finally, the words faded away. She stood there, drenched in perspiration, trembling. She opened her eyes. It was hard to adjust to the reality of what she saw. The smiling faces around her, the cries of "Jesus loves you," and "Praise God, Athaliah has spoken in tongues at last."

She couldn't believe it. She *had* been speaking in tongues. How did she get carried away? What had caused it? Fear? Hysteria? She did not know. But it frightened her. She hadn't realized how close they had come to really brainwashing her. She had told herself that she would never be drawn in. At least, her conscious mind had told her that. But here she was, speaking in tongues, and knowing that in fact they had really gotten to her unconsciously, in some subliminal way. She had almost been ready, she was only a hair away from becoming a true Soul for Jesus, a loyal member of the cult.

Amid all the congratulations, she felt a sense of panic.

She knew she *had* to get out, now, and soon. Before it was too late . . .

Her eyes caught the robed figure of Henoch, standing on the platform. He was smiling broadly at her, and he raised his hand in benediction.

A voice spoke in her ear.

"Congratulations, Athaliah."

She turned to see Tobiah standing there. He was smiling, and his eyes shone. They seemed more greedy than ever, they devoured her. She shuddered a little, knowing exactly what he was thinking.

She's one step nearer to Purification now.

Two days later, she was summoned to Hezekiah's office.

It was Tobiah who had given her a very strong personal recommendation. He and Henoch were both there to congratulate her. Once she worked on the streets, if she did well at it, it would only be a very short time before she was deemed worthy of Purification.

Hezekiah assigned her to God Squad Six. She was to go to work the next morning.

She thanked them profusely. They responded by telling her warmly that Jesus loved her, and hinted that He would love her even more if she did well in selling her booklets. She left the office, exhilarated.

Now, she could get out on the street. Bide her time. Wait for her chance.

And then, run for it.

She went to the Wardrobe Room in Building Four. There she took off her coarse heavy robe and put on the regular earth-clothes worn by girls in the God Squads, powder blue blouse with the insignia SFJ stitched under a pocket in red letters, neat dark blue skirt, black shoes. She washed and set her hair, and looked into the mirror, and was stirred by what she saw. In fact, she had trouble holding back the tears. The girl she saw in the full-length mirror was someone she had almost forgotten.

The girl she saw was Cindy Hyland.

The way she had looked, before all this happened.

The next morning, the members of the various God Squads boarded the big blue bus at Ashtaroth. Each was neatly groomed and freshly scrubbed. And each carried a kind of shoulder bag, filled with booklets.

The electric gates opened, and the bus started down the canyon toward the Pacific Highway.

Later, it stopped at intervals, dropping off the various God Squads at their appointed locations. Two of them were dropped at the public beaches in Santa Monica. This was not only a favorite location on hot days, but the beaches were also excellent for "witnessing," or proselytizing new members.

The bus turned up off Pacific Highway, and dropped another Squad at the big shopping mall on Santa Monica Boulevard. Then it headed east for the Los Angeles locations.

God Squad Six was headed by two Deacons named Heman and Shem. It was assigned to the Farmers' Market, which was considered a choice location since it was a big tourist attraction, and always busy.

The bus came south down Fairfax, and turned left into the parking lot of the Market at West Third.

The members of God Squad Six stood up. The driver waited a moment, while Heman stood at the front of the bus, facing them. Then he shouted:

"What are we going to do today?"

"We're going to *sell!*" came the answering shout.

"And what are we going to sell?"

"The *Sayings of the Master.*"

"And who is the Master?"

"The Messenger of God."

"And what does the Messenger preach?"

"The word of Jesus."

"Jesus loves you, every one," said Heman. "Now go out there and *SELL!*"

That was the crazy thing about it, thought Cindy. They *wanted* to work. Programmed or not, they were sincere. They really believed in what they were doing. They considered it a privilege.

The driver opened the door, and God Squad Six filed out.

Cindy Hyland stood for a moment, enchanted, staring at everything around her. This was the first time she had been outside the walls of Ashtaroth in a month. She had the feeling that this was another world, another planet. Everything seemed strange to her, fascinated her. The flow of traffic on Fairfax Avenue. The names of the shops, shown on discreet signs: Pants World, Buttons and Bows, Far East Trader, Indian Trading Post, Fun Shop, Today's Girl, Little Mexico, Polynesian Casuals.

But most of all, most wondrous of all, were the people, all dressed in earth-clothes, in bright colors, in shorts, and slacks and Hawaiian shirts, and not a monk's robe to be seen anywhere...

"All right, Athaliah." She turned to see Shem, watching her. "Let's get going."

The Deacon waved a finger at a girl who had been on God Squad Six for some time. She was older than Cindy, a true and trusted Soul for Jesus, and it was expected she would become a Deaconess any day now. She was named Zipporah, after the wife of Moses. "Athaliah, you stay close to Zipporah here. She'll show you the ropes. Pretty soon, you'll get the hang of it yourself."

They began to sell, thrusting the booklets toward people coming out of the cars and tour buses, heading for the gates into the Market itself. They moved in and out among their prospective buyers, aggressively shouting the various slogans and sales pitches they had been taught, selling the word of the Master, and therefore, God. If someone bought a booklet, he always got a reward. A warm "Jesus loves you" from the saleswoman.

Many of the Japanese sightseeing buses stopped at the Farmers' Market, and throughout the day disgorged hundreds of tourists from Tokyo, Osaka and Kyoto. All were armed with cameras, and they seemed fascinated as they watched the young SFJ salesmen in action. They were heavy buyers of the booklet. Perhaps they considered it some kind of bizarre religious souvenir. Or maybe they felt some curious Japanese obligation to buy the booklets in return for the privilege of taking the pictures.

Cindy was a little slow at first, perhaps not aggressive

enough. But very shortly, she caught on and was selling as hard as anyone else.

She was aware that the two Deacons, Heman and Shem, were watching her closely. She sensed that they were not concerned with her selling technique, but were watching her to see that she stayed with the group. After all, she was new on the streets. And they were still not yet convinced that she was a true and loyal and totally brainwashed Soul, even though she had spoken in tongues.

Cindy looked around her, a little desperately. She saw there was no use in trying to make a break for it here. The two Deacons stayed too close to her. She was sure they were poised to go after her, if she even tried. The parking lot was a big open area, there was no place to hide.

After about an hour, she said to Heman, "I've got to go to the ladies' room."

It occurred to Cindy that maybe, if she could get inside the Market building, among all the food and fruit stalls, she could possibly make a run for it. But you were never left alone on a God Squad, even if you only wanted to go to the john. Heman assigned Zipporah to go along with her.

The ladies' room was located within the great roofed and awninged structure of the Market itself. Cindy had forgotten what real food was like. The diet at Ashtaroth was dull and monotonous: oatmeal, mush, boiled vegetables, macaroni, mashed potatoes, beans, and the like. She found the treasures of this place heady; her senses reeled at what she saw and smelled. They passed booths piled high with jumbo oranges, Hawaiian papayas, Ribier grapes, D'Anjou pears, Golden Delicious apples, Crenshaw and honeydew melons. They passed booths selling chestnuts, filberts, almonds, walnuts, macadamia nuts, peanuts and popcorn, chocolate and fudge, old-fashioned hard candy and lush, ripe cheeses. Jeff had brought Cindy here once, on a trip they had made into town, and again memory stirred.

She walked along, or rather was propelled along, by her companion's firm hand on her elbow.

"Zipporah, let's stop and look for a while."

"We don't have any time. We have work to do."

"But all this—it looks so marvelous."

"I know," said Zipporah. "But we must resist such temptations, Athaliah. You know what the Bible says. We must abstain from fleshly lusts, which war against the soul. Our bodies belong to Christ, and we must feed His spirit, and not the flesh."

Cindy stared at her companion. Zipporah was a pretty girl, she looked so clean and fresh and innocent in her blouse and long skirt, so real, so *normal*. Yet, here in the middle of the Farmers' Market, she was mouthing the same stilted phrases from the Bible they used all the time at Ashtaroth. It occurred to Cindy that in a way, Zipporah was insane, the words came out of her as though stamped from some machine, her brain had been damaged and programmed to respond by reflex in the same way to any given situation.

She's crazy, thought Cindy. They're *all* crazy. Maybe *I'm* crazy, at this point.

And she screamed to herself, *I've got to get away, I've got to get away, soon, soon*. Otherwise they would have more time to work on her, and in time she would become another zombie, like Zipporah, and no matter how much she resisted, she knew they could do it.

They passed the restaurant area. People were sitting at tables, in the shade of awnings, and devouring a variety of foods purchased at the restaurant stalls. She felt a little faint as she inhaled a mélange of delicious smells, hamburgers and hot dogs, lasagna and tacos, tortillas and spare ribs, shrimp and crabmeat, fish and chips, corned beef, roast beef, baked ham.

She thought of the box lunches the members of God Squad Six carried, containing an egg-salad sandwich, a tomato, a hard apple, and perhaps a piece of cheese, and she had an insane desire to buy herself a tremendous hamburger, with slaw and mustard and onions, and devour it on the spot, then and there, buying it with the money she had on her through sale of the booklets. And to hell with Zipporah, or what she would say.

She rejected the fantasy, and studied her chances of escape. Trying to be cool, to analyze the situation.

It was possible to make her move right here. Zipporah's hand was grasping her arm, but with the advantage of surprise, she could tear it away, run up the alleys between the stalls, get lost among all the shoppers and tourists, and come out through one of the exits on the south side of the Market.

She steeled herself for the try. She tried not to let her body go tense and alert Zipporah. She was just about to wrench Zipporah's hand away, and make her run for it, when she stopped short.

She saw Shem a few yards away. He was strolling along casually, looking at the goods in some of the stalls. He did not even glance in their direction.

She knew that either he or Heman would stay close to her. Tomorrow. And the day after that. Again and again.

Until they were sure of her. Absolutely sure.

15

It all happened by accident. Or more specifically, through an accident.

The next morning, the big SFJ bus was moving south down Little Santa Monica Boulevard. At the intersection of the Avenue of the Stars, in Century City, there was the sound of a vicious crash up ahead. The traffic slowed with a squeal of brakes, and came to a stop. A police car came up fast, racing to the scene.

The bus itself had stopped at the intersection. It could not go forward on Santa Monica. But there was a narrow open space between the rear of the stalled car just ahead and the front of the bus. It was possible, barely possible, that the big bus could squeak through this space, and thus avoid the tie-up by turning right and going down Avenue of the Stars.

Heman went up to the driver, a Deacon named Tikvah. They both eyed the situation through the windshield.

"Think you can make it, Tikvah?"

"I don't know. I have to swing the bus around to make the turn and I don't like the angle. We could scratch some paint.

Or we could get stuck between that car just ahead and the curb."

"Maybe we'd better not try. The police are around, and the last thing we want is any problem with them." He motioned to Tikvah to open the bus door. "Maybe we won't be stalled here too long. Let's see what's going on ahead."

Tikvah opened the door, and he and Heman got out of the bus.

Cindy had been sitting in the second seat from the front, on the opposite side. Through the open door, she could see the Avenue of the Stars, running straight through Century City. It was an open invitation.

She did not even pause to think about it. She leaped from her seat, jumped out through the bus door, and began to run. Someone inside the bus yelled something. Heman, who was standing with the driver, turned, startled. He made a futile grab at Cindy. She began to run down the Avenue of the Stars.

She ran hard, on the south sidewalk of the Avenue, past the Bank of America and the First Los Angeles Bank. She turned her head slightly to see Heman and Shem running after her. She could hear the pounding of their feet on the pavement, and faintly heard them yelling for her to come back.

Vaguely, she was aware of people turning quickly to watch her, their faces startled. She saw the Avenue stretching straight ahead, looked back a moment, and saw that the Deacons were gaining. She knew that if she continued to follow the Avenue, they would ultimately catch up with her. She had to hide somewhere, to get into one of the buildings.

When she reached Constellation Avenue, she saw a big blue sign, at the entrance to an underground garage in one of the huge buildings. Just across from the Señor Pico restaurant, it read "Century City Parking."

She turned right on Constellation, then ran down the ramp and into the garage.

She ducked under the yellow automatic lift bars, which allowed cars to pass through, and raced straight ahead, through the vast garage. A moment later, she could hear the pounding feet of the Deacons as they came into the garage after her. She caught flashes of a bewildering number of directional signs: "Levels C and E," "Guest Parking," "Monthly Parking," "Blue Zones," "Red Zones," arrows pointing to "Exit" or "Escalator."

She tried to elude her pursuers by dodging among the parked cars. They stayed close to her, grimly, never letting her out of their sight. They shouted at her, "Come back, Athaliah," and "Jesus loves you," but she kept right on going. Their yells echoed through the vast garage; they sounded distorted, tinny. She ran on.

Directly before her she saw the ramp marked "Guest Parking." It was a down ramp, leading to a lower level of the garage. She ran down it, and heard them follow.

She was panting now. Fire seemed to burn in her chest, she fought for air. Panic gripped her, she could smell her own fear in her perspiration. She knew what would happen if they caught her. They would bring her back to Ashtaroth and put her through a hell called Mortification and Penitence, which was a special process of Purification applied only to backsliders.

She would be kept in a room, totally naked, to symbolize her mortification at betraying Jesus Christ. She would be given only bread and water, to sanctify and purify and cleanse her body to receive the new soul they would give her.

During this time, they would never let her sleep. They would hammer away at her, with the sayings of the Master, with quotations from the Bible, with exhortations to repent. They would tell her that they loved her, and Jesus loved her, and she had gone the way of Satan, but Satan could be repulsed, Satan could be conquered, if only she would accept Jesus, and never betray him again.

It was something like the Purification she and the others had already undergone, but a thousand times worse, and more intense.

She knew that if they ever caught her, and if she ever went through this, she would come out a true and loyal and glassy-eyed Soul for Jesus, loving Him and working for Him forever,

141

and never dreaming of ever going into the earth-world again. There was no way she could hold out. The mind damage and the brain damage, after this ordeal, would be total.

And so now, in a very real sense, she was running for her life.

She found herself in another vast garage, in a section labeled "C-Red." In the distance, she saw the entry to an escalator, its wall marked with a huge white "C" against a square red background. She turned her head to see Heman and Shem pounding down the ramp and into the garage after her.

Gasping, she ran toward the escalator. She could feel them gaining on her. They had longer legs, they could run faster, they always seemed to be shortening the distance. She reached the up escalator, ran up the steps, jostling startled riders as she did so. She reached an upper level, took another escalator to still another level, and still another section of escalator moving higher.

Finally, she emerged into a section of the great plaza of Century City itself. Above her towered huge buildings, one of them the American Broadcasting Company. Below her, there were twisting, curving concrete levels and malls, lined with multilevel shops, banks and restaurants. She turned right, and ran toward a sign marked "Century Plaza Towers" that pointed to the entry of the Century Plaza Hotel. She caught glimpses of shops all around her, Harry's Bar and American Grill, Jade West, Connoisseur, La Cuisine, Creative World Travel.

She raced through the wide entry, in the center of which was a big illuminated model of a ship, enclosed in glass, advertising "Princess Tours." The Century Plaza Hotel itself was on the other side of the Avenue of the Stars, but the entry through which Cindy ran was actually an underpass beneath the street; she could hear the traffic roaring over her head, louder than her pounding feet.

She glanced back again, and saw that the two Deacons were no more than a hundred yards away from her now, and closing the gap. They had stopped yelling at her. Their faces were grim, and red from exertion, and they simply kept coming.

She ran for the hotel entrance, past the Café Plaza, where people sitting at the outdoor tables, shaded by pink metal umbrellas, were having breakfast. They stared at her as she went by. Straight ahead, looming high over her, was the great, curved, many-windowed front of the hotel itself.

She had been nurturing an idea in the back of her head, somewhere she could hide, and she paused for a moment to look around her. But she did not see what she wanted. At the Granada Room and Bar she took an escalator leading up to the main lobby. Just as she stepped on the escalator, she saw Heman and Shem burst through the door. They sighted her and ran for the escalator.

She came out in the main lobby, just opposite a sunken cocktail area where a number of people sat, drinking coffee or having a morning pickup. Through a window, opposite, she caught a glimpse of a huge swimming pool, or a connected series of them, with small fountains spouting up within the pools themselves. She blurred past a series of elegant lobby shops. She ran blindly to the right, hotly pursued by the Deacons. They were so close to her, she could hear them gasping. They bumped and jostled people as they ran. Some man in a uniform, a security guard or somebody, was yelling at them. She was so tired, she wanted to die. Her lungs shrieked in agony, they wanted to explode.

She caught glimpses of offices to her right, Western Airlines, Hertz Rent-a-Car. But she was looking for a different kind of sign.

And at last, she saw it.

"Ladies Room."

She ran inside, closing the door behind her. A moment later, she heard the two Deacons pounding on the door. And yelling loudly:

"Athaliah, come out of there! *Athaliah!*"

Suddenly, there were voices outside, loud argumentative

voices, the sound of a slight scuffle and then silence. Cindy went into one of the toilet booths, closed the door, and sat on the john, gasping, trying to catch her breath. A few moments later, a lady came in. She seemed flustered. Cindy heard her say, to another woman at the mirror, "You wouldn't believe what was going on outside!"

"I could hear *something* happening. What was it?"

"The craziest thing. There were these two young men pounding on the door here, and yelling someone's name. For a moment, I thought they were actually coming *in*."

"Into the *ladies' room?*"

"Honestly, I actually thought they would. I mean, they were breathing so hard, and they were so angry and upset . . . "

"What happened then?"

"Well, these men came from the hotel. I guess you'd call them security people. And they grabbed the two men, and hustled them away, and told them to leave the hotel. That's the last I saw."

Cindy heard the shudder in the second woman's voice. "It's horrible. Absolutely frightening. The kind of awful people you're liable to run into these days—perverts, muggers, rapists, psychopaths . . . "

"These two young men looked perfectly normal. I mean, they were good-looking, well-dressed . . . "

"That's just what I mean," said the second woman. "Those are the kind you have to watch out for. You never can tell, these days. A man may *look* perfectly normal. But for all you know, he could be another Charles Manson."

At that moment, Cindy came out of the booth. Her hair was awry, her face streaked with perspiration, and she looked disheveled. The two women, both matronly and with dyed blue hair, stared at her. They knew she had been the quarry the two men had been pursuing. They waited awkwardly for some kind of explanation from Cindy. Finally, one of them said, "Were those two men after you?"

"Yes."

"For heaven's sake, why?"

Cindy shook her head. She didn't feel, at this point, that

she wanted to use up any more of her breath explaining it all to strangers.

"It's a long story," she said. "And you probably wouldn't believe it."

They looked at her suspiciously, and then left. She washed her face and hands, fixed her hair, looked at her reflection in the mirror, and then tried to think of what to do next.

She wanted to get home, back to her mother's apartment in Santa Monica.

But how?

She could wait here for an hour, and then leave. Hoping that the two Deacons would have given up by that time and gone away. But then she thought it through. She didn't dare leave this sanctuary alone. She had no guarantee that Heman and Shem might not be lurking around outside the hotel entrances, waiting for her to come out. Maybe they had already hired a car, and were waiting to snatch her into it the moment she stepped outside. She knew the SFJ was terribly tenacious. It never lost a Soul if it could help it. Not if they had a chance, any chance at all, to bring her back, and brainwash her, this time for good.

In the pocket of her blouse, she had five one-dollar bills. This was given to each member of a God Squad before he or she mounted a bus, in order to make change for larger bills when they sold their booklets.

There was a pay phone in the ladies' room.

She decided to call her mother, tell her she was free, and ask her mother to drive down and pick her up. It wouldn't take Elizabeth Hyland long. Their apartment was no more than a half hour's drive from the Century Plaza.

A woman came in, and Cindy asked her if she could change a dollar. Luckily, the woman had the change. Cindy went to the phone and dialed her mother's number.

There was no answer.

She dialed again, and then again. And after that, every ten minutes. Still no answer. Sooner or later, Cindy reassured herself, her mother would be back. Maybe she was out marketing. Or visiting friends. Or playing bridge. She could be anywhere. But what if her mother had gone out of town? Maybe she'd gone to visit her sister Evelyn in Palm Springs. Or her mother, in Houston . . .

Desperately, she continued to dial.

Finally, after what seemed forever, her mother answered. "Cindy!"

"Mother, I've been trying to get you . . ."

"I just got back. From the beauty parlor. Cindy, Cindy darling. Are you all right?" Elizabeth Hyland was so excited, she could hardly speak. "Are you all right, dear? Are you . . . ?"

"I'm okay."

"My God, I haven't heard from you in a month. Where are you? Where are you calling from? From that awful place?"

"No. I've just run away from Ashtaroth, Mother. I'm free."

"Thank God. Thank God for that. I don't know why you ever joined that horrible cult in the first place. For the life of me, I'll never understand why you . . ."

"Mother, look. I don't want to get into all that now. All I want to do is come home. But I have no way of getting there. Unless you come down and pick me up . . ."

"Yes," said her mother, breathlessly. "Yes, yes, of course, darling. Where are you?"

"At the Century Plaza Hotel."

"All right. But where . . ." Suddenly, her mother stopped. "Hold on, Cindy. Just a moment. Somebody's at the door, I'll send whoever it is away, and be right back." Cindy waited a little while again, then her mother came on again. "Isn't that strange?"

"Isn't *what* strange?"

"I mean, it's quite a coincidence. Here you call me on the phone, after I don't hear from you for one solid month, and then these two young men ring the doorbell, asking for you . . ."

"Oh?" A chill ran up Cindy's spine. "Did they say who they were?"

"No. They looked like nice young men. Said they'd met you on the beach somewhere, and asked if you were home . . ."

146

"What did you tell them?"

Elizabeth Hyland noted the sudden anxiety in her daughter's voice.

"Darling, what's wrong? What is it?"

"Mother, *what did you tell them?*"

"I don't know. Why is it so important? I told them you'd be home some time later. In a few hours. After all, I didn't want to stand there talking to them forever. Not with you on the phone. Now, you said you were at the Century Plaza? *Where* in the Century Plaza? It's an awfully big place. Where do I find you?"

"Mother, I want you to go to the window."

"What?"

"Go to the window. Tell me if they've gone away, or they're still there."

"Dear, for heaven's sake, what . . ."

"Please, Mother. *Do* it. Do as I say."

Their garden apartment was on the second floor, facing the street. Cindy knew her mother would have an unobstructed view. In a little while, Elizabeth Hyland came back to the phone.

"They're still there, Cindy."

"They *are?*"

"I watched them both get into the car. They drove down the street just a little way, then they stopped the car." She seemed puzzled. "They just seem to be sitting there, and waiting. I don't know why. I told them you wouldn't be back for . . ."

"Mother, I'll call you back later."

"Cindy. What on earth . . . ?"

"I can't come home right now. I'll call you back later."

"Dear, wait a minute . . ."

Cindy hung up. A shudder went through her. They hadn't wasted any time. They really wanted her back, and they had acted swiftly. Ashtaroth wasn't too far away. They had sent a couple of Deacons from there, ready to trap her if she came home.

As far as she knew, Heman and Shem could still be somewhere outside the hotel, waiting to pick her up. She imagined that they had even called for reinforcements, to watch every possible exit. Maybe they had other Deacons already in the hotel waiting to seize her when she came out.

Almost in echo of her thought, two women came through the door. She recognized them immediately. They were Sara and Chelcias, Deaconesses at Ashtaroth. It was clear they had hurriedly been summoned from one of the other God Squads to come in and get her.

As they came toward her, Cindy, in panic, dodged into one of the booths and locked it behind her. They began to pound on the door.

"Jesus loves you, Athaliah. Open the door!"

"Come out, Athaliah. Come with us, and all will be forgiven. We promise you this."

She stood there, paralyzed. They wheedled and threatened, continued to pound furiously on the door. A group of women came into the rest room. Cindy heard them talking about some convention they were attending. The pounding stopped abruptly. The newcomers had seen the Deaconesses pounding on the door, and they wanted to know what was going on. They called in to Cindy, asking who she was, and whether she was all right. She told them she was. They wanted to know why she had locked herself in, and what this was all about. She told them it was nothing, nothing at all. Finally, she heard people leaving, and there was silence.

She stood on the toilet seat and looked over the top of the door. The rest room was empty. She unlocked the door and came out, cautiously, realizing that the Deaconesses could come back at any moment. If they did, they would not hesitate to drag her out by force.

Sooner or later, she would have to leave. She couldn't stay in here forever. Panic gripped her. She felt trapped, closed in. The very walls of the ladies room seemed to close in on her. The room seemed to become smaller, more stifling. The women who came in stared at her curiously. There were only so many times she could pretend to wash her face, or fix her hair, or go to the john before she got so tired of pretending that she really didn't care any more.

She thought of calling some of her friends. But the cult would know who her friends were, through their own people, who knew everyone on the beach, and perhaps through Jeff Reed, who knew most of her friends, anyway. They would find who she was staying with, sooner or later. She thought of calling the police. But she was sure they wouldn't take her story seriously. And on the face of it, it *did* sound ridiculous. She was only seventeen, and they might put all this down to some girlish hysteria, some juvenile urge to get attention. And even if they did come down and get her, they'd probably take her home.

And at home, they'd still be waiting for her.

Then she had an idea. Someone to call. Someone who could help. If that didn't work, then she would call the police. Or call her mother again. After that, she'd have no option, anyway.

She put a dime in the box, dialed the operator, and asked for Santa Barbara Information. When she got it, she asked for the number of Frank Reed, Jeff's father. The operator gave her two numbers, home and office, and Cindy asked for the office, person-to-person and collect, Mr. Frank Reed.

His secretary answered, and asked who was calling. When Cindy identified herself, Frank Reed came on immediately. Quickly, she told him what had happened. She had nowhere to go, she needed help and protection, she had to stay somewhere for a little while where they couldn't find her, until it all blew over, and she had thought of him because he was Jeff's father, and he would understand . . .

He didn't even let her finish.

"Cindy, where are you?"

She told him and he said, "You stay there, and don't move. I'm starting out right now, and it'll take me a couple of hours. I'm taking you to my house. Don't even stick your head outside the door until I get there."

When Frank Reed arrived at the hotel, he sent one of the women employees into the ladies room to get Cindy. He walked her through the lobby, and they stood at the entrance while he waited for his car to be delivered.

She looked around uneasily. None of the Deacons were to be seen. But she had the uncomfortable feeling, probably imagined, that they were still watching her from somewhere. Still, she felt secure now, with Jeff's father beside her.

"You'll stay at our house for a week or two, Cindy," he said. "Until they get tired of you, or just lose interest."

She told him that when they got to Hope Ranch, she'd call her mother and swear her to secrecy as to where she, Cindy, would be staying. She added that she had an aunt and uncle in Palm Desert, near Palm Springs, and perhaps she could stay there for a while, until it was safe to go home. She explained that if the cultists couldn't get her back in a day or two, while they still considered her vulnerable to programming again, they would probably lose interest in her.

He thought Palm Desert was an excellent idea. In fact, it made all kinds of sense. The resort area wasn't too far from Big Bear. John Morse had told him, back in Memphis, that when the crunch came, they could use all the help they could get. Not only from Jeff's family, but anyone else close to him.

They drove up Santa Monica Boulevard, and Cindy confessed that she was hungry. They stopped at a coffee shop, and she ordered two enormous hamburgers. It was the first meat she had eaten in a month. She consumed them ravenously, and topped them off with a piece of apple pie and chocolate ice cream.

Back on the road, they turned off Santa Monica onto the San Diego Freeway, took the Ventura cutoff, and headed for Santa Barbara.

Mr. Reed said, "You know, Cindy, there's one thing I've never understood."

"Yes, Mr. Reed?"

"I've never really had a clear idea how you and Jeff ever got mixed up with this cult. What was there about the Souls for Jesus you went for, anyway? How did it all happen?"

She tried to explain, knowing how insane it must all sound now.

It all began on the beach at Malibu.

Jeff had been surfing with some others, and Cindy had been sitting on the sand watching him, when she had met a girl named Stephanie, who was a friend of one of the other surfers, a boy named Bob. They had all become friendly, and later on had gone to Alice's Restaurant on the Pier for something to eat.

At first, it was all small talk, but then both Stephanie and Bob began to talk about the Souls for Jesus, of which they were members. They both raved about the experience, claiming it was marvelous, it got you higher than any drug, that it blew your mind so that you never were quite the same again.

Then they invited Cindy and Jeff to spend a weekend at the Church up in Topanga Canyon, to see for themselves. They told them it would be a fun weekend, and they would meet a lot of new friends, fantastic people, really, who were into Christ and had found that He had TM or est or anything else of the kind beaten by a mile. In short, they would find the weekend an "absolutely incredible experience."

Jeff and she were far from religious, but they liked Bob and Stephanie. Cindy hadn't really wanted to go. She had met a few Jesus freaks, and they had turned her off. But Jeff wanted to see what it was all about, just out of curiosity. Reluctantly, she had gone along.

When they got there, she realized that they had been duped. That Bob and Stephanie had "witnessed" or recruited them. And that Ashtaroth, far from being a fun place, was a nightmare.

From the beginning, they were subjected to prayers, to voices from loudspeakers extolling the Master, to individual meetings with the Elders, who seemed to exert some kind of hypnotic influence. They had wanted to leave after a while, but the gates were kept closed and they were not allowed to. Instead, they were surrounded by members of the SFJ, who said they loved them, who reproached them for wanting to leave before they had "Found Jesus."

Hour after hour, they were bombarded with lectures on the glory of His Divinity, and the sacred mission of saving souls for Jesus. The loudspeakers never stopped haranguing them, even in the bathrooms. They were given nothing to eat, and were not allowed to sleep. They sat on the hard floor, weak with hunger, numb from lack of sleep, while the lectures continued, and liturgical music and the Voice of the Master incessantly assailed their eardrums. They were never allowed to leave the building, even to walk out for a little air.

The central theme of the lectures was always the same. They had to surrender themselves to Jesus in order to achieve salvation. They belonged to a new spiritual family. They had a new father now—a confidant of the Lord, the Messenger of God whom they called the Master. But in order to enter the Kingdom of Heaven, they had to abandon and reject their families. Their fathers and mothers were corrupters, creatures of Satan. They were the enemies of spiritual peace.

Hour after hour, the process went on. Gradually, under the constant assault, they became confused, disoriented, mesmerized by the incessant attack on their brains and nerves, the steady weakening of their bodies. Finally, as though in a trance, under some kind of hypnotic spell, they started to babble the same prayers, repeat the same slogans. Have faith in us, the Elders told them, every doubt in us is a blow for Satan. Hour after hour, they sat there dazed, under the continuing assault, their thoughts manipulated.

After some thirty hours or more, they were allowed a few hours' sleep on the hard wooden floor, and a fifteen-minute walk outside. Even outside the building, the loudspeakers continued to blare at them from trees and walls. Then they were brought in again for more of the same.

This, they learned later, was the first step in the process they called Purification.

Finally, under the incessant attack, under this kind of "mind control," the newcomers were broken. She, Cindy, had almost gone over the edge herself. But somehow, by dint of enormous concentration, by mentally trying to shut out that incessant religious bombardment from her ears, she had barely managed to keep her sanity.

In the end, the newcomers became Neophytes, Souls for Jesus. They no longer wanted to leave Ashtaroth. They *liked* being Souls for Jesus now. They *wanted* to serve the Lord. Not only that. They wanted to give Him everything they owned. Ashtaroth had a separate storeroom full of radios, television sets, stereo equipment, cameras, everything you could imagine, waiting to be sold.

If you protested giving up your car, for example, they would say: "You want to go to heaven? Then you can never get there in your Mustang. Christ died on the cross for you, did He not? He gave His life to you. Are you saying you're not willing to give Him your car?"

Everybody signed over whatever he or she had, bank accounts, everything, and they were also told to write their families telling them they needed money.

Finally, in a special ceremony, they were christened with biblical names and given their robes to wear, and assigned to their dormitories at Ashtaroth.

An hour after they arrived at Hope Ranch, the phone rang. It was a long distance call from Memphis.

"Reed, John Morse. Everything ready out there?"

"We're all set."

"The house? Everything?"

"Everything."

"Okay. I've just finished here. I'll be flying out to Los Angeles tomorrow."

"I'll drive in and meet you at the airport."

"No. I've already made other arrangements. You stay in Santa Barbara till I contact you."

Reed told Morse about Cindy, and Morse sounded pleased. Then Reed asked anxiously:

"You really think we can get Jeff out of this?"

"We'd better," said Morse, grimly. "Otherwise, you'd better forget you ever had a son. Because you'll never see him again."

PART THREE

16

John Morse had reserved a window seat in the first-class compartment of the plane.

Now, as the big jet left Memphis and began its long trip west, he stared out of the window and thought, Here we go again. For a while, he watched the state of Arkansas slide by beneath him.

Then he turned to the newspaper he had bought in the airport. It was a copy of *The Washington Post*. On an inside page, a story caught his eye. It was datelined Denver, and had come over the wire services.

The story was about the girl he had deprogrammed in Denver just before he had gone to Memphis. Her name was Angie Michaels, but as a Neophyte in a Souls for Jesus commune called Hamath, she had been named Jedidah, after the mother of Josiah. She had told her story, in depth, about the horrible brainwashing she had undergone at the commune, and how happy she was to be back with her family and friends.

The reporter who had interviewed Angie, however, had

leaned far back to write what was called a "balanced story." He was over-careful to present the other side. He had quoted a Doctor Ralph Mantree, a psychoanalyst from Columbia University and a leading authority on adolescent behavior:

"I've talked to several of the young people who belong to the SFJ. My impression is that they've never been happier. They feel they've left a corrupt, rotten society for a better world, where greed is unknown, where spiritual values count. They enjoy a warm, trusting togetherness they had never found on the outside of their commune walls. There is no sibling rivalry, the kind they encountered in their regular family situations. Behind the walls of the SFJ communes, everybody is brother and sister. There is no pressure from parents or peers to perform, to make it, to achieve success. Everybody is equal. There are no demands made except two—to love God and to love each other."

Bullshit, thought Morse, savagely.

Didn't the good doctor know about the competitions of Purification? Didn't he know how hard you worked to make Deacon or Deaconess, or what it took to enter the executive suite robed and cowled as Elder some day?

The reporter went on to quote a statement from the star of an enormously popular television cop show, about a detective named Hinge, seen by millions each week:

"My son belongs to the SFJ. And that's okay with me. Let him do his own thing. If he finds it reasonable and productive, then who am I to tell him no? It's his life, right? And maybe these people living in religious communes know something we don't. Maybe they've got the kind of faith we don't understand. Let's give them credit where credit is due, right? These people, like my son, are living something spiritual twenty-four hours a day, which is a distinction from other religions, which usually practice forty-five minutes on Sunday."

My God, thought Morse, what was the matter with these people? They were obviously intelligent. It was so damned hard to get the message across that these cults were dangerous. The general public simply wasn't aware of what was going on. Or didn't care.

He stood up, reached into the luggage compartment overhead, and took out the Bible from his bag.

He sat down, opened it, and started to study it. Now and then, he made penciled notes in the margins. His concentration was intense. He was a little weak on the gospel according to Saint Luke, and he could use the time to brush up on I and II Corinthians.

The plane landed at Los Angeles International Airport a little ahead of time. He still had ten minutes to kill before he would be picked up. He always traveled light, with just the two pieces of hand luggage he carried aboard the plane, so he had nothing to wait for at the baggage counter.

He stood indecisively, trying to decide whether to make the phone call or not.

Then, smiling grimly, he thought, Why not? This was as good a time as any. He had been relishing the thought all along.

He went to a phone booth, took out his address book, checked the number George Glennon had given him, and dialed the operator.

"Operator," he said, "I'd like to make a person-to-person, collect call to this number."

"Whom do you wish to speak to, sir?"

"His Divinity, the Messenger of God."

There was a pause at the other end of the line.

"I'm sorry, sir. Who was that again?"

"His Divinity, the Messenger of God. They'll know who I want at the other end."

In a few moments, a male voice came on. Not that of the Reverend Hodges. Probably one of his Deacons.

"Yes?"

"This is long distance, calling collect for His Divinity, the Messenger of God." The operator sounded incredulous. "Is there such a party there?"

"Yes. Who is calling, please?"

"This is the Devil," said Morse.

The operator waited awhile. As though trying to decide

whether to simply cut off this crazy, or call her supervisor. Then she said, tentatively and carefully, to the man at the other end, "Will you accept charges, sir?"

"Yes," came the answer. "Yes, operator, we will. One moment, please. I'll connect this man to his party."

Morse grinned. When he had received the message from Glennon, he had debated whether to call Hodges at all. Maybe he should just ignore the son-of-a-bitch. Let him dangle. If the Reverend Hodges was uptight now, as his desire for a dialogue indicated, then he might become even more so if Morse never called him.

Not that Morse really believed this. One thing about Buford Hodges. He was shrewd, and cool, and very tough. Not the kind of man you could shake up in small ways. In his heart, John Morse had known that he couldn't resist the temptation to make the call. It would be interesting to talk to the sanctimonious bastard, just to hear what he had to say. It would be more than just interesting. It would be amusing . . .

"Morse, I've been waiting for you to call."

"Jesus loves you, Buford."

"Thank you, Brother Morse. But He doesn't love you. You seem to be interfering heavily in His work."

Morse grinned. "That's my job, remember?"

"Let's dispense with the fun and games. Morse, I'm getting pretty damned tired of these deprogramming stunts of yours. They're beginning to irritate me, and they're becoming more than just an inconvenience. They're becoming a problem."

"So you want to make a deal?"

"Yes."

"And I presume that, as Godfather of the SFJ, you're going to make me an offer I can't refuse."

"Put it that way."

"Well?"

"What'll you take to quit?"

"What am I offered?"

"You can practically name your own ticket."

"I'll let you name it."

"Let's say—a quarter of a million dollars. In cash."

"Buford, you must be joking."

"On the contrary, I'm very serious."

"You want me to turn in my pitchfork for that?"

"It's a lot of money."

"But not enough," said Morse, quietly. "Nothing's enough. You know that."

"Even the Devil has his price, Morse."

"Does he?"

"I'll double my offer."

"A half million?"

"In cash. A private transaction. Tax free. Just to get you off my back."

"That's a lot of money, Reverend."

"It is indeed. And the offer is final." Hodges paused for a moment, and then: "Well?"

"Get thee behind me, Reverend."

"All right, Morse. I just thought I'd try." Hodges spoke coolly. He showed no anger whatever. He had made an offer, it had been refused, and it was just as simple as that. "You know, Morse, you're obsessed. You hold me personally responsible for something I never had anything to do with. I understand your motive, but you're sick. No matter what you think, it wasn't our fault. Worse than that. You're unbalanced—insane. You claim we warp minds. Yours is warped far more. You're letting this crazy vendetta eat away at your guts, your brain. I made you a legitimate offer—a generous one. Now when are you going to stop playing David, throw away your slingshot, and quit?"

"Right after *you* quit, Reverend."

"There's no way I'm going to do that, Morse."

"Then I'll just have to go right on squeezing your balls."

"You do that," said Hodges, coldly. "But be careful you don't get your hand cut off while you're doing it."

Morse hung up and walked through the airport toward the exit. He took the Master's threat very seriously. Hodges was not only shrewd, he could be ruthless and dangerous. The Messenger of God had an investment worth millions of dollars to protect, and he would stop at nothing to protect it.

Not even murder.

Still, thought Morse grimly, it was nice to know the divine shoe was really pinching now. There were a lot of troubled souls in the SFJ now, at least on the Disciple level. Otherwise, the Reverend Buford Hodges, who really loved money more than the Lord, would never dream of offering a half million dollars in bribe money, tax free, right off the top. It was the best possible proof that he, Morse, was really bugging them now.

He came out of the terminal at the American Airlines exit, near the baggage pickup area. He waited on the sidewalk for about a minute. There was a row of taxis waiting a short distance away. The driver of the front taxi in the rank looked at him hopefully. But he made no sign.

Suddenly, a cab moving along the road swerved in to the curb, in front of the waiting line of taxis. The driver jammed on his brakes, stopping his cab directly in front of Morse. Morse opened the door, threw in his hand luggage, and sat down.

The cab drivers waiting in line blew their horns angrily at this sudden and greedy intruder.

"Welcome to Los Angeles, Mr. Morse."

"Thank you, Charlie."

As Charlie started the cab, they heard shouted obscenities behind them. The driver of the lead cab was on the sidewalk, shaking his fist at them. The others continued to blast at them with their horns.

"They seem pretty unhappy," said Morse.

"I don't blame them," grinned Charlie. "Squeezing in ahead of them like that. I'd feel the same way myself. But what the hell, this is a private pickup." He stopped the cab for a moment to let some pedestrians cross a white-striped walkway from the parking lot to the terminal. "Let's see, Mr. Morse. I know we worked San Francisco, San Diego, and Fresno. But this is your first job here in Los Angeles. Right?"

"Right."

"Will you need me on this one?"

"I'm pretty sure of it. Any trouble getting this taxi?"

162

"Not as much as I did in Fresno and San Diego. This is my home town, and I picked it up through a friend of a friend of mine. The guy who owns it worried a little. You know, about an accident, or losing his permit. But he decided to take the money."

Morse was pleased that the taxi had presented no problem. They might use it, or they might not. It all depended. But in the past, it had been an important part of his technique, and he had found it very valuable.

"Where am I staying?"

"Got you all set up at the Holiday Inn. Reserved a room for you, beginning tonight, and one for Mr. and Mrs. Reed beginning tomorrow."

"We may need another room for the older Reed boy and his friend in a few days. They're coming in to provide some extra muscle."

"Right. And from what I've already seen, Mr. Reed is going to need all the help he can get."

"Where is this Holiday Inn?"

"On Sunset Boulevard, at the San Diego Freeway exit. Good halfway location between Ashtaroth and the main part of Los Angeles, depending on which direction you want to go."

"Have you seen Ashtaroth?"

"Drove up and took a look at it yesterday."

"And?"

"And it's a bitch. A real bitch."

Once settled in his room, he got on the phone. First, he called George Glennon, told him he'd come up to Santa Cruz for a few days, right after this Los Angeles job was finished. They had a lot to talk about, particularly in trying to arrange for television exposure and newspaper coverage of the kids he had already deprogrammed. Glennon told him of some increasing resistance to this.

"The cult's just instituted some new lawsuits against a few television stations and newspapers for libel and slander. Not that they have much of a case. But this kind of thing *does* tend to make the media a little cautious—especially the TV stations. You know how it works—Hodges' people in Washington get to the FCC and complain that this particular TV station or that is attacking a religion in the way they present the news. The TV owners start to get chicken—worry about their licenses being renewed. But that's only part of it, John. I've just got in some reports in the last few days. The SFJ's started a new attack. And this one is *really* low down and dirty."

"Yes?"

"The cult's threatening those kids you've busted loose with violence. The parents have gotten these anonymous phone calls, sometimes in the middle of the night, warning them to keep their big-mouthed kids quiet, or else."

"They can't shut *everybody* up."

"No. But they're making a damned good try at it. And I'm still high on their list. They're on the telephone, threatening my publisher, almost every hour on the hour. But the hell with all this. What I really want to know is—did you call His Divinity?"

Morse told him of the dialogue he'd had with Hodges, and Glennon whistled.

"He went to five? Praise Jesus. He *must* be hurting."

"But not enough. Not yet."

After Morse hung up, he called Frank Reed in Santa Barbara. He told Reed where he was staying, and that he was registered under the name of Richard Stevens. Also, that he had a room at the Inn reserved for Reed.

"When do we start, Morse?"

"Today, if you can make it."

There was a pause at the other end. Then:

"I can make it."

Morse checked his watch. "It's three o'clock now. When can you get down here?"

"Give me two hours. Do I bring Kate?"

"No. We're not ready for action yet. This is just surveillance. We'll call your wife in when we need her."

"What about the boys? The ones who are going to help us? My son Ken and Jeff's friend Joe Peterson . . ."

"It's too early for them, too. All I need at the moment is you. But alert them to be ready."

"Okay."

"By the way, Reed, what kind of a car have you got?"

"A Mercedes."

"Two-door or four-door?"

"A four-door."

"Leave it home. Rent a two-door, and make sure it's not a compact, but a big car. With plenty of room in the back. Get a common make. You know, the kind that doesn't draw attention. And I repeat, it has to be a two-door. And while you're about it, bring a pair of field glasses. The higher the power, the better. Okay?"

"Okay." Reed hesitated, and then: "After we meet, then what?"

"Then we're going to Ashtaroth."

17

From a vantage point on a nearby hill, overlooking Ashtaroth, the two men studied the physical layout of the SFJ commune.

They had found a rough dirt road leading off the side road to Ashtaroth, and climbing above it. They had driven up the canyon in Reed's rented car, a Pontiac sedan, hidden the car in the brush at the side of the road. They lay on their stomachs in the brush. Both men were equipped with field glasses, with which they swept the terrain.

They were able to see clearly the main building, with its shining tower and huge cross; the dormitory buildings, topped by the smaller crosses; and the garage and service buildings to the rear, all surrounded by a high fence. Now and then, they heard the barking of the huge mastiffs which were kept in some kennel they could not see, in the rear of the garage area. Occasionally, they sighted the robed and cowled members of the cult, as they walked from building to building. They were close enough and their glasses were powerful enough to make out even the faces. The sun, at their backs and to the west, was sinking toward the rim of the Pacific.

"This brings back memories," said Reed.

"Yes? Of what?"

"Of Korea. Recon missions. Survey enemy territory and report. God, it seems like a thousand years ago. The big difference was we were freezing to death then, and sitting ducks for the Chinese and North Korean patrols who circled around in back of us." He lowered his glasses. "You must have been through the same thing."

"No," said Morse. "I was in a different line of work."

He volunteered no further explanation. And Reed asked for none. He waved down toward the commune.

"Well? What do you think?"

"No way," said Morse. "There's no way we can snatch your son out of here. The setup's impossible. This damned place is a fortress."

"Do we have any other options?"

"It depends."

"On what?"

"On whether he's with a God Squad or not. If he is, we can take him out somewhere on the street."

"And if he isn't?"

"Then we're licked. There's nothing we can do." He paused. "How long has your son been in the cult?"

Reed thought a moment. "About five weeks, I think."

Morse frowned. "That's bad."

"Is it? Why?"

"I may have made this trip for nothing."

Reed stared at him. "I don't understand."

"My fault. I should have asked you. I just assumed Jeff had been in longer. You see, they put these kids through a de-braining they call Purification. It's usually two or three months before they think they've zombied a Neophyte enough to be trusted on a God Squad. Now and then, when it comes to certain kids, they make exceptions." He shrugged. "Still I wouldn't count on it."

"If I read you," said Reed, bitterly, "you're saying we might as well *both* go home."

"Look, I told you. It's my fault. We can always wait a

while, and I can always come back. Say in a month, just to be on the safe side." Morse was angry with himself. "Godammit, how is it I could possibly forget to ask you . . ." He cut off sharply, staring down at the commune. "Oh, oh." Then he raised the field glasses to his eyes. "Wait a minute. Do you see what I see?"

Reed raised his glasses to his eyes. "A big blue bus. SFJ painted on the side in big white letters. Rolling up from the garage toward the entrance to the main building."

"That's the bus they use for God Squads," said Morse. "Except they rarely go out selling in the evening. Must be some kind of special event going on in town."

The bus stopped at the entrance. Now they saw the Neophytes, led by their Deacon leaders, begin to file out and enter the bus. They kept coming out in single file, and the bus was rapidly filling up when Reed almost shouted:

"There he is!"

"Jeff?"

"Yes."

"Quick," said Morse. "Which one? Point him out to me before he gets into the bus."

"The fourth one from the front."

"The tall thin one, with the blond hair?"

"Right. He's just getting into the bus. See him? He's moving toward the back."

Morse put down his field glasses, and heaved a sigh of relief.

"Well, Reed," he said. "Jesus must love us. It seems we're in business after all."

"What do we do now?"

"Follow it."

The bus started to move toward the electric gate, and the two men waited until they saw which direction it would go. It turned up the canyon and headed east, toward the San Fernando Valley.

They raced for their car and began to tail it.

It turned onto the Ventura Freeway, then the Hollywood Freeway, and then took the Highland Avenue cutoff. It was already dark, and the Avenue was jammed with traffic, turning into the Hollywood Bowl. Thousands of cars were being waved into the several entrances by uniformed police. They were waved even further in by parking lot attendants, who signaled the cars into parallel lines, bumper to bumper, on the multi-leveled parking areas. The signs advertised an all-Brahms concert tonight, with Ormandy conducting, and Isaac Stern the soloist.

The Pontiac, driven by Frank Reed, hung on to the rear of the bus, three cars behind.

They watched the SFJ bus park, and were waved into the same line by the attendants, so that they were still three cars to the rear. The bus emptied, and the members of the special God Squads assigned to this location followed their Deacons toward the entrance of the Bowl itself.

The two men got out of the car. Morse took a quick look around, noticed the hundreds of cars, each in line, each trapped, bumper to rear, so that it could not move.

"Nothing we can do here," said Morse, wryly. "No way to get out. You can see that for yourself."

"Then if they come here every night, we're licked."

"No. This is a kind of special event. The Elders will work their kids nights as well as days, so long as they see locations where they can really make a big profit. And all these thousands of people here—well, you can see what the market could be for *Sayings of the Master*. Chances are these kids were on their regular assignments during the day, and they're moonlighting now. We'll go up into the canyon early tomorrow, and check the bus when it leaves."

"What now?" said Reed.

"Nothing. Our car's trapped in, until the concert's over."

Reed nodded in the direction of the God Squads, slowly making their way through the crowds of people, along the walk leading to the entrance of the Bowl itself.

"Let's follow them. I'd like to see how they operate."

Morse seemed doubtful, shook his head.

"Too dangerous. They might see us . . ."

"Look," said Reed. "I've been here before, and I know where they're headed for. There'll be thousands of people milling around down there, all over the place. We could stand off to one side. Stay hidden behind the edge of the crowd. They'd never see us." He seemed to plead a little now. "And I'd like to see my son. The way he is now—close up. I haven't seen him since—well, since he got mixed up in this thing."

"You may not like what you see."

"I know," said Reed. "I'm prepared for that."

"Okay," said Morse. "Let's go. But we'd damned well better stay out of sight. They know *me,* too."

They followed the God Squads, now some distance ahead. They walked up an incline, jostling shoulders with music lovers carrying picnic baskets, thermos jugs, and blankets in case the night turned cool. Some distance off, they could see escalators carrying people to the upper levels of the Bowl.

Just beyond the ticket booths and turnstiles was a large open area, surrounded by refreshment booths selling popcorn, soft drinks, packaged picnic dinners, hot dogs and coffee. From this point of convergence, the patrons moved off toward the different entries into the Bowl itself, graded according to the value of the tickets.

It was in this area that the God Squads set up shop. It had already been preempted by three street musicians, long-haired boys in faded blue jeans, entertaining the crowd with violin and two guitars. True to the occasion, they did not play rock, but classical music instead.

But once the SFJ salesmen took over, the trio did not last long. It was drowned out, and quit in disgust.

Reed and Morse watched from a safe distance.

They saw the boys and the girls begin to exhort the patrons. They seemed to swarm all over their prospective buyers, yelling loudly, "Save a soul for Jesus" or "Read all about God" or "Make an investment in Christ," and rewarding purchasers with a warm smile and a hearty "Jesus loves you."

By their very aggressiveness, they sometimes embarrassed people into buying the booklets, just to get rid of the salesmen. Then again, some reasoned, these were clean-cut American kids, you could see that. They looked thin and overworked, but they were obviously dedicated to their beliefs, and if they were into Christ instead of drugs, well, that was a change for the better. Anyway, how much was two bucks these days, and what harm could it possibly do? Besides, this Reverend Hodges was all over the television screen—maybe he really had something. And, as these young salesmen kept pointing out, the money was going for orphanages and homes for the aged.

Frank Reed turned to Morse, puzzled.

"I didn't know they had orphanages and homes for the aged."

"They don't. They're lying. It's part of their antinomian philosophy."

"Their *what?*"

"Antinomian. It comes from the Greek, *anti* meaning against, and *nomos,* the law. The word refers to a rejection of all the usual moral obligations, values like loyalty, honesty, truth and so on. Some of the early Christian sects practiced antinomianism. Their members believed that as true Christians, they could lie and cheat, steal, as long as it was in the service of God. As long as they were spreading His word, He would forgive them. They would never be liars or cheats in His eyes. And furthermore, you could use the worst weapons you could find against the world of nonbelievers, which you labeled as rotten and corrupt, and which would never purify itself anyway. As long as it was in the service of God, you could shoot, kill, hang, or screw your neighbor, and still go to heaven."

Reed was incredulous. "And the cult teaches *that?*"

"All you have to do is listen. The way the SFJ sees it, all they're doing is ripping off the System."

"Why, the bastards! The goddamn hypocrites!"

Frank Reed glared at his son. He saw Jeff, or, as he was now called, Simeon, as busy and as aggressive as the rest of them. Jeff looked somewhat thinner, but otherwise all right. Better than the way Kate had described him when she had gone into Ashtaroth to see him. Morse had told Reed that after the Neophytes had made the God Squads, they were given better food to fatten them up somewhat so that they

171

wouldn't create too negative an appearance on the streets, and hurt the cult's image.

The anger rose in Frank Reed as he continued to watch his son. It was hard to believe what he was seeing now.

Here was his own boy, running around in that damned ridiculous red blazer, squeezing and begging money out of people, breaking his ass to do it, and then turning everything over to the monkish bosses who were exploiting him. From there, most of the money would go into the pockets of His Divinity, the Reverend Buford Hodges, and be used to run his various businesses, and that big yacht of his, and buy presents for the young Neophytes and Deaconesses he was screwing, and all the time this pious creep was laughing all the way to the bank, thumbing his nose and saying fuck you, not only to the parents of these kids he had sucked in, but to the Bureau of Internal Revenue as well...

This was Jeff Reed in the Hollywood Bowl, like some animated pest, annoying people, haranguing them, and what was more, looking as though he loved every minute of it. It was unbelievable, absolutely unbelievable. This was a kid who lived in Hope Ranch, who had had everything, *everything*, who right now should be a freshman at Stanford, who at this moment should be studying for his future, making something of himself, becoming a *man*, a kid who should be driving his own car, and taking out girls, and having some decent respect for his father and mother, and living a *normal* life...

Frank Reed's gorge rose, just watching his son's performance. The anger built in him. He remembered how many times he and Kate had talked about it, tormented themselves. *Where have we gone wrong, what did we do wrong?* He knew the answer now. Not one damned thing. *They* hadn't done *anything* wrong. It was that kid of his. Jeff's fault. *He* had gotten himself into this, nobody else. He'd been weak, naive, stupid. And so he'd been ripped off.

Still, maybe it was everybody's fault. A combination of everything. Frank Reed did not know. But there was his son, only a few feet away from him now. He had the feeling that if he just walked over, grabbed Jeff by the collar, and told him

172

they were going home where they belonged, that they would talk this thing over, man to man, they could straighten everything out. And if any of these red-coated creeps tried to interfere, he'd break their heads.

He saw Jeff through a kind of haze now, and he tensed his muscles and took a step through the crowd toward the shouting God Squad when he felt a strong hand on his arm jerking him back.

"Don't," said Morse.

He turned to look at Morse. "It's worth a try. If I can only get to him, talk to him."

"You'd get nowhere," said Morse, harshly. "Damn it, Reed, don't you understand? Nothing you can say will change him. Nothing. He won't listen to reason, he *can't*."

"I know, I know," said Reed. "But what harm will it do if I just *try* . . ."

"I'll tell you what harm it'll do. You'll never see him again. I keep telling you that, but I don't seem to get through to you. Just show your face once, and they'll transfer him to some other commune." He snapped his fingers to illustrate. "Just like that. He'd be out of Ashtaroth tomorrow morning, and on his way to some commune like Ephesus or Joppa, or some other place of theirs two or three thousand miles from here. And you'd never know where to find him."

"I see." Reed was apologetic. "I'm sorry. It was just the idea of standing there . . . just a few feet away . . . watching him . . ."

"I know," said Morse, gently. "I know exactly how you feel." He slapped Reed on the back. "Come on, Frank." For the first time he used Reed's first name. "No use just hanging around till the concert's over. Let's buy a couple of tickets, sneak by these kids, and go in ourselves. I happen to be a Brahms buff. And my God, how many chances do you get in a lifetime to hear Isaac Stern play the Brahms violin concerto?"

18

Shortly after dawn, the two men drove up Topanga Canyon. Morse was at the wheel. They turned up the side road, parked the car just off the road in an area shielded by bushes, and watched Ashtaroth from the same observation post they had used before. They had come at this hour because, as Morse explained, sometimes the God Squads went to work very early, depending on their destinations.

They had been there no longer than ten minutes when they saw a strange procession emerge from one of the buildings. This time, none of the cultists wore the familiar monks' robes.

Instead, they wore clothes of biblical times, some in flowing white robes, others in the uniforms of Roman soldiers. The sun, still low, glinted red gold on their shields and spears.

Frank Reed stared. Then he turned to Morse.

"What's all this?"

"It's one of the SFJ rituals. Every month or so, they run their own version of the Passion Play."

They were too far away at this point to hear what was

174

said. But Morse, who seemed to know intimately every detail of what was going on, began to interpret.

"You see that boy carrying the big wooden cross on his back?"

"Yes."

"That's Simon of Cyrene. In the Bible, he was just passing by, a stranger, and they forced him to carry the cross."

Suddenly, the crowd put up a clamor. Even from this distance, they could hear the faint shouting. The crowd was shaking their fists at the building, and making motions with their hands as if to say, Come out.

"They're shouting for Jesus to come out of the Praetorium now."

Just as he spoke, a tall youth wearing purple robes came out, guarded by other Roman soldiers. He wore a gold crown on his head. The crowd ripped off his purple robes, and wrapped him in a simple white one. They tore the gold crown from his head, and replaced it with a crown of thorns. Then they saluted him and got down on their knees in jeering worship.

"They're mocking Him now," said Morse.

The procession turned, and started up a hilly rise. The boy playing Christ walked slowly, head high, and with dignity. Through their glasses, they could see Simon just behind Him, knees bent, staggering under the weight of the cross.

"Now, they're on their way to Golgotha."

"Golgotha?" Reed was puzzled. "I thought it was Calvary."

"It is, if you read the Gospel according to Luke. But if you read the Gospel according to Mark, John and Matthew, it's Golgotha—which means the 'place of the skull.'"

Reed stared at Morse. He and Kate rarely went to Mass or to church, unless it was for the funeral of some friend. He hadn't looked at a Bible in years. Morse's expertise amazed him.

"You really know your Bible."

Morse nodded. "I have to. It goes with the territory, as they say."

Reed looked through his field glasses again. He was fascinated by what he saw. It was all so damned eerie, a grotesque fantasy.

This was early in the morning, in Topanga Canyon, California, and just beyond those walls, a few miles down the canyon, the Pacific Highway was beginning to buzz with traffic, people were going to work, gas stations were starting to open, there were early joggers on the beach. But down there behind those walls, the walls of Ashtaroth, they were engrossed in playing an ancient drama some two thousand years old. And somehow, watching it, Frank Reed shuddered, and wondered if his son were in this make-believe biblical crowd. He scanned the faces of all the young people in the procession. But he did not see Jeff.

As the mob walked up the hill, some of its members were dancing around the figure representing the Son of God, taunting him. He endured all this without flinching. Finally, they reached the crest of the rise. The soldiers ran forward, took the cross from Simon's shoulders, and stuck it into some supporting pipe, apparently embedded in a block of concrete. Immediately, two other crosses, smaller in height, were set up, in other concrete blocks nearby. These were for the two criminals who were to be crucified with Christ, and who had already stepped forward, minor actors in this scenario, virtually unnoticed.

As he stood at the base of the cross, the crowd ripped the garments from the young Christ, so that he stood naked. Finally, one of the crowd offered him a bowl, containing something to drink. But he refused it.

"What was in it?" asked Reed.

"Vinegar mixed with gall, if you like Matthew. But if you read Mark, it's wine mingled with myrrh. Take your pick."

Now, they hoisted the boy up on the cross. Reed glanced at Morse, a little alarmed. Morse smiled slightly, and shook his head.

"No. All they'll do is bind his hands and feet with leather thongs. And then draw a little blood to make it look authentic."

After the boy was securely straddled on the cross, the soldiers repeated the same procedure with the two criminals. They pricked the wrists and feet of all the actors, to draw the symbolic blood. Then they stepped back. The crowd then stood back, peering at the figure on the highest cross, haranguing him.

They could hear nothing, only watch all this in pantomime.

Through his glasses, Reed saw something that puzzled him. The boy hanging on the cross had a beatific smile on his face. It wasn't a spiritual kind of smile. It seemed smug, almost self-satisfied.

"I don't get it," he said to Morse. "If he's being crucified, why does he look so happy?"

"It's the biggest honor an SFJ Neophyte can make. The biggest kick there is. To play Christ for a day. That's one of the things they work for."

"Work for?"

"Exactly. It's a work incentive. The way you qualify for the job is to prove that you've served Jesus better than anyone else. You've given Him more than anyone else of your heart, soul, and spirit. In other words, you've sold more booklets than anyone else." He smiled at the stunned look on Reed's face. "It's just as competitive down there at Ashtaroth as anywhere else. If you sell more electrical appliances than the next guy, you get a cruise to Nassau or maybe a week in Acapulco. Here, you get to play the Son of God, at the time of His suffering. Providing your sales figures entitle you to it."

"What about the two criminals on those other crosses?"

"Oh," said Morse. "They placed second and third."

They watched as the crowd suddenly turned and walked down the hill, leaving the three hanging on the crosses alone. Reed saw that they had already started to sag a little, in their uncomfortable positions.

"How long will they keep them there?"

"Oh, they'll let them hang in the sun all day. Then they'll cut them down. After that, they'll play part of the Resurrection. Joseph of Arimathea, with Pilate's permission, will wrap the boy playing Jesus in fine linen. They'll carry him into a sepulcher somewhere inside. After that Mary Magdalene, Mary the mother of James, and Salome will come to the sepulcher with sweet spices to anoint him. And so on."

"You're serious? You mean they'll really let those kids hang in the sun all day long?"

"As long as they can stand it."

"The bastards," said Reed. "The dirty bastards."

"You don't understand," said Morse. "The kids love it. The suffering, I mean. You hang on the cross, and suffer as He suffered, you *really* get close to the Savior."

They were silent for a while and then Reed said:

"Look, maybe we're wasting our time here."

"What do you mean?"

"This could be some kind of holiday down there. Maybe they won't send out the God Squads, as usual."

Morse laughed. "Forget it. They'll be out, all right. This is still a business day."

Morse turned out to be right.

A half hour later, they saw the bus leave the garage, and move to the front of the main church building. Morse was a little concerned that Jeff might not appear. Sometimes a squad which had worked the night before was given other duties around the commune the next day.

But when the God Squads came out to get into the bus, Jeff Reed was among them.

They followed the bus down the canyon, onto Pacific Coast Highway, and down the Santa Monica Freeway. Its ultimate destination turned out to be the Los Angeles International Airport.

The bus stopped at United Airlines, American Airlines, TWA and Western Airlines. At each, it dropped off a squad, which immediately assembled for duty. The squad of which Jeff was a member was assigned to TWA. The group gathered on the sidewalk, perhaps a hundred feet away from the actual entrance itself, but still near enough to accost people coming in or out.

"Keep your head down when we drive by," warned Morse.

But Jeff and his companions were too busy getting their booklets ready to notice the occupants of any cars passing the terminal.

Morse drove a short distance beyond the group, then put on his brakes.

"Something I want to check out here," he said.

He opened the window, stuck out his hand and signaled to a porter who was checking in baggage at another entrance. In his hand was a five-dollar bill. The porter came over.

"Those kids over there," said Morse. "You ever seen them here before?"

"Yes, sir," said the porter. "They're here every day."

"The same bunch?"

"Yes, sir. They never change. Come here around this time, quit every day around six."

"Thanks," said Morse. He gave the man the money, and began to drive again. He seemed pleased at what had developed.

"Check and double-check," he said. "You know, Frank, this is a break for us."

"Yes? Why?"

"All things being equal, airports are good locations for making a 'hit.'" This was the term John Morse constantly used for a kidnapping. "Now, let's find somewhere to park where we can see them, but they can't see us. I need to study this setup for a while."

Morse circled the airport, came back and drove into a big parking lot opposite the TWA entrance. They found a space, opened the car windows, and with the aid of their field glasses, had a pretty good view of the God Squad at work, across the road and some distance away.

Reed watched Morse's face. It was tight in concentration. He swept his field glasses left and right, studying the area in front of the TWA terminal. Finally, he said, "I like it. You make your hit tomorrow."

"Tomorrow?"

"Why not? The sooner the better."

"Exactly how do I do this?"

"I'll brief you as we go along. But first, there are some things I want you to see for yourself."

They sat there for another half hour, without speaking. Morse was busy, studying the area in front of the TWA terminal with his field glasses. Reed felt a little queasy, and his skin prickled with excitement. It was the same way he had felt years ago, in Korea, just before going into battle, or on some risky patrol. He tried to cover his anxiety by making conversation.

"Does the cult usually work airports?"

"Almost always. They're great locations for business. Lots of traffic, people coming and going, and always in a hurry. No time to stop and argue, and in no mood to be bothered. They're rushing to catch a plane, or a taxi, or to meet somebody, so many of them just pay the pest to get rid of him."

"I'm surprised they're allowed to sell here."

"So are a lot of people."

"Isn't it some kind of violation? Don't they need a permit?"

"There was a test case on it. Right here at this airport, some time ago. It was brought up by Hare Krishna. They claimed they had a First Amendment right to sell their literature here. They won. A Superior Court judge ruled in their favor, as long as they stayed outside of the buildings, and away from the entrances themselves." Suddenly, he grabbed Reed's arm. "Watch. Those two breaking away from the group."

Two of the Neophytes said something to one of the Deacons. He nodded; the two walked together toward the entrance of the TWA buildings, and went inside. Morse turned to Reed.

"Mean anything to you?"

"They're probably going to the john."

"Right. Or they could be going in to buy a bar of candy. Or whatever. But they always go in twos. To keep an eye on each other, of course. No Soul for Jesus is *ever* left alone. Now, in a little while, we'll come to what they call the moment of truth. That is, as far as you're concerned."

"I don't understand."

180

"Keep watching," said Morse. "This is something I want you to see for yourself."

A short time later, the two Neophytes came out of the building. They walked up the sidewalk and they joined the rest of the God Squad. Morse said, "Notice anything interesting?"

Reed looked at him, puzzled. "No."

"Right after they came out of the building, the two of them were alone for about a hundred feet. Separated from the others. You saw that?"

"Yes."

"Sometime during the day tomorrow, hopefully, your son will have to go inside the terminal. You'll have to wait till he does, no matter how long it takes. When he comes out and starts walking toward the others is when you make your move. That's the point where you and your helpers drive by, stop, grab him, and pull him into the car before the others hear his yelling and come running over to help him. Clear?"

"I think so. Yes."

"Now, before I give you the details of how you move, I want to emphasize one thing. Once you commit yourself, once you and your helper grab Jeff, you'll have to move fast. And I really mean *fast*."

"Just what does that mean, in terms of time?"

"I'd say twenty seconds. Maybe thirty on the outside to grab him, and drive away with him."

"Seems pretty tight."

"If you take longer than that, it'll be too late. You'll have blown everything. By then, the others in the God Squad will have time to run over and get to you. *You* may be the one who's grabbed, instead of your son. And those Deacons can be pretty rough. They regard you as some incarnation of Satan. In Tulsa, a boy's father I was working with was too slow. He froze in the middle, tried to persuade his son to go with him by talking to him, which never works. Anyway, he and his helper couldn't get him away in time. The helper got away, but they caught the boy's father, broke his arm, and slammed him to the sidewalk. They would have killed him if the police hadn't pulled them off. You see what I mean?"

"Yes."

"When you and your helpers get to Jeff, you won't drag him into your own car. You'll use a taxi."

Reed stared at his companion.

"A taxi? *What* taxi?"

"It's a procedure we've worked out at a lot of other airports. I'll arrange the whole thing." He turned the ignition key and started the motor. "Well, I've seen all I need to see here. When we get back to the motel, call your son and his friend. Tell them to come down today. When you're all together, I'll brief you on the whole operation."

"What about my wife, Kate? And Cindy. You want them down here, too?"

"Yes. But we won't need them until you get your son to Big Bear. After that, we'll need all the help we can get."

"Something I've been meaning to ask you," said Reed.

"Yes?"

"Where will you be when all this is happening?"

"Oh, I'll be somewhere nearby. Watching."

19

Later that afternoon, Ken Reed and Joe Peterson drove down to Los Angeles and brought with them Kate Reed and Cindy Hyland.

They checked in for an overnight stay, and then John Morse brought Frank Reed and the two boys into his room. There, he gave them final instructions on how they would make the hit in the morning. He was very specific and very thorough. Wherever he went, he carried a pair of handcuffs in his bag, beside the Bible and the field glasses. He taught Frank Reed how to use the cuffs, made him snap them on Ken's wrists, again and again, until Reed was letter perfect. They would come in very handy later. Finally, he warned them again that any slipup in the operation, any deviation, could bring disaster.

He was impressed by Reed's two young helpers. Ken, who resembled his father both in face and manner, was tall, solidly built, and moved with the grace of the athlete he was. There was nothing nervous or jittery about him, and he had a certain self-confidence. When Morse had finished his briefing, he had said, calmly, "I think we can handle it, sir."

Joe Peterson, who had been closer to Jeff than anyone else, was a different kind of boy. He was a freckle-faced blond, excitable in nature, and in the way he moved around the room, he seemed charged with energy. But he was big and he was strong, and all he said was, "Man, we got to get Jeff out of there, and flip him back to where he was." Morse decided that Joe would work best as the "inside" man, while Ken would work "outside" with his father.

After that, the Reeds, Joe Peterson and Cindy went out to an early dinner. They invited Morse to come along, but he told them he was too tired, he wanted to rest.

For some reason, the night before a hit and a deprogramming he always preferred to be alone. It was as though he wanted to gird himself for the battle privately. He wondered what kind of kid Jeff Reed would turn out to be. Easy? Tough? You never knew until you met them face-to-face.

He had a bottle of Scotch with him. He took one drink, then another. He lay on the bed, feeling a little more relaxed, his head propped against two pillows. He lit a cigarette, and turned his thoughts again to the Souls for Jesus.

In a sense, it and the other cults were an American phenomenon. When Americans tried to find their own individuality, strangely, in order to do so, they joined a group. This was a country of multi-religions, and sub-religions splintered off from these, usually led by some charismatic leader who had heard God's voice whisper in his ear, showing him new maps to salvation, new turnpikes and freeways to the Promised Land Up There. A case in point, the Reverend Hodges. And they usually found followers looking for answers that the established religions did not give them, or they became a haven for young dropouts and misfits, kids looking for acceptance, brotherhood, love, security, psychological support, the feeling of being part of something very important and exciting, the magic of feeling and believing that now you had a direct line to God, a dialogue with Him, He listened when you spoke, He patted you on the head and considered you Chosen.

And so you were no longer perennially lonely, you no longer

were a dropout physically or socially from a normal life, you were *accepted*. And in the SFJ, you found that when you accepted Jesus, when you accepted the ritual, the rules, the Purification, everything, when you stopped thinking of yourself and thought only of Christ, then the pain eased and left. If the price was to give away your mind, then you did not know it. Or did not care.

And it did not matter if you wore monk's robes, or if you wore mala beads, saris, turbans, or you burned incense and drank ginseng tea and lined your walls with mandalas. The trappings and symbols were different, but the idea was the same.

When you thought about it, he reflected, the earth was only a speck of dust revolving around a fourth-rate star, somewhere in infinity. And covering this speck of dust were microorganisms known as men. And these infinitely tiny microorganisms split into clusters, dividing into tiny cells, and then subdividing, each a different color or race or tribe or community, each inventing a different God, each claiming that *its* God was the only true God, the members of each cluster on this ridiculous speck of dust claiming that *they,* and only they, worshipped the true God, only *they* had contact with Him way out somewhere in outer space. Where, they were not sure, but for lack of a better name, they called it heaven.

Of course, thought Morse, it was absurd, sheer *chutzpah,* for these sub-micro-organisms called humans to make this claim. It was incredible arrogance to believe that even if God existed, he would give any notice to these tiny mites crawling over this particular grain of sand drifting through space. It was easy for His divine eye to miss them altogether. But it was the old story. You needed a God, so you invented one. And inventing one, you believed it. And if you believed it hard enough, it was true.

Everybody needed something to fill that empty place. The broad, general answer was love. But the choice of panaceas was almost infinite.

There were all the Therapies—Reality Therapy, Reichian, Primal, Gestalt, Client-Centered, Logotherapy. Take your choice of Psychosynthesis, Open Encounter, Psychodrama, Hypnotherapy, and Megavitamin Therapy. Were you looking for new mindstyles? Then here we were with Silva Mind Control, Mind Probe One, Arica, est, Lifespring, Re-evaluation Counseling, Living Love Center, and Biofeedback.

Everybody needed something. If not God, nor love, then something else.

Did you want the Body Beautiful, yearn for it, and through it, find harmony with the Cosmos? Try Bioenergetics, Functional Integration, the Alexander Method, Rolfing, Do'in, Shiatsu. And there were always Polarity Therapy, Reflexology, Relaxation Response, Chronobiology, all full of those ultradian and circadian rhythms, and Directed Massage, to put you in touch with the somatopsychic. And of course there was yoga, with fifty-seven different flavors—hatha, karma, bhakti, raja, japa, jnana, laya, krija, niyama, tantra, kundalini.

And if your lifestyle problem was Sex, there was always Dr. Reuben, or Masters and Johnson, or Hartman and Fithian, Lonnie Barback and Barbara Roberts, and other gurus to instruct you. You could read the *Joy of Sex* and *More Joy of Sex*. Or just for kicks, you might try Sandstone, or Elysium or Ipsa, the school for sexual surrogates.

The point was, he, John Morse, knew what he wanted. He knew he was sick, and he knew exactly what the disease was.

The disease was hate. And the only cure for it was revenge. In a curious way, the cure made him even sicker than the disease.

It was the reason why he had no permanent home, no roots, and why, for the past three years, he had lived in a succession of motel and hotel rooms, until he could remember none of them—they all became blurred in memory, and they all looked the same as this room, in which he lived now. It was the reason why he had traveled incessantly, under a hundred assumed names, from one city to another after the job was done, riding in planes, walking through endless airports, moving by rented car or taxi, each trip always ending in the same place, facing some angry and hostile young boy or girl.

He knew that he had to be mad, or at least on the edge of madness, to do what he was doing. He knew that in his own way he had become a kind of zombie, fanatically programmed to achieve his own mission. John Morse, relentless enemy of mind control, yet finding it hard to control his own.

He rose and took another drink, straight from the bottle this time, and looked at his reflection in the mirror, and he saw the words form on his lips, the same incredulous words he had spoken to himself so many other times: *What am I doing here? And why?*

There was pressure in his head, he felt it mounting, he feared it would explode, and he knew tonight he was close to the edge, very close, and what he needed was release. He needed to bring himself down, to find some kind of normal level, to immerse himself in something besides the SFJ, to put aside his obsession and sweep it under the rug, at least for this night, this one night, or else he would, in fact, go mad.

He knew exactly what he needed. He looked at his watch. It was still early.

He remembered her name was Sarah Brand, and she was in fashion of some kind. Her home was in Los Angeles, but he had met her in New York. They had slept together, and she had reminded him of Nora, or rather the woman Nora *had* been before the terrible business at Sidon. She had given him her phone number, had told him to be sure and look her up if he ever came to Los Angeles. And she had sounded as though she meant it.

He dialed her number; she was in, and delighted to hear from him, and although she had another date for the evening, it was nothing she couldn't cancel, and eight o'clock would be fine, just fine.

Later, when he saw her standing before him, naked, he was again struck by her resemblance to Nora, the lift of the head, the cut of the face, the tilt of the neck. And when they were in bed, he was sure she used the same perfume Nora had, and her flesh was as soft and as sweet and as warm. And to him, for this night, this was not some woman named Sarah Brand in his arms; he thought of her as Nora Morse, she became

187

Nora, she *was* Nora, and everything, at least in his mind, was the way it was, for this one night, this one night only.

When he finally got back to his hotel room, he felt good and relaxed, and altogether ready for Jeff Reed. He hoped that this deprogramming would be short, two or three days perhaps, a week at the outside. But you never knew.

He slept for a few hours. Then, in the morning, he drove to the airport, and into the same parking lot where he and Reed had been the day before. He found a space up fairly close, across from the TWA terminal, where he could easily see all the action.

All he could do now was watch. And wait.

20

The next morning Frank Reed, his son Ken, and Joe Peterson left the hotel in the two-door rented Pontiac. Reed carried a briefcase under his arm. They drove to a location Morse had designated, on a quiet residential side street off Sepulveda, about a mile from the airport.

They parked and waited.

A few minutes later, a yellow taxi turned the corner and stopped behind them. The driver, a thick-set man with twinkling blue eyes, got out and came over to them.

"I'm Charlie," he said. "Charlie O'Connor." He shook hands all around, and then said, "Let's go."

They left the Pontiac and got into the back seat of the cab. On the ride to the airport, Charlie said, "Let's go over it together. One for the road. Just to make sure we don't foul anything up."

They went over the procedure once more. Finally, Charlie brought the cab into the airport area, and headed for the TWA terminal. In the tactic they were about to use, a private car would have been impossible, simply because it could not park anywhere in front of the terminals for any length of time. But a taxi was entirely feasible in the congested airport areas. It could cruise slowly. It could park almost anywhere, temporarily at least, without being conspicuous. And, if it took a position in a cab rank, the line of cabs waiting at the curb to pick up passengers, it could park indefinitely.

But Charlie did not park immediately. He cruised slowly around the airport, two or three times, until they saw the blue SFJ bus come in. It discharged the members of God Squad Three at its usual location, and they saw that Jeff was among them.

There was another entrance into the airport, which led to a baggage receiving area. This was about a hundred yards from where the SFJ group solicited. Charlie O'Connor stopped the cab, and let his three passengers out. They quickly went into the entrance, and stood there out of the line of sight of the God Squad, working on the sidewalk a short distance away. Morse and Reed had noted that members of the squad, whenever they went inside the terminal, used another entrance, much nearer to where they were located.

Charlie then parked his cab at the curb, opposite the entrance where the three waited. From this position, he could observe God Squad Three straight ahead, although those waiting just inside the entrance could not. He set up his off-duty sign and made himself comfortable behind the wheel. But he never took his eyes off the group working the sidewalk ahead.

They waited just inside the entrance for an hour. Then two. Always watching Charlie, sitting at the wheel of his cab. And finally, Ken said:

"You know, Dad, we may wait here all day."

"If we have to, we will."

"What if Jeff doesn't leave the sidewalk and go inside at all?"

"Sooner or later, he's bound to."

"Man," said Joe Peterson. "I can't imagine old Jeff getting into a thing like this. I mean, he never took any interest in religion before. All he talked about was surfing, mostly. And cruising around State Street, watching the low riders. Or

Cindy." Joe shook his head. "You know, Mr. Reed, it's really hard for me to believe. I mean what Cindy told us. Talking the Bible half the time. And calling himself this other name, what is it?"

"Simeon."

"Yeah. Simeon. And wearing all that monk stuff, when he's inside that place. Man, he's really blown his mind. We've got to get his head back on straight."

"That's what we hope to do, Joe."

"Dad! Look!"

Frank had been temporarily distracted by his conversation with Joe. He turned his head to look at Charlie. Charlie was giving them the signal they had been waiting for. He was motioning them to come out and get into the cab.

They walked across the sidewalk to the cab, and got into the back seat.

"Your son just went inside with another boy, Mr. Reed." Charlie started the motor. "He'll be out in a minute or two. The minute he comes out, everybody hang on. Because I'll move in fast, and then jam on the brakes."

"Ken," said Reed. "When I push open the door, and jump out in front of him, you come on right behind me."

"Right, Dad."

"Don't say anything, don't ask any questions, just do what we have to do."

"Okay."

"Joe, you know what *you* have to do."

"Right. I'll be ready."

"Jeff's a pretty strong kid. He may give us a lot of trouble."

"We'll handle it," said Ken.

They waited tensely, staring at the TWA entrance directly ahead. God Squad Three was busy, buttonholing everyone who passed. Their voices were strident, their sales pitch loud and aggressive. The time seemed to pass slowly as they waited. There was no sign of Jeff as yet.

"He's taking a long time in there," said Joe, nervously.

Frank Reed checked his watch. "It's only been five minutes."

"Stay cool, everybody," said Charlie.

But his knuckles whitened as his hands rested on the wheel. A police car had cruised by a moment ago. One of the men in the car had turned and stared at Charlie curiously. He had been struck by the oddity of what he saw. People didn't ordinarily sit in a cab and just wait. They either got out, or got in. Moreover, a narrow concrete island separated the outer road from the inner road here. And normally, pickup cabs were supposed to be on the other side of the island.

It was possible, thought Charlie, that the police car would turn around and come back. It depended on how really curious the cop was. Sometimes they were lazy, just said the hell with it, and didn't bother to turn around and come back. Other times, they would do just that. You never knew. But if they came back, they could blow the whole thing. They would tell Charlie he wasn't supposed to be here, and would order him to move.

He decided not to tell the others in the back seat about his fears. He would only upset them. They were tense enough as it was. He hoped Reed would do exactly as Morse had instructed him to do. No talking. Just hit and run.

"There he comes," said Reed.

Jeff and another Neophyte were just sauntering out of the entrance.

"Okay," yelled Charlie. "Here we go!"

The cab shot forward, as Charlie accelerated. The cab barely missed a passenger car just ahead, which had just started to move out and away from the curb. In what seemed to be only a second or two, Charlie jammed on the brakes.

"Okay," he yelled. "Go get him!"

Frank Reed had already opened the cab door just a crack as they had moved up, hanging on to the door handle. Now, he flung the door wide open and stepped out onto the sidewalk, in front of Jeff. Ken was just behind him.

Jeff froze. His eyes widened.

"Dad! Ken! What . . . ?"

Reed grabbed his son's arm. "You're coming with us, son."

"No," yelled Jeff. "No, I'm not!"

Ken had Jeff by the other arm now. They started to wrestle him toward the cab door.

"Let me go, damn you," yelled Jeff. "Let me go!" He turned his head to his companion as he struggled. "Help! Help me, Zebulun!"

The other Neophyte, frozen in astonishment at what had suddenly happened, now moved in. He was a tall, thin boy, and he started to scream at the top of his voice, as he grabbed Ken around the neck. Ken let go of Jeff for a moment, tore away Zebulun's stranglehold, and hit him hard in the face. Zebulun fell to the pavement, his nose bleeding. Meanwhile, Jeff was shouting hysterically, as he fought to get out of his father's grasp, yelling at the God Squad some distance away.

"Ephraim! Shechem! Help!"

God Squad Three had become aware of what was going on. The two Deacons whose names Jeff was calling started to run toward the taxi.

"For God's sake," yelled Charlie, "get him inside!"

Jeff fought his father and brother tooth and nail, but they had him halfway through the cab door now. Joe Peterson, who had stayed in the cab, reached forward, grabbed Jeff by his shoulders and yanked him inside, while the others pushed from behind. Ken and his father jumped into the cab, while Joe Peterson wrestled with Jeff and Reed slammed the door virtually in the angry contorted faces of the two Deacons. One of them grabbed the handle of the car door, as Charlie stepped on the gas. He hung on for a moment or two, then let go and fell to the sidewalk. Through the rearview mirror, they could see the other Deacon standing on the sidewalk shaking his fist at them in rage, shouting something at them.

Inside the car, Jeff fought insanely. They tried to keep him down, low and away from the windows, by sitting on him, so that they wouldn't attract attention. But Jeff squirmed and twisted and fought.

"You bastards!" he yelled. "Scum of Satan! Let me go, let me go!"

He lunged toward the door, made a grab at it, had it half

open, before they pulled him back. Jeff was tall and gangly, but he was strong and wiry, and his anger magnified his strength. He continued to struggle for a while, then suddenly went limp, realizing it was no use.

"Come on, Jeff," said Joe Peterson. "Relax. Nobody's going to hurt you, man. This is me. Joe Peterson. Remember?"

"My name is Simeon," screamed Jeff. "Simeon, *Simeon!*"

Frank Reed saw the reactions of both Ken and Joe to his younger son. They looked stunned, incredulous. They had envisioned him as the Jeff Reed they knew. This boy was a stranger, a maniac, a crazy. Reed tried to speak quietly to his son.

"Your name isn't Simeon. It's Jeff. And there's no use trying to put up any more of a fight. You're coming with us, and we're going to make you well."

"Satan," yelled Jeff, staring wildly at his father. "You were all sent by Satan to steal my soul from Jesus. But I belong to Jesus, do you hear? To Jesus."

"All right, Jeff. But you also belong to yourself, and to your family, and your friends . . ."

Jeff spat full into his father's face. Both Ken and Joe sat there, shocked. Frank Reed quietly took out his handkerchief and wiped the spittle from his face. He did not even try to reproach his son.

"They're all like this, when you grab them," said Charlie, from the front seat. "Nothing you can do about it. Just take it."

He had driven the cab out of the immediate airport area, and now they were moving down Sepulveda. He turned the cab up the side street, where the Pontiac was waiting, and stopped the cab alongside of it.

The trick was to effect the transfer of Jeff from the taxi to the car, without attracting attention. There was a man up the street watering his lawn, and beyond that a woman wheeling a shopping cart full of groceries. Jeff sensed their dilemma. Again, he became a screaming, scratching wild man. And even while still inside the cab, he started to yell:

"Help! Help!"

"I'm afraid we'll have to shut him up," said Charlie, reluctantly.

He got out of the cab and opened the back door. He reached in, avoiding Jeff's kicking feet, and pressed his thumb against a point at the base of Jeff's neck. Jeff immediately subsided, and went limp.

"He'll be okay in a minute or two," said Charlie.

They transferred Jeff from the taxi to the Pontiac, supporting him between them, without any trouble. They got into the Pontiac. Ken took the wheel, while Frank and Joe sat in the back seat, flanking Jeff.

"Good luck, Mr. Reed," said Charlie.

"Thanks, Charlie. For everything."

"No sweat. I know your boy is going to make it. I'd better get this hack out of here. We may have attracted some attention back there."

Charlie waved goodbye, got into the taxi, and drove away. Jeff stirred, and started to scream, "Satan, Satan, Satan!"

He reached out with his fingers, tore at his father's face. Joe Peterson grabbed his arms, pinned them behind his back. Frank Reed reached for his briefcase, took out the handcuffs, and locked them on Jeff's wrists.

From his vantage point in the parking lot, John Morse had seen the hit work perfectly.

He stayed there, watching for a while, as a police car came up, apparently summoned by onlookers who had stood there, dumbfounded, as they witnessed the action.

He saw the patrolmen talking to the Deacons. They simply shrugged, shaking their heads. He smiled grimly. He could not hear what they were saying, of course. But he could guess.

"One of our people simply took a taxi and went home. Violence? What violence, Officer? We didn't see any violence. We're not charging anybody with anything. We don't know about anything. If these people saw some violence being done, we didn't. The name of the boy who took the taxi? Forced into it, you say? I doubt that, Officer. I doubt that very much. This boy here who has the nosebleed. He gets them often.

They just come out of nowhere. He's had a terrible cold, lately. The name of the boy who got into the taxi? Well, if you insist. His name is Simeon. Simeon what? Just Simeon, Officer. He had some earth-name once, but we don't even know what it is. He is a Soul for Jesus, and his name is Simeon. That's all we can tell you."

Finally, the police left. So far, thought Morse, par for the course. The SFJ was not about to make a complaint about anything, or anyone. This would mean undesirable publicity. Questions. Statements would have to be made. Complaints filed. They didn't want to lift any large, flat rocks and let everybody see what was underneath. They'd rather take the loss of a Soul here and there than expose themselves.

John Morse drove out of the parking lot, and headed for the Holiday Inn. He would pick up Kate Reed and Cindy there. Then they would all head for Big Bear.

Now, it was his turn.

21

On this same morning, the Master woke to face a busy day in San Francisco.

First, he had a business breakfast meeting aboard the *Messenger of God* with some of his Disciples. After that, there would be a huge SFJ crusade program at Winterland, called Jamboree for Jesus, which would also be filmed for national television syndication. Finally, he had a luncheon with some reporter-researchers from *Time* Magazine.

The Disciples at the breakfast meeting were Digby, Caswell, Garvey, and the media representative and producer for all the cult's TV productions. His name was Arthur Ames, of the advertising agency of Gordon, Jessamyn, Ames and Alexander. But when he wore the monk's robe and the black belt of the Disciple, he was known simply as Timothy.

They first went over the computer readouts of the God Squad sales for the one hundred and eight SFJ church-communes throughout the country. The Master was pleased with the total. But he was highly displeased with the figures for recruiting new members.

"What's wrong with our witnessing?" he wanted to know. He looked directly at his business manager. "What's happening here, Billy?"

"It's the competition, Buford."

"*What* competition?"

"The thing is, you have these new churches springing up all over the country. Like a bunch of damned mushrooms. Most of them are small and pretty way out, they don't mean anything. But every time they get one, we lose one. And there are only so many fish in the barrel. Now, some of these small churches have leaders who draw kids because they have a certain charisma. You take, for instance, Mother Prophet."

"Who?"

"Mother Prophet. Full name, Elizabeth Clare Prophet. She's leader and chief revelator of the Church Universal and Triumphant. She teaches the scientific use of energy through the spoken word—prayer and mantras—and what she calls 'the teachings of the ascending masters.'"

"Mother Prophet." Caswell grinned, his public relations mind spinning. "That's a hell of a name for anybody running a church. Man, could I do a job on *that*."

"I couldn't care less about Mother Prophet," said Hodges.

"Don't forget those kids John Morse has deprogrammed," said Garvey. "When they get on television or in the newspapers, they're not helping us any. They turn off a lot of prospects we might have witnessed, otherwise."

"Nobody has to tell me about Morse," said Hodges. "I *know* what he's doing."

"I still get back to the same thing," said Digby. "There's a lot of competition for Christians these days. They use commercials on TV, newspaper ads, bumper stickers. In some cities, they'll have this special telephone number. All you have to do is dial Jesus, J-E-S-U-S, and you get them on the phone. They go in for big names. For instance, one of them baptized Eldridge Cleaver and his wife, in the pool at their center in San Bernardino. People like that. And like us, they're fully computerized." Digby hesitated. "But that isn't all."

"No?" Hodges eyed Digby. "What else is there?"

"The thing is, some of them are legitimate Christian organizations, and the public sees them that way. They're movements, not cults. Their policy is to steer converts into their local Christian churches. Every time they persuade one, we lose one. At least, as a prospect."

"Which brings up a point, Buford," said Caswell. "From a public relations point of view. We've got to figure out ways to look more legitimate. Change *our* image."

"I agree," said Hodges. "It's something to think about."

"Maybe we ought to get rid of the monk's robes," said Caswell. "You know, that kind of thing."

"Maybe," said Hodges. "I'll think about it. Maybe we can phase it out gradually, if we have to. But that's what these kids go for, Dick—the ritual. The weird stuff."

"Some of them. Not all."

"I'll think about it," repeated Hodges. He turned to Ames. "The program all set up for this morning, Art?"

"Yes. We've got a sellout crowd and standing room only. Packed the house from communes all over northern California, plus our regular members on the outside."

"Good," said the Master. "Very good."

"You sure you want to tell your Miracle Story again, Buford?"

"Got to," said the Master, drily. "Got to remind them once in a while how the Lord and I got to walk together, hand in hand."

In the taxi, on his way to his show at Winterland, the Master reflected on what had been said at the breakfast meeting. His business manager had been right. He, Buford Joe Hodges, had come a long way, but still not far enough. He wanted, above all, respectability. He wanted the SFJ to be regarded as legitimate, not some cult at all. He, personally, wanted to be *accepted*, in the way the other nationally known evangelists were. Maybe it was the matter of the right publicity. Maybe they should make an effort to get the really big names, the Pat Boones and Johnny Cashes and so on. Maybe some day he'd get rid of the communes, the mumbo-jumbo ritual and the rest of it, and make them into separate colleges for Christ, part of a national SFJ University.

But before he could move forward, he had to get the Devil off his back.

That was priority Number One.

In his special television broadcasts, the Reverend Buford Hodges used several formats.

This one, the Jamboree for Jesus, began with a film sequence showing the wonders of God through nature, backed by the muted and reverent singing of the Resurrection Singers.

Now, the nature films faded into a full shot of the amphitheater, the choir and audience. As usual, a smiling young woman appeared in a circle at the lower lefthand corner of the screen using sign language to bring the message to those who were deaf or hard of hearing. The camera moved in on a soloist in the choir. She was a lovely girl, fresh-faced, with long blond hair, dressed in a long, flaring chiffon dress. Her voice was pure and sweet. She sang a hymn, backed by the Resurrection Singers.

Then the spotlight spun to the Master, standing on the stage of the huge amphitheater.

"Now," he said, "I want every one of you to turn around, look at the person sitting next to you, and shake hands with him."

There was a rustle in the great crowd as everyone did so.

"Now, say to your neighbor—Jesus loves you, and so do I."
There was a swelling chorus from the audience.

"Jesus loves you—and so do I."

The Reverend Buford Hodges smiled benevolently. "Now, today I am going to speak of a Miracle. It happened to me, and I promise you an incredible experience you will never forget. But first, I want you to meet a young friend of mine. Once this young man had an earth-name, but it does not matter now. He has just given his Soul to Jesus. His name is Amasiah, a brave captain of Judah, who, as it is related in 2 Chronicles 17, offered himself and his men to the Lord.

"Amasiah has a word or two to say to you, from his heart." He stepped aside to give the spotlight to the boy.

Amasiah was about eighteen, clean-cut and handsome. He wore his SFJ street jacket, and he spoke in a low voice, full of humility.

"I always knew I'd meet Jesus some day. But I didn't know I'd meet him as a friend. I am sorry I did not meet him long ago. My parents, my friends, never knew him, and never really told me about him.

"I found that He doesn't run a credit card system. His only real currency is Love. Love for God, love for each unto one another. Now, I am happy, I am content, I am at peace. Now, I am on the good and holy path to Heaven and Salvation. I hope there are kids out there who are ready and willing to give Jesus a chance, as I did. Because He will give *you* a chance. If you only let him."

Then he spread his arms.

"I love you all. And Jesus loves you."

The Resurrection Singers sang a swinging gospel, backed by guitars, piano and bass. Then the Master stepped forward: "I have promised you a miracle. And now you shall hear one. The miracle that happened to me."

The lights went down, leaving the Master in a spot. The interpreter for the hard of hearing remained in her small, illuminated circle at the lower left of the screen.

Now, the Master began to relate his Miracle. It had happened in the mountains of Tennessee, on the Holston River in Hawkins County. As an itinerant young preacher, he had gone from town to town, through burning heat, rain, and cold preaching the Word wherever he could.

He had stayed up all night in a town called Rogersville, giving spiritual comfort to a sick woman, and in the morning, he had wanted to go into Greene County across the river, to preach to the folks there. The pedestrian bridge was upstream a distance, and he was very tired, and he decided to take a shortcut across a long trestle that spanned the river. He was warned that this might be dangerous, but he was very tired, and he decided to chance it anyway, and deep inside, he had the conviction that, since he was doing the Lord's work, no harm would come to him. During the night, a fog had risen, and it remained early that morning, and when he had started to walk across the trestle, he could see only a few feet before him.

Then, when he was about halfway across, stepping from one railroad tie to another, he heard a dreaded sound.

The sound of an oncoming train.

Now, as the Master continued to speak, the rumbling of a train was heard, distantly, through backstage sound effects. It was blowing its whistle intermittently. Gradually, it came closer and closer.

"I heard that train come on," said the Master. "And I knew I was trapped. I knew it would catch up with me because I could never get to the end of that trestle in time. I knew the engineer would never see me, because it was so foggy, until it was too late to stop." The Master began to wave his arms. "I knew I could not jump off the trestle into the river. It was very high, and there was nothing but a dry bed and sharp rocks below . . .

"I knew then, brothers and sisters, that my time had come."

The sound of the train gradually came nearer, its whistle shrieking.

"I knew that train, coming on and on, was a tool of Satan, come to get me. I knew, brothers and sisters, that it was like the Devil himself breathing fire and smoke, coming down to crush me, because I had dared to defy him, and preach the Word. I knew the engineer driving that train, without knowing it, had been possessed by the Antichrist because he kept that train coming on, faster and faster, never slowing it up.

"Suddenly, brothers and sisters, I heard this voice. It came from nowhere. It spoke in my ear. It was gentle and full of love. I could not believe it. I asked myself, could it be? Oh my God, oh, Lord, could it possibly be?"

The Master paused. On this instant, a voice was heard, coming from limbo somewhere, echoing through the amphitheater. It was deep, eerie, yet gentle. It was entirely unexpected. The voice of some hidden actor. The audience sat up straight, startled. Then they realized that the Master, with his flair for showmanship, was presenting the Miracle in the form of a dialogue:

ANGEL: The Lord has heard your prayer, my son.
MASTER: (incredulous) The Lord?
ANGEL: It is true, you now walk through the valley of the shadow of death. But fear no evil. For I am with you.
MASTER: Who is that? Who speaks?
ANGEL: I am an angel of the Lord.
MASTER: An angel!
ANGEL: Rise up, my son. There is work for you to do.
MASTER: But I am about to die.
ANGEL: Rise up. For the Lord has decreed that you shall live. He restoreth not only your soul but your body as well. For you have been chosen to do His will.
MASTER: (unbelieving) I?
ANGEL: He has chosen you from among the multitudes to spread His word. He has given you life, so that you may become His Messenger. As such, you will possess the divine power of prophecy. You, before anyone else, will know and predict the coming of the Messiah.
MASTER: All this?
ANGEL: And more. You shall start a Church of your own, in His name. And save souls in His name. So it is decreed, and so it shall be. And ye shall be blessed, my son. Not only thee, but all those who follow you, in the name of Jesus, blessed be His name.

Now, the sound of the train was very close, it was coming on with a roar, the wheels changed pitch as they hit the track on the trestle, the ties rumbled.

MASTER: But Death is upon me now. How can I live to do the Lord's bidding?
ANGEL: Look ahead of you, my son, and down at your feet. And there, you shall find life and Salvation. And this, ye

shall remember for all times, and relate it as a Miracle of the Lord.

The voice vanished abruptly, and now the Master shouted to his audience above the din of the oncoming train:

"And then I saw what the Angel had pointed out to me. One of the railroad ties was missing, a few feet ahead of me. Somebody, or something, had broken it, or ripped it out. It left just enough space for my body to get through. I ran to it, wriggled through it, dropped my head and body just beneath the track, just in time. The engineer had seen me just ahead, through the fog, and he tried to stop the train . . ."

There was the shriek of brakes, steel sparking against steel in the sound effects, the train coming to a grinding halt.

"That train, that tool of Satan, passed just over me, and the Lord had stayed it. There was a girder just below that missing tie, and instead of falling onto the rocks, I caught it and hung on to it for dear life. The Lord had given me His hand there, as well. The men got off the train, expecting to find me crushed under those cruel iron wheels. Instead, they saw me hanging on the girder, below the trestle, and they lowered a rope and pulled me up. They could not believe how calm I was. And I *was* calm, brothers and sisters, I was calm, because I knew I had been held in the hand of the Lord, I was in God's righthand pocket, you might say.

"After that, I got down on my knees and prayed. After that, they told me it was a miracle that I was alive. The day before, a trackwalker had walked that very trestle, and found not one of the ties missing. They could not believe the Lord had removed this with His own hand. They said again, it was a miracle, and I told them, truly, this is what they had witnessed. And I told them what it was, and how the Angel had spoken to me, and what he had said. And there were many there who took off their hats, and stood dumbfounded when I spoke, and believed.

"And that, brothers and sisters, was the Miracle. And as you know, I have tried to do His will, from that time on."

The Master paused. He waited until the Resurrection

Singers began to hum a gospel for background. Then he raised his arms dramatically:

"Brothers and sisters, stand up in the name of the Lord. Bow your head, and pray as I did, if you want to be healed, if you want to be saved."

After that, there was the usual pitch for desperately needed money to help the church by buying the booklets, and another pitch for building funds for the planned new SFJ main church and administration center, a highrise building to be constructed in the shape of a cross. It would be located high in the San Bernardino Mountains, or possibly near Disneyland in Florida, and at night it would be brilliantly illuminated, so that it could be seen for miles around.

Later, in the dressing room, the Master was alone with his producer. He sat at the mirror, wiping the makeup off his face, and asked, "How do you think it went, Arthur?"

"Great, Buford. You were never better."

"I've been thinking about that miracle sequence we use."

"Yes?"

"Maybe it's a little overdone."

"No," said Ames. "You've done fine with it so far, Buford. People love it. It gives them a mystic experience, and gives you a special pipeline to God."

"Still, I think we ought to raise the level of our programs from here in."

"In what way?"

"I don't know. Make them more sophisticated. Dignified. Cut out some of the razzle-dazzle—you know, the production numbers. Make them more straight from the shoulder—sincere."

"Buford," warned Ames, "you've got to remember one thing. People want to be informed, sure. And they want to be inspired. But they also want to be entertained. We're in show business."

"I know that," said the Master, irritably. "But let's just put our heads to it. Think along some new lines. We're Number One. And the only way we're going to stay that way is by coming up with something new, now and then."

22

The luncheon with the people from *Time* was held in the Redwood Room of the Clift Hotel.

It was a place of Buford Hodge's choosing. They wanted to meet him aboard the *Messenger of God,* but he had vetoed that idea. He believed that first impressions were important and he did not want to project his initial image as someone wearing a monk's robe and cowl. Psychologically, no matter how objective they might claim they were, they would judge him as weird, way out, or at the least, highly exotic. And they would see the SFJ in the same way.

There were four people from *Time* present.

All were involved in the SFJ cover story. First, a senior editor, Henry Bedell, who was in charge of the entire project; second, a senior writer, Michael Allen; third, a reporter-researcher named Amanda Tompkins, who wore huge glasses and recorded the discussion in shorthand, rather than by tape recorder; and finally, an art director named Giorgio Favio, who was there to observe the Reverend Hodges, and suggest ideas that one of the artists could use on the cover.

They had attended his show and, in a guarded way, they said they found it fascinating. They did not question him on the authenticity of his miracle. A miracle was something you believed in, or something you did not. Clearly, they did not. But this did not bother Buford Hodges at all. He was aware they were studying him intensely, and curiously. But he had now met and measured his interrogators, and he felt he could handle them all. He knew that Allen was hostile, had already prejudged him. But he was confident that he could field any questions any of them might throw at him.

It was the senior editor, Bedell, who led the questioning, although the writer, Allen, came in now and then. The art director said nothing through the interview. He seemed to be doodling, although he actually was drawing one sketch after another of Buford Hodges. The reporter-researcher's fingers flew, as she recorded the interview in shorthand:

BEDELL: Reverend Hodges, I want to be fair and aboveboard with you. We want to be as objective as we can. But we intend to ask you some hard questions here.

REV. HODGES: Ask anything you like.

BEDELL: They're questions people all over this country are asking. Some of them you may possibly find offensive.

REV. HODGES: I'm prepared for that. I'm not the first religious leader in this world who's been maligned. I refer you to one great example you already know . . .

BEDELL: Now, as of today, you are the leader of what is perhaps the biggest cult in the country today . . .

REV. HODGES: Now, that's a statement I do find offensive, sir.

BEDELL: Yes?

REV. HODGES: The Souls for Jesus is not a cult. It is a church.

ALLEN: Excuse me, Reverend. But the popular conception . . .

REV. HODGES: The word "cult" is greatly misused, Mr. Allen. Just how do you define it?

ALLEN: You'll have to give me a minute to think about it.

REV. HODGES: Please do.

ALLEN: I'd say a cult, and I'm speaking of a religious cult here, is any small group of people who break away from an established religion, and form their own. There's something exotic about it, with unusual rituals, something mystic, and not quite legitimate in the eyes of the general public.

REV. HODGES: Then, if that is true, Jesus formed a cult when he broke away from the established religion. All He had was Himself and His disciples. Would you call Christianity a cult?

ALLEN: No, of course not.

REV. HODGES: How about Joseph Smith? The founder of the Mormon religion. They called him a cultist, and a mob in Illinois shot him. What about Mary Baker Eddy, the founder of Christian Science? She was denounced as a crook and a lunatic. And the Quakers. They were denounced as a crazy sect, and were fiercely persecuted in Europe.

BEDELL: I think you have a point there, Reverend Hodges.

REV. HODGES: I know I do.

BEDELL: What you're saying is that although all these started as cults, they're recognized today as respectable religions. Simply because they've been around long enough, and people get used to them.

REV. HODGES: Precisely. And this is the case with my Souls for Jesus. They may *call* us a cult, but actually we're simply a new Christian church that's broken away from the established church. Unorthodox, to be sure. But I make the point again. A *church*.

BEDELL: Reverend Hodges, there's a prevailing impression that you witness or recruit members, get them into your communes, and then control their minds—in effect, brainwash them. Is that true?

REV. HODGES: I expected that question.

BEDELL: And you have an answer?

REV. HODGES: Of course. The answer is yes. Yes, we do brainwash our young people. We clean their brains of all the lies, of the greed, of the false values they have learned in a corrupt world. We wash their brains of hate and materialism, and teach them love of each other, and of God.

ALLEN: And that's the way *you* see it, Reverend.

REV. HODGES: That's the way every church sees it. Every religion brainwashes its young people into whatever it wants them to believe. Your religion does it, Mr. Allen. The Catholic Church does it, almost from a child's birth. *Every* church does it. Why should *we* be any different? Why should anybody point the finger at *us*?

BEDELL: Reverend, there's a story that the SFJ is a conglomerate worth twenty or thirty million dollars. Is that true?

REV. HODGES: I don't know. I am not concerned with these earthly matters. I leave this to others. But of course, that figure is totally absurd, a fantastic exaggeration.

BEDELL: That's all you have to say about it?

REV. HODGES: Yes. Other than to say that every dollar we get goes into the Church.

ALLEN: Your so-called God Squads collect money for orphanages, hospitals that apparently don't exist. How do you account for that?

REV. HODGES: They will exist shortly. The plans are already finished. If you want to see the blueprints, I can show them to you. We're starting construction as soon as we can finance it.

ALLEN: A personal question, Reverend.

REV. HODGES: Yes?

ALLEN: I hope you don't take offense.

REV. HODGES: I'll tell you if I do.

ALLEN: You seem to live well for a spiritual leader. To use the slang: "Pretty high on the hog." How do you square that with being the—er—"Messenger" of Christ, who was ascetic, simple in his wants . . . ?

REV. HODGES: Nobody ever said that the head of a church should live like a pauper. Solomon and the other kings of Israel lived in great splendor. Look at the Pope, and the way *he* lives. You wouldn't call the Vatican a slum, would you? And the Cardinals and Bishops don't live poor mouth either. You take the other evangelists, the ones you see on television. Wherever they go, they go first class. Why shouldn't I? God Himself was in favor of it. It's all in the Bible.

BEDELL: It is? Where?

REV. HODGES: Do you know anything about the Bible, Mr. Bedell?

BEDELL: To be honest with you, very little.

REV. HODGES: I quote you Job 40, verse 10, where the Lord instructs Job, who he has appointed to serve Him: "Deck thyself now with majesty and excellency; and array thyself with glory and beauty."

ALLEN: I assume you interpret that to mean a yacht, a private jet, and other accessories.

REV. HODGES: I interpret it as I read it in the Bible.

ALLEN: Getting back to this difference between a cult and a church.

REV. HODGES: Yes?

ALLEN: What would you call Dr. Moon's Unification Church? Or Hare Krishna? They claim they are religions, or churches. Are they basically any different from your Souls for Jesus?

REV. HODGES: You must be joking.

ALLEN: On the contrary.

REV. HODGES: To even compare us to them is an outrage. Souls for Jesus is a *Christian* religion. And more than that, it's pure, one hundred percent American. These other outfits are run by foreigners, Orientals, and they're extremely peculiar. They're practical jokes thought up by Satan, to ridicule all religions, and confuse the public. And they fill their followers with the most amazing ideas. Why, do you know how the Krishnas welcomed their chief swami when he arrived in Frankfurt one day?

BEDELL: No. How?

REV. HODGES: His converts lay flat on their bellies in the dust. Then they washed his feet with rosewater, fanned him with a peacock whisk, and offered him marzipan. Then they blew horns, and beat drums, and danced around him yelling "Hare Krishna." Now, *that* is what I call way out, gentlemen, really beyond the fringe.

BEDELL: Reverend Hodges, of late, we've been hearing a lot about parents abducting their children from the SFJ, and then having them deprogrammed.

REV. HODGES: Yes? What about it?

BEDELL: Aren't you concerned about it?

REV. HODGES: Not really. When you think of it, it's pretty hypocritical. Here are the parents, accusing us of programming their children. Then what do *they* do? They hire a deprogrammer who does exactly the same thing. Here is the pot calling the kettle black.

ALLEN: Maybe they have good reason.

REV. HODGES: Oh, they're sincere enough, Mr. Allen. But wrong-headed. And this whole idea of parents trying to kidnap their own children from some religion is nothing new. It's hundreds of years old. In fact, you people at *Time* made that point yourself.

BEDELL: *We* did?

REV. HODGES: In one of your own issues. I have a copy of the article right here.

Amanda Tompkins put down her pen, as the Reverend Hodges reached into his wallet and took out a faded yellowed clipping. She was glad of the break. Her fingers ached from taking down the shorthand. She watched Hodges. His face was smug, amused, as he surveyed the group.

"I don't know which one of your people wrote this," he said. "But in my view, he hit the nail right on the head. Shall I read it to you? It'll only take a minute."

"Go ahead," said Bedell.

The Reverend Hodges put on a pair of Benjamin Franklin reading glasses, and then read what had been written, almost tasting each word, as though it were a delicious morsel of food.

" 'Parental abduction is, to be sure, not novel in the annals of religion. St. Clare's family tried to retrieve her bodily after she ran away from home to join St. Francis of Assisi and his band of pious mendicants. Legend has it that St. Thomas Aquinas' family locked him in a room with a whore to dissuade him from joining the Dominican order.'" Hodges read what came next with particular relish: "'But the deprogramming practiced by today's soul-snatchers seems suspiciously like a religious version of the Ludovico technique—that brain-blowing treatment administered to Alex, the anti-hero in Anthony Burgess' A Clockwork Orange. It was designed to make him acceptable to society by ridding him of his sado-sexual violence. In the process, Alex also lost his free will.'" He folded the clipping, and smiled. "Well, gentlemen, do I make my point?"

"Interesting," said Bedell. "When was that written?"

"Way back in 1973 . . ."

They were interrupted by a waiter who came in and said there was a telephone call for the Reverend Hodges. He excused himself, and the waiter led him to a private phone booth. The call was from Caswell.

"Yes, Dick? What is it?"

"Buford, he's done it again."

"Morse?"

"Who else?"

"Where did it happen, and when?"

"Just a little while ago. At L.A. International Airport. A Neophyte out of Ashtaroth. A boy. And give the Devil his due —they pulled off the job perfectly. The First Elder, name of Nehemiah, tried to reach you on the *Messenger of God*. You were out, so he called me. I thought it was important enough to interrupt you. How are you doing with the *Time* bunch?"

"Fine."

"I wish you'd let me come along. If you give them an opening, they can really stick it to you."

"Look, Dick," said Hodges, irritably, "I can take care of myself. This boy Morse snatched—what was his name?"

"Simeon."

"Damn it, I mean his real name!"

"It's some kid named Jeff Reed. Lived in Santa Barbara."

Buford Hodges said nothing for a few moments. He was deep in thought. Then he came to a hard decision. A decision he had been turning over in his mind for some months now.

"Dick, I want that boy found."

"That's going to be pretty hard to do, Buford. Morse has him hidden somewhere. He'll keep the kid salted away, until he's deprogrammed. After that . . ."

"Look, Dick. I *know* what Morse is going to do. I know we probably won't be able to get to that boy till after Morse brainwashes him. But I don't give a damn. I want that boy found, even if you have to hire a detective agency to do it."

"What have you got in mind, Buford?"

"A showdown."

"What kind of showdown?"

"Between Morse and myself. He's pushing me too hard, Dick, and I've had it. This time, I'm going to get him for good."

"How?"

"I'll go into that with you later."

"What's this kid, Jeff Reed, got to do with it?"

Buford Hodges laughed. "He's my secret weapon, Dick. That's why I want him found. And quickly."

While the Reverend Hodges was on the phone, the group from *Time* drank their coffee and eyed each other. Finally Bedell said, "Well? What do you think of him?"

"He's a fraud," said Allen. "A snake oil salesman, of the first order."

"But he does seem well-informed," said Bedell. "And you'll have to admit, Mike, he not only has charisma, he's news."

"Oh, he's news all right," said Allen. "Bad news. You note he wouldn't meet us on his yacht, or let us examine one of his communes. And he's working the old respectability image. Meets us at a good restaurant in his best Sunday suit, abandons the arm-waving evangelism, and talks about the history of religion in a nice, sweetly reasoned, professorial way."

"That's true," said Bedell. "He's another man, totally, on television."

"Basically," said Allen, "I see him as one hell of a politician. He can wear any hat to suit any occasion. And he's smooth." He turned to the reporter-researcher. "Amanda, you haven't said a word. What do you think of His Divinity?"

She stared at them all through her owlish glasses.

"You won't believe what I'm going to say."

"Say it anyway."

"It isn't just that he has this charisma. He's sexy, too."

They stared at her. Allen said:

"Amanda, you are kidding?"

"No. I mean it. You can smell it in a man. Feel it. He's got it. The Reverend Buford Hodges is a very sexy man. He reminds me of a character, Merle, in that old television show 'Mary Hartman, Mary Hartman.' You know, the evangelist. The one who lusts for all the girls. Sometimes it's power that attracts women, sometimes money. This man's got something different, and it makes some women curious. At least, it does me. Call it a crazy and purely female reaction."

"Yes?"

"He runs a religion. They call him His Divinity. I know it sounds crazy, but women fantasize about what it would be like to go to bed with certain men. They might wonder how divine His Divinity would be between the sheets. Just curious. You know?"

"Well," said Allen, "I'll be damned."

Bedell turned to his art director.

"Giorgio, you haven't said a word. Just sat there doodling. What's your opinion?"

Favio said nothing. Instead he picked up a sketch and held it up with both hands so that they could all see it. He had drawn a figure, with the face of the Reverend Hodges, dressed in a monk's robe and cowl. Reverend Hodges had a Bible hanging from his neck. He was looking up toward the sky, his arms raised high in prayer and supplication. In his left hand, he held a cross. In his right hand, a fistful of money.

Favio grinned. "How do you like it?"

They stared at the sketch for a moment. Then Allen said, "It'd make a great cover."

"Yes," said Bedell, ruefully. "It would. Except they'd be afraid to go for it upstairs."

23

For a time, as they moved up Route 10 toward San Bernardino, Jeff Reed kept shouting and screaming. He tried to bang the windows with his fists, wave to people in passing cars, and show them his handcuffs. He twisted and turned, struggling fiercely, so that his father and brother had to wrestle him down. If they attracted the attention of passing motorists, Frank and Ken Reed smiled and waved, pretending that they were just engaging in a little horseplay in the rear seat. The motorists would smile and wave back, then move on.

Meanwhile, Reed cautioned Joe Peterson at the wheel.

"Drive carefully, son. Stay under the speed limit. Keep in the right lane as much as you can. We don't want to give the police any reason to stop us."

Meanwhile, Jeff continued to scream at them. "You're all shits. Shits, do you hear? You're going to pay for this. You wait and see. You're all working for Satan, he put you up to this, and Jesus will get you all for this!"

He continued to rave and rant, and finally Reed said, "Take it easy, Jeff."

"My name isn't Jeff, you filthy bastard. It's Simeon. Let me out of here. You hear me? Let me go!"

"You're not going anywhere, son, except with us."

"You call me son?" Jeff spat at his father. "I'm not your son. You're just a big motherfucker. You fucked my mother to get me, and she lay there and let you put your big cock into her, and then you called me son. But I never really belonged to either of you. I have a new father."

Ken and Joe listened, shocked, stunned by this outburst. Frank Reed went white. He half raised his fist. He wanted to smash his son's face. He wanted to take Jeff by the neck, and twist it till he screamed, and then pry open his mouth, and stuff it with soap. The nausea rose in his throat. He wanted to throw up. It took him a moment or two to calm down. He lowered his fist. John Morse had warned him that he must discipline himself against every insult. He had warned Reed that for the time being, his son was sick, mentally sick, and not responsible for his actions or his words.

Now, Jeff turned his abuse on Ken and Joe.

"You stinking bastards. You creeps. I thought you were my friends."

"We are," said Joe. "Look, Jeff, you don't understand. They've blown your mind back there."

"Joe, you're just a stupid jerk. You're just a dumb asshole. You don't know what you're talking about." He paused, and then: "'A fool's mouth is his destruction, and his lips are the snare of his soul.'"

Ken stared at his brother. Jeff had spoken mechanically, as though he'd memorized by rote.

"Now, what's *that* supposed to be?"

"A quotation from the Bible. The only true book, the only sacred words. It's from Proverbs, stupid. And I've got one for *you*, Ken. 'A foolish son is a grief to his father, and bitterness to her that bare him.' That's from Proverbs, too. But you don't read the Bible, do you, Ken? You're too busy up there at Stanford, reading all that shit they give you, riding around in your car, screwing all the girls, living and thinking lust. Giving your soul to Satan."

216

Ken was silent. He knew it was no use talking to his brother. Jeff, exhausted for the time being, leaned back, and for a while lapsed into silence. Frank Reed studied him covertly. It seemed impossible that this boy, sitting between himself and Ken, his hands manacled as though he were some common criminal, could actually be his son. The face was his son's face, the body his son's body, but there the resemblance ended. He was sure now that Jeff was too far gone to ever come back. He began to doubt that John Morse could turn that sick mind around, no matter what his skills. And once again, he thought, This isn't my son. *It's a Thing*. Human, to be sure, but still a Thing. A zombie.

After a while, Jeff turned and looked at his father. At this moment, surprisingly, he seemed calm, rational. At this moment, there was a flash of the old Jeff Reed they used to know.

"Where are you taking me?" he said, quietly.

"You'll find out when we get there."

"I know. You're taking me to meet *him*."

"Him?"

"The Devil." Nobody answered, and Jeff continued, calmly, "Oh, we've been warned about being kidnapped, and then taken to meet Satan. We've been warned that Satan will try to talk to us, and poison our minds against God." He smiled confidently. "But I am not afraid of the Devil. Because my soul belongs to Jesus now. 'Whosoever putteth his trust in the Lord shall be safe. He is a shield unto them that put their trust in Him.'"

"Son," said Reed. "All we're trying to do is help you."

"I *told* you," said Jeff. His eyes were burning. "Don't ever call me son again."

After that, he withdrew into silence. Shortly before San Bernardino, near Fontana, a sign on the freeway said: "Rest Area—2 Miles." Jeff said to his father, "Better stop for a minute."

"What for?"

"I've got to go to the john."

Frank Reed thought about it for a moment. He didn't want to make the stop. It would be awkward.

"It can wait till we get where we're going."

"That's up to you. But the thing is, I *can't* wait. I mean, I've got these terrible cramps." There was the ghost of a smile on his face. "When you've go to go, you've got to go. If I don't, it's going to smell real bad in here. I mean, it's going to really *stink*. Not that it doesn't already."

Again, at least for the moment, he seemed calm, totally rational, and he spoke quietly. Joe turned his head to look inquiringly at Reed. He nodded, and Joe swung the Pontiac into the right lane, and then into the parking lot of the rest area.

It consisted of a brick restroom in the center of a grassy area. There was a drinking fountain, a kind of brick-roofed patio to provide shade, and a glassed-in display stand, showing a map of the area and depicting a little of its history. The place at the moment was comparatively deserted. A truck driver sat dozing at the wheel of his rig. There was one other car present. Its occupants, a woman and two children, were resting on the grass, watching the traffic hum by on the nearby freeway.

"All right, Joe," said Reed. "You wait in the car, and stay at the wheel. Ken and I will take him inside."

Jeff raised his handcuffed wrists.

"What about these?"

"What about them?"

"I *told* you I've got cramps. How am I going to take my pants off and sit on the john wearing these? And how am I going to wipe my ass?" He grinned at his father, mockingly. "Unless *you* want to do it for me, Big Daddy. You know, just the way you and Big Mama did, when I was just a little baby." He glanced at the people lying on the grass. "And of course, if they see me wearing handcuffs, they might start asking a few questions. You want *that* to happen, you motherfucker?"

Again, Frank Reed managed to swallow his anger. He realized that Jeff had a point, and he took out his key and unlocked the handcuffs.

"Remember, Jeff, Ken and I will be standing very close to you. So don't try anything funny."

218

"Look," said Jeff, "I'm in a hurry. Let's get there, okay?"

They left the car. Both Ken and Reed held on to Jeff's arms, as inconspicuously as they could. Reed stopped a moment to study the brick restroom. There was no window through which Jeff could possibly escape. They released Jeff so that he could go inside, and posted themselves at the entrance.

It all happened so quickly, they were unable to react in time. They had expected Jeff to stay inside for a while, and had automatically relaxed as they stood at the entrance. An instant after Jeff had entered, he surprised them by turning and rushing back out. His body hurtled between them, and he took to his heels.

They ran after him. Jeff had lost weight, he was undernourished and in poor condition. Ken immediately drew ahead of his father, his long legs eating up the terrain in an athlete's stride, and he gained rapidly on Jeff. At the end of the parking lot, he caught Jeff, and they began to struggle, Jeff screaming at the top of his lungs.

Frank Reed came up. He saw the woman and her two children turning to stare at them curiously. Jeff continued to scream and, with sudden decision, Frank Reed hit his son on the jaw, stunning him. Meanwhile, Joe Peterson, instantly sizing up the situation, swung the Pontiac around and drove to the point where they were holding Jeff. They piled him into the back seat, and Joe boomed the car back onto the freeway.

They had no way of knowing what the woman had seen, or what she would do about it. It was possible that she might call the state police and tell them she had seen some men scuffling. It was also possible, and more probable, thought Frank Reed, that she would not. People were the same everywhere. They didn't like to get involved if they could help it.

See-no-evil, hear-no-evil, know-no-evil.

He could only fervently hope that it was true. At least in her case. The last thing he wanted in this world right now, the very last thing, was a witness. Or some state cop pulling up and telling them to pull over to the side.

He looked at Jeff. His son was sitting quietly, stunned,

his head lolling. Frank Reed rubbed the knuckles of his right hand. They felt sore. He had had to hit his son, and now he felt sick about it. And guilty. It had been a long time since he had done that.

Later, he hoped Jeff would understand, and forgive him. *If* he ever got back to being who he once was.

When they reached the cottage at Big Bear, they locked Jeff into one of the upstairs bedrooms. This was an elementary precaution, keeping him away from the ground floor, if he attempted an escape. Then they boarded up every window in the house, including those in both the upstairs and downstairs bathrooms. Morse had told them that on three or four occasions, members of the cult, desperate and under severe strain, had tried to get away by jumping out of windows.

It was early in the evening when Morse arrived with Cindy and Kate Reed. They had stopped at a supermarket, and the trunk of Morse's rented car was loaded with brown paper bags filled to the brim with bread, rolls, cheese, steaks, delicatessen foods, chickens, cereals, staples like sugar and coffee, stacks of paper plates and napkins. All this was in addition to the canned food they had purchased previously.

They hauled the bags in, and the two women started to put the food away. Reed was puzzled, and he said to Morse, "There's enough food here to last a month."

"That's right."

"You mean, we may be here *that* long?"

"No. Hopefully, we may get Jeff out in a couple of days—a week, at most."

"Then what's the point of buying all this stuff?"

"It's just a trick to impress your son."

"I don't understand."

"When he sees all this food, he'll *think* we're ready to stay here a month, if we have to. And that's exactly the impression I want to give him."

After Kate and Cindy put together a hasty meal of cold cuts, Kate Reed began to prepare some sandwiches for Jeff, locked in the bedroom upstairs. But Morse stopped her.

"Sorry, Mrs. Reed. But no dinner for Jeff."

"But I don't think he's even had lunch," she protested. "He must be starved."

"Fine," said Morse. "The hungrier he is, the better."

"Look," she said. "I don't know how you work, but I just can't understand how keeping him hungry is going to help anything. He's lost enough weight as it is." She sounded upset. "He's lost at least ten pounds, maybe fifteen, since he went into that horrible place . . ."

"Mrs. Reed," he said. "I'm trying to do a job here. It'll have to be done my way."

"All right," she said.

"Besides," he said with a mirthless grin, "he wouldn't eat those sandwiches you made anyway."

"No? Why not?"

"Because they've got meat in them. And every good Soul for Jesus is a strict vegetarian."

After the dishes were washed, John Morse briefed the group on the procedure to be used.

"First of all, remember this Jeff Reed waiting upstairs is someone you've never really known. He's someone else entirely, a different personality, at least for the time being. But you've all seen that for yourself. Now, at Ashtaroth, he was programmed, or brainwashed in a certain way. As Cindy here can tell you, they make you go hungry, they don't let you sleep, you sit on hard floors, they keep at you and at you. Is that right, Cindy?"

"You better believe it," said Cindy. "They blast at you with all these quotations from the Bible, and they keep tape recorders going day and night with sayings of the Master, and there are all these lecture groups, and Bible discussions, and rap sessions, and all you hear is Jesus, Jesus, Jesus loves you, and finally you're so hungry and tired you can't stand it any more. And all that goes on night and day, till they just wear you out . . ."

"Okay," said Morse. "You understand how they program a Neophyte. Now, in order to deprogram Jeff, I've got to do the same thing in *reverse*. Re-brainwash him back to normal, so to speak. Using some of the same techniques, the same methods they use. Fighting fire with fire."

Kate Reed looked a little pale.

"He'll have nothing to eat at all? No sleep?"

"I didn't mean that literally. But he'll get just enough to keep him going. The point is, he's going to be very uncomfortable."

"It all seems so cruel."

"It is. Unfortunately, it's the only way we have."

"Jeff's a pretty stubborn kid," said Reed. "How do you know he'll break at all?"

"I think I can break him," said Morse, quietly. "Hopefully he isn't totally insane, or psychopathic, at this point. I'll do everything I can to reach him. It may take some time, depending on how tough he is, and how deep they've really hit into his psyche. I ask you all to be patient."

He went on to explain that he would not see Jeff on this first evening. It was better for him to get used to the idea that he was being held, but that it was his family that was really keeping him up there in the bedroom, not he, John Morse.

"If I walked in right away," explained Morse, "it would scare hell out of your son—maybe drive him into doing something crazy, perhaps even try to kill himself. You see, I'm pretty well publicized as the Devil Incarnate in every SFJ commune in the country. I'm the Big Daddy of all the devils. They've told the kids who are boys that I'll torture them, stick burning cigarettes in their stomachs, blind them and finally kill them. And the girls that I'll rape them first, make them perform all kinds of indecent acts, and then cut off their breasts, and strangle them. In short, the fiery tail, sharp horns and red-hot pitchfork aren't enough. I'm the monster to end all monsters." He paused a moment. "So you see, if he knows his family is around, friends, anyone like that, he'll be reassured. And he'll understand that you won't let me hurt him, and all I want to do is talk to him."

"Can we see him?" asked Cindy.

222

"I was coming to that," said Morse. "I want you each to see him tonight. Not all together, each take a turn. I want you to see him in relays, and keep it up all night, so that he gets no sleep. Talk to him. Say anything you want to him. Tell him that you love him, you miss him, you want him back. You won't be able to reach him, of course. Not deep down. But you may make some kind of small, surface impact. At least, he'll be reassured, and ready to take the shock when I walk in on him."

"What about security?" asked Reed. "I mean, isn't it possible he may make a break for it when anyone walks in?"

"That would be possible, yes. Except that we're going to make it impossible."

"How?"

"Well, let's say Cindy goes in first. In fact, that's a good idea. You're most recent in his memory, Cindy. You were there on the inside with him. He'll feel a little easier with you. You go in first then. Okay?"

"Okay."

Morse turned to Reed. "Now, when she goes into the bedroom to be with Jeff, you lock the door behind her. Keep the key. Stand guard at the bottom of the stairs. When she's tired and wants to go, she'll knock. Then you open the door and let her out. After that, you and your wife go in, and the door is locked behind you, until it's Ken or Joe's turn to go in and keep him awake. Understood?"

"Yes."

"Barred windows and locked doors," said Kate Reed. "My God, it's like a jail."

"Jeff *is* in a jail," said John Morse, quietly. He tapped the side of his head. "A different kind. Far worse than San Quentin. The difference is, he's got a chance to get out of this one." He hesitated. "One more thing. All of you. No matter what Jeff says to you, stay calm, don't lose your cool, don't yell back at him, don't get angry. Just try to show him that you love him in any way you can, even if he doesn't realize it now." He turned to Cindy. "Well, let's get started.

No better time to begin than right now. As I said, we'll keep Jeff awake all night by working in shifts, or watches. Are you ready, Cindy?"

"Yes," she said, quietly. "I'm ready."

"Okay," said Morse. "Ken, you stand guard outside the door for the first shift. The rest of you get some sleep, until your turn comes. You're all going to need it. I'm dead tired, and I'm going to need some sleep myself, before I tackle Jeff in the morning. If he gets violent, or starts attacking somebody, you're to wake me up, and I'll take it from there. Understood?"

They all nodded. Morse turned to Cindy, and smiled warmly.

"Good luck. Don't let him upset you."

"I won't."

"You'll get him back in a little while."

"You don't know how much I want him back," she said.

Cindy walked into the bedroom and heard the click of the lock behind her, as Ken turned the key.

The room was hot, stuffy, and airless. No light came in through the boarded-up windows. John Morse had given specific instructions as to how the room was to be furnished. It was illuminated by a single, naked electric light bulb, hanging down, so that its glare was in the subject's face. There was only one chair; a hard mattress on the floor served as a bed. There was no pillow, and no sheets on the mattress. A bathroom led off from the room.

Jeff was sitting on the mattress, his back propped against the wall. He was tired, drawn, disconsolate. He looked gaunt and undernourished, even thinner than when she had seen him last.

He said nothing when she came in, simply stared at her.

"Hello, Jeff."

"My name is Simeon, Athaliah."

"Jeff, I am not Athaliah. And you're not Simeon. That's just what they called us in that terrible place."

"Your name is Athaliah," he said. "Daughter of Jezebel and Ahab, and you were the only ruling queen of Judah. And I am Simeon, Jacob's second son by Leah."

She saw that he was elsewhere, his mind was totally back in Ashtaroth; he had no idea of what reality was at this moment.

"Jeff, listen to me. You're not in Ashtaroth any more."

"Why did you run away? We all missed you so much. Your friends all missed you. Rahab, and Jochebed, and Tamar and Zillah—they all asked for you." He was plaintive now, accusing. "Why did you run away? You gave your soul to Jesus, then took it away. Jesus loves you, Athaliah."

"Jesus loves you, too. But so do your father and your mother. So does your brother Ken. So does Joe Peterson, your best friend . . ."

"I hate them," he flared, suddenly. "I hate them all. They stole me away. They brought me here. They are all tools of Satan. They are Satan's shit for doing this. They had no right, Athaliah, they had no right."

"They're only trying to help you, Jeff."

"Not Jeff!" he screamed at her. "Not Jeff, goddamn you. Simeon, Simeon!" He beat his fists on the mattress in frustration. "How long are they going to keep me here?"

"I don't know."

"Look." He rose and came to her. He grabbed her blouse, wild-eyed. "Help me get away. I'll go to the police. Report them all. They can't do this to me, Athaliah. If I want to give my soul to Jesus, I have a right. Do you hear? I have a right!"

"You don't want to go back there, ever."

"I do, I do. I do, you damned whore, I do."

"Don't you remember me? I'm Cindy. Cindy Hyland. Don't you remember all the good times we had, before we went in there? The things we did? The surfing and swimming, and just lying on the beach, and riding in your car, and eating hamburgers at Oscar's and the Burg, and driving up to Palo Alto and seeing Ken, and after that, up to San Francisco, and Sausalito, and Mill Valley and Tiburon and seeing all our friends there. And don't you remember how it was when we were in bed, how marvelous it was, what we said and what we did . . . ?"

"Shut up," he said.

"Listen. They made you sick. They almost made me sick. Listen to me . . ."

"Fuck you. All you are is shit."

"Just listen to me . . ."

"Get out of here! Do you hear me, get out of here and let me alone."

"Just try to remember . . ."

He closed his eyes, and raised his hands toward the ceiling: " 'I call thee whore, woman. Ye are of your father the Devil, and the lusts of your father, ye will do.' "

"Forget about the Bible. Just for a minute, will you? Try to remember the way it was . . ."

" 'Blessed is the man that endureth temptation; for when he is tried, he shall receive the crown of life.' " He opened his eyes, and smiled triumphantly at her: "You know where those came from, Athaliah?"

"No, and I don't care."

"The first was from the Book of John, and the second from James."

"Oh, shit," said Cindy, impatiently. "When are you going to start to talk sense, Jeff? And you are Jeff—not Simeon. When are you going to begin to *think* again?"

He went back to his mattress, and lay on his back. He stared up at the ceiling, totally ignoring her. She tried to get him to talk to her again, but he ignored her. He tried to sleep, but she continued to talk, rambling about the way it had been between them, and kept him awake. Finally, he sat up and screamed at her, called her bitch, and demanded that she leave because he wanted to get some sleep.

She stayed on a while, until she could stand it no longer.

Then she rapped on the door, and the Reeds came in next.

24

Just after dawn the next morning, they had breakfast in the kitchen. Everyone looked haggard. Since every window was boarded up, it had been difficult to sleep in the airless rooms. Besides, it had been unseasonably warm, uncomfortably so, even at Big Bear. In addition to this, each had served a stint with Jeff, and each had found it terribly upsetting. They all looked like mourners who had lost a loved one, and had just come back from the funeral.

To John Morse, all this was a familiar scene. He had seen it a hundred times. There was always this feeling of depression on the part of the family and friends, on the first day of deprogramming. They all went into a kind of shock. They all had an image of the boy or girl, as they remembered him or her before. But this was after, and the shock went deep.

"He's crazy," said Frank Reed. "Totally gone."

"You can't imagine what he called me," said Kate. "The names he called me. Worse than those he called me when I saw him at Ashtaroth. They were—filthy."

"Jesus," said Ken. "I didn't even know him. My own brother."

"Ken," said Joe, "do you *have* to use that word?"

"What word?"

"Jesus. I know it's the name of the son of God, and I believe in Him. But that's all I heard from Jeff. And when you hear it from him, it sounds different. He kept yelling it at me so much I thought I'd go out of my skull."

"I'll tell you this, Morse," said Reed. "None of us got through to him."

"I didn't expect you to."

"I said it before, and it makes me sick in my gut to say it again. But I really think the boy is insane."

"I doubt it," said Morse. "I'll tell you more when I see him."

"Suppose you're wrong? Suppose you can't snap him back? I mean, let's put it on the table. If you fall down, what do we do then? Send him to an institution? Send him back to Ashtaroth, where he came from?"

"Take it easy, Reed," said Morse. "Take it easy. If he turns out like the others, he's going to be fine."

"God, I hope you're right," said Kate Reed. "God in heaven, I hope you're right."

Morse drank the rest of his coffee and rose. He checked his watch. Joe Peterson had spent the last watch with Jeff. That had been an hour ago. On Morse's instruction, they had let Jeff sleep for an hour. Long enough to refresh himself just a little. There was a point where if you kept the subject up a little *too* long, he could go over the edge. That is to say, he might be able to hear what you said, but his brain would be too numbed with fatigue to either understand or interpret it. The weariness had to be incessant, it had to be devastating, but it also had to be monitored, carefully controlled in order to get maximum results.

"Well," said Morse. "My turn."

He picked up a small black bag he had brought with him. They all stared at it curiously. Nobody really knew what was in it. Ken had asked Morse what it contained, but he had only smiled pleasantly and said only that it held the tools of his trade.

He walked up the stairs, then turned and told them, "Now

and then, I'll need one of you to relieve me, for a little while. But I'll be alone with him from here in, most of the time. This could be anywhere from a few hours to a week. So you might as well just settle in and relax. But don't leave the house if you can help it. When he breaks, I'll need you all here."

Then he went into the room, and Frank Reed locked the door behind him.

The room was hot and stifling. Its air was stale now, foul from lack of ventilation. Good enough, thought Morse. The more miserable his subject, the better. The trouble was that he, as the boy's deprogrammer, would have to suffer as well. He had sweated through many a long hour with a hundred subjects in rooms more or less like this one. He could only hope for a quick break. He had had cases where it had taken only a few hours to do the whole job. But they were rare.

The light had been turned out, and the room was dark, except for slivers of light filtering through the boarded windows. Morse turned on the naked light bulb overhead. Jeff Reed was lying on the mattress, legs bent close to his chest, arms crossed, lying in the fetal position. He had undressed to his shorts, and his body was wet with perspiration.

Morse noted that Jeff's slacks and SFJ jacket were hung neatly on hangers in the closet, his shirt and tie hung on a hook. They were always very neat about their God Squad outfits the first day. Later on, he hoped, Jeff's clothes would furnish him with another kind of clue. He noted also that the lock on the bathroom door had been taken off, according to his instructions. And there was no phone in the room.

He put his bag on the table, and stood over the sleeping boy for a moment. The face was thin, the ribs showed through the young body, and John Morse felt a quick rush of compassion. It was the only moment he could afford this luxury. Afterward, it would be all business.

He reached down and shook Jeff. The boy twisted and turned, and mumbled something. Morse shook him again.

"Wake up, Jeff. Wake up."

Finally, Jeff Reed opened his eyes. He stared up into the

strange face looking down at him. Dazed, still drugged with sleep, he looked at the room around him, unaware of where he was, for the moment. Then: "Who are you?"

"My name is John Morse."

Suddenly, Jeff stiffened. He sat up straight, staring at Morse. Recognition came suddenly. His eyes widened. He blanched with fear. Then he shouted, "You're a liar. I know who you are!"

"Okay," said Morse. "Who am I?"

"You're *him!*"

"Him?"

"The Devil!"

"Now come on, son," said Morse. "That's just plain silly. Unless you think I left my tail and horns at home . . ."

"I know your face. They have pictures of you at Ashtaroth."

Morse drew up the single chair in the room. He brought it close to the mattress on which Jeff sat, so that he could look down at him. They were almost eyeball-to-eyeball now. Jeff, hypnotized by Morse's eyes, tried to shrink back further against the wall.

"Relax, Jeff. I'm not going to hurt you."

"My name is Simeon."

"From now on, it's Jeff."

"Simeon, Simeon, *Simeon!*" yelled Jeff.

"Jeff, Jeff, *Jeff*," mimicked Morse.

Jeff sat rigidly, his mouth working nervously. His whole body was tense, his eyes still fearful, but watchful now, waiting and wondering what the first move of his seducer would be. The gooseflesh popped out all over his body. And he began to sweat more profusely than before.

"You might as well relax," said Morse. "Because you and I are going to do a lot of talking. We're going to talk and talk and talk, until we finally wash out of your brain all the shit that's been put into it, and until you finally see what he did to you."

"He?"

"The Devil. The *real* Devil."

"I don't know what you're talking about!"

"I'm talking about the phony you call the Master. His Divinity, the Reverend Buford Joe Hodges. He claims he's the Messenger of God. But you know what that is, Jeff? It's a big lie. It's pure crap. You know what he really is? He's a fraud and a hypocrite. A bigmouth and a thief."

"That's a lie," shouted Jeff. "A lie, a lie!"

"Is it? What's the Master ever done for you?"

"He introduced me to Jesus. He taught me love. He gave me peace. He showed me how to serve the Lord."

"*That,* Jeff, is so much shit. He showed you how to serve Buford Hodges. What he did for you was take everything you had, your car and your money. He half starved you, and then he took your mind. After that, he made you go out with the God Squads, and work like a dog. He *really* ripped you off, Jeff. And where do you think all that money you collected went to?"

"It goes in the service of God."

"Does it?" Morse reached into his black bag, and took out a series of photographs. "Take a look at this yacht, Jeff. Old bigmouth, bloodsucking Buford lives on it. It's called the *Messenger of God.* Pretty nice, eh? You know how much that yacht is worth? A million dollars. And who do you think paid for it? You did, you little fool. You were jerk enough to go out on the street in front of the airport, and break your ass collecting money, and lying to people about what it was for, and work ten hours a day doing it. And the son-of-a-bitch took your money and put it into this nice plush yacht, with a big living room and luxurious cabins, and a galley full of booze and steaks. Man, you're pitiful. You are stupid. You don't even know when you're being ripped off!"

There was a gleam of triumph in Jeff's eyes.

"Get thee behind me, Satan. Now *you're* lying."

"Am I?"

"A Soul for Jesus doesn't eat the flesh of any living thing, or drink alcohol."

"Does that include all Souls for Jesus?"

"Everybody."

"Including the Master himself?"

"Especially the Master. It's *his* law."

"That's interesting," said Morse. "Very interesting." He grinned, and then took another photograph from his bag. It showed the *Messenger of God* moored to a pier. It seemed to be in some southern location—there were palm trees in the background. There was a truck on the pier, standing just beside the gangplank. A legend on the side of the truck read, "Jamaica Meat and Produce." The rear of the truck was open. Two men were seen carrying what was clearly a side of beef up the gangplank.

"This picture was taken on the island of Jamaica, Jeff. And that isn't a bag of sugar those two men are carrying into the yacht. Right?"

Jeff studied the photo. He was a little shaken. But then he rallied: "Okay, it's meat, all right. But it's for the crew."

"Something you forgot, Jeff. The *Messenger of God* is the main church of the Master. It's a floating commune. That means everybody aboard, the crew, everybody, is a Soul for Jesus." He grinned. "Oh, for your information, the Master likes his steaks rare. And he likes bourbon and sour mash. Before dinner, and after. Now, you know why he won't let the rest of you eat meat? You know why that bastard says every Soul for Jesus has to be a vegetarian? Himself excluded, of course. It's because it's cheaper to feed you poor, deluded little jerks carrots and celery and cucumbers than meat. Don't you see it? How stupid can you get, Jeff? I tell you again, you're being ripped off by this bastard in a way you wouldn't believe. The Reverend Buford Hodges happens to be the biggest con man of all time."

Jeff stared at him, then smiled. "Oh, I know what all this is. Lies, lies. Trying to break my faith."

"Somebody ought to break your ass, Jeff, for being so stupid. Your friend and my friend, the Master, is quite a boy. He not only starves you when it comes to food, but what about sex?" Jeff was silent. "What about it, Jeff? When was the last time you got laid?"

"I don't want to talk about it."

232

"I do. It's been weeks hasn't it? Weeks since you've balled anybody. Right?"

"That's because I'm going through Purification."

"Oh sure. You're going through Purification. You're taking cold showers, or jerking off, because you haven't had a woman in weeks. But what about his Divinity, dear old Reverend Buford Hodges, righthand man to God Himself, direct pipeline to heaven? While you're taking cold showers and masturbating, what is *he* doing most of the time? Let me show you." He took more photographs from the bag. He showed one of the Reverend Hodges in a bathing suit, lying on a tropical beach. There was a beautiful young blonde lying next to him. The Master was smoking a cigar, and he had his hand on the girl's leg, caressing it. It was a candid shot, and Hodges had had no idea he was being photographed.

"There's the holy head of your church," said Morse. "While you're stuck in Ashtaroth, sleeping on a hard cot, praying all the time, working ten hours a day, what's Mr. Big doing? Cruising in the Caribbean, or in the Bahamas. A different young girl every cruise. Fucking himself blind, and drinking himself blind." Morse showed Jeff another photograph.

This time the Master was sitting at a table in what appeared to be a nightclub. There was a sensuous looking, heavy-lidded brunette with him. Her face was of a Mexican-Indian cast, and she was beautiful. Her dress was low cut, so that her breasts were almost popping out. There was a bottle of bourbon on the table, and a Mexican waiter was seen, just taking a bottle of champagne from an ice bucket, ready to pour. The Master had just caught sight of the candid cameraman, and he had reacted angrily. But a moment too late. He had flung his hand up to hide his face, but he hadn't quite been able to cover it.

"Old Buford likes them young, Jeff, as you can see. But sometimes, the little Deaconesses he picks from some commune and takes along don't do it for him. He gets a little bored with them. He likes his fucking a little special, you know what I mean? A little kinky. So he hires some high-class

233

call girl, like the one you see here in this picture. Two hundred dollars a night, Jeff. Figure out the booklets you have to sell in front of the airport, in the service of the Lord. In the service of the Lord, my ass!"

"Lies, lies, *lies!*"

"How old are you, Jeff? Eighteen? And you've given your soul to Jesus. You haven't touched a girl in weeks. How long do you think you can fight nature? How long do you think that can last? There are a hundred girls out there who'd love to get into the sack with you. They'd love to grab you by the cock. They'd love a roll in the hay with you. There's Cindy, waiting downstairs. She's yours, Jeff. She's crazy about you. She loves you. Remember what it was like to go to bed with her? Remember what it was like to lie on the beach with her, or between the sheets? What kind of damned fool are you, to deny yourself all that? Because his Holiness, one of God's great cocksmen, tells you you can't?"

"Stop it!" Jeff put his fingers to his ears. "I won't listen to you."

"Then look." Morse took another photograph out of the bag. "Here's our friend getting ready to enjoy a little session. Something he allows himself, but denies you."

The photograph was a composite, the kind sometimes put together in cheap sex magazines. It showed the grinning head of the Reverend Hodges atop a cutout of some other man's naked body. The penis was enormous, and in full erection. The picture was obscene, and deliberately designed to be. It was meant to shock Jeff, and ridicule his leader, symbolically portray his obscenity. Jeff gasped when he saw it. Then he tried to grab it away from Morse.

"Give me that!"

Morse made no resistance. He smiled and let Jeff take the photograph. Jeff angrily ripped it into shreds.

"It's a fake. A fake!"

"So is your leader, Jeff. Can't you see that?"

"You've said enough. Now let me alone!"

Morse leaned back in his chair and lit a cigarette. "Oh, I can't do that, Jeff. We've got a lot to talk about yet."

"I'm not going to listen to you."

"You're going to have to, Jeff. Because you're not going anywhere, and neither am I. We're going to sit in this stinking room and talk and I'm going to put your head on straight ahead, no matter how long it takes."

"I *told* you, I won't listen."

"Okay. Then it'll just take a little longer. Not just hours. But days. Weeks. And, if necessary, months."

Morse saw Jeff's eyes flicker a little. He was trying to conceive what it would be like to spend weeks in this room. And he didn't like the thought. Then, remembering something, he took courage and smiled.

"I don't believe all your lies, Satan. And you can't change me."

"What makes you think I can't?"

"Because it says so in the Bible."

"Does it?"

"It's right in the Bible. 'Resist the devil, and he will flee from you.'"

Morse went into the black bag now, and took out a Bible. He handed it to Jeff.

"Show me where it says that."

Jeff shook his head. "It's somewhere in there. But I don't know where."

"Then *I'll* tell *you*," said Morse. It's the Book of James, Chapter 4, Verse 7. And since you love to shoot your mouth off quoting the Bible, and you think I'm old Beelzebub himself, let's play games. Do you know another passage about me in the Good Book?" Jeff stared at Morse, then shook his head. Morse jeered, "Oh, you don't."

"I don't remember."

"You mean you don't know. Okay, I'll give you another lesson. It's in the First Book of Peter: 'Be vigilant; because your adversary the devil, as a roaring lion, walketh about, seeking whom he may devour.'" Morse sneered. "Now, Jeff, I ask you, do I look like a roaring lion? You're already being devoured, but by somebody else. All I'm trying to do is pull you *out* of the lion's mouth, not stuff you into it. Okay? Now, why don't you face it? You don't really know that much about the Bible. All you can remember is what they tell you to remember. Those creeps at Ashtaroth are lousy teachers. You'll have to admit that. All they know how to teach you is hate."

"They teach us love."

"Hate, Jeff. Hate, hate, hate. Hate the rest of the world. Hate your friends, hate the people who love you. Hate your father and mother."

"I have no father and mother."

"That, Jeff, is a crock of shit. Think about it. You weren't born out of some moonbeam or cloudburst. The stork didn't bring you. Your father and mother created you, and your mother bore you in pain, and nursed you when you were helpless, and loved you, and still does. Yet those pious, phony bastards at Ashtaroth, those creeps you respect so much, the Elders, taught you to hate them. They taught you to call your mother a whore, and your father a blob of greedy shit, and spit in his face. They taught you to turn your back on your friends, on everybody, everybody except *them*. Hate is what they taught you, Jeff. Hate, not love.

"You love Jesus? Well, Jesus preached love. Nothing but love. But he preached love for *everybody*, rich or poor, halt, sick or lame, black or white, *everybody*, family, friends, strangers, all humanity. Love of all humanity. That's what the Catholics teach, and the Protestants and the Jews, and any other good religion worthy of the name, whether it's Christian or not. Now, Jeff, you don't know a hell of a lot about the Bible. But when it comes to your parents, it teaches love, not hate. You ever hear of the Ten Commandments?"

Jeff was silent, his face sullen, and Morse continued, "All right. You know what's in it. Honor your father and mother. What does that mean? Love or hate? You know what you did, Jeff? You spit in your father's face, you called your mother a whore. Like to hear what the Bible says about that? I quote you Exodus 21. 'He that smiteth his father, or his mother, shall be surely put to death.' That's Verse 15. Or let's try Verse 17. 'And he that curseth his father, or his mother, shall

236

surely be put to death.' The Elders didn't teach you Exodus 21, did they, Jeff? Did they? *Did* they?"

John Morse stayed with Jeff Reed for ten straight hours. During that time, he talked incessantly. He could see Jeff slowly begin to wilt, but the boy was stubborn, he hung on, he blocked his ears, he would not listen or believe. Morse knew that he was making inroads, he could tell by certain telltale reactions on the part of Jeff. But it would take some time before he really got through.

When Morse left, Reed came in to relieve him. His son sat crumpled on the mattress, soaked in perspiration. His thin face was drawn in exhaustion.

"Go away," he said. "I want to go to sleep."

"Not quite yet, son. We're going to talk awhile."

"You son-of-a-bitch," yelled Jeff. "You just want to keep me awake. You just want to tire me out. I know all about what you're trying to do. Now, get out of here and let me sleep."

"I'm going to stay awhile," said his father quietly.

"Get out, you bastard! You dirty shithead, you scum of Satan, get out!"

Jeff's eyes were blazing wildly. He ran at his father, seized him in a bear hug, tried to fling him against the wall. Frank Reed was strong and fresh. They grappled for a moment. Then Reed broke his son's hold, and flung him back onto the mattress. Jeff lay back, and started to weep.

"Go ahead," he said. "Go ahead and talk. My soul belongs to Jesus, and you can't take it away from me, no matter how long you stay, how much you talk."

"We're not trying to take your soul from anybody," said his father, quietly. "We're just trying to give you back your mind. Don't you understand, Jeff? Your mother and I, we both love you."

"Come on, Big Daddy," Jeff sneered. "Still handing out the old bullshit, right? The way you've been handing it out all your life. All you *love* is yourself, and your money, and the big house, and the yacht club, and all those fatass friends of yours you play golf with at the club. You don't know what love is, Big Daddy. And neither does Big Mommy. So why don't you just fuck off, and go downstairs, and let me get a little sleep. Okay?"

25

After Jeff's father had finished, his mother took over. Then his brother. Then Joe Peterson. Each stayed with him for a couple of hours. Then John Morse, who had slept for a while, took over again.

He continued to hammer at Jeff with the same theme. The Master is a phony. He's one of the biggest ripoffs of all time. And his young Neophytes are out on the streets, working ten hours a day to give the Master his yacht, his women, his four-hundred-dollar suits, and all the rest.

"You know what old Buford likes to do, Jeff? He likes to travel. He's hardly ever in the United States. He's usually cruising the Bahamas, living it up with one or more of his ladies. About four times a year, he flies to Switzerland. Not because he likes to look at the mountains, Jeff. Not because he likes to ski, or buy cuckoo clocks or watches. It's because he's got numbered bank accounts in Switzerland. And they hold millions.

"And what happens to you and the other poor Souls for Jesus? Why, you sleep on hard mattresses, just like you're doing here. You eat oatmeal mush and other crap three times a day. You stand out in the hot sun or the rain and sell the *Sayings of the Master.*"

Morse took out one of the booklets. "You know how much each of these costs to make? A quarter. You sell them for two dollars. Pretty good profit, right? And all in old Buford's pocket. And for this, you lie to people. You tell them the money's for orphanages, old people's homes. You want to know something, Jeff? There aren't any SFJ old people's homes. There aren't any SFJ orphanages. That's just a snow job to make you work harder, to squeeze people out of their hard-earned money. That pious, hypocritical son-of-a-bitch you call the Master lied to you. And you lie to the people."

Jeff sat huddled on the bed. He professed not to listen seriously to what Morse was saying. Instead he raised his eyes upward: "'O, thou deceitful tongue. Deliver my soul, O Lord, from lying lips, and from a deceitful tongue.'"

"A nice little quote from Psalms, Jeff. Now, if you want to play Bible games again, let's play them. We've got hours, and days, weeks to play them. How about this? A little something to fit old Buford, and his twenty- or thirty-million-dollar rip-off of stupid young suckers like you. This one's from Matthew. Chapter 7, Verse 15. 'Beware of false prophets, which come to you in sheep's clothing, but inwardly they are ravening wolves.' Doesn't *that* say something about your big phony leader?"

"Damn you, you keep lying to me."

"Do I?"

"The Master is a true prophet."

"The Master is a fat cat, and a con man."

"All he preaches is love."

"Like loving your parents. And your brother. Right? This makes you a hypocrite, Jeff. You'll find it in the First Letter of John. 'If a man say, I love God, and hateth his brother, he is a liar.'"

Keep at him, thought Morse, keep hammering at him. The same themes over and over, repeat and double repeat until they begin to sink in ...

"You're talking about my earthly family. They don't exist any more for me. It's right there in Proverbs. 'He that loveth father or mother more than me is not worthy of me.'"

"Jeff, you don't know your ass from your elbow when it comes to the Bible. Neither do these creeps up at Ashtaroth."

"What?"

"Those words you just gave me aren't in Proverbs. They happen to be in Matthew. If you'd like a little wisdom from Proverbs, why, be my guest. In Proverbs it says differently. 'Who curseth his father or his mother, his lamp shall be put out in obscure darkness.' Proverbs 20, Verse 20. 'Hearken unto thy father that begat thee, and despise not thy mother when she is old.' Proverbs 23, Verse 22. Or let's try *this* one on for size, stupid. Proverbs again: 'He that wasteth his father, and chaseth away his mother, is a son that causeth shame, and bringeth reproach.' Maybe you'll remember that one when you think back to the time you had your mother kicked out of Ashtaroth."

All this, Morse knew from his experience, was par during the deprogramming process. The boy or girl had been taught to protect himself or herself against the wiles of Satan by constantly thinking of the Bible, and quoting it. Repulse Satan, and he would flee from you. They did this to defend their senses, to insulate themselves from the blandishments of Satan, the voice coming at them, hour after hour, trying to unsettle them, confuse them, persuade them, tempt them. But they were always upset by the fact that the man the Elders told them was Satan knew the Bible better than they did. Better, indeed, than the Elders who had taught them. And it always shook them up; they became aware that there was some crack in their armor, that Satan knew of this Achilles heel and would keep on exploiting it.

"Had enough, Jeff? Or shall we keep on playing Bible, Bible, who's got the Bible?"

Jeff lapsed into sullen silence. He decided not to pay any attention to Morse, to shut off his mind. He tried to let Morse's voice simply drift into one ear, and out of the other. He

241

thought of other things, a thousand other things. How nice it would be back at Ashtaroth, with his brothers, his friends. How nice it would be to be back on the streets, serving the Lord. How nice it would be not to have to think, to make decisions, but just to go on loving Jesus and each other.

But the words came at him, hour after hour. The Devil sat in the chair, and looked at him, and simply went on talking. He felt more and more tired. The talk was like a waterfall, words came tumbling out, they simply never stopped. Jeff felt hot, tired, uncomfortable. He stank from his own perspiration. He needed a bath. They wouldn't even let him take a bath. He was tired, so tired now. He needed Jesus. He had to talk to Jesus.

Suddenly, he felt the Holy Spirit within him. Jesus had come into him, to give him strength. God was speaking to him now. He could hear all the words. They started to come out of his mouth. He felt removed now, he didn't even know Satan was there. God began to speak to him, giving him strength to resist the Devil. Jeff rose from the mattress. He did a little dance. He closed his eyes, he felt wonderful, exalted. He raised his arms. He felt light, free, drifting, almost as though he could float. He could hear the Lord speaking to him now, he could feel his own mouth moving, as he poured out the sacred words:

> Corda, semo, bora, bosa,
> Dano, taka, ogla du
> Fana, fano, dia, dena,
> O, nantao, muta, drona, du.

The words pouring out of his mouth were strange to him. But in his trance, he understood them perfectly. He understood what Jesus was saying to him. *Watch ye, stand fast in the faith, be strong, resist Satan and he will flee. I am Jesus, and Jesus loves thee, Simeon . . .*

It was marvelous. He was sure Satan had fled. He had vanished in a flash. He was no longer there to tempt him, to

242

tease him, to torment him. Finally, the words faded. God had finished talking to him. He came out of his trance, trembling, feeling exalted, blessed, released. He opened his eyes.

Then he saw that the Devil was still there.

Worse than that. The Devil was smiling. He seemed to think all this was a big joke.

"Marvelous," said the Devil. "This speaking in tongues. It's very relaxing. I use it myself, once in a while."

Then the Devil got to his feet and closed his eyes. He raised his arms to heaven. He did a little dance. Jeff noted with horror that it was the same sanctified dance the Elders had done at Ashtaroth when *they* spoke in tongues. Then the words began to babble from the Devil's mouth:

> Baca, munto, zoonta, lat,
> Gosta, mida, mista, mas,
> Staro, setto, domin, du,
> Pator, maso, seka, voo.
> Paka, pako, tromo, toom,
> Romo, toom, cabra, droon,
> O, vio, vio, labo, tu
> Masa, meda, homa, dru.

Finally, the Devil finished. He opened his eyes, and stretched his arms. Then he grinned at Jeff.

"Very relaxing," he said. "Very. I'd recommend it to anybody. It's great therapy."

Jeff was staring at him in shock.

"You're lying," he said. "You didn't speak God's words at all. You just made them up. You were just putting me on."

"That's just the point, Jeff," said Morse. "Almost anybody can speak in tongues of some kind, if they can get themselves worked into a trance. Even me, the bad old Devil. Now, I'm not really knocking it. A lot of people in some of the Protestant churches do it, and are spiritually inspired by it. That's okay with me. But you just said it yourself. It can also be a big put-on. That's the way the boys who run the SFJ communes, the Elders, use it. As one big put-on, to impress their Neophytes."

"That's a lie," said Jeff. "It's a religious experience."

Morse shrugged. "To some people, yes. To the creeps at the top of the SFJ, it's just another gimmick. And it's time you understood it. Like to hear something choice?"

Jeff didn't answer. He simply glared at Morse. Morse grinned and took a small tape recorder from his black bag. He inserted a cassette, and turned on the recorder. A voice came on. It was shrill, hysterical, it sounded insane, mad. It was speaking in tongues. The words were weird, strang sounding, a gabble run together.

"Recognize it?" Jeff said nothing. Morse grinned. "You should. It's your Master's voice."

The strange words continued to pour forth from the mouth of the Reverend Hodges. They rose and fell, rose and fell, in an eerie, almost chilling cadence. Morse had turned the sound up loud. The babble and gabble of the strange, meaningless words continued to flow, the voice of the Master sounded obscene. It was harsh, unpleasant, the whole performance sounded like that of some demented maniac.

Jeff listened. He looked shocked.

"Turn it off."

"You don't mean that."

"Turn it off."

"That's blasphemy," said Morse. "You're listening to your Master and God, talking to each other. You wouldn't want me to turn off a conversation like that, would you?"

He turned the recorder up to maximum loudness. The obscene voice assaulted the eardrums. Morse had used this tape before. It had been spliced together from two or three tapes bootlegged from one of the SFJ communes. He himself had gotten used to it, having heard it so often. But to the boy or girl he was deprogramming, hearing it like this, naked, exaggerated and unmodulated, it came as a shock.

"I've heard the Master before," shouted Jeff. "You can turn it off now."

"Oh," said Morse, settling in the chair. "Let's just listen

awhile. We've got an hour and a half of tape here, and of course, we can play it over and over again. It's very interesting. I mean, I just keep wondering what he's saying to God, and what God is saying to him. I really can't figure it out. But since you're a Soul for Jesus, and so much closer to Him than I am—maybe *you* can."

"You bastard," said Jeff. "Oh, you dirty bastard. This is just one of your filthy tricks . . ."

"Why, Jeff. I thought *you'd* enjoy this, appreciate it. This is your Master's voice, remember? In a dialogue with the Almighty. And *you* want me to turn it off. Now, I call *that* sacrilege."

Jeff half rose. He was wild-eyed. He looked as though he was getting ready to jump up and make a grab for the tape recorder. But he saw that Morse was alert, and was blocking the tape recorder on the table with his body. He knew it was no use. He lay back, and stared up at the ceiling. The voice of the Master shrieked through the room, the weird words smashed against his eardrums. He felt as though his head would burst. He really began to hate the Master's voice. He grabbed the pillow, turned over onto his face, and covered his face and ears with the pillow.

But even the pillow wasn't nearly enough to obliterate that constant, maddening yammering. He writhed at its impact, he banged one fist on the wall in frustration, held the pillow over his head and ears with the other hand.

Finally, he sat up, grabbed the pillow and flung it at Morse.

"Turn it off, damn you," screamed Jeff. "That's enough." Then he moaned. "Please, please . . . !"

"All right, Jeff." Morse turned off the recorder. He didn't want to overdo this particular procedure at the moment. You had to know when to put on the pressure, and when to take it off. There were parameters within which you could reasonably work to get results. There was also such a thing as over-kill. Your subject would break down, confess to anything in order to get relief. But this would be a false brainwash, not a true one.

Morse had been fooled once or twice that way, and he

didn't propose to go over the edge this time. Each kid was different. You had to play each like a fish. Tighten the line, let him run a little, then pull him back again. But you could always use the threat of further punishment. Threat was one of the most potent weapons in the deprogramming arsenal. Jeff Reed wouldn't forget the effect of those decibels quickly. Already, Morse knew, he had created an unpleasant association in Jeff Reed's mind regarding his hero, the Master. And he, Morse, would not hesitate to exploit it later.

"We can hear more of your Master's voice later," he said to Jeff. "I mean, how many times do you really hear God and His Messenger talking to each other, with your own ears? You don't seem to appreciate that, Jeff."

"My name is Simeon," said Jeff, wearily.

"Your name is shit right now," said Morse. "Because you're getting no place, and you're going nowhere. You're going to sit in this room, and we're going to talk, and you're going to think about what we talk about. You're going to sit here with me, as I told you, if it takes days, or weeks or months. I couldn't care less. I've got all the time in the world. We're going to talk, Jeff, and it won't be in tongues, because you're going to understand everything I say. And until you understand what they did to your mind, and screw on your head where it belongs again, we're just going to sit here and—"

"Yeah," said Jeff. "Yeah, yeah, I know. But I'm tired. I want to sleep. And I'm starving. I've gotta get some sleep. And I don't want to talk. That's all we've been doing. Talk, talk, talk."

"I know," said Morse, quietly. "Now let's talk some more."

"Fuck you," said Jeff. "*You* can talk if you want to. I won't even listen. Not if you keep me here forever!"

He stared defiantly at Morse. But his aggressor seemed unruffled. He lit a cigarette, leaned back in his chair, took a long swig from a can of beer, which Jeff eyed thirstily. It was the second can of cold beer he had drunk in the hot, airless room, and he had offered none to Jeff. He studied Jeff for a moment, and then said, "You know, you may be right about one thing."

"What's that?"

"We may *have* to stay here forever."

Hour after hour, Morse kept after Jeff relentlessly, taking only short rest periods. In between, he was spelled briefly by the others.

Jeff had been allowed very little sleep, only an hour or two at long intervals. He was given just a little to eat, a bowl of oatmeal mush, soaked in skim milk; a small plate of boiled vegetables. Just the kind of food he had been served at Ashtaroth. Just enough to keep him going, yet keep him hungry. He was not allowed to bathe, nor even change his clothes.

Once, Jeff tried giving Morse the silent treatment. He stared straight ahead, hands on his knees, back rigid, lips tight, his face a set mask. He had put himself into a state of altered consciousness, a self-imposed daze or stupor. Morse knew, from long experience, that in this situation any words he spoke would fall on barren ground, they would literally not even be heard, much less understood. But he had been given the silent treatment, and he knew exactly what to do.

He took out the tape recorder, played the Master speaking in tongues again, and turned the volume up loud. After five minutes of this, Jeff Reed suddenly woke up, and screamed to Morse to turn it off.

Once, while he had been busy working on Jeff, Cindy had come in to bring a tray of food to Morse. As she had opened the door, Jeff made a sudden break for it. He had knocked her to one side and rushed downstairs. There was no way he could dive through a window, since they were all boarded. He headed for the door leading to the outside. But before he could make it, his father and brother had caught him, wrestled him back. He had fought like a wildcat, knocking over chairs and smashing lamps. Joe Peterson, who had been sleeping, joined them, and the three of them half pushed, half carried Jeff up the stairs, pushed him into the room, and locked the door behind him.

Morse had never even left the room. He was sitting there calmly, waiting for Jeff to return. When Jeff flung himself on the mattress, Morse turned to the lunch Cindy had brought him. It was a steak, medium rare, with french-fried potatoes, and coffee. It looked delicious, it smelled delicious, and from the look on Morse's face, it *was* delicious.

Jeff watched Morse hungrily. The smell of the steak began to get to him. The french fries made him salivate. He stared at the food, fascinated. Morse knew what Jeff was thinking, and commiserated with him: "Too bad you're a vegetarian, Jeff. Otherwise, we'd have your mother cook you a steak like this. But then, as a good and true Soul for Jesus, you'd be committing a mortal sin. And we wouldn't want that to happen, would we?"

John Morse slipped off his clothes, and crawled between the sheets, in the downstairs bedroom he had assigned to himself. Frank and Kate Reed had another, and Cindy occupied the last bedroom. Joe and Ken bedded down in sleeping bags in the living room.

At the moment, Cindy was upstairs on watch with Jeff, who was now asleep. The subject was never left alone in the room for a moment. There was always the possibility of a suicide attempt, and Morse was taking no chances

He looked at his watch, as he crawled between the sheets. It had been just thirty-eight hours since he had started to deprogram Jeff.

He had to admit Jeff was stubborn. Tougher than most. He began to worry a little about breaking him at all. Once in a great while, you lost one. You ran into some kid who was a brick wall, some boy or girl too far gone ever to bring back. It was rare, but it happened. There was nothing you could tell the distraught parents then, except that you had failed. After that, the boy or girl was returned to the cult, a permanent reject from real life. And that was the end.

Mind control. It was a strange and frightening thing. It could be used for good or for evil. Hitler used it in a mass way, with his propaganda and speeches. He could hypnotize crowds. But it could be used in a positive way, too.

Once again John Morse speculated, as he had so many

times, as to what might have happened if a good deprogrammer had had a chance to get at Squeaky Fromme and Susan Atkins and the rest of Charles Manson's followers, or a Patty Hearst, when she had been first terrified, then intimidated and finally brainwashed by the S.L.A. The results might have been different, all around . . .

He was just drifting off to sleep when the phone rang. It was George Glennon, calling from Santa Cruz.

"How are you doing with this Reed kid?"

"I don't know. I never know till it happens. How are you doing with the book?"

"Finished. Just cutting and editing and inserting little pieces here and there."

"Like it?"

"I do, I do. But that isn't the question. Will my publishers like it? Enough to find the guts to print it, I mean. Incidentally, you *are* coming up to Santa Cruz, aren't you?"

"Right after this job. I'm pretty tired, George. I need to rest a little."

"Well, after what you've been doing, no wonder. We've got a big spare room, an unlimited supply of booze, and, as you know, Ellie's a great cook. And if you happen to feel a little carnal, there are a lot of unattached ladies in the area, all devoted to Women's Lib, and just dying to assert their sexual rights and independence."

"I can't wait."

"Oh, John." Suddenly, Glennon sounded worried. "One more thing."

"Yes?"

"Something's stirring in the top echelon of the SFJ. There's a story going around that our friend, Buford Hodges, is going to make a big move. And it concerns you. The story is that he's finally figured out a way to dig you out of your hole, skin you alive, and hang you up to dry."

"He's always trying to do that."

"No. This time, according to my underground, he's going for the jugular. Nobody really knows what the hell he's up to, but there it is. So be on guard, friend. Okay?"

"Okay."

"See you in a couple of days, then. Ellie sends her love."

Jeff Reed lay stretched out on the mattress. His eyes were closed, but he could not sleep. He was aware that Cindy was sitting in the chair, at the opposite end of the room, reading a paperback.

He thought of the Devil, who called himself John Morse, and who had talked to him, and talked to him, and talked to him, and never seemed to tire, and never seemed to stop.

This was the monster they had told him about, over and over again, at Ashtaroth. Henoch, the Elder in charge of Purification, Prayer and Penitence, had lectured them, again and again, about how devious Satan could be, how shrewd and clever, how he could appear in any disguise, he could be man, woman, or even a voice inside of you. But the Devil, Henoch had said, when trying to steal a Soul for Jesus, always took the shape and guise of this man who was trying to drive him crazy now.

Henoch had been right about the ways he said the Devil worked, how he lied and tried to seduce you with soft words, and then abuse you. He would tempt you with lust, he would tell you how much your earth-parents loved and missed you, and bring them face to face with you so they could tell you their own lies about loving you. Henoch had said they would keep you awake almost all the time, and starve you, to break you and finally make you give in, and he had been right in that. Henoch had even said that once you finally yielded up your soul to him, to the Devil, he would not hesitate to torture you and kill you and take you to hell with him and throw you in the fire so you would burn in eternal flame.

Yet, Jeff was confused.

His mind spun around and around. This man they called the Devil knew more about the Bible than he did. More than even Henoch knew. But the Bible was God's book. The Devil would burn God's book, not read it. And then all those questions this man Morse asked him. He had made him, Jeff, look foolish. They were questions he couldn't answer. Especially about the Master. I mean, all those pictures he had shown. The yacht, the girls, the rest of it. They could have been faked. But in his heart, Jeff knew they were real. What *did* the Master do with all the money they collected? *I mean, what did he really do?* He didn't want to doubt the Master. The Master was head of the Church, the Messenger of God, the purest Soul for Jesus. My God, he thought, *I'd better be careful. Careful, Simeon, careful.* The Devil has made me doubt the Master.

Already, he had sinned, in his mind. He *wanted* to have some of that steak the Devil ate in front of him. He drooled for it. *Thou shalt not eat of the flesh of animals,* they told him at Ashtaroth, *for they, too, are living creatures created by God.*

Yet, the sight of the steak evoked dim memories from somewhere far back in his mind. Memories of sizzling meat, of hamburgers, and roast beef, and fried chicken, and chili, and barbecued meat and hot dogs roasted over beach fires. And there were other things he began to remember dimly.

Cindy.

When she sat in the chair and talked to him, and he looked at her legs and her tits and the swell of her hips, he remembered caressing them all; he fought to erase these memories, since they were sinful, but no matter what his head said, his prick said something else. It would not listen, but it stood straight up, as it was doing now, just thinking about her. His earth-mother had cried when she had come in to sit with him, and his father had tears in his eyes—and he had laughed at them, because he hated them, they were so much shit—yet, way way back, deep in his mind, he had felt something, something had quivered and stirred, and he had hated himself for it, and told himself again that he was Simeon and a true Soul for Jesus, and to turn off this earth-parent hangup.

His mind continued to reel, words popped in and out of his head like flashing neon signs, the Master, Souls for Jesus, Ashtaroth, Henoch and Hezekiah, Old Testament and New, Matthew and Moses, Luke and John, the Books of Job and

251

Joel, Proverbs and Revelation, Judges, and Kings, Purification and Penance, and Thank you, Lord, and *Jesus loves you, Simeon.*

He was confused, and he was tired and hungry and miserable, and he wanted a bath, and he couldn't stop thinking of Athaliah.

He cocked an eye open, and saw her reading the paperback, and her smooth, young lovely legs were spread a little, so from his position on the mattress, he could see partly upward, almost upward into the crotch, and he formed a picture of it in his mind now, the softly silky hair, the warm, dark and wonderful place, the way it felt when he slid it in, and then began to thrust, slowly at first, then faster and faster, harder then harder . . .

He wanted to go to her, and yank her onto the mattress, and tear off all her clothes and fuck her till she screamed in ecstasy, but he knew if he did that, she would scream, but it would be in a different way, and the others would come running up. Besides, he was still a Neophyte, and not yet a Deacon, and he was forbidden to take a woman, especially during Purification.

He wanted to get up and go into the bathroom and stand over the toilet bowl and masturbate, but there was no lock on the bathroom door, and whenever he went to the john they all kept the door open and watched him to see that he did nothing to hurt himself, and that was terribly humiliating and embarrassing. And so there was nothing he could do, since Cindy was sitting right there. And anyway, he wouldn't give her the satisfaction.

Finally, he fell asleep.

A moment later, or so it seemed, someone was shaking him, waking him up.

He opened his eyes to look into the face of the Devil again.

26

Jeff Reed was sleeping in his shorts. As Morse shook him awake, he glanced into the boy's closet.

The slacks were no longer folded neatly on the crossbar of the coathanger. They hung loosely from one of the hooks. And the jacket itself lay on the floor in a crumpled heap. Morse found this interesting.

His subject sat up and looked at him blearily: "Lemme sleep."

"Not now, Jeff."

"Got to sleep," mumbled Jeff.

He tried to lie down, but Morse yanked him upright.

"We've got to talk some more."

"Don't want to talk. Can't."

"All right, Jeff. Then we'll listen to some other people talk for a while."

He took out the tape recorder again, and inserted a cassette. The voice of a young girl came on:

"My name is Betty Lorimer. But as a Soul for Jesus I was called Haggith, named after the fifth wife of David. I was a

Neophyte at a commune called Shunem. That's near Louisville, Kentucky. You know, after they robbed me of my mind, about which I'll go into more later, I became a kind of Thing. I mean, a body. I washed and cleaned, and mopped the floors, and worked on a God Squad for a while. But then I guess I caught the eye of our First Elder, Ashur. I mean, he became real horny for me. I mean, I'm nineteen, and he was about sixty, but that didn't make any difference.

"He sent for me, and I slept with him, and then when he got through, he turned me over to Zebul, who was our Elder in charge of Witnessing and Recruiting, and I slept with him for a while. They all said it was all right, it was moral, because it was in the Bible, you know? Men had many wives and concubines and whatever, so that made it all right. The way all us girls looked at it, it was a real honor, you got closer to Jesus that way, because the Elders were very close. But the real honor was to be taken by the Master himself. I mean, nobody from our commune had ever been taken by the Master, but we'd heard about it.

"Anyway, I got pregnant, and I wanted to have the baby, but they said no. So they got this doctor in from the outside, and he performed an abortion, and I lost my baby. They have these people on the outside, you know, lots of them, doctors and lawyers and business people and so on who are members of the cult, and whenever they need somebody, they call him in . . .

"But that's all over now. Thank God, my father and some of his friends got me out of there, and thank God for Mr. Morse, he talked to me and talked to me, until I got my mind back, and everything back there now is a dirty dream, a nightmare, I mean a real bad trip, *real* bad . . ."

Morse put on another tape of another deprogrammed Soul for Jesus. And another. And another. He watched Jeff's face as he did so. He knew Jeff was trying not to listen. His lips were mumbling prayers, snatches from the Bible, as he tried to distract himself from listening. But Morse knew the words of the boys and girls on tape were getting through. He saw it in the subtle shifting of the eyes, in the occasional tremble of

Jeff's lips, in the way he clenched and unclenched his hands.

He continued to play tapes for three hours. Each voice came from a different deprogrammed boy or girl, each was a unique story but each had a repetitious core.

"My name is Bernstein. Michael Bernstein. I was brought up by good Jewish parents. I guess you'd call them the permissive type. They loved me more than anything on this earth, but I was too stupid at the time to understand it. I thought the world was a crock, with all its values screwed up, everybody in it for himself, greed, you know, that kind of thing. So I was a real pushover for the Souls for Jesus. Man, was it incredible! I got to be a crazy, and didn't know it. I was in a commune called Bethsaida, which is just outside of Pittsburgh. But now that I've got my head back, I always think of it as Zombieville, U.S.A. . . ."

After that, Morse kept hammering at Jeff. His head was gone. There was a chance to get it back, and put it on straight ahead. The way these other kids had. He, Jeff, had heard the tapes. He had heard what they had all said, he knew the way they felt. He had the same chance to come back as they did. Once again, they were thinking for themselves. If he would only listen, let go . . .

Some of the kids simply hadn't been able to take it, Morse told Jeff. They had gone mad, their minds had cracked. He reached into his black bag again, pulled out a folder. He showed Jeff a series of horror stories. One SFJ Neophyte on a God Squad had gone mad, running around berserk, hitting out at everything near him, smashing the faces of his Deacons. Then he had run out in front of an oncoming truck, and had been crushed under its wheels. He showed Jeff a story of another SFJ member, who had jumped a wall of his commune during the night, gone crazy, broken into a house and murdered a mother and three children with an axe, and was now in an institution for the hopelessly insane.

Then he took out two grisly photographs. One was of a body wrapped and tied in a body bag, being taken out from the entrance of a commune. The sign on the commune said "Megiddo." The body was being carried out by the police.

"This one cut his wrists, and bled to death," said Morse. "He thought that Jesus had abandoned him, and didn't love him anymore."

Then he showed Jeff another photo. He held it with steady hands, in front of Jeff's eyes. It was a photo of a winter scene. There was deep snow all about, and in the center of this a tree. A body hung from one of its naked branches. It was the body of a young girl. Her shapeless gray monk's robe had flapped open in the wintry wind, to reveal her pathetic, thin and naked body. Her monk's hood had been pulled halfway down her face, her head hung grotesquely to one side. Around her broken neck was the green braided rope, the belt of the Neophyte, which she had used to hang herself.

"This one couldn't take it either," said Morse, evenly. "They called her Reumah, after the concubine of Abraham's brother, Nahor. Not that anybody really gives a damn, Jeff. But Reumah happens to be the first concubine recorded in the Bible and so designated."

He put the pictures away. Now, he started to talk to Jeff about his parents again.

"Your father and mother are downstairs, Jeff. They're waiting to take you in their arms. They love you. They had dreams for you, ambitions. They're downstairs now, and I can't tell you how many times your mother has wept for you. And your brother, Ken. Your brother loves you, too. He'd do anything for you. And Joe Peterson. Did you ever have a better friend? Someone you could talk to, confide in?

"And Cindy. Cindy loves you, Jeff. She got out of Ashtaroth by herself, and she knows what went on in there, and you don't have to hear *her* voice on tape, because she was with you. You're lucky to know her. You're damned lucky that she cares enough about you, enough to come out here with us, and go through all this, while you just sit there like some zombie and tell yourself what they told you to think. Hate, Jeff. That's what they told you to think. Hate, hate, hate. But if you want love, it's there. If you need love, it's there. It's waiting for you downstairs. And I'm going to keep talking to you, Jeff, I'm going to sit here for weeks and months and forever, until I make you understand . . ."

Suddenly, Jeff began to cry. Huge sobs racked his body. Tears ran from his eyes. His body shivered and shook as he sobbed. He covered his face with his hands.

"Ohgodohgodohgod," he cried. "Where have I been, where have I been? What have I done?"

Morse watched the boy carefully. He had seen false breaks before, and had the experience to identify them, whenever they happened. But he knew this one was true.

Jeff Reed was out of it. He had become himself again.

Almost automatically, Morse looked at his watch, and calculated the time. This particular deprogramming had taken forty-four hours and ten minutes. Almost two days.

Not bad, he thought. Not bad at all.

He knocked on the door. Joe Peterson opened it, and Morse called everybody into the room.

He watched as Jeff walked to his mother, put his arms around her, sobbing her name, crying that he was sorry, sorry, sorry. He embraced his father, Ken, Joe and Cindy. All of them were openly crying, unashamed.

"I love you," Jeff was saying over and over again. "I love you all, Dad and Mom and Ken and Joe and Cindy—my God, what have I done to you? I love you all."

John Morse watched this tearful reunion for a moment. His face showed no particular emotion. All this was an old story. He had seen it many times. But still, in his special way, he was quietly pleased.

That's another one you've lost, Buford.

Then, while the happy reunion was going on, he went downstairs to make a phone call.

The job wasn't over. Not yet. There was still one more hurdle to jump.

Afterward, Jeff Reed showered and changed into some fresh clothes his mother had brought—a white crew-necked sweater he had always liked, a pair of faded blue jeans.

Meanwhile, the men ripped the boards off the windows, opened them to fill the house with fresh air and sunlight, and replaced the lock on the bathroom door. Kate Reed, with Cindy's help, prepared an early dinner.

Finally, Jeff came down, carrying his SFJ jacket and slacks. He smiled at them as he stuffed them in the large garbage can on the porch just outside the kitchen. It was a ceremonial little gesture, and it was obvious that he enjoyed it hugely. It was remarkable how he seemed to change, wearing his normal clothes. His whole body seemed to have magically filled out, gained a few pounds, there was new color in his face, his eyes sparkled, and he radiated a new zest for living.

They had steak and French fries, a huge salad, and apple pie with ice cream. Jeff ate ravenously, as though trying to replace all at once the twenty pounds he had lost.

This was the old Jeff Reed, the boy they had known before he had gone to Ashtaroth. He seemed to have no memory of Ashtaroth, or if he did, he never mentioned it. He laughed and reminisced, and asked a hundred questions about what had happened in his absence. They had had no radio, no newspapers, and no television at the commune. At least not for the Neophytes. It was as though he had gone on a vacation to some distant place, and had just returned. Or as though he had been, for a time, a resident on some far planet.

But it was a gay dinner, a joyful family reunion, and everything was a laugh, and a joke, and Jeff talked mostly of what he would do when he got back home, to Hope Ranch, the hundred and one things he would do, the surfing, and catching up with his friends, and making application to get into college at the beginning of the midyear term. But he had been a long time without any real sleep, and finally he dozed off over the dessert.

Instead of leaving the house immediately, they decided to spend the night there, so that Jeff, exhausted both physically and spiritually, could catch up on his sleep. This even though they hated the house, had spent so many anxious hours inside of it, and never wanted to see it again.

After Jeff had gone to bed, the others expressed their

heartfelt gratitude to John Morse. But he cautioned them that it was not over yet, as far as Jeff was concerned. He still had some distance to go before he was fully deprogrammed.

"To begin with," Morse explained, "he can't go home with you tomorrow. Not right away. That would be a bad mistake."

"I don't understand," said Kate Reed. "Hope Ranch is his home. He'd be happy there. We'd all be together . . ."

"I know how you feel. But there are a couple of reasons why you'll have to get along without him a little longer. In the first place, it's possible some people from the cult will be watching Hope Ranch. At least for a couple of weeks. They may try to snatch Jeff back, bring him to another commune, and then reprogram him back to where he was. Right now, and for the next two or three weeks, he'll still be vulnerable, and they'll still be able to brainwash him again, if they can lay hands on him. They've done this successfully a couple of times, and there's no reason to believe they wouldn't try it again."

Frank Reed stared at Morse.

"But I thought he was out of the woods. I mean, totally."

Morse shook his head. "Not quite yet. Don't forget, he's just come out of a long nightmare. He's just walked into what, to him, is a whole bewildering world. He's still open to the possibility of psychological reflex. For the first couple of weeks, there's always the danger that Jeff might 'drift.' That is to say, regress, or backslide. Go back to being Simeon. It's been so long since he's had a chance to think for himself, he isn't going to find it easy to accept his own, real identity."

"My God," said Kate. "You're beginning to scare me."

"I didn't mean to. I think Jeff is going to be fine. But it takes a while to make the total transition from a trance-induced zombie to a thinking person. So, the next two or three weeks are critical. Once he gets through those, and there's absolutely no reason why he shouldn't, they'll never be able to get at him again, no matter what they do. He'll be completely out of their reach. The important thing now is to send him on a kind of vacation, away from everything familiar, even his own home. Give him a chance to relax, have some fun, unwind. Get to know himself. Be with somebody he likes . . ."

"Somebody like me?" asked Cindy.

"Somebody like you," smiled Morse.

"Then I've got just the place."

"Yes?"

"Palm Desert. It's near the Springs. My Uncle James and my Aunt Sarah Hyland have a place there. They're retired. They've got a big house, with a swimming pool, and this smaller guest house back of the pool, you know, set away from the main house and really private, and I'm sure they'd love us to stay there . . ."

"Sounds fine," said Morse. "If you can manage it."

"Don't worry," said Cindy. "My aunt and uncle are just crazy about me. Consider it done." She looked at the Reeds. "That is, if it's all right with you."

"Sounds good to me," said Frank Reed.

Kate looked anxiously at Morse.

"Would we—would we be allowed to visit him?"

"I'd wait a week. After that, why not? It'd be good for him. Figure he'll need three weeks out there, a month would be even better." He turned to Cindy. "Now, Cindy, a few instructions. They're important, so listen closely."

"Yes?"

"The thing to do is keep Jeff busy. You know, physically active, occupied at all times, so busy he doesn't have time to think. He'll need good food to get his strength back, and lots of sleep. Another thing. He should see people of his own age, as much as possible."

"I'll take care of that," said Cindy. "I know a lot of kids out there. Real desert rat types."

"Another thing. Keep him away from the Bible. I mean, if there are any Bibles around, in bookcases or anywhere else, hide them. Okay?"

"Okay."

"Do your uncle and aunt go to church every Sunday?"

"Why, yeah. I guess they do. Once in a while, anyway."

"Then will you ask them to skip it? Just for a couple of Sundays, as long as Jeff is around. I don't want anything to remind him of church, or religion. I know this may be an imposition on your uncle and aunt, but if you explained the situation to them . . ."

"They're marvelous people," said Cindy. "And as I said, they're just crazy about me. They'll go along."

"Another thing. Keep him away from the telephone so that he won't be tempted to call the cult in a weak moment. If there's a phone in the guest house, ask your uncle to disconnect it for a few weeks."

"You really think something like that could happen?" asked Reed, incredulously.

"It *has* happened," said Morse, grimly. "I lost one girl back to the cult that way. It isn't likely to happen with Jeff, especially with Cindy around, but it's best not to take any chances."

Kate Reed looked distressed. "You make him sound like a—well, like a reformed alcoholic."

"In a way, he is. Except his hangup is memory, not alcohol. But once he's home, he'll be home for good." He turned back to Cindy. "One more thing."

"Yes?"

"Most important of all, don't leave him alone. Not for a second. And don't let him talk about the SFJ, or his experiences at Ashtaroth. If he tries to, change the subject. Get his mind off it. Make him think of something else. Okay?"

"Okay, I'll try."

"That's important, Cindy. Try hard. Don't even let him discuss it with friends. Just change the subject. Otherwise, God bless you, and good luck."

Cindy looked at Morse for a moment. Then, impulsively, she went to him and kissed him on the cheek.

"You know what, Mr. Morse?"

"What?"

"You're sweet. And thanks. Thank you so much. For Jeff."

"He's a nice kid," said Morse. "Take care of him."

He told them that he would not stay the night, but was leaving immediately. His job was done, and the rest was up to them. He would stay in Los Angeles overnight, and then would drive north the next day to visit George Glennon in Santa Cruz. He was very tired, he needed a rest, and after that, there was a lot more for him to do.

"You know something," Cindy said to him. "Here we've all been together in this house for a couple of days now, and we don't know a thing about you. You never talk about yourself."

"Nothing to talk about."

"Who are you, Mr. Morse? I mean, who are you really?"

"It isn't important."

"Yes, it is. Here, you come into our lives and you perform this miracle, I mean this real miracle, and then you go running off like some shadow, and we don't even know who you are, or why you're doing what you're doing, or anything." He was silent, watching her, and she said, "Where do you live, Mr. Morse? Do you have a wife? Children?"

"It's a long story, Cindy. And I really don't want to talk about it."

Then he picked up his bag, shook hands all around, and went out of the door.

Driving back to Los Angeles, he felt drained, exhausted.

He always did, after a deprogramming. The process was almost as hard on the interrogator as it was on the victim. Physically, it was really an ordeal. Emotionally it always drained him.

Because whenever he came face-to-face with one of these kids, he thought of Sidon. He couldn't help it. It only renewed the nightmare. And he couldn't help thinking what might have been, what could have been, if he'd only had a little more time . . .

Now, he needed to forget Sidon, and Jeff Reed and the SFJ and Buford Hodges. He needed to refresh himself, body and soul. He needed a drink or two, he needed to laugh, he needed to think of other things, he needed to *feel*, to touch somebody, to join the real world, at least for a little while, until George Glennon told him this call had come in, from the father or mother of this boy or girl in Beersheba, or Maktesh, or Bethphage...

27

At Palm Desert, Jeff and Cindy enjoyed themselves thoroughly.

The Hyland house was situated on a road called Silver Spur Trail. It was located just opposite the Irongate Golf Course, and it had an unparalleled view of the open desert, lying in a bowl ringed by rock-colored mountains, topped by Mt. San Jacinto.

The guest house was perfect. It had a small kitchen, and Cindy cooked many of their meals. Occasionally they went to the big house for dinner. But outside of this, they saw Cindy's aunt and uncle rarely. He played golf almost every day, she was busy with tennis and her bridge club and her social events. By tacit agreement, they discreetly and cheerfully left Cindy and Jeff by themselves.

Each day was a golden day, dry and hot, the sun shining from a cloudless sky.

They rode, played tennis, swam, went to the movies, saw their friends at night. They spent long, lazy quiet afternoons, lying on mats at the pool's edge, toasting themselves in the sun. The pool area was totally enclosed, and when the Hylands were away for the day, they stripped and stood in the Jacuzzi, naked, reveling in the steaming hot water bubbling from submerged outlets in the sides. After that, they dove into the cool pool, swam and then floated together, played together, and made love together. Sometimes, late in the soft, balmy night, after they made love, they would come out and swim naked under the moon.

And they made love. Every night.

John Morse had taken her aside once, and told her that sometimes the twisting of the mind by the cult led to weird physiological effects. He had said that often the endocrine system could get all fouled up. A number of deprogrammed girls had stopped menstruating, temporarily. Some of the boys had been impotent for a time. They had found they no longer had to shave, and they developed adolescent problems like acne. It had something to do with a mental reversion back to infancy, since the decision-making process had been taken away. And he suggested to Cindy that if any of this showed up in Jeff, all she needed was a little patience.

But there was no problem whatever. Jeff was a young bronzed bull.

After their horrendous experiences at Ashtaroth, Cindy felt closer to Jeff than ever. She never let him out of her sight. He started to put on weight. Each day he learned to laugh a little more. His face lost its pinched, wan look; it began to tan and fill out.

At the end of the first week, the Reeds came to visit Jeff, and Cindy's mother came out to see her, as well. There was one phone call. It was for Cindy, and she took it in the big house, since there was no phone in their own quarters.

It was from John Morse, who was still staying at George Glennon's place in Santa Cruz. He wanted to know how Jeff was getting along, and he was delighted at Cindy's report. He also reported that one of the big national networks was interested in doing a documentary on Jeff, as well as some of the other deprogrammed kids, as soon as he was well enough to surface. But there was plenty of time for that. The thing was to keep right on with what she was doing, until Jeff was completely well.

They continued to while away the golden days. They took the aerial tramway in Palm Springs up to the top of San Jacinto, admired the view, and had lunch at the restaurant. They hiked through Taquiz and Palm Canyons, explored the Agua Caliente Indian reservation, and went power boating and water skiing at the Salton Sea.

Then, on the tenth day, it happened.

They were driving through the Joshua Tree National Monument, through a desolate area of the park, admiring the strange trees, some of which were thirty or forty feet high, and three hundred years old. They stopped the car to admire a stand of rocks weathered by the desert sun and winds. They were eroded in eerie fashion, shaped like human skulls, sliced loaves of bread, sailing ships and prehistoric mastadons.

The rocks had been near the road, and Jeff and Cindy had hiked a distance toward the rocks to get a closer look. They rested in the shade of the rocks for a while. When they turned to go back, they saw another car parked behind theirs.

It was a gray Cadillac, and they had seen it cruising along slowly behind them. It did not seem strange that it had stopped directly behind their car. Just some other tourists admiring the view. But when Cindy and Jeff were just a few yards away from their car, they saw three young men get out of the Cadillac. They were dressed in slacks and sports shirts, clean cut and neat young men with short haircuts.

The men stood there patiently, without moving, their bodies throwing long, grotesque shadows as they waited for Cindy and Jeff to approach.

Cindy and Jeff froze. They stared at the waiting men. They were all smiling, in a friendly fashion. A chill swept through Cindy. She began to panic.

"Jeff, you know who they are. And why they're here."

"Yes."

"Let's get out of here. Let's run."

"Run?" he said, hopelessly. "Where can we run in this desert? There's no place to run to."

They walked toward their own car, not knowing what else to do. The three Deacons watched them idly. Then one of them, the leader, said:

"My name is Ahaz. This is Jotham and Hazael. Jesus loves you, Simeon."

Jotham said, "Come with us, Simeon. Jesus wants you back."

"No," said Jeff. "I don't want to go back."

"We know how Satan tried to seduce you, Simeon."

"My name is Jeff," he said. "Not Simeon. That's all over."

"We know how you struggled against the temptations he offered you." Ahaz was talking now. "You gave yourself to him for a little while. We understand, Simeon. He tormented and tortured you. Your flesh was weak. But you have committed no mortal sin. You can be washed clean, by prayer and meditation."

Ahaz continued to speak to Jeff, softly and persuasively. Jeff stood paralyzed, staring at him. Cindy saw that Jeff's eyes had become glassy, and that he was beginning to tremble. Ahaz seemed to tower over Jeff. His smile was warm, benevolent.

"We've missed you, Jeff. All your friends, your whole family has missed you. After you have purged yourself of your sin, and given your soul back to Christ, you may join them again forever, here, as in heaven."

"Jeff," said Cindy. "Don't go. Please don't go with them!"

He did not seem to hear her. She knew she wasn't getting through to him. Already, it was too late. He simply stood there staring at Ahaz. Cindy began to scream, and tried to tear Jeff away. They pulled her from him. She bit at them, fought them with her nails.

"Let him go!" she continued to scream. "Let him go!"

The rocks nearby merely echoed her screams across the desolation. She hung on to one of the Deacons. He knocked her sprawling to the ground. She lay there stunned, watching. She saw them leading Jeff to the Cadillac. He walked as though he were in a trance. They were all speaking to him softly now.

She could not hear what they were saying, but she saw

what was happening to Jeff. He was standing still, listening, frozen, as though hypnotized. They continued talking to him, softly, quietly, a barrage of words.

She saw Jeff's face grow dreamy. He smiled at them, and they smiled back. They put their arms around his shoulders, and embraced him, hugging him close. He returned their hug.

One of the Deacons came back to Cindy's car. He reached in and took the ignition key from the dashboard. He threw it as far as he could, out into the soft desert sand. He smiled down at her, and went back to the Cadillac.

Cindy watched them all drive off. Then she put her face in the sand and wept.

They drove to Los Angeles, but did not take Jeff to Ashtaroth. Instead, they turned in the rented Cadillac at the airport, and they all boarded a plane for Kansas City.

A car picked them up at the airport, and drove them to a commune called Edom.

At Edom, Jeff was stripped of his clothes. He was taken to a room, virtually a small cell. It was totally empty of furniture, and its only decoration was a painting on the wall—the Cross and Crucifixion.

He was given a single piece of bread, and a bowl of water. Then he was allowed to sleep on the cold floor for a few hours, before he was brought to Penance.

Penance was attended in the main church, and witnessed by all the inmates of Edom, Elders, Deacons and Deaconesses, and Neophytes as well.

As at Ashtaroth, Edom had five spiritual leaders. The First Elder was named Hoshea. The others were Hadad, Hezron, Obed and Naphish.

The five robed and hooded Elders each sat on a high chair on the altar floor. Each of them held a red candle in his left hand, and a white candle in his right. The flames flickering from the candles provided the only light in the great room. The rest of the church was in total darkness.

Jeff entered, with an escort of Deacons. He was led up to

the altar. His face was bathed in an unearthly glow from the trembling light of the candles. It looked drawn, infinitely sad. He sank on his knees before the high chair on which Hoshea was sitting, and bowed his head.

"Jesus loves thee, Simeon," said the First Elder. "Ye have met Satan, and ye have listened to him. And he has tempted thee, and for a time rendered thee impure. Ye have given him thy Soul. Yet the Lord loves you still, and He is all forgiving, and your Soul shall be returned to Him in time. Dost thou understand, Simeon?"

"I understand, Hoshea."

"All men are torn between two great forces, Simeon. In my left hand, the red candle, symbolizing the Devil, Satan, Beelzebub, the Spirit of Evil himself, archenemy of Christ. In my right hand is the white candle, which represents the goodness of Jesus and His purity. Which hand shall ye grasp, Simeon? Which flame shall light your path through life?"

"The right hand, Hoshea."

"Think well, Simeon. Reflect and meditate. Red for the Devil, white for Christ. Which hand?"

"The right hand. The hand of God, blessed be His name."

"I ask thee to reflect once more. In the left hand there is sin, the pleasures of the flesh, lust and greed, worldly things. In the right, there is only abstinence, sacrifice, denial of all worldly things. In this choice, most worldly men would choose the delights of Satan, the pleasures of sin. And for these, they would sell their soul to the Prince of Darkness. This thou hast done, and found it a delight. Yet thou choosest, at this moment, my right hand. Tell me why, Simeon. Tell all those assembled here. Why?"

"Because it is the hand of Jesus Christ. I want to take His hand, and walk with Him, hand and hand through all eternity. I want His light to shine in my soul, and show me the way."

There was a long silence. Then Hoshea said, "Well said, Simeon. Ye have spoken well. The Devil has polluted your soul. He infects you still. Now thou must begin to cleanse thyself. How shall ye begin, Simeon?"

According to the ritual, Jeff rose to his feet. He took

Hoshea's red candle, blew out the flame, and threw the candle on the floor, crushing it under his sandal. He did the same with the red candles held by Hadad, Hezron, Obed, and Naphish. Now, the Elders held only the white candles.

"It is a beginning, Simeon," said the First Elder. "But this is only symbolic of what lies in thy heart. Ye had Jesus in thee, Simeon. And ye knew well what was written in the Book. 'Reject Satan, and he will flee from thee.' But ye did not do so. Therefore, ye must repent. There can be no Purification for thee until ye serve Penitence. Repent ye therefore and be converted, that your sins may be blotted out. Thus it is written, in the Book of Acts."

After that, according to ritual, each of the other Elders quoted from the Bible on the benefits of repentance and the washing out of sin.

After that, there was a moment of silence. Then, the First Elder again: "All have spoken truly, and well. This is the task before you, Simeon. First Penitence, then Purification. Ye shall wear no belt on your robe, so that thy nakedness shall be revealed. Ye shall fast every Friday and Monday, as did some of the ancient prophets and saints. And thy food and drink shall be bread and water. Ye shall work only with the women, and do the most menial of labor. Pray for your salvation, and ye shall be saved, Simeon. Purge yourself of Satan's poison, and purify yourself. And ye shall once more become a Soul for Jesus."

There was a loud amen, and then cries of "Praise the Lord" from all those assembled there. The Elders rose, holding their white candles high.

The ceremony ended with a closing ritual, as the congregation sang a hymn from the Master's Hymnbook: "Forgive Him Lord, Lead Him with Thy Light..."

In the main cabin of the *Messenger of God,* His Divinity, the Reverend Buford Hodges, was on the phone. With him were his lawyer and his public relations man.

The Master was irritated, impatient.

"God damn it," he said. "You'd think *someone* was around

out there to answer the phone. I don't know where the hell..."

"Yes?" It was a man's voice on the phone. Grave, and solemn.

"Is this Edom?"

"This is Edom," said the voice.

"Let me talk to the First Elder."

"I am sorry. The First Elder is asleep. I cannot disturb him now."

His Divinity's voice was soft, gentle, and pious now.

"Whom am I speaking to?"

"I am Zibeon, a Deacon of Edom. I serve as secretary to Hoshea, First Elder. Who is this?"

"This is the Master."

There was a stunned pause at the other end. Then: "Praise the Lord. His Divinity."

"Tell Hoshea I must speak to him at once."

As Hodges waited, he grinned at both Garvey and Caswell. They did not return the grin. On the contrary. They looked worried, grim.

"This is Hoshea, Your Divinity."

"Jesus loves you, Hoshea."

"Praise the Lord. What can I do for you, Master?"

"You have a boy there, Simeon. On my instructions, he was sent to Edom."

"Yes. He has already arrived. He begins Penitence tomorrow."

"I want you to take him off Penitence, Hoshea."

There was a moment of silence on the other end. "But Master, he has consorted with Satan."

"True," said Hodges. "True. But I need him for a special purpose. A divine purpose. One that I cannot reveal now."

"I see. Then I shall take him off Penitence, as you instruct."

"I want you to do more than that," said Hodges.

"Yes?"

"I want him to be well fed. To be given the best food you have at Edom. In fact, I want him to dine at the Elders' table, with you."

271

Hoshea drew in his breath. He sounded shocked.

"A Penitent? At the Elders' table?"

"I know. I know this is highly, well—unorthodox. But we must treat him well. This boy has been chosen."

"Chosen?"

"Chosen by Jesus. To perform a special mission. Through his soul, we shall save thousands of others. It is not just a mission, but a revelation. It shall be known to all of us later. Do you understand, Hoshea?"

"Praise the Lord. I understand, Master. And of course, I shall do as you say."

The Reverend Hodges hung up, and turned to the others:

"Yes, sir, I want that boy. I want that boy fattened up and looking good, when he sits in that witness chair. I want him to look apple pie, clean cut, as All American as you'll ever see. I want the whole damned country to fall in love with him."

"I think you're making a mistake, Buford," said Caswell.

"A hell of a mistake," agreed Garvey.

"I don't think so. Sooner or later in life, there comes a time when you have to bite the bullet. I've got this boil festering on my ass, gentlemen. Only way to get rid of it is lance it, and let the pus pop out."

"What if you stick the needle in too far, Buford?" said Caswell. "You could really hurt yourself."

"He's right," said Garvey. "You might even kill yourself."

Buford Hodges studied his two advisers for a moment. "One thing about you two boys," he said evenly, grinning. "You've always underestimated me. I am personally going to Edom tomorrow, and spend some time with that misguided boy. I am gently going to show him the error of his ways, and guide him to the Light. What I've got here is a righteous cause. Yes, sir, I've got the Lord on my side, gentlemen." He smiled at them. "Now, why don't we all just relax and have us a drink."

PART
FOUR

28

It had all begun when Jeffrey Reed, a member of the Souls for Jesus, commonly known as the SFJ, made a formal complaint to the Office of the District Attorney, County of Los Angeles. This was on the third of November. The complaint stated that he had been kidnapped, and falsely imprisoned by persons known to him, against his will.

The Grand Jury had taken testimony from the complainant and witnesses, had issued indictments, and finally warrants were issued stating the bail.

The trial was set for the 16th of January in Superior Court Department 102, on the ninth floor of the Criminal Courts Building in Los Angeles. There were six defendants in all. Officially, the case was called *The People of the State of California versus Frank Reed, Kate Reed, Kenneth Reed, Joseph Peterson, Cindy Hyland, and John Morse.* Cindy had just turned eighteen before Jeff had been taken, and since she was now an adult, she could be tried with the others.

The charges were officially listed as kidnapping and conspiracy to commit kidnapping; false imprisonment and conspiracy to commit false imprisonment.

The oncoming trial created immediate and national attention. The issues were sensitive, bizarre, and highly charged emotionally. It was given sensational play in the media, both newspapers and television. Reporters from all over the country had flown in to cover it. Some of the legal profession called it a landmark case in the history of American jurisprudence. There was a cover story in *Time* on the Reverend Buford Hodges and the SFJ, with a general treatment of the burgeoning rise of cults in America. The issue was published just a week before the trial, fanning further interest.

District Attorney Thomas Hatch had decided not to assign this case to any of his assistants, but to conduct the prosecution himself. The defense attorney was Matthew J. Blake. He was one of the top criminal lawyers in the State of California, shrewd, flamboyant, with an imposing record of wins, nationally known as a personality with charisma, a public figure in his own right. Each defendant was entitled to his own lawyer but, by mutual consent, they had all agreed to be represented solely by Blake.

The judge was Harlan F. Brenner, and the trial was due to begin promptly at nine o'clock on a Monday morning.

At eight-thirty, Matt Blake and Saul Goodstone, one of his bright young assistants, stepped out of a chauffeur-driven Cadillac onto the sidewalk in front of the Criminal Courts Building. Blake was a big, florid man in his middle fifties. He had a thatch of snow-white hair, and he wore, as always, a blue polka-dot bow tie, which had become a kind of personal trademark.

Temple Street, fronting the building, was crowded and seething with excitement. Four huge SFJ busses lined the curb, and a great crowd of young SFJ Neophytes, neatly dressed in their God Squad uniforms and led by their Deacons, patrolled one side of the street, walking slowly back and forth in an orderly and dignified way. It was a kind of silent demonstration. Every minute on the minute, at a signal from the lead Deacon, they all chanted in unison: "Jesus loves you!" Otherwise they said nothing, and did nothing, except continue their slow march.

On the other side of Temple Street, there was a different kind of crowd. It consisted of parents of sons and daughters already in the cult. They were shouting angrily, the same slogans printed on the placards they were carrying: *Free Our Children! We Want Our Kids Back! Put the SFJ Away! Turn Off the Master's Voice,* and *Buford Doesn't Love Jesus; He Loves a Buck.* There were representatives present from organizations that offered information about cults and counseling for parents and children.

Blake looked up and down Temple Street. He loved what he saw. It was his kind of scene. He noted the TV trucks set up with their portable equipment. He smiled as he saw the photographers and reporters heading toward him.

"It's a beautiful morning, Saul," he said. "A beautiful, beautiful morning."

"Yes, sir. It certainly is."

Blake looked across the street at the SFJ marchers. Then he grinned: "The Reverend Hodges is losing a lot of revenue. Taking all those kids off the streets, and having them demonstrate here. Yes sir, losing all that collection money must gall him. Still, I suppose he feels it's worth it."

Then the photographers and newsmen were upon him, shooting his picture, asking him what he had to say, and he made the usual amiable answers, *No comment, boys,* and *The trial hasn't even started yet,* and *We'll have something to say later, boys,* and so on.

There were several police on duty, on the possible chance that some riot might develop; they cleared a passage for Blake and Goodstone to enter.

The corridor on the ninth floor, just outside the courtroom, was jammed, a crush of people. Some were spectators simply trying to get inside, others were more people of the media. TV cameras were set up, the sweating crews trying to keep the cables on the floor clear. Spotlights, set up in strategic corners of the corridor and on the black cushioned benches, glared brightly. Their light was pitiless and obscene. They made the corridor look like a movie set, instead of the real thing. They made actors out of the flesh-and-blood spectators jamming the place. Fantasy upstaged reality here.

A short time later, Matt Blake was seated next to his clients at the defense table to the right, facing the bench. The jury had already been seated. It was the moment before the judge appeared.

Blake's quick eye checked the scene. He felt good, ready to go, confident. He loved it all; everything in this courtroom spoke of home to him. The furniture and fittings were all to his taste, the dark mahogany paneling of the walls, the indirect lighting through the glass ceiling, the great bronze circular official seal of the State of California on the wall above the bench.

Now he turned his attention to his battlefield. He looked to his left at the prosecutor's table. He studied his opponent, Tom Hatch. Hatch was thin-faced, well-tailored, clean-cut, Los Angeles Country Club, the Jonathan Club, and a house in Truesdale. Blake didn't blame Hatch for taking on the job himself, instead of giving it to one of his hotshot assistants The district attorney would be a damned fool, just plain stupid not to handle this plum himself. There was all that publicity, and he knew Hatch had his heart set on being attorney general of California some day. He also had a big ego. And this particular case, because it was so bizarre and was making headlines through the country, could possibly make Hatch an instant celebrity, as Vincent Bugliosi had become, after the Manson case.

Next, Blake studied the complainant, Jeff Reed. The boy, wearing his neat SFJ jacket, was freshly bathed and combed. He was smiling and talking to one of Hatch's assistants; he seemed animated, and very likable. A real clean-cut American boy, thought Blake, the polite, yes-sir and no-sir kind of American boy, the rich and well-bred boy who played quarterback at USC or Michigan or Harvard, the kid next door who you hoped would marry your daughter one day.

278

And yet, thought Blake, there's something about him, something strange, something a little weird.

Maybe he's just *too* damned clean-cut, too damned nice, too damned animated and bright-eyed, too damned *what?* Blake didn't know exactly. He really couldn't put his finger on it. But this was going to be the chief witness for the prosecution. Matt Blake was a man who prided himself on reading character, he wrote his own personality profiles, and they were almost always accurate, but this kid, this Jeff Reed, he found a little baffling. The boy never once looked to the right, toward the defense table, where his family and the others were sitting. He never even glanced at them once, never acknowledged them even as strangers. He did not simply ignore them. He acted as though they did not even exist. Anybody human, thought Blake, had to feel *some* kind of emotion in a situation like this. After all, this was his father and mother he was trying to put into jail. Not to mention his brother and his best friend, and even his girlfriend.

Nothing. Blank. Nothing.

Blake glanced at the jury. He was satisfied with the selection. He looked at the empty, high, green-backed chair behind the bench, at the black sign on the bench spelling out the name: *Harlan F. Brenner, Judge.* He knew Brenner, and found him unpredictable. Factor X. Sometimes he could be lenient, and sometimes he could be very tough when it came to the letter of the law. It depended on his mood. You never knew whether he was going to throw you a fastball or a changeup.

He thought of his defense, and he felt good. Very good. It was classic, a dream case tailored especially for Matt Blake. It was the kind he loved to argue, and the kind he almost always won. The prosecution, he knew, basically had to argue the law, and the strict interpretation of the law.

But on his side, he had mother-love, father-love, brother-love, girl-love and buddy-love. All jury shakers, guaranteed to make you cry. But his sixth defendant, John Morse, was something else again.

He had to be careful. Jack-be-nimble, Jack-be-quick. Morse

was an outsider when it came to Jeff Reed. The jury would see him as someone, or something, else.

Yet Blake wasn't too worried.

The jury did not know it yet, but Morse had his own story to tell. It was one hell of a story. And in Blake's view, it could make the difference.

He smiled to himself, popped a mint into his mouth, caught Tom Hatch's face and smiled. Hatch nodded toward him, looked confident, and smiled back. But Blake saw the smile as merely a slash in a false face.

He leaned forward and spoke softly into Saul Goodstone's ear.

"You know what, Saul?"

"What?"

"I'm going to beat their asses off this time. I'm really going to beat their asses."

That is, he thought, if the jury didn't go off its collective rocker. Jesus, he really loved the big ones like this, the really big ones that made the national headlines, the flamboyant ones with that special twist, that certain unique issue, the kind that were always chosen as a lead item in their newscasts by Cronkite, or Reasoner, or Chancellor, or Brinkley. Manson, of course, or Hearst, one of those. He was positive if he hadn't gotten that damned angina at the time, and had to have a heart bypass, he would have been chosen to represent Patty Hearst, rather than F. Lee Bailey. He loved to speculate on the defense he could have put up for her. Actually, this case was similar in one big respect. There was this whole thing about brainwashing . . .

At this moment, the door to the judge's chamber opened, and Judge Harlan F. Brenner came out, robed in black, his thin, ascetic face expressionless as he adjusted the glasses on the bridge of his nose. At the exhortation of the bailiff, everybody rose.

After the jury was sworn in, Judge Brenner picked up a piece of paper and read: "This is the case of the People of the State of California versus Frank Reed, Kate Reed, Kenneth

Reed, Joseph Peterson, Cindy Hyland, and John Morse." He read off the charge and asked, "Are both sides ready?"

Both Hatch and Blake indicated they were, and Judge Brenner said to Hatch, "Does the prosecution wish to make an opening statement?"

"I do."

The district attorney rose, bowed to the court, and took his place in front of the jury.

He paused for a moment, smiling at them in friendly fashion, trying to make them feel at ease. Then: "Now, ladies and gentlemen, I do not have to tell you what the First Amendment to the Bill of Rights tells us. It gives us the right to freedom of religion, to worship in any way we please, to join any church we please. It is an inviolable right of any adult American citizen, black or white, rich or poor. You on the jury may be Catholic, Protestant, Jew, Mormon, Holy Roller, Seventh-Day Adventist, or anything else. It does not matter. You have the right to worship God in any way you please. And nobody in this state or government has the right to stop you.

"In June of this year, the victim Jeffrey Reed, being eighteen years old and therefore an adult in the State of California, exercised his right. He decided to leave home and join a church called Souls for Jesus, Christian in its beliefs, charismatic and Pentecostal in nature, a church founded right here in America.

"This was his inviolable right, then, under the First Amendment.

"But his parents conspired to deny him this right. They did it by committing a major and very serious crime, one of the very worst anyone can possibly commit.

"We intend to prove that Frank Reed and Kate Reed had long conspired with the defendant, John Morse, to kidnap their son, Jeffrey Reed. That on the morning of October 6, they did, indeed, kidnap him. That with the help of the defendants Kenneth Reed and Joseph Peterson, they violently seized him, against his will, forced him into a car, and thereafter placed handcuffs on him.

281

"We intend to prove that they then drove him to a remote place, a house at Big Bear, where he was placed under imprisonment, cruelly treated, starved and not allowed to sleep, and held at all times under guard. We intend to prove that the conspirator and the real architect of this cruel and depraved procedure, the defendant John Morse, then confronted the victim, tormenting and torturing him for endless hours, trying to get him to accede to the wishes of his parents . . ."

Blake listened to the rest of Hatch's opening statement with only half an ear. He could have written it himself. Instead, he was busy studying the jury.

Ah, he thought, say what you will. There's where it's all at. God on the Mount, in this courtroom or any other.

The jury.

There were seven men and five women. Generally speaking, they were to his liking. He had traded very carefully with Hatch in the paneling. Two of the men were blacks. He considered that, on balance, a plus. They were middle-class blacks, solidly part of the Establishment. They wouldn't buy this cult, as a younger and poorer black might. They would equate it with Black Muslims, groups like that, which were anathema to them, on their upward-mobile road. And secretly and deeply, they still were hostile to the strict application of the law. Because it was white man's law. It had been created and enforced by "the Man," and used against the blacks for two hundred years. And Tom Hatch's case was based on the letter of the law.

But there was a minus as well as a plus in their selection. They might, unconsciously or consciously, resent the Reeds, because they were so rich, and lived in Hope Ranch, which they saw as being for "whites only." He knew Tom Hatch considered that as a kind of edge.

Of the twelve jurors, ten were parents. Blake was gambling on the fact that there was an emotional issue here, that these people would identify with the Reeds, and hopefully sympathize with them. Of course, you could never tell about a jury. Never. But you tried for the edge. The Reeds were Catholics, even if they were not churchgoers. Two of the people on the jury were staunch Catholics and family men, the strict type when it came to their children, conservative. On balance, he had traded well with Hatch, but when you picked a jury, you had to give as well as get.

Win a few. Lose a few.

A jury was a collective thing, and you never could tell about it, even if you broke it down, individual by individual. There was the evidence, of course; some of the jurors would be more persuasive than others, some were leaders and some followers; some would be able to bury what their hearts said and vote with their heads, and some would react the other way around. A jury could be many things. A monster. An angel of mercy. An irrational collection of idiots. An assembly of wise men. A riddle wrapped in a mystery. He had made a confident statement to Saul Goodstone earlier. He was still high on his chances. But goddamn it, you never really *knew*.

Blake watched Hatch as he bowed to the court, returned to the counsel table, and sat down.

"Does the defense wish to make an opening statement now, or reserve the right?" Judge Brenner asked.

"No, your Honor," said Blake. "But I would like to reserve the right."

"Very well," said Judge Brenner. "The State will proceed."

29

The prosecution began by quickly establishing its case that the victim had, in fact, been physically and violently kidnapped.

A sidewalk porter for TWA named Leroy Harris was brought to the stand and sworn in; he testified that he had been close by, and had seen the victim seized by two men whom he identified in the court as Frank and Kenneth Reed. He had seen the victim struggle, trying to free himself, before he was forced into a taxi.

A man named Salvatore Ratazzi, the driver of an airlines hotel bus that had been parked across the road, had witnessed the same event, and gave the same testimony.

A lady who identified herself as a Mrs. Amelia Crane was brought to the stand. She had been resting in the grassy section of a rest area on the San Bernardino Freeway with her two children that day; she testified that she had seen the plaintiff trying to escape from two captors, and identified them in court.

A fourth witness was brought on and sworn in; he testified

that his name was Herman Ernst, that he was the rental agent for a cottage at Big Bear, and that this cottage had been rented for two months by a man he identified in court as Frank Reed.

Reed had actually used the place for a few days. Neighbors had suspected there had been mysterious goings on in the place, because the windows had been boarded up. Ernst had found the boards lying in a pile in the backyard, and noted the nail holes in the window sides and sills. There were evidences that a number of people had been living there for the short period of occupancy, including some women.

After each witness, Judge Brenner asked the defense if it wanted to cross-examine. And Blake's answer was the same each time. "No questions."

Judge Brenner looked at the clock, then addressed the district attorney. "Who is your next witness, Mr. Hatch?"

"The victim, Your Honor. Jeffrey Reed."

"Then I presume his examination will take considerable time."

"Yes, Your Honor, it will. He is, in fact, our principal and only remaining witness."

"It is now eleven fifty. There is no point in putting the victim on the stand for ten minutes, and then finding it necessary to interrupt his testimony for lunch. This court is now recessed, and will reconvene at one forty-five." He turned and addressed the jury. "The jurors are warned not to permit themselves to form any opinion as to the merits of the case, nor will they discuss the matter among themselves, nor permit it to be discussed in their presence."

He banged the gavel once. Everyone rose, and the courtroom started to clear.

John Morse and Matt Blake had decided to lunch together, and they were joined by George Glennon, who had come down from Santa Cruz for the trial.

Temple Street was still paraded by the noisy picketers, the angry parents shouting and brandishing their fists. Across the street, the Neophytes and the Deacons of the SFJ continued

285

their slow, dignified walk in silence, except for their loud declaration, each minute on the minute. They walked with heads down, as though humbly enduring this pain, this ridicule, this humiliation and blasphemy, as Jesus had done almost two thousand years ago, when he, too, had suffered the jeers and barbs of the mob.

There wasn't enough time for an elaborate lunch, so they had a sandwich and coffee in the cafeteria. Morse asked Glennon how the book was going and he said, "I thought it was done until this trial came up. Now, I've got to write the last chapter."

"I've read some of your work," said Blake. "And I admire you for it. You've got real guts."

"Thank you, Mr. Blake."

"Not at all. People who still tell it the way it is—well, there aren't too many left any more. And look, the hell with all this formality. I'm Matt, and this is John, and you're George. Okay?"

Morse studied the lawyer. Blake's smile was charming. It was professional but still dazzling. No question about it. The man had charisma. It emanated from him like a scent. He did not even have to turn it on. Morse hoped Blake would be able to enchant the jury with his charm, when the time came.

Glennon took a sip of his coffee and said, "Guess where our friend Buford Hodges is right now."

"Where?"

"Well, you noticed he wasn't in the courtroom. Actually, he's cruising around, just outside of the Bay. The story is he's found a new young Deaconess to be his secretary, quote unquote. The whole country's interested in this trial, it's one of the biggest things of its kind since Patty Hearst, and His Divinity is acting as though he couldn't care less." Glennon laughed. "But I guarantee he does. He's got his ear to the water, every second he's out there on that ocean."

"One thing I've wondered about, Matt," said Morse.

"Yes?"

"How does it happen you never subpoenaed His Divinity?"

"No point in it. First of all, he'd be a hostile witness. That's something you try to avoid, if you can. Second, even if I put him on the stand, I couldn't get him to testify."

"Why not?"

"Because as a minister, anything he says or has to do with the penitent is privileged. The penitent in this case being the victim, Jeffrey Reed. In other words, he could simply refuse to testify for or against the boy. The same holds true for a lawyer-client, doctor-patient, or husband-wife relationship."

"That's too bad. I'd like to see the son-of-a-bitch up there on that stand, taking it."

Blake looked at his client. "You really *do* hate him, don't you?"

"Do you blame me?"

"No. I guess if I were in your place, I'd feel the same way. I'd want to kill him."

"I'd really like to see him in court," said Morse, almost wistfully. "I'd like to see somebody like you peel his skin right off."

"It's always tricky when you examine a man of the cloth," said Blake. "Any cloth, any color. Hodges may be a conniving, greedy son-of-a-bitch, but he's still a minister, and most juries take ministers and priests seriously, with great respect. On top of that our friend Hodges is very clever, very shrewd. He's smart enough to turn the whole thing over to his side, if he surprised us by agreeing to testify. So if you don't mind, John, I'd just as soon have him sail all over the Pacific Ocean till this is through." He laughed and turned to Glennon. "I tell you, George, I never saw it to fail. Once we get into a courtroom, everybody wants to get into my act."

"Especially your clients."

"Particularly my clients."

At five minutes of two, Jeffrey Andrew Reed took the stand.

He put his hand on the Bible, and swore he would tell the truth, the whole truth, and nothing but the truth, so help him God.

His voice shook a little as he took the oath. He looked very young and very vulnerable. He sat in the witness chair stiffly, back rigid. He seemed ill at ease, shaken by stage fright, a little awed at sitting here before all these important people in this awesome place. He looked very neat in his freshly pressed SFJ jacket, slacks, and well-shined black shoes.

His gaze swept around the courtroom. He never even glanced at his father and mother. His eyes caught those of the jurors. He smiled shyly at them. He was very appealing, his face asked for their sympathy and understanding. It told them how innocent, how really vulnerable he was. Some of the jury couldn't help but smile back.

District Attorney Hatch stepped forward, and began to examine the victim. His manner was gentle. He asked a few preliminary questions, and then:

"Why did you leave home, Jeff? Why did you abandon the idea of going to college, and become a Soul for Jesus?"

"Because I was looking for love, and I wanted to give it. There was nothing like that at home."

"Would you explain that still further?"

"We were supposed to be a family. But everybody was for himself. My mother and father fought all the time. They hated each other. My mother was only interested in bridge and her clubs, stuff like that. My father was interested only in making lots of money, you know, business deals. He and I, well—we fought all the time."

"What did you fight about?"

"He wanted to make me over in his own image. He wanted me to go to the college he went to, and do what he did, and become what he was. I didn't want all that. I just wanted to be myself. To do my own thing."

"And what was that?"

"I wanted to love, and be loved. I felt there was too much corruption and materialism in the world. I felt, deep in my heart, and in my soul, that I wanted to really help people. And the only way I could do that was to serve the Lord."

"And so you saw your chance to do this by becoming a Soul for Jesus. Is that correct?"

"Yes."

"And did you find what you were looking for?"

"Yes. I couldn't believe the love and warmth I found with the other kids in the SFJ. It was just incredible. We all became brothers and sisters. It was as though I'd found a new family. I felt I *belonged,* you know? I felt I wanted this to be my life. To live in peace, and serve the Lord. I guess you could say that becoming a Soul for Jesus gave me the one answer I was looking for."

"And what was that answer?"

"God is when you live for other people. Evil is when you live for yourself."

"Do you now have any desire whatever to return to your family, to the society you knew?"

"No."

"Did you ever entertain any such desire?"

"No."

This was not the Jeff Reed of Ashtaroth. There was nothing wild-eyed about him now. He spouted no biblical quotations. He never even mentioned the Devil once. He called nobody Satan. This was no crazy, no weirdo, no freak of any kind. His demeanor was entirely normal, and so was the way he answered the questions.

"Then when you were kidnapped at the airport, was it against your will?"

"Yes, sir." Jeff Reed was very emphatic on this.

"You *knew* you were being kidnapped? Is that correct?"

"Yes, sir."

"You were not living in some dream world? You were not confused? You knew *exactly* what was going on? Is that right?"

"Yes, sir."

"Did you fight to get away?"

"Yes, sir. I did."

"Did you struggle when they forced you into the car?"

"Yes, sir. I did. Very hard."

"How did they subdue you?"

"They put handcuffs on me."

The district attorney then went into the details of the ride, and the rest stop.

"What happened at the rest stop?"

"I tried to escape."

"Tell us, in your own words, how you tried to escape."

"I was in the men's room. I ran out and tried to get away. My brother Ken ran after me and caught me. I tried to fight. Then my father came up and hit me."

"How did he hit you?"

"With his fist."

"Where did he hit you?"

"He smashed me in the face."

"What happened after that?"

"Well, he punched me hard, and I was knocked out. I couldn't fight any more, and they dragged me into the car."

He then went on, through Hatch's questioning, to relate how he had been imprisoned at the cottage at Big Bear. How Mr. Morse, sitting there at that table, had tormented him, beaten and abused him, ridiculed and humiliated him, and shown him pornographic pictures, keeping him up hour after hour, trying to get him to renounce the new religion he had chosen.

"How long did you resist him?"

"Forty-four hours. Almost two days."

"And all this time, were you given any food?"

"No."

"Were you allowed any sleep?"

"No."

"You were faint and weak, then, from lack of sleep and hunger? Is that correct?"

"Yes, sir."

"And because of this, you finally gave in. Is that correct?"

"No, sir. I didn't really give in. I only *pretended* to. I only wanted them to think I did."

"But you still intended to remain a Soul for Jesus. Is that true?"

"Yes, sir."

"You resolved to do this of your own free will."

"Yes, sir."

"Then Mr. Morse failed in his effort to deprogram you. Would that be true?"

Through Hatch's questioning, the Court and jury were told that Jeffrey Reed, the victim, had then planned to escape his kidnappers at an appropriate moment. He had gone along with them for a while, made them really believe him so that in time they would abandon their precautions, and be off guard.

In Palm Desert, they had assigned Cindy Hyland to stay close to him, never to leave him for a moment. At the first sign of his backsliding, she was to call them, his father and Mr. Morse, and they would come again. So he had been patient, and continued the game.

Then, he managed to evade Cindy for a few moments, and get to a phone. He telephoned Ashtaroth, and told them where he was. He told them that the next day, he and Cindy would be taking a drive through Joshua Tree National Monument.

After that, they had come and rescued him. They had sent him to Edom, a commune in Kansas, in order to make sure he was safe. The Church had finally decided that the time had come to press charges against such kidnappers.

"Jeff, are you happy back in the Church?"

"Yes, sir. I am very happy."

"Do you hate your parents for what they did to you?"

Tears sprang to Jeff's eyes. He took out a handkerchief and wiped them away. His voice broke a little as he answered the question.

"No. I think what they did was wrong, and it was evil. But I love them still."

"And your brother, Ken? And Joe Peterson? Do you feel the same way about them?"

"Yes, sir. I do. It wasn't their fault at all. I mean, they were brought into this by my father and mother and Mr. Morse there. They just didn't know what they were doing. But I love them still. As a Soul for Jesus, I have learned to love every human being in this world, even my enemies, because we are all creations and creatures of the Lord, and we all have the divine spirit within us."

The district attorney paused for just a moment. Then he said, "No more questions."

Throughout, Jeff Reed had been enormously sincere, entirely believable. The jury listened intently, and their faces were sympathetic. It was clear that some of them were touched by the victim's ordeal, and his dedication.

John Morse sat there listening in fascination. What a job of programming, he thought. What a hell of a performance Jeff Reed had given. *Buford, my friend, even though I hate your guts, I have to take my hat off to you.*

When Jeff had finished, Judge Brenner checked the clock. Five minutes past four. The district attorney had timed his examination beautifully. It was excellent strategy. You finished with your client just before time ran out, so that the defense had no chance to cross-examine. The jury would go back to their hotel, knowing only what, in this case, the victim had said. The jurors would have all night to think about it, and the victim's testimony would have a chance to sink in.

"It is past the hour of the afternoon adjournment," said Judge Brenner. "Court will recess until nine o'clock tomorrow morning."

Once again, he cautioned the jurors not to discuss the case, or express any opinion as to its merits.

Immediately after adjournment, Matt Blake spent two hours with his clients in a small conference room, briefing them on the proceedings for the next day. He would cross-examine Jeff. Then, unless the district attorney produced some new surprise witness, the State would rest. After that, he, Matt Blake, would begin their defense.

When the meeting broke up, the Reeds, Cindy Hyland and Joe Peterson went back to their hotel. Morse found himself alone with Blake. Morse, in a sense, was Blake's key problem vis-à-vis the jury, since he was the one real outsider involved, and they still had much to talk about. The lawyer, who knew the area, suggested that they have a drink and dinner on

Olvera Street. He said it was something a little different, and only five or ten minutes' walk from the Criminal Courts building. That is, he said, they would go if Morse liked Mexican food.

They passed a large cross commemorating the founding of Los Angeles and entered Olvera Street. It was a colorful replica of a Mexican market street, with shops on either side and rows of stalls down the center. Somewhere, they heard mariachi music. The shops sold Mexican curios, souvenirs for the tourists, candles, leather goods, pottery, books, glass and Mexican art.

The restaurant Blake had chosen was called the Casa la Golondrina.

They both ordered margaritas, to be followed by the combination taco and enchilada special, with rice and refried beans.

Over their drinks, Blake remarked, "Funny thing."

"Yes?"

"The Souls for Jesus are very high on the Bible. Every word in the Good Book is the word of God. Yet this kid Reed put his hand on the Bible, swore to God he was telling the truth, and lied like hell."

"So?"

"So at the very least, it's inconsistent. Either that, or these SFJ kids are all total hypocrites."

"No. They're not. They really believe what they're programmed to believe. The Bible is the only true book, its ethic the only true ethic."

"Then how in hell could this kid swear on the Bible, and then lie through his teeth?"

Morse explained the antinomian philosophy again, as he had explained it to Frank Reed. "You can lie, cheat, steal or even kill, and God will forgive you if you do so in His service. As long as you do His work, you're clean."

"I'll be damned," said Blake. "Learn something every day." He thought for a moment. "Man, did that kid lie. You know, I can't wait for the cross tomorrow. I'm going to rip Jeffrey Andrew Reed's skin right off, and hang him up to dry."

"I wouldn't count on that, Matt."

"No? Why not?"

"You'll find him tough to cross-examine. As I told you, he's been programmed for this. By none other than Buford Hodges himself, who spent a lot of time with him at Edom, getting him ready. In fact, you might be better off *not* cross-examining him at all."

Blake stared at him. "You must be kidding."

"No. I'm serious. I know what happens to these kids. All the lies they tell will really seem the truth to them. And Reed will stick to his story, no matter how you try to trap him. If you cross-examine him, he may make you look bad."

Blake smiled. "Look, John. I've cross-examined witnesses you wouldn't believe. Expert liars, cast-iron liars, liars who could make any lie detector ever built stand up and cry in frustration. I mean, *liars*. I've never seen one yet that I couldn't beat, or at least, shake up. I said it before, and I say it again. I expect to skin the victim alive tomorrow morning."

"Okay." Morse shrugged. "You're the doctor."

"No," said Blake. "I'm the lawyer."

At the moment, the waiter came in with two heaping plates. Blake took one look at the hot, aromatic food, and he moaned softly, "My God. There goes my waistline!"

At eight forty-five the next morning, the corridor outside the courtroom was again jammed with people, television operators trying to set their cameras in position, reporters trying to get a word with Hatch and Blake before they came in.

Thirty seconds after nine, when the courtroom was jammed with its restless and whispering audience, after the jurors had solemnly filed in and taken their seats, after counsel for both prosecution and defense, as well as their clients, had been seated at their tables, and after the courtroom artists had straightened out their drawing pens and charcoal and opened their sketch pads, Judge Harlan F. Brenner entered.

The bailiff pounded his gavel, and intoned: "Everybody stand up, please."

All rose, and the judge took his high-backed chair. He glanced at the jurors and the spectators and then he said,

"Please be seated. The defendants and all attorneys are in court, the jurors are all present."

Judge Brenner looked at Blake. "Do you wish to cross-examine?"

"Yes, your Honor. I certainly do."

"Call Jeffrey Reed to the stand."

When Jeff sat down, Blake deliberately delayed rising for a few moments. Instead, he wasted a few moments fiddling with some papers. A witness who expected a hostile interrogation was always uptight to begin with. Waiting in the witness chair, watching his interrogator take his time, unnerved the witness just a little more; it heightened his tension, made him more vulnerable. Matt Blake was a man who believed that, in a courtroom as well as elsewhere, it was the little things that counted.

Finally he walked up to the witness chair. He looked Jeff directly in the eyes. Blake was conscious, out of the corner of his eye, that the courtroom artists were now furiously busy, sketching him. Yesterday was Tom Hatch's day. This was his. Idly, he wondered how the sketch of himself would look on the television news programs later tonight.

"Your name is Jeffrey Andrew Reed."

"That is the name I was given at birth."

Blake smiled warmly. "Do you have any objections if I call you Jeff?"

"My name is Simeon now, but under the circumstances here, I have no objection."

"All right, Jeff. Now, you have told the Court that you loved your father."

"Yes, sir."

As Blake proceeded, he kept looking into Jeff Reed's eyes. But what he saw there, at close range, was strange. What he saw was nothing. The eyes seemed glazed, they reflected nothing. Under the eyelids, they were small blue opaque curtains. They showed no uneasiness, no fear, no life. They might have been painted there, or made of glass. They might have belonged to some robot.

Matt Blake found this disturbing. His interrogative attack,

although set, could vary depending on what he saw in the witness's eyes. Here, he could make no reading whatsoever. No reading of any kind.

Gently, he continued to cross-examine Jeff. He had testified to this, he had testified to that. Was this true, and was that true? He set little traps for Jeff. The traps stayed open, Jeff refused to step into any of them. The district attorney intervened often with objections. The question is argumentative; it calls for a conclusion of the witness; it is leading and suggestive. The witness cannot testify to a conclusion. Judge Brenner overruled most of the objections. But Hatch scored with a few.

Blake continued his questioning. Again, and again, he tried to trap the victim. He tried to muddle him, confuse him, upset him, tried to get him to change his testimony. Each time, he was frustrated. Jeff Reed stuck to his story. That is, he stuck to the pyramid of lies he purported to be the truth. Matt Blake had the weird feeling that the boy *believed* the lies he was telling, actually thought they were God's truth. Morse had been right. The boy *had* been programmed, in a way that was eerie, frightening.

Wind him up, and he will walk. Wind him up, and he will talk. Wind him up, and he will smile.

Wind him up, and you will hear the Master's voice.

Blake was not a man who was easily shaken. But he shuddered a little as he continued to ask questions of the victim and continued to be frustrated. He had the distinct impression that he was talking to some kind of machine, one made of flesh and blood and brains and nerve centers, but a machine nevertheless, some kind of engineered robot. He felt the gooseflesh pop out all over him.

He was also aware that the jury was listening intently, watching this combat with keen interest. None of the jurors coughed, or rustled restlessly. He knew they were impressed by the way the victim was sticking to his story, and by the fact that the defense attorney could not shake him. They were impressed by the boy's calmness under fire. He sensed that some of them were beginning to believe that he, Matt Blake, was harassing this boy needlessly.

Blake began to sweat a little. For the first time in his long career, he felt shaky, insecure in a cross-examination. He sensed that he was a loser. Frustrated, he decided to cut his interrogation short, quit early to cut his losses. And lose he had. He knew it. At least, for this round. He could almost hear the wheels turning in the heads of the jurors.

Why is he keeping this up? Anybody can see the boy is telling an honest story. Anybody can see he's sincere. Look, the defense attorney hasn't been able to trip him up once. Not once. Right?

"That's all," said Blake. "I have no further questions."

Jeff Reed left the stand and Matthew Blake walked slowly back to the defense table. He glanced at Morse, expecting an I-told-you-so look on the deprogrammer's face. But tactfully, and mercifully, Morse was looking the other way.

Judge Brenner looked at Hatch, inquiringly.

"We have finished, your Honor," said Hatch. He smiled smugly at Blake. "The State rests."

Judge Brenner looked at Blake.

"Is the defense ready?"

"We are, your Honor."

"Very well." The judge rapped his gavel. "This court will recess for fifteen minutes. When we resume, the defense will begin its case."

Matt Blake found he was still perspiring a little. He mopped his brow. Then he went directly to the men's room, where he washed his face in cold water.

He was glad the judge had called the recess. He needed this rest stop. He had to admit it. He had found the cross-examination of Jeffrey Reed unnerving. He should have taken Morse seriously. Jesus, what had they done to the kid, how did they manage it? It was scary. What if this SFJ thing snowballed? They could program five million kids like young Reed. Ten million. Any number.

Theoretically, if they could do that, they could take over

the whole goddamn country. Not theoretically. *Actually*. And these cults were growing. Getting bigger and bigger . . .

The importance of this case suddenly came home to him. Its implications stunned him. It was not just another feather in his cap, not just another notch in his gun, another digit on the personal and public scoreboard of Matthew J. Blake. Now he felt *involved*. And concerned. In a whole new way. This case had taken on a totally new dimension.

By the time he walked back into the courtroom, he had completely recovered.

And, he thought grimly, *This one's for blood.*

Real blood.

30

Matt Blake opened his defense by calling Frank Reed to the stand.

Under Blake's gentle and expert questioning, Reed told of the high hopes he and his wife had had for their son, how he had been a healthy, entirely normal boy in every respect. He had been a good student, and was due to enter Stanford in the fall, where his brother Ken had already been enrolled. Like any father who loved his son, he had fretted about Jeff, and worried about some of his young idiosyncrasies and ideas, and they had clashed on some things, of course, but that was normal enough. A teenage boy wanted to be independent of his father, and make his own decisions, and certainly that was understandable.

But then this terrible thing had happened. Jeff had suddenly joined this cult, given it his car and all his money, rejected his family, told his parents he despised them, and called them obscene names. He then said his true father was the Reverend Buford Hodges.

"What opinion did you form from that, Mr. Reed?"

"My wife and I concluded that this cult had somehow poisoned his mind, twisted and corrupted it. This was not our son at all. This was some stranger."

"Objection, your Honor," said the district attorney. "The defendant is not stating a fact, he is merely giving us an opinion. His own."

"Overruled," said the judge. "The opinion is based on perceptions by the parent of the child."

"Did you formulate some plan of action after this?"

"Yes, sir. I did."

"What was the substance of that plan?"

"I wanted to save my son. To force the cult to return him to us, so that he could resume a normal life."

"What steps did you take to accomplish this?"

"I went to the district attorney's office in Los Angeles County, and asked them whether this was legally possible."

"What did they tell you?"

"They said they could do nothing to help me. My son was eighteen, and an adult. The Souls for Jesus was officially a church. There was no legal way they could intervene."

"And that was when you consulted Mr. Morse?"

"Yes, sir."

"You saw no other way to get your son out of there? No other possible way? Is that correct?"

"Yes. If there had been some other way, I would have taken it. I wanted to save my son, and I took the only option I had. It was either that, or stand helplessly by and watch my son ruin his life and his future."

"Thank you, Mr. Reed. No further questions."

The jury listened intently, and the men in it particularly seemed impressed. As fathers, they seemed to identify with Frank Reed. And when the district attorney cross-examined, he was quite gentle. He made Frank Reed admit that he and his son Ken had indeed seized Jeffrey Reed by force at the airport, that Jeffrey Reed had struggled to get away, and that they had forced him into a car and handcuffed him, and thereafter, and against his will, held him imprisoned for many hours in a house at Big Bear.

Next, Blake called Kate Reed to the stand.

Her testimony was roughly the same as her husband's, except that it was tearful and moving. Once or twice, in the middle of it, she wept. She kept looking at Jeff, but her son avoided her eyes. The jury seemed touched by her testimony, and especially interested in what had happened when she had gone behind the walls of Ashtaroth to see her son.

On cross-examination, the district attorney was especially gentle with Kate Reed. He had no intention of antagonizing the jury. He was content simply to establish that she had known about her husband's plans to take Jeff back, she had known all about John Morse and his part in the taking of Jeff, and that she had been present at the house at Big Bear where Jeff had been held. In short, he simply established the facts that she too was involved, that she had had full knowledge of what was going on at all times, and that she was, therefore, a co-conspirator.

Then Blake called Cindy Hyland to the stand.

She told her story, and Hatch cross-examined. He reminded her of the incident at Joshua Tree.

"Did the victim, Jeffrey Reed, try to run away?"

"No. But there was no place . . ."

"I ask you to simply answer the question, Miss Hyland. Did he or did he not try to run away?"

"No. He didn't try to run away."

"Did he put up any resistance when the Deacons asked him to get into the car?"

"No."

"He did not fight, nor did he try to run. Is that correct?"

"Yes."

"Then he entered that car willingly? Isn't that correct?"

"Objection," said Blake. "Counsel is trying to lead the witness."

"Sustained," said Judge Brenner.

"Now, you have already testified that one of the Deacons knocked you to the ground."

"Yes."

"Did he attack you first?"

"Well, no. But you see . . ."

"He did not attack you first. Is that correct?"

"Yes."

"Did any of the victim's rescuers attack you first?"

"Objection," said Blake.

"Sustained." The judge looked at the district attorney. "Please rephrase that question, Counselor."

"Did any of the Deacons attack you first?"

"No."

"Isn't it a fact that *you* attacked *them* first?"

"No. I . . ."

"Isn't that a fact, Miss Hyland? You attacked them first?"

"Yes."

"You fought and scratched and tried to tear Jeffrey Reed away from them. Isn't that true?"

"Yes."

"And as a result, you provoked a reaction in force from one of the Deacons. Isn't that true?"

"I . . . well, yes, I guess it . . ."

"No more questions," snapped the district attorney.

Blake had decided there was no point in calling either Ken Reed or Joe Peterson. The reasons for their participation were obvious.

He called John Morse to the stand.

The crowd stirred. This was the defendant in whom they were really interested. And so was the media. To the public, he had become a kind of mystery man, a shadow who appeared, struck quickly, and vanished, a hit-and-run guerrilla, a one-man army and self-appointed avenger who had haunted the Souls for Jesus for months, for years.

He had become a kind of romantic figure, an instant celebrity. *Time*, in its cover story, had mentioned the fact that those in the SFJ really believed he was the incarnation of the Devil himself, they actually called him Satan instead of his true name, his photograph had been posted in every commune in the country, and this information fired the interest of the public still more. The magazine had tried to contact him for an interview but he had never come forward. And although there were many rumors as to *why* he was doing all this, no one really knew for sure. It was apparently something he simply did not want to talk about. The story was that the Reverend Buford Hodges, and a few of the hierarchy, really knew Satan, his true identity and why he was hounding them. But they, too, had been silent.

Morse took the oath and sat down. As he did so, the court artists went to work, pens working furiously. They knew these were the drawings the networks were interested in, the ones they really would want to show on the news programs that evening.

Blake began by asking a few preliminary questions of a routine nature. Morse answered that he had been born in Flint, Michigan, that he was forty-eight years old, and that his last permanent residence had been in New Haven, Connecticut.

The defense attorney began by establishing Morse's expertise.

"What is your profession, Mr. Morse?"

"I am a psychologist."

"What is your educational background?"

"I am a graduate of the University of Michigan, and took my postgraduate work at Cornell, where I achieved my Doctorate."

"Are you presently engaged in your profession?"

"No, sir. Not in its strict application."

"When were you last engaged in your profession?"

"Three years ago."

"Where were you so engaged?"

"I was a professor of clinical psychology at Yale University."

"A full professor?"

"Yes, sir."

"How many years did you occupy that position?"

"Fifteen years."

"What were your specialized areas in this field?"

"Psychopathology, cognition, learning and perception in human development. Also the psychophysiology of motivation and behavior analysis and programming."

"Then would it be fair to say that as a professional, you already had a certain expertise in programming?"

"Yes, sir."

Blake then asked Morse whether he had been published in this field. Morse named articles in several professional journals on psychology and two authoritative books on the subject which he had written.

"When did your interest in programming and deprogramming begin?"

"In 1953."

"How did it begin?"

"With my doctoral dissertation at Cornell. Its title was 'A Study in Mind Disorientation Due to Stress Factors Imposed Under Confinement and Deprivation.' Much of it concerned work with prisoners released from long terms in jail, whose minds had been programmed to accept the routine of prison life."

"And your study concerned the restoration of their minds to accept civilian life?"

"Yes, sir."

"Was this dissertation published?"

"Yes, sir. It was."

"What happened after that?"

"It came to the attention of the United States Army. This was shortly after the Korean War had ended, after the armistice at Panmunjom. The Army then had a problem with certain returning American prisoners of war. A few of them had been totally brainwashed by the Chinese communists. Or to use another word, programmed. The Army asked me to come to Korea to help find a solution to this problem."

"Did you go to Korea?"

"Yes, sir. I did."

"What were your activities there?"

"I worked with Military Intelligence and the Secretary of Defense's Advisory Committee on Prisoners of War. Specifically, with certain returned prisoners in the 2nd and 24th Infantry Divisions, both of which had been in heavy combat.

Later, I was brought into what was called HumRRO, or the Human Resources Research Office, an Army research contractor. After that, back in the United States, I continued the same deprogramming work at the Walter Reed Army Institute of Research and Valley Forge Hospital."

"What were your professional findings in this work, Mr. Morse?"

"The Chinese used everything in their mind control arsenal, and it had been extremely effective. They were able to coerce, instruct, persuade, delude, threaten, frustrate, and manipulate the mind, by constant repetition of the same themes, meanwhile weakening the resistance of their victims through starving them, and refusing them sleep. We found that these men would respond to no known methods of psychiatry, or other therapy. There was only one way we could deprogram these men, and restore their minds to normality."

"What was that way?"

"By fighting fire with fire. That is to say, by using the same harsh mind control techniques used by the Chinese themselves."

"And this was the *only* way?"

"Yes, sir. There was no other way."

"Now, Mr. Morse, you stated you left your professorship at Yale three years ago."

"Yes."

"Why did you leave at that time?"

"There was an event in my life that caused me to move in a new direction, although related to what I had previously been doing."

"What professional activity did you take up at that time?"

"I became a full-time deprogrammer."

"What was the event which brought about this change?"

He remembered it had been a cold winter's day, in New Haven, when the phone call had come. He remembered distinctly that it had started to snow; he was staring out at the flakes drifting down past the window of his study as he listened dumbly to the voice at the other end. When he hung up, he told Nora, and neither of them even bothered to pack a bag.

They had gotten into the car and driven, and the drifting snowflakes became a howling blizzard as they headed north. The snow had glazed his windshield, blinding him, but still he kept going. A state trooper had stopped them at the northern Massachusetts line and advised them not to try to go further, to stay overnight and wait for the snow plows to clear the roads, but he still kept going.

By some miracle, they had finally gotten to the place from which the call had come, Essex Junction, and there was a delegation of men waiting there, the Sheriff of the county and the Medical Examiner and some state troopers and some other men they did not know, and they brought Nora and him inside a building, and showed them Suzie's body and told them what had happened.

At that point, his wife fainted and went into shock, and they took her to the hospital in Burlington. They had taken some police photographs at the scene; he wanted to see them, but at first they did not want to show the photographs to him. They told him it was much better if he did not see them. But he insisted, telling them that it was his right, nobody had a better right than he. Finally, they showed him the photographs, and the way it had all happened at Sidon . . .

He had looked at the photographs, and seen the way she had hung herself from the tree, with the green belt of her robe, and her twisted face in its last agony, and the robe open in an obscene way to reveal the thin pathetic body. Then he had turned aside and felt very sick, and he had run to the bathroom and had vomited, and when he came out, he felt cold, very cold, and some big trooper asked him if there was anything he could do, and he remembered asking to be driven to the hospital, so that he could see Nora.

Later, he had issued a complaint and it had been answered by the Reverend Buford Hodges, who, on behalf of the SFJ, claimed that Suzie had been mentally disturbed *before* she had entered Sidon, that she had simply taken her problems with her, and that the Souls for Jesus had tried to help her find some peace and serenity, but she had gone beyond that, and it was too late. But he, John Morse, knew the real reason, he knew *they* had destroyed her mind, frightened and confused her, mixed her all up with their damned Purification, and finally she hadn't been able to take it any more . . .

"I'll repeat the question, Mr. Morse. What was the event that brought about this change?"

Morse stared at Blake. The voice of the defense lawyer seemed to come from a long distance away. He roused himself, and slowly became aware that the courtroom was silent, waiting for his answer. And he said:

"The suicide of my daughter."

His voice was flat, toneless. The jury sat rigid, staring at Morse. The court artist stopped his sketching abruptly. There was dead silence in the courtroom. Then, as though no one had heard him, as though fearing no one had heard him, he said it again:

"The suicide of my daughter."

"What were the circumstances of her suicide?"

Quickly, the district attorney got to his feet.

"Objection, your Honor. That's irrelevant."

"Objection overruled," said Judge Brenner. "The defendant has just testified that this event changed the course of his professional history. This event, therefore, is in context with his testimony on that history." He nodded to Blake. "Proceed."

"I'll repeat the question. What were the circumstances of your daughter's suicide?"

"My daughter Suzie had just completed her freshman year at Wellesley. That summer she went to a girls' camp near Windsor, Vermont, as a counselor. She was eighteen at the time. A few weeks later, my wife and I received a letter from her. She had abruptly left the camp, decided not to go back to college, and had joined a cult known as the Souls for Jesus."

Morse stopped. It became difficult for him to speak. Tears sprang to his eyes. He closed his eyes for a moment, enduring his agony in silence. Finally, Matt Blake said:

"Go on, Mr. Morse. What happened after that?"

"She had been witnessed, proselytized, or to put it in plainer words, seduced into joining this cult by another counselor in her own camp, with the help of a counselor from a boy's camp across the lake. Witnessing, or recruiting by cults, is often done by two or more people. Anyway, she wrote us that she was now living at a Souls for Jesus commune with the biblical name of Sidon."

"And where was Sidon located?"

"Not far from a town called Essex Junction, near Burlington, in northern Vermont."

"Did you make an attempt to see your daughter?"

"Yes. My wife and I flew to Burlington, rented a car, and drove to Sidon."

"What happened then?"

"We were refused admittance."

"Was that letter the last communication received by you from your daughter?"

"No. There was one more. A telephone call."

"What was the substance of that telephone call?"

"She wanted to sign over her car to the cult, and she needed some papers we had at home. She also wanted us to send her a few hundred dollars she had in her bank account. She was giving everything she had to the Souls for Jesus, in the service of the Lord. She did not sound like Suzie at all. She sounded strange, and for lack of a better word, weird, as though she were automatically mouthing words she had learned by rote. I knew then that she had been programmed, and I knew precisely how they had done it."

"Did you agree to your daughter's request?"

"No. I did not."

"What was her reaction?"

"Very hostile. She called me all kinds of filthy names. She told me that neither I nor my wife would ever see her again. Then she hung up."

"What did you do then?"

"I knew that if I could get to Suzie, if I could get her out of there, I could help her. I was sure that either I, or some of the other deprogrammers I had worked with, could save her, return her own mind and the power to think for herself, bring her back to health. The question was—how could I get to her? And I knew I had only one option."

"What was that option?"

"To physically snatch her away from these cultists, bring her to some safe and secluded place, and use the techniques I had learned."

"And did you put that plan into motion?"

"I had just begun to. I had enlisted the aid of two of my young assistants at Yale. I made another trip north, this time to survey the territory around Sidon. I had planned to make still another trip, this time with my two aides, when I received another phone call from Vermont."

"Whom was this call from?"

"The Sheriff of Chittenden County."

"And what was the substance of the call?"

"The Sheriff told me that some time during the night, my daughter had left her bed, gone outside, walked through deep snow, and through a snowstorm, found a tree in an area within the walls of Sidon, and, using the rope belt from her monk's robe, had hanged herself."

Morse stopped abruptly. He closed his eyes and he rocked his body backward and forward a little, caught by his grief, and memory. Finally, after he regained his composure, Blake continued:

"What did you do then?"

"My wife and I left immediately for Sidon. We identified her body as it lay on a slab. They had cut her down from the tree, but had taken an official photograph of Suzie, while she—while she was still hanging. It—it was horrible. Sickening. Indescribable . . ."

"What happened after that?"

"My wife collapsed. Went into shock. A week later, she broke down completely."

"Where is she now?"

"She is at a place called Hillbriar, in upper New York State."

"And what is Hillbriar?"

"It is a private institution for the hopelessly insane."

"What is her present medical prognosis?"

"She has completely lost her mind. She is what is commonly called—a vegetable. And will be—for the rest of her life."

"It was immediately after the incident at Sidon that you decided to change your whole life. Is that correct?"

"Yes."

"You notified the authorities at Yale that you would no longer teach there, that you had taken up a new career. Is that correct?"

"Yes, sir."

"You decided then to become a deprogrammer. Is that correct?"

"Yes."

"With what object, Mr. Morse?"

"I had already lost my wife and daughter to the Souls for Jesus. I was now alone. I wanted to devote my life to saving young people who had been duped or coerced into joining the SFJ. I was determined, insofar as I could, to spare other parents the grief and loss my wife and I had suffered. And finally, to do everything in my power to discredit this hideous cult. This is what I've been trying to do for the past three years. I suppose you might call it a personal crusade."

Blake then asked Morse how he had been employed by Frank Reed, and why. He asked for the details of his connection with the victim, Jeffrey Reed.

"Mr. Morse, did you have anything to do with the actual physical taking of Jeffrey Reed from the cult?"

"No, sir."

"Were you present at the immediate scene? By that, I mean the sidewalk in front of the TWA terminal, where Jeffrey Reed was taken?"

"No, sir."

"Then you never laid a hand on him, so to speak. Is that correct?"

"That is correct."

"Were you present in the car which transported him to the house at Big Bear?"

"No, sir."

"That's all, your Honor," said Blake. "I have no further questions."

Judge Brenner looked at the clock.

"It is past the hour of adjournment, gentlemen. I do not wish to interrupt the cross-examination of this defendant. Court will recess until nine tomorrow morning."

Early that evening, the *Messenger of God* came into San Francisco Bay, eased into its slip, and was secured tightly.

Later, the Reverend Buford Hodges lay naked in his king-sized bed with his new "secretary," a straw-blond Deaconess he had detached for temporary duty from the commune called Midian, near Fort Worth. There she had been named Michal, after King Saul's daughter and David's first wife, but her earth-name, the one she used aboard the *Messenger of God,* was Elizabeth.

At the moment, she was lying close to Hodges, gently caressing him, delighting in the stiff, hot fleshy spike she felt tingling at the end of her fingers. He leaned over and picked up the remote control that operated the television set at the foot of the bed.

"Time for the eleven o'clock news, baby."

"Oh, not now, Buford."

"Got to see what's going on down there in court."

She began to protest again, but he interrupted her.

"It'll keep." He flipped on the television set and the screen began to light up. "Time for that, later."

He took her hand away. "I want to concentrate."

She rolled over, and gave him her hostile back.

"Oh, damn," she said. "Damn, damn!"

At the moment, Buford Hodges was a little tired. He had had a long meeting with some of his Disciples earlier. They had discussed some fresh new possibilities. There was big money in gospel music now. The whole born-again thing had really taken hold in the country. People had stopped asking each other for answers, and were looking to heaven, instead. Gospel singing groups like Sweet Honey and the Rocks, the Gospel Warriors, the Ecclesiastics, the Edwin Hawkins Singers, and the Monument of Faith Choir, had become names, other groups had followed, and now gospel was big in records and on the charts, very commercial, selling in the hundreds of thousands. He had recognized that there was gold in gospel, and they had discussed the idea of having an SFJ group tour the country and sing gospel for the evangelical faithful, now estimated at about fifty million. There could be money, too, in the group's cutting a few albums, and the organization certainly had the capital and muscle and connections to promote them.

In addition, they had discussed the idea of having an SFJ basketball team tour the country, professionally managed and coached, with the athletes praying and delivering sermons between the halves. There wasn't much money in this, but you had to do a certain amount of public relations, and this would be good, very good, for the SFJ image.

All this, of course, after the trial down there at Criminal Courts was finished, and the case won.

But it was relaxing now, lying here in the big bed with this new girl, watching the news. The trial was the lead item on the program. First there were shots of the activity on the street—the angry parents picketing, and his own troops marching silently and with dignity, back and forth, back and forth, on the other side of the street. Then there were shots in the corridor outside the courtroom—the defendants coming out, the camera featuring the Devil, John Morse, and reporters badgering Blake. Hodges studied the drawings made by the court artist, and thought they were very good; he half-wished he'd been there, but it had been better, all around, simply to stay away.

He felt good about this trial, very, very good. And he was not worried. Buford Joe Hodges was not worried at all. He looked forward to tomorrow. Tomorrow, the cross-examination would start, and Satan would sit there and squirm, and Morse was the one he, Buford Hodges, really cared about, Morse was the one the district attorney really wanted, and considered the most vulnerable.

When the announcer went on to other news, he switched off the set. A few moments later, he had forgotten all about the trial.

31

Promptly at 9:00 A.M., Judge Brenner called the court to order, and John Morse took the stand.

District Attorney Hatch studied Morse for a moment. He stared directly into the defendant's eyes. The defendant's return stare was steady, and it was stony. He refused to flinch.

"Mr. Morse, were you paid for your services by Frank Reed?"

"Yes."

"How much were you paid?"

"Twenty thousand dollars."

"How much actual time did you devote to this deprogramming?"

"About a week."

The district attorney paused. He wanted to let that one lie there for a moment. He walked back to his table, shuffled some papers, just to give it a little time to brew. Twenty thousand for a week's work. He glanced at the jury box. The jurors looked a little stunned, unbelieving. Some of them were

314

hard-working stiffs who were lucky if they made that kind of money in a year.

He walked back and faced Morse again.

"Mr. Morse, you have testified that you have been a deprogrammer for three years. Is that correct?"

"Yes."

"How many young men and women have you deprogrammed during that time?"

"A substantial number."

"I ask you for a more specific answer, Mr. Morse. An *exact* answer."

"One hundred and six."

The district attorney gave that one a little time to lie there, as well. He could hear a slight buzz rise from the spectators. But he was watching the faces of the jurors again. He could see them mentally multiplying. One hundred and six times twenty thousand dollars, in three years ... equals ... *wow!*

"Would it be fair to say that the *real* reason you're in this quote profession unquote is for the money you can make?"

"No, it is not. I have a very large overhead. Some of the money goes for traveling expenses, and assistants I employ in various cities. A very large part of it goes to pay for my wife's upkeep at the institution. I might add that I charge only what the traffic will bear."

"Twenty thousand dollars is a lot of traffic, Mr. Morse. Would it be fair to say you took heavy advantage of your client?"

"Mr. Reed could afford the fee I named. Very often I have charged my client only for expenses. In a number of cases, I have charged a client nothing at all, and paid my own expenses."

"Name someone you didn't charge, Mr. Morse."

"Well, I could name a dozen or more."

The district attorney sensed that Morse could do precisely that. He suddenly realized he had dug a small hole for himself, and abruptly changed his line of questioning. He set about to show bias and prejudice on the part of the defendant.

"You hate the Souls for Jesus, don't you?"

"Yes."

"You hate everything it stands for, and the minister who heads it, don't you?"

"Yes."

"As a matter of fact, that's the only organization you do any deprogramming against. Isn't that true?"

"Yes. But I share my knowledge with other deprogrammers throughout the country."

"You hold this church responsible for the death of your daughter. Is that correct?"

"The SFJ is not a church. Not in the legitimate sense of the word. It is a cult."

"Mr. Morse, we are not here to quibble about words. I will repeat the question. You hold this church responsible. Is that true?"

"Yes."

"Do you have any proof that it was responsible?"

"I know it was."

"That is only your opinion. Do you have any *proof?*"

"I don't know what you mean by proof."

"Did your daughter, for example, leave a suicide note, stating that she was going to take her life, and blaming the SFJ?"

"No."

"Did she ever tell you she was going to commit suicide, and that the SFJ was responsible?"

"No."

"Do you know anybody she told this to?"

"No."

"Isn't it possible she might have been seriously disturbed before she entered Sidon? Disturbed enough to take her own life?"

"No."

"Isn't it possible that she might have been in a deep depression, that she might have lost a boyfriend, or been rejected by her peers, or had other emotional problems with which she could not cope?"

"No," shouted Morse. "Suzie was a healthy, normal girl. She

was sensitive, was not disturbed. She would have never taken her own life."

"Did your daughter discuss all her intimate and personal problems with you, Mr. Morse?"

"No."

"Then you don't know for sure what all her problems were, and *why* she was disturbed . . ."

"It was the SFJ that disturbed her. And it was the SFJ who hanged her! Damn it, don't you understand? She couldn't take the Purification. She went mad with all their programming, they broke her, she lost her mind. When she couldn't argue the money out of me, they kept after her . . ."

Morse was standing on his feet now, glaring at the district attorney, fists clenched. Judge Brenner pounded his gavel.

"The defendant will sit down, and calm himself."

Finally, Morse regained his composure. He sat down slowly, still glaring at Hatch. The district attorney was unruffled. He then went to the facts of the case. He asked how and when the defendant had first come in contact with Frank Reed, and his activity subsequent to that.

"Would it be fair to say that you discussed the kidnapping with the parents of the victim?"

"Yes."

"And instructed them how to proceed?"

"Yes."

"And conspired with them to bring it off successfully?"

"Yes."

"And provided certain facilities, to help them in that enterprise? The taxicab, the driver, and so on?"

"Yes."

"Isn't it true that you deprived the victim of a normal ration of food while you deprogrammed him?"

"Yes."

"And is it true that you deprived him of sleep for long periods of time?"

"Yes."

"And isn't it true that you beat him, in order to make him cooperate?"

"No. That's a lie."

"Is it a lie, Mr. Morse, that you used the same techniques the Communists used?"

"Only some of them."

"Is it a lie that you used the same technique you alleged the SFJ were using?"

"No. But that's what deprogramming is all about . . ."

"In other words, it's all about not only brutally mistreating the victim, but holding him prisoner against his will . . ."

"It wasn't against his will. He had no power of free choice or decision because he had already been brainwashed by the cult. All I was trying to do was to restore his free will, and give him back his mind."

The district attorney turned to Judge Brenner.

"Your Honor, I move to strike the answer as not responsive."

"The motion is denied. The defendant, as an expert, has a right to explain his expert opinion."

Hatch turned back to Morse.

"Let us be clear. You did know the parents would take the son."

"Yes."

"You did receive the victim, and hold him in that room, in spite of his resistance, didn't you?"

"Yes."

"He wanted to leave, didn't he?"

"Yes."

"And you prevented him from doing so, didn't you?"

"Yes."

"No further questions."

Hatch turned away abruptly. Judge Brenner looked at the defense attorney.

"Mr. Blake, do you have any further witnesses?"

"No, your Honor. The defense rests."

District Attorney Hatch took his place in front of the jury for his closing statement.

He paused for a moment, smiling at them in friendly fashion, trying to make them feel at ease.

318

"May it please the court, and you ladies and gentlemen of the jury. We are here because a crime has been committed. It happens to be one of the worst, one of the most serious, the most heinous crimes anyone can commit. Now, outside of a few insane people—psychopaths, who have no idea of right or wrong—most people *know* they are committing a crime, when they are in the process of doing it. They *know* what the law is, and they *know* when they are breaking it. I am not talking here of some crime of passion, a jealous man killing his wife on the spur of the moment, or an accidental crime, where a man shoots a friend entering his house, mistaking him for a burglar. I am talking about a crime conceived in conspiracy, deliberated upon, carefully planned, and finally carried out.

"Now, whoever commits a crime, and is caught during or after the act, can always tell you *why* he did it. Oh, yes, he can do that, folks. He can do that very well. He can say, I killed the man because he stole my wife; I killed the man because he swindled me, ruined me financially; I killed the man because I was afraid he was going to kill me first. I killed the man because he threatened his family. I know I broke the law, but I had a reason. I had this reason, or I had that reason.

"Ladies and gentlemen, here in this court, the fact that you have a reason means nothing. As I have pointed out, *everybody* has a reason. The fact is, the hard fact is, that the criminal involved broke a law. A law that is *your* law, folks. It was made by you, to protect your persons, and those of your children, and the rest of society, and placed on the books for just that purpose. The criminal who broke it had no respect for it. He, in effect, spit in your faces. He trampled on your law, and made his own law.

"You have heard the evidence against these defendants. Clearly they did kidnap the victim. Clearly they broke the law.

"Naturally, the criminal doesn't want to go to jail. The last thing he wants is to be punished for his crime. So he discusses his reason, whatever it is, with the lawyer defending

319

him, and they hope they can build it up into what is called extenuating circumstance. They hope they can play upon the sympathy of the jury. He had these reasons, you see. He was frightened, he was threatened, the man stole his wife, and so on and so on. Sure, he says, I killed the man, or I killed the woman, but you see, I had this reason.

"Now, what is the reason two of the defendants here, Frank Reed and Kate Reed, father and mother of the complainant, give? Why did they hire the defendant John Morse, a professional at this hideous and dirty business, to help them?

"Listen to this. You have already heard it in evidence, but let me repeat it again. Just to see how absurd it is.

"They committed this crime simply *because they didn't like the church their son was going to.*"

The district attorney took a long pause, to let this sink in. The members of the jury looked at each other. There was a small snicker from the audience. Matt Blake nodded to himself. He appreciated not only a good point well made, but also a good piece of acting.

After that, Hatch pointed out to the jury the fact that even if two of the defendants were parents of the victim, it had no bearing in this court. They had willfully broken the law, as had all these defendants, and all must accept total responsibility for their actions. There was no condoning their guilt, when proved.

"For these crimes," he concluded, "coldly planned and cynically executed, there can be no real or valid extenuating circumstances. These defendants must be punished to the full extent the law allows . . ."

Now, Matt Blake stepped forward to make his closing statement.

"May it please the court, ladies and gentlemen of the jury. It is true that a crime has been committed here. A crime that beggars description. A crime so weird, so bizarre, and so frightening that it boggles the mind to even consider it possible. A crime so monstrous that it goes far beyond the mere confines of this courtroom; it has, as we shall see, nationwide significance.

"Yes, folks, a crime has been committed in this case. In this one respect, the district attorney and I agree. What is that crime? It is stated in the charge. As attorney for the defense, I freely admit it. I not only admit it, I insist on it. The crime is—indeed—*kidnapping*. And it is, indeed, false imprisonment!"

He paused. The jury looked startled. They stared at him as if he were bereft of his senses. There was a buzz in the courtroom. Judge Brenner gaveled it quiet. Blake's face was grim, but he smiled to himself. He was savoring the moment. Hit them with something hard going in, on the opening. Turn them on with a little surprise. They'll remember it, when they forget a lot of other stuff . . .

"Yes, ladies and gentlemen of the jury, a kidnapping has been perpetrated. The victim sitting here is indeed the victim. But the defendants sitting here are not the defendants at all. They should not be in this courtroom today. The State has imposed on their time and their patience. They should be outside on this fine California day, going about their business. They have no business here, folks, I assure you, no business at all.

"The real defendant here is a cult known as the Souls for Jesus, whose leader purports to have a direct line to God, calls himself a Messenger of God, and in due time promises to favor us with a timetable in which the Messiah will appear.

"The real kidnapping here was committed by this cult. But it was not physical, it was not violent. Instead, it was subtle, sinister, pernicious, and depraved. Jeffrey Reed, the victim here, was *psychologically* kidnapped. That is to say, he was seduced into the cult by blandishment, and then his mind was stolen. He was falsely imprisoned both in body and mind, at one of the centers of this evil cult, at a place called Ashtaroth, surrounded by high walls and guarded by fierce dogs. He was starved, allowed no sleep, blasted incessantly with the cult's propaganda, hypnotized as a snake would hypnotize a bird, until his will to think was destroyed, and his mind belonged to him no more.

"The final result was this. This fine American boy, born in

the Catholic faith, seduced away from his loving parents, finally became a human automaton, a zombie, a robot. Wind him up and he would talk. Wind him up again, and he would walk. Wind him up still again, and he would eat, or sleep, or go to the bathroom. But no matter how much you tried to wind him up, there was one thing he was unable to do.

"And that was to think. Think for himself. He was able to obey, yes. Follow, yes. But think? No. Make his own decisions? No. Order his own life? No. Jeffrey Reed was a slave. He was literally owned, body and soul and mind, by his masters, the monk-robed, fanatic Svengalis of the SFJ called Elders and Deacons.

"The defendants sitting here at that table, the people who should not even be here at all, did not, I repeat, did not try to kidnap Jeffrey Reed.

"Frank and Kate Reed, the loving father and mother of the victim, tried to *save* him from a kind of living death, return him to himself, to give him back his mind and his manhood. They needed help to do this, and they acquired it. But his monk-robed jailers held him in a terrible prison. Not just the walls of Ashtaroth, but also another kind of prison—the walls surrounding the mind of Jeffrey Reed himself.

"And so Frank and Kate Reed had to take desperate measures, to restore their son to sanity.

"Ladies and gentlemen, most of you are fathers and mothers. You have heard Mr. and Mrs. Reed here today. Surely, you must have understood, and identified with, their agony. What would you have done in their place? Sitting in that jury box, you all heard what happened and *how* it happened.

"What would you have done?" He paused, then he said: "Ah, I do not need an answer. I already know the answer. I see it in your faces. You would have felt the same stunning horror the Reeds felt. And if you could save your child from these monsters, you would. If you saw one tiny glimmer of a chance to restore your son's mind, or your daughter's mind, you would.

"The prosecution has told you that a physical kidnapping was done here, that Jeffrey Reed was seized and forced into a car against his will. Now, ladies and gentlemen, I ask you to consider that phrase carefully. *Against his will.* The fact was he *had* no will. The fact was that he was out of touch with reality, and was not capable of judging whether he should go with his father or not. Since his capacity of decision had been removed by the obscene programming of the cult, since he was unable to *think,* then the prosecution cannot say he consented or did not consent, the prosecution cannot say whether it was against his will or not, because, ladies and gentlemen, I repeat, he did not know himself, he could not think for himself, he could not decide for himself.

"Now, nobody here will condone the physical kidnapping of any person. But we have seen the motive here, and it is unique, it is special, it is logical and entirely understandable. There is justification here, and legal precedent to support it, in common law. Sometimes it is called justification by necessity. When a man has two evils to face, and has to face the necessity of choosing one, he chooses the less evil of the two. No crime has been committed when the man takes the course he believes to be necessary to avoid some terrible situation, some evil or consequence . . .

"No one can object if an adult decides to join any church of his choice, ladies and gentlemen, practicing any religion he wishes. This is a right guaranteed by the First Amendment. The Souls for Jesus calls itself a 'church.' They insist they are not a cult. The prosecutor has echoed their shopworn arguments. But the Souls for Jesus is a cult, and always will be. It cannot call itself a Christian church, because it is a fraud. Any legitimate religion or church I know of, Catholic, Protestant, or Jewish, preaches love. Love for one's brother, love of God, love of humanity, *love.* The SFJ professes to teach love for Christ, and love for each other. But that is all. Otherwise, it preaches hate. Hate your father, hate your mother, hate your brother and sister, reject your friends, hate everything but the commune, despise the world itself.

"Any so-called church built on hate, ladies and gentlemen, cannot last. At the moment it is the largest cult in the country, and has seduced thousands of our best young people, and robbed them of their minds, and it is still growing. We must view this with alarm. But I repeat, ladies and gentlemen, it cannot go the distance. Because it is built on hate, not love.

"Some day, the Reverend Buford Joe Hodges and his Souls for Jesus will gradually drop from view. Its tax-free real estate will be taken back by its mortgagees. Its victims may, in time, regain their minds, and return to their parents, or college, or whatever they decide to do. And the country will be better off for it. Thank you, ladies and gentlemen."

32

The members of the jury voted one of their number, a man named Edward Dorn, to be their foreman.

In a jury made up in large part of retirees, housewives, and people from minority groups, he seemed to be the obvious choice. He was about fifty, conservatively dressed. His hair was prematurely snow-white, he had a warm smile, and there was a certain maturity and dignity about him. He was a used-car dealer, and some of the jurors vaguely remembered seeing his ads in the classified columns of the *Los Angeles Times:* "Make Your Deal at Dorn's." Moreover, he had served on a jury once before, and they felt his experience would be valuable.

He had been very reluctant to serve. He had been the foreman of the jury on which he had previously served, and he had found it a great responsibility. But as one of the jurors, a Mrs. Evelyn Paton, put it, "Just being here is a responsibility for all of us, Mr. Dorn. And all of us just think you're the man for the job."

The vote for him had been unanimous. Now, as they all sat around a large round table, Dorn said:

"Look, people. Before we start, let's make sure and do this. Everybody keep the same seat you're in right now, and don't sit anywhere else. That way, we can sort of get used to each other, know each other."

"Like a family sitting around a dinner table."

"Something like that," said the foreman. "Or put it this way, we're like the numbers on a clock. I mean, there are twelve of us at this round table. Now, I'm going to go around the clock, make a list of your names, and give you a number and I'd like to know what each of you do, as well. Just to give me some background. I'll be calling on you a lot for questions and answers and votes, things like that, and it'll make it easier for me to remember."

"That's very clever," said one of the jurors. "Making each of us a time of day."

"*Very* clever," said someone else.

"It's something I figured out on the last jury," said the foreman, modestly. "And as I said, it's for my benefit, not yours. Now, I'll be Number One. I'm going to go around the table clockwise, Number Two and Number Three and so on. You give me your names, and what you do just for background, and I'll write them down."

They did as he suggested. He went around the table and, when finished, he read off his list to the others:

ONE	Edward Dorn	*Used-car dealer*
TWO	Fred Muller	*Retired*
THREE	Sarah Steinberg	*Housewife*
FOUR	Evelyn Paton	*Housewife*
FIVE	Leroy Williams	*Owner, liquor store*
SIX	Anthony Caruso	*Building contractor*
SEVEN	William Gatling	*Retired*
EIGHT	Barney Cohen	*Retired*
NINE	Ethel Jordan	*Housewife*
TEN	Gloria Diaz	*Supermarket checker*
ELEVEN	Jonas Frazer	*Postman*
TWELVE	Agnes Nealy	*Housewife*

After the foreman had read off the names, Number Eight commented: "You know, it's very interesting. I mean, we've got two famous names sitting right here. Patton and Caruso."

"You're right, Mr. Cohen," smiled Four. She was a sweet-faced woman with blue-tinted hair and a motherly manner. She was a little overweight, and wore a blue print dress. "Only the General spelled his name with two *t*s. Mine has only one. P-a-t-o-n. But we pronounce it the same."

"Actually," said Seven, "there are *three* famous names here. You can add my name. Gatling."

"Gatling?"

"You never heard of the Gatling gun?"

Seven looked around the table, incredulously. The others squirmed a little, embarrassed. But then Two snapped his fingers.

"Wait a minute. I remember. The Gatling gun. They used it in World War I."

"Now you've got it," said Seven. He was a small man of about sixty, with a pinched face and mottled skin. "Only it was used as far back as the Civil War. It was a kind of machine gun with revolving barrels, and was invented by my namesake, Richard Jordan Gatling, in 1862."

"That's interesting, Mr. Gatling," said Twelve. "Very interesting."

Juror Five looked up at the vent on the wall.

"They got the air conditioning up too high here," he complained. He was a thin black man on whose face there was a perpetual look of complaint. "It's bad for my sinuses. I get these sinus headaches and, man, you wouldn't believe how bad they can be."

"It *does* seem a little high," said Nine.

"The thing that gets me is, they're supposed to be having an energy crisis. Right? And what do they do? They waste the taxpayers' money, freezing us to death..."

"I hope we're not here too long," said Three. "I've got four cats at home. I asked the little girl next door to feed them while I'm away. But I don't know, I think she's unreliable. Anyway, I just hope we're not here too long..."

The foreman listened to this chatter for a while. He recalled it had been the same way in the previous jury on which he had served. The jurors avoided any discussion of the case for the first few minutes. They chattered with each other like this, almost as though they needed a breather, some relief from the recent tension of the courtroom, and the concentration they had to demand of themselves.

Finally, he rapped the knuckles of his fist on the table.

"Ladies and gentlemen," he said. "Twelve good citizens and true. We'd better get on with it. Right? I mean, we have a job to do here."

They all agreed, and listened to him intently as he said, "Now, we've got six defendants here. And that makes it complicated. My idea is that maybe we ought to separate them. Discuss the family first. The Reeds, I mean. Decide on them. Plus Cindy Hyland and Joe Peterson. Then take the deprogrammer separately. Decide on him. But that's only my opinion. This is a democratic body here. What do you say?"

"Sounds okay to me," said Six.

"Right on," said Eleven. "Makes it simpler all around."

Everybody else agreed, and One said, "All right. We're now in discussion on Frank Reed and Kate Reed. The father and mother. We'll talk about the two boys and the girl later. Now, I guess the best way to start, get the ball rolling so to speak, is to get a vote on how we all feel going in, without any discussion. Okay?" They all nodded, and he went on: "All those who think they're guilty of kidnapping and false imprisonment, raise their hands."

Two and Four raised their hands. The foreman himself, Number One, joined them.

"All those who think they're innocent of the charges?"

Seven of the jurors raised their hands. Ten and Eleven were undecided.

"All right," said One. "Guilty votes, three. Not guilty votes, seven. Two undecided." He paused. "Now, the best thing to do, I'd say, is to go around the table seat by seat and ask each one *why* they voted as they did." He looked to his right. "Two?"

"I agree with the district attorney. The law's the law. I understand why the father and mother did what they did. But they still broke a serious law. Maybe they took their own son, but on the books it goes as kidnapping. So I say—no matter if it *is* their own son—guilty."

"Three?"

"I feel for the parents," said Three. "And the defense lawyer made a good point. If someone was trying to steal your child, or to kill him, wouldn't you do anything, *anything*, to save him? I know I would. To me, these people are innocent."

"Four?"

"Well," she said. "I guess I disagree with Mrs. Steinberg here. I don't see where anybody was stealing the boy, or hurting him. All he wanted to do was worship in his own way. Join the church of his choice. That's a right guaranteed by the First Amendment. We all heard that in court. The boy's eighteen, and he's old enough to know his mind, and I don't think the parents had any right to—well—butt in."

"Five?"

"I just feel they're innocent," said Five. "I mean, I think this SFJ is a real weirdo thing. You see them marching outside? Crazy. Just like some of the laws we got. If it were my kid, I'd have gone in after him, too."

"Six?"

"Me?" Six was Anthony Caruso, a short, barrel-chested Italian with beetling eyebrows and a nose that looked as though it had been broken in two places. "I go with the father and mother. Here's this crazy kid, comes from a good Catholic home, tells his old man he's quitting college, tells everybody he knows to get lost, and goes into this here cult and walks around in the monkey robes . . ."

"Monk's robes," somebody corrected.

"Monk, monkey, what's the difference?" said Six, impatiently. "The thing is, the kid came from a good, religious home. Okay, the parents didn't go to Mass or anything like that, but that don't matter, Catholic is Catholic. The kid could be excommunicated for doing a thing like that. If it was my boy, I'd get him out of there, and wallop hell out of him—

pardon me, ladies—and teach him a little *real* religion, you know what I mean?"

"But the boy's eighteen," interjected Four. "He's an adult. I have a teenage boy of my own. I know I can't hold him. I know I haven't got a right to hold him. He wants to make his own life."

Six stared at Four.

"Yeah? Well, lemme tell you something, Mrs. . . ."

"Mrs. Paton."

"Right. A lot of these eighteen-year-old kids never grew up. Never had to work hard, with their hands; everybody gave them everything. Like this Reed kid. Had everything handed to him on a golden spoon. Living in that high-class section of Santa Barbara, the whole thing. Kids nowadays, they have no guts, no ambition. Spoiled rotten. All they do is keep busy putting down their parents, spitting in their faces."

"I think you're exaggerating, Mr. Caruso. Really, I do. All the boy wanted to do, as far as I could gather, was to serve the Lord, to be close to Jesus . . ."

"If he wanted to know about Jesus," said Six, "he could go to his priest. He could find out all about Jesus in no time flat. I vote innocent here. And there's no way I'm going to change my mind. As of now, anyway."

"Seven?"

"I felt for the parents. I think I'd have done the same thing. Otherwise, I have nothing to say. I pass."

"Eight?"

"I believed them. And I didn't believe the boy."

"No?" One was curious. "Why not?"

"I don't know. Did you see his eyes? There was something funny about them."

"In what way?"

"They seemed—well, I don't know. Funny. Like he memorized everything. Like he was reading a script, or something. I think he *was* programmed by these people. You know, something like Patty Hearst was."

One looked at the others.

"I didn't get that impression. Does anyone else here have the same feeling?"

A number of them shook their heads, but Nine said:

"I'm next, and I do. That boy's so charming, so neat, so polite, well—he just doesn't seem real. I guess, in a way, I agree with Mr. Cohen here." He searched for words. "You know, he's almost too good to be true. He just doesn't sound— well, natural."

"It seemed to me," said Four, "he was a healthy, normal boy."

"Well," said Nine, "I had my say and I said it."

"Ten? You were undecided."

Ten was a thin Chicano girl. "I dunno. I just can't make up my mind. I'd like to hear more, you know?"

"Eleven? Any change?"

"No opinion," said Eleven. "Not yet."

"Twelve."

"Being a mother, I felt for the mother." Twelve was a large, matronly woman, with pendulous breasts, who wore tight slacks, much too tight for her. "Of course, I don't have a son, I have a daughter, but the idea's the same. When you think of that poor woman, going up to that place, what's it called—?"

"Ashtaroth," said someone.

"Yes. Going up to that place, and then being turned back by her own son, and their not even letting the father *see* his own son, well—I put myself in their place. I mean, suppose it were my Tammy, my daughter. How would I feel? You know? So I guess I'd do what they did. I don't think they're really guilty of anything. They just loved their boy, and wanted to save him. If there's a law against that, then they better change the law." She paused. "And one more thing."

"Yes?" said the foreman.

"I agree with Number Nine here. Mrs. Jordan. The boy *did* sound a little funny. The one I really believe is the girl. What's her name? Cindy Hyland. She sounded very honest, very sin- cere. She's very sweet, and I feel sure she was telling the truth about everything. You know, she reminded me a little of Tammy, you know, my own daughter."

Now, it was One's turn. They all looked expectantly at the foreman.

"I have to say, I honestly have mixed feelings," said One. "Being a parent myself, and the father of two sons, I guess that's natural enough. But being a father, in itself, doesn't mean you can ignore or break the law. You kidnap anyone, and that includes your own son, and it's still a very serious crime, no matter how you cut it. Any kidnapping is a terrible thing. I believe the law regards it in the same class with murder. The law is the law is the law, and it's there to protect all of us, you know, everybody, and you can't take the law in your own hands."

"He's right," said Four. "You're absolutely right, Mr. Dorn. If everybody did that, we'd have anarchy in this country."

"Now, don't get me wrong," said One. "I sympathize with these parents, I feel for them. But in my opinion, the rule of law has suffered in America. There's entirely too much crime, too much lawlessness. People being mugged on the streets, and so forth. In my view, the first place you learn respect for the law is the home. Mr. and Mrs. Reed *knew* they were breaking the law. That's the point I'm making. They knew it, and they went ahead anyway. So I think they ought to be punished in some way. I have to vote with Mr. Muller and Mrs. Paton here—guilty."

After that, the jurors went into a general discussion. For an hour or two, they held their positions. Those voting not guilty seemed to be more positive. "There's no way I'm gonna change my vote," said Six, stubbornly. "Even if I have to sit here a year."

Number Two, who had initially voted guilty, now swung over to the not guiltys. That left only One and Four. For three more hours, One and Four held steady. Four was the first to capitulate. And she did it gracefully:

"Well, I don't want to seem harsh or cruel. As I said, I'm a mother. I guess way down deep in my heart I might, I just *might* have gone along with this whole thing, the way Mrs. Reed did. I still don't see any harm in this Souls for Jesus church. It's still a Christian church, and they worship Jesus.

That's good enough for me, no matter how they do it. I mean, it isn't one of these crazy foreign cults, like those Hare Krishnas or Moons, you know? I still think the parents broke the law, but their intentions were good, maybe they made a mistake in trying to prevent him from living his own life, but whatever they did, they did out of love. You could see that. There's mother love and there's father love, and maybe we should show them mercy here, above the law. I have to tell you I still don't like it, I still feel uneasy about what they did, I still respect the law and feel that everybody should observe it, no matter who they are, high or low, rich or poor. Most of you seem to feel that the parents shouldn't be punished. All right, then. I still feel unhappy about this—but I'll go along with you. Not guilty."

"Hear, hear," said Eight.

"Beautifully spoken," said Nine. "Very well said, Mrs. Paton."

"I agree," said Twelve. "It takes a big person to have an open mind like that. We really respect you for what you just said, Mrs. Paton."

"Thank you," said Four.

They all turned to look at One, expectantly. He fiddled with some paper scraps on the table. He was the last holdout, and obviously, he was uncomfortable.

"That makes it eleven to one," said Seven, pointedly. "That's what you'd call a real majority. You know?"

"It's almost eight o'clock," said Eleven. "And we haven't had dinner. Maybe this is the time to see it our way."

"At least," said Eight, "think about it."

"I *am* thinking about it," said One.

"You're entitled," said Eight. "Nobody says you have to change your vote. Nobody's forcing you. You have the right of dissent here." He turned to the others. "That right, everybody?"

They all chorused agreement, but the chorus was weak. The foreman looked at them. They were waiting expectantly, hoping he would see reason.

Suddenly, he capitulated.

"All right, all right," he said. "If eleven of you think one way, then maybe it's unreasonable for me just to stand here and hold out. I see merit in what you've all said. Like Mrs. Paton here, I have an enormous respect for the law. But I guess I would have to say there were extenuating circumstances. I mean, the parents did the wrong thing, they were beating the wrong horse. I agree with Mrs. Paton here when she says that the Souls for Jesus is a Christian church. Maybe they're not Baptists or Presbyterians or Episcopalians, but there's room for everything. If they want to worship Jesus in their own way, that's good enough for me, too. But I understand your point of view. I can't wholly agree to it, but I've decided to come around to it. So I'll make it unanimous. Not guilty."

Quickly, the jury agreed that Ken Reed and Joe Peterson and Cindy Hyland were innocent as well. Then One looked at the clock.

"Well, people, it is almost eight o'clock. I move that we adjourn. We're all tired and hungry and tomorrow morning we can start discussing the programmer, John Morse. Are we all agreed on this?"

They voted unanimously to adjourn.

The foreman pressed the button, and the bailiff opened the door.

"We're finished for the evening," said One.

They all rose and filed out into the empty courtroom, making their way toward the exit.

Number Eleven yawned. "I wonder if they let you order anything you want at the hotel? I could go for a big steak and some French fries."

"I could go for a couple of Scotches," said Six.

"Why not?" said Eight. "Enjoy, enjoy. It's all on the house."

"I have a bad back," said Twelve. "I hope they have a bedboard I can use at the hotel."

"They usually do," said Three. "I can't wait to get to a telephone. I wonder how my cats are doing?"

"That goddamn air conditioning," said Five. "My sinuses are killing me."

33

The jury returned at nine o'clock in the morning.

As the bailiff opened the door to the jury room, he said, "Sorry, folks. Air conditioning's broken down. But they'll probably get it fixed in a little while."

"Well," said Ten to Five. "No air conditioning. You got your wish."

"What I got is a sinus headache," complained Five. "Couldn't sleep all night, and I still got it."

"We had someone like you at Food Giant," said Ten. "She was another checker. Our supermarket's got this air conditioning. I mean, it's real heavy. So she had to quit, you know?"

They took their seats at the round table. Nine looked at Three.

"How about your cats, Mrs. Steinberg? Were they all right?"

Three beamed. "Oh, they were fine. The bailiff phoned and spoke to the little girl—she was right on the job." Then she looked a little worried. "Only she can't take care of them today and tonight. She's staying over at a friend's house."

"Maybe you could get someone else," said Nine.

"I hope it won't be necessary to try. I mean, I hope we can finish up today." She turned to Twelve. "Did they get you a bedboard at the hotel?"

"Yes, they did. But I couldn't sleep anyway."

"Nothing like your own bed at home," said Four.

Six looked at the foreman.

"I hope we can finish this up by sometime this afternoon. My son's playing basketball tonight in San Bernardino, and I want to get out there in time. I wouldn't wanna miss seeing him play for anything."

"Oh?" said Two. "You have a son who's an athlete?"

"Athlete?" Six beamed with pride. "He's more than that. He may make the All-State High School team. You should see Guido play. He's got a hook shot you wouldn't believe, and the way he grabs rebounds—well, you've got to see it to believe it. He *owns* those backboards. He's had a couple of offers already, different colleges, but he's sort of holding out for UCLA."

"You must be very proud of him," said Nine.

"I am."

"Speaking of getting out of here," said Number Nine, "I hope we can finish up before evening, too. My little daughter Betsy's having a birthday party tomorrow. Ten of her friends. And I've got so much to do." She looked at One. "What do you think our chances are, Mr. Dorn?"

"Well, Mrs. Jordan, I guess that's up to all of us." He laughed. "But the longer we just sit here and chatter, the longer it's going to take."

"He's right," said Seven. "Let's get to it."

"All right," said One. "Now the only defendant we're discussing here is the deprogrammer, John Morse. Right?"

They all agreed and One went on: "Now, let's think back about what the judge said. You know, his instructions. There are four different charges here. Right? Kidnapping; conspiracy to commit kidnapping; false imprisonment, and conspiracy to commit false imprisonment."

"Man," said Eleven, "you could go crazy trying to figure all those out."

336

"Well," said One. "First things first. Let's vote on the charge of kidnapping first. Without discussion."

He asked for a show of hands.

One, Two, Four and Seven voted guilty. Three, Five, Six, Eight, Nine and Eleven voted not guilty. Ten and Twelve were undecided.

"Six for not guilty, four for guilty, two undecided," tallied the foreman. "Now, let's open it up for discussion."

Number Six was the first to speak up.

"For my dough, he's innocent."

"Why do you think that, Mr. Caruso?"

"He was only helping the father grab his kid from a bunch of creeps. That's the way I see it."

"And you can't blame him," said Eight. "I mean, after what happened to his daughter."

"But no matter how you slice it," said Seven, "it's still kidnapping, isn't it? And there's a law against that, right?"

"I'd say it wasn't kidnapping," said Five. "I mean, this dude Morse didn't lay a hand on the boy. The boy's father and brother did. So it really isn't kidnapping."

"I disagree with you," said Four. She seemed very positive. "This man Morse planned the whole thing. Right down to the last detail. He told the boy's father just how to go about everything. That remind you of somebody famous?"

"Somebody famous, Mrs. Paton? Who?"

"I'm talking about Charles Manson," said Four. "That's who. He wasn't there at the Tate-LaBianca murders. I mean, he didn't shoot or stab all those people himself. But he plotted the whole thing, planned it, you know? It was just the same as being there, just as bad, if not worse." She looked at One. "You voted guilty. What do *you* think?"

"I agree with you, a hundred percent," said One. "In my view, he deserves the maximum under the law. He was a stranger to the victim. He wasn't even emotionally involved. He didn't know the father, or the boy. You can understand the motives of the father and mother. They were concerned about their son. But it seems to me this deprogrammer's real motive was money."

"I'd call it revenge," said Nine.

"I'd call it psychopathic," said One. "I mean, when you think of the number of kidnappings he was involved in."

"One hundred and six," said Two.

"And getting paid for each one," said Four. "Look at how much he got from Mr. Reed. Twenty thousand for a week's work. A *week*. He must be a millionaire by now, he has to be."

"He said he deprogrammed a lot of these kids for just expenses, or charged nothing.

"I don't believe it," said Four. "I don't believe that for a moment."

Suddenly, the air conditioner went on. It blew in a blast of cold air, colder than before.

"Oh, God," moaned Five, "my head."

"I've got some aspirin if you want it, Mr. Williams," said Twelve. "Maybe it'll help."

"The only thing that'll help is to get out of here."

"Getting back," said Eight. "I'm against the kidnapping charge. I mean, outright kidnapping. If we're talking about anything here, it's *conspiracy* to kidnap. You can argue that, not the other."

There was lively discussion for a while, after which everybody but One and Four agreed that if John Morse was guilty at all, it was more like conspiracy. That was really how he was involved. One and Four fought for two hours, but finally gave in.

"All right," said One. "We'll take up the charge now of conspiracy to kidnap."

"As far as I'm concerned," said Four, "there's no doubt about *that*. I mean, the defense admitted he was involved in court."

"Yeah," said Six. "But the question is—is he guilty?"

"And if so," said Ten, "how much does he get?"

"The judge decides that, Miss Diaz," said One, gently.

"Oh," said Ten. "Yeah, you're right, Mr. Dorn. I forgot."

"Now," said One, "may I make a statement? Give you *my* point of view?"

338

They all were anxious to hear what he had to say. Somehow, whether they agreed with him or not, he seemed to talk sense.

"Look, everybody," said the foreman, "I know we're all people of compassion here. I knew that when we all felt for the parents, and finally decided they were innocent. But this deprogrammer is different. I mean, whatever his motives were, money or revenge or whatever, he still went around conspiring to kidnap, to inflict false imprisonment, on some boy or girl he didn't even know, or wasn't involved with, emotionally. Each one, you might say, was a kind of number with him. He was just doing an impersonal job. You know, like the men you see in those movies. The killers the gangsters hire to kill other people."

"You mean, hit men?" said Six.

"Exactly, Mr. Caruso. That's the term they use. Hit men. Anyway, the hit man doesn't even *know* his victim. He simply kills for a fee. This man, Morse, it seems to me, is doing the same thing. For a fee. Only he doesn't kill. He kidnaps. But in principle, there's no difference."

"Hear, hear," said Four. She beamed at One. "You put that very well, Mr. Dorn."

"Thank you, Mrs. Paton."

"I still say he's innocent," said Six. "And I'll say it again. This Souls for Jesus ain't even a legitimate church. I mean, like the Catholics and the Protestants, and even the Jews. It's a big con job, a rip-off. This Hodges, who runs it, gets all the dough, and lives it up on his yacht and wherever. You ask me, this man Morse isn't just innocent. He's doing everybody a favor."

"I don't think that's a fair statement, Mr. Caruso," said Seven.

"No?"

"I don't think you can use that argument. The Pope lives in luxury, too. You ever been in Rome and seen the Vatican? Well, I have . . ."

Six glared at Seven, and was about to say something, when

One rapped his knuckles on the table and said, quietly:

"Gentlemen, this is no place to discuss religion or politics. I think we ought to get back on the track."

"All right," said Six. "Let's do that. I still say not guilty."

"So do I," said Nine.

"Will you give us your reasoning, Mrs. Jordan?"

"I don't know. I guess I just can't blame Mr. Morse, after the terrible thing that happened to his daughter. I've got a girl about the same age, she's in high school now, and I guess I identify."

"I'd like to say something," said Four.

"All right, Mrs. Paton. You've got the floor."

"I can understand how this Mr. Morse felt about the horrible thing that happened to his daughter. But we're missing a point. A law has been broken. If you break a law, you have to be punished. You take the law in your own hands, like this Manson, or the Symbionese Liberation Army, or people like that, and you've got a terrible situation. If we don't respect the law, then crime all over is going to go even higher than it is. All of you, and I'm speaking right to the women now, know how dangerous it is to go out on the street at night. You can be mugged, and raped, and killed, and heaven knows what else."

"She's right," said Ten. "I won't even go out on the supermarket parking lot at night. And my boyfriend drives me home."

"All I'm trying to say is," continued Four, "if we walk out of here and deliver a not guilty verdict for *everybody*, we're going to look pretty funny. I think the newspapers would get after us, and so would the public."

"Not to mention the judge," chimed in One. "He's liable to rebuke us for the decision. Really let us have it."

"Can he do that?" asked Nine.

"I'm not sure. But I think he can."

"I *still* say this guy Morse hasn't done anything wrong," insisted Six. "And to hell with the public, we're the jury here."

"No," said Four. She was very quiet and determined. "A person has to draw the line somewhere. I've been talked into letting the parents off. But I won't be moved when it comes to this Mr. Morse. He's broken the law. Not just once. But one hundred and six times. And he should pay for it."

They argued until it was time for lunch. Then after the break they began to argue again. Ten, one of the two undecided jurors, came over to the "guilty" side. She was joined by Five, who continued to sniffle and sneeze, his face perspiring in spite of the cool room.

At three o'clock in the afternoon, Twelve made up her mind to vote guilty.

"I guess you're right." She looked at One and Four. "We all should obey the law, no matter what. I'll go along. Anyway, I don't think I could sleep in that bed another night. Even with a bedboard and a sleeping pill."

At four o'clock, Number Three thought of her cats, and the possibility of their going without food still another day, and, playing with her conscience, decided the same way. The law was the law was the law.

At twenty minutes after four, Number Nine thought of her small daughter, Janie, and the birthday cake she had ordered and had not yet picked up, and the decorations and the candles and the paper hats she had to pick up at the notions shop, and all the details of giving a birthday party for eleven little girls, and she could not bear the thought of having to stay overnight and perhaps not being able to have the party at all if their deliberations ran well into the next day, and she finally agreed, on balance, that Morse was guilty.

A little later, Eleven went along because it was his bowling night, and he bowled in a league formed by postal clerks and letter carriers, and he was the highest scorer on his team, and the team would miss him, it would really miss him, and besides, it was his only night out, the only night he could be free of his stupid and nagging wife.

Finally, Eight went along because he had a history of angina and he was getting what seemed to be some of the chest pains. Although it could be indigestion from the food he had had at lunch, still he had to be careful, he'd better get home and lie down and take care of himself. They were very mild now, nothing to worry about, but still if anything happened he'd be at home with Mollie, and they could call the cardiologist.

That left Six as the only holdout.

Eleven to one, and still he was convinced that Morse was doing everybody a service, instead of committing a crime, and he held fast to this until five o'clock. He looked at the clock, and thought about the San Bernardino Freeway, and how crowded it would be at rush hour, and if he wanted to get out there and have a bite and see Guido play at all, it'd have to be now, or never. And finally, he said:

"Okay. I still think you're all wrong, you're giving this Morse a lousy deal. But you're eleven and I'm only one and who am I to fight City Hall? Maybe you know something I don't know, or see something I don't see. So, I'll go along. Guilty."

They all agreed that if Morse was guilty of conspiracy to commit kidnapping, he was also guilty of conspiracy to commit false imprisonment, so they threw that in, too.

Then One pressed the buzzer, and the bailiff opened the door and the foreman said:

"We're ready."

Three weeks later, Judge Brenner sentenced John Morse to one year in prison.

There was a further condition of probation. The judge ordered him to refrain from any and all deprogramming activities for the period of probation, which was set at ten years.

After that, Morse was led out by the bailiff.

34

~~~~~~

The gray Pontiac turned off the main canyon road, onto the dirt road.

It took the switchbacks carefully, crawled along the hairpin turns veering off into the deep canyon. Finally, it swung around the last S-curve marking the final approach to Ashtaroth.

The car stopped with its hood pointing at the gate. A man and a woman got out of the car.

They were Juror One and Juror Four.

They walked back to the trunk of the Pontiac. One unlocked and opened the trunk. He took out a package, and handed another to his companion.

They opened their packages, took out their monkish robes, and put them on, securing them with belts of red braided rope.

After they were fully robed, they turned to look at the great golden cross gleaming in the sun. It seemed to loom high on the building behind the walls, higher than they had ever seen it before, and it shone more brilliantly in the sun.

One looked at Four and smiled.

"This is a big day," he said.

"Oh, yes." She smiled back at him. "This is going to be a beautiful, beautiful day."

They heard the dogs inside the walls begin to howl. Number One walked to the communications panel. He pressed the button, and the voice came over the speaker.

"Who is it?"

"Zadok. I am here with Tirzah."

"Jesus loves you," said the voice. "And we are all waiting for you. Enter."

One and Four got back into the car. The electric gate slid open. They drove up the long driveway and stopped at the entrance to the building.

The five Elders of Ashtaroth were waiting at the door to greet them. Their faces were wreathed in broad smiles.

The First Elder stepped forward.

"Jesus loves you, Zadok. And you, Tirzah."

"Jesus loves you, Nehemiah," said One and Four, together.

"Let us go inside," said the First Elder. "We are all waiting." He held out his hands. "But first, give me your belts."

They took off their red belts, and gave them to Nehemiah. Then the five Elders escorted them into the church itself. It was illuminated only by candles. The church was filled to capacity. Everyone in Ashtaroth was there to do them honor. When they entered, the entire assemblage began a soft hymn.

The five Elders escorted One and Four up to the altar. For the moment, it was dark.

Then a spotlight was turned on.

In its glow stood His Divinity, the Master himself. He looked majestic, like some imposing prophet straight out of the Bible, his gray robe held closed by his gold belt, wearing his golden sandals. He smiled down at One and Four, and it was a beatific smile.

"Jesus loves thee, Zadok," he said. "And thee also, Tirzah. Ye have both done well in the service of the Lord."

Then he asked them to come forward to receive their reward.

344

In each hand, he held a white belt.

They took the belts he offered them, fastened their robes with them, and knelt before the Master for his benediction.

After that, the hymn sung by the congregation swelled into a mighty chorus.

EPILOGUE

35

From the Los Angeles Times *of March 6:*

LOS ANGELES—Judge Harlan F. Brenner of Superior Court today released John Morse pending appeal, and set bail of $100,000. The bail was raised by a number of organizations consisting of parents who have lost sons or daughters to the Souls for Jesus cult.

The cult has come under strong attack in recent weeks. The trial in January drew national attention, and resulted in a rising storm of criticism against the religious group. Advance copies of a new exposé on the SFJ, written by best-selling author George Glennon, has revealed that there have been several suicides among the neophytes in the cult, as well as severe psychiatric disturbances. It will be recalled that Morse's daughter, Suzie, took her own life while undergoing the SFJ processing for neophytes called Purification.

The Reverend Buford Joe Hodges, the titular head of the cult, and called by his followers His Divinity, or the Master, has also come under severe attack. The Treasury Department has begun an investigation of his personal finances, as well as a review of the cult's present tax-exempt status. The attorney general of California and those of several other states have begun to conduct investigations into the cult's activities, as have the district attorneys of a number of counties where the church-communes are located.

Some of the counties have already begun, under pressure from frantic or worried parents, to adopt a legal formula first used in Tucson and Pima County, Arizona. This instrument is usually called a "temporary conservatorship." Through it, parents may gain custody of a cult member for 30 days through a court order. The document is issued by a judge on the basis of testimony from psychologists, physicians, former cult members, and often the parents themselves. During this period, a programming team takes over, and tries to persuade the SFJ member to leave the cult and resume a "normal" life.

But there is strong opposition to this. Not only from the Souls for Jesus, but from many of the other cults as well. They are hiring expensive lawyers and preparing for an all-out battle. And some psychologists, ministers, and civil-liberties leaders are expressing increasing concern, one of them stating: "This is an outrageous and nationwide conspiracy to deprive people, and especially young people, of their personal, civil, and religious rights. It is clearly a blatant attack on the First Amendment."

The Reverend Buford Hodges has just returned from a cruise to the Bahamas. When interviewed aboard his yacht, the *Messenger of God*, he complained of being harassed simply because he served God, and was a servant of God.

"I resent all these vicious innuendos and activities against my church," he said. "If they continue to persecute me in this country, as Christ was persecuted in another country in other times, and finally drive me out, it does not mean the end of the Souls for Jesus. There are millions of Christians in Europe and elsewhere, waiting for God's message, and I can always preach the gospel, wherever I go."